Ensign James Lockwood

The Rebellion of 1798

Ensign James Lockwood
The Rebellion of 1798

by

Mark Bois

www.PenmorePress.com

ISBN: 978-1-957851-06-8 (paperback)

ISBN: 978-1-957851-05-1. (Ebook)

BISAC Subject Headings:
FIC032000FICTION / War & Military
FIC002000FICTION / Action & Adventure
HIS018000 HISTORY /Europe/Ireland

Edited by Chris Wozney

Address all correspondence to:

Penmore Press
920 N Javalina PL
Tucson, AZ 85748

Dedication

For those first in my heart: Charmin, Jonathan, Lauren, Kevin, Tiffany, Eliza, Rosie, Catherine, Genevieve, and Patrick, and for those who may one day join our merry band. I have such love for you.

Chapter One

Moira Carney had gone into domestic service at age eight, and by age fifty she had risen to the position of housekeeper at Lockwood House. It was a hard life, especially in that house, but she knew no other. She thus had no compunction in addressing one of the few maids left in the house in an uncompromising tone, well before dawn. "First, I'll need you to open the shutters and light the kitchen fire. You'll then sweep and dust the halls, but for God's sake, be quiet or you'll wake the family. Next, lay the hearth and help take breakfast up. Then make the beds and empty the slops. After that you'll make your apple tart, as Master James is coming home today, and you know how he loves your apple tart."

The maid was young, small, plain, and already inured to the drudgery of service, but she brightened and smiled like a girl for the first time in a long time and said, "Oh, is Master James truly coming home?"

Moira looked up from her list and said, "Yes, young lady, and you had best remember your place. If you give Master James just one of your little smiles, Mr. Lockwood will have you out the door, alone and penniless in the ditch. Recall what happened to our Mary last week: one sassy reply and she was dismissed without recommendation, and Mr. Lockwood seeing her family turned off their land as well. You mind me now, child." They were speaking in English; Mr. Lockwood had forbidden the use of Irish, even below stairs.

As Moira turned to tend to her own duties, duties no lighter than those she had assigned the maid, she too was pleased by the notion of Master James coming home. He and Mrs. Lockwood were the only members of the family with a Christian bone in their bodies. Mr. Lockwood was the very devil, and it was a blessing that Master John and Miss Susan were still away at school, as they were every bit their father's children. Master James, though, was such a sweet boy.

*****

At the same moment the household staff of Lockwood House was pondering his merits, James Lockwood—tall, lanky, and shy—was trapped in a whore's bed.

He was traveling home from school in England, taking his time in doing so, and had spent the final night of his journey in Dublin, resolved to lose his virtue. He had just turned seventeen, and was determined not to return to his father's house a boy.

There had been several obvious whores in the crowded public house he visited, coarse, older women who intimidated him, and he kept to himself as best he could. But eventually, a young woman, a pretty thing about his age, offered a modest smile from across the room, and had then come over to say hello. Typically, he had difficulty speaking to girls, especially pretty girls, but three beers on an empty stomach, a young man's desperate urges, and the girl's sweet nature gave him the courage to invite her to sit down. He asked what he might get her, and when she admitted to being hungry, he ordered up beer and stew for two. She ate quickly, embarrassed to confess it was the first real meal she'd had in days. With an unaffected, manly tone he called, "House, there! Two more bowls of your fine stew! And more beer, do you hear me, there!"

Her name was Saoirse, and she talked rapidly between mouthfuls. "I came to Dublin this Michaelmas past, as my cousin told me of how she had found me a position at a milliner's shop. Oh, but that cow lied to me, showing away like she does, and there was no job at all, was there? But I dared not return to Stradbally. I had such a row with my Da when I left, didn't I?" Without looking up she poked at her meal and added, "Since then, I have been forced to rely on the generosity of strangers."

They were polite to one another, and soon kind as well. She had a bubbling laugh that delighted him, and together they ate, drank, and shared the happy, inane chatter of young people who have had too much to drink. She told him excitedly of how the stained-glass windows of St. Patrick's sparkled during the monks' evening prayers, and with wide eyes he leaned forward and burst out, "Let's go and see!"

"Oh, yes, let's!"

He threw some coins onto the table, and they dashed out into the darkening streets. As they ran and laughed up Wine Tavern Street he recklessly took her hand, and when he did so, she stopped, smiled up at him, and said with great earnestness, "It's like we're sweethearts, aren't we? Like real kind-hearted folk? Can we be sweethearts, even if it's for just a bit, even if it's just pretend?"

By the time they reached St. Patrick's it was dark, and the view of the cathedral was achingly beautiful from the gloomy streets. He turned and told her, gushing and grinning, that she was as pretty as the windows, and she went up on her toes and kissed him on the cheek. They held hands and strolled for a while longer, earnestly chatting, until she mentioned she had never tasted wine, and he marched into a shop and bought two bottles of something resembling claret.

Shyly, she invited him back to her room. As drunk as he was, he was hesitant, particularly when she shared the fact that she lived in the crowded network of streets and alleys between Dame Street and the Liffey. James had been to Dublin often enough to know that well-bred young gentlemen from Malahide did not walk there, especially late at night. There were some thoroughly disreputable people about, but still, he followed her, her hand tugging at his, down the dark streets to the narrow alley that led to a cluster of shabby apartments. Once inside her door, though, she lit a candle, and he was touched to see the little room was clean, tidy, and intimate.

They drank the wine from two chipped crystal glasses, in her family since the days of the Armada. They were laughing and chatting, young, drunk and growing wildly flirtatious. She leapt to her feet to say, "Oh, now, Jamie boy, let me show you how we dance in the country, on a full moon night at Garron's Cross, in the shadow of Cnoc na mBráthar!"

James was clumsy, drunk, and ponderously affectionate. After a romping turn around the room, he took the first opportunity to tumble into her bed, and she happily tumbled in beside him.

She said wistfully, "I have not been so happy in such a very long time." She then fell fast asleep.

As James soon determined, the cumulative effects of Irish stew and generous amounts of beer and wine had rendered the girl deeply insensible, immune to any stimuli short of cannon fire. With the illogic of a desperate young man he whispered, "Saoirse? Saoirse, *a grah*?" He wiggled a bit, thinking it might rouse her; it did not. He gathered his courage and touched her arm, to no effect. He took the outrageous liberty of gently kissing her, and shamed himself by casting a furtive glance at her softly rising bosom.

In an unfocused tumult of lust, disappointment, indecision, and not a little affection, he sighed, glanced once again at her bosom, and sighed once again. She was lovely and vulnerable and he thought of her as his responsibility, even if for that short time. She had likely slept with a hundred men, but he found her willingness to sleep beside him trusting and intimate, a thrilling new sensations for him. He closed his eyes and fell asleep beside her.

He woke as dawn filtered through the girl's thin curtains. He soon became aware that he might need to be sick, he was certain he needed to piss, and was very sure that he needed to hurry to be at his inn at eight o'clock, where he had left his trunk, and where he would meet the carriage he had booked to drive him the final miles to Malahide. James had, in short, a great deal to tend to, but with his back to the wall, the sleeping girl had essentially trapped him, and he was loath to wake her. He was certain that morning would shatter the spell of their laughing evening, and if she woke, there would be an awkwardness to their conversation which would embarrass them both. He was easily embarrassed, and he had grown expert in avoiding situations which might prove uncomfortable.

In the end it was fear of missing his carriage and angering his father that drove him to act. Slowly, he placed his hands and the tips of his feet on the bed's side rails, and although he was thin, he was strong and so was able to lift himself over and past her.

Saoirse slept on.

James padded to the door and slipped outside, the dawn air chill and damp. He paused, until with a grin and a subtle shrug he turned back inside and laid this last two guineas on the table beside her cherished crystal glasses. Out on the street he walked quickly through the tendrils of fog toward his inn, *virgo intacta*, but still he felt much less a boy than he had the day before, his father be damned.

*****

Lockwood senior was a tall, heavy, imposing figure, his arms folded across his chest. "Well, here you are at last. You took your time getting here; we looked for you all this past week." There in the echoing hall of Lockwood House he shook his son's hand absently, then eyeing him, went on, "Taller now, I see. But did they not feed you in England? Christ knows I paid them enough to feed you like a fighting cock. I trust you are not grown particular in your appetites; you will find no elegant fare here."

"No, Father."

"I have some news to share regarding your future, but I am determined that your sudden arrival shall not interrupt my sherry and newspapers." With a dismissive wave toward the stairs he went on, "For now you had better get upstairs to see your mother. She will be pleased to see you, I suppose."

James turned and bound up the stairs two at a time.

Sophia Lockwood was a fading beauty, her mind slowly but relentlessly failing her. Still, she sprang from her bed, her eyes alight, when her youngest child came to her door. He was her dear boy, and her sole ally.

They were both happy, sitting side by side on her settee, falling into loving conversation as if they had never been apart, though he had been away for nearly a year and half.

He successfully masked the sadness he felt as he studied the absence in her eyes.

"Now that you are home," she said, "I am determined that you shall never leave me again."

"Now, Mother, dear, we have discussed this at length. It is the fate of every second son of our class: John shall inherit, Susan shall marry well—"

She sniffed and said, "God help whoever marries your sister."

"—and as the second son," he said with a wry smile, "I have little choice but to become a soldier or a sailor or a man of the cloth."

Sophia looked confused for a moment, twisting a kerchief in her fingers, quietly saying, "Oh, you must not go to sea. You must not go to sea. My father went to sea and never returned. The sea is very dangerous. Oh my, not the sea...."

He patted her hand, leaned over to catch her eye, and said, "No, mother, not the sea. I shall be a soldier, don't you think?"

She rallied, gave him a trembling smile, and said, "You'll not take holy orders, James?"

He laughed and said, "No, Mother, I think we both suspect that is not the life for me."

He told her about school, and was sharing a somewhat edited account of his journey home when they heard Lockwood senior's thumping approach from down the hall. An observer would have noted how the two went silent at the same moment, tilted their heads in the same manner and listened intently, both trying to discern the mood and intent of the lumbering master of Lockwood House.

When Lockwood entered the room, James saw his mother look at her husband askance, her last private space invaded, and he saw in turn his father falter, just for an instant, before the mask of command returned. Lockwood said, "By God, I swear you two conspire like a pair of thieves. No more of your scheming, now, it is time to discuss this commission business."

Lockwood did not sit, instead towering over his wife and son as he said, "James, I am surprised, nay, astonished, sir, by the tone of your last letter, and your petulant insistence upon a commission in a line regiment. Four hundred pounds, sir! And then uniforms, kit, weapons, and a horse! A horse, sir! God's my life, I will not fund such a wild extravagance!"

Sophia said nothing, her eyes down, still twisting her kerchief, as James nodded, his eyes also on the floor, and he muttered, "Yes, Father."

Lockwood, pleased with their meekness, rocked forward on the balls of his feet and went on with triumph in his voice, "I have, however, applied my influence on your behalf. You may recall that Mr. Youngblood of the Honourable East India Company is a member of my club. Last week I treated that gentleman to an elegant dinner, a most expensive dinner, I might add, all on your behalf. After considerable discussion I have obtained for you a lieutenancy with the 1st Madras Native Infantry! India, boy! John Company does not insist on this extravagant purchase of rank. There is no expense to your family for you to join the regiment, other than the odd coat or two, and I am certain we might find you a second-hand sword at a reasonable price. And best of all, in future years your promotion is based on seniority, so you never need beg for outrageous amounts of money every time you feel yourself deserving of promotion."

James was all too aware of the nature of service with the HEIC, as three older boys from his school had sailed to India two years before. Word had soon come back that two of the three had died of fever within months of their arrival, and the third had been hacked to bits at Trincomalee. James did not, however, need to address his father's suggestion, as his mother quickly turned on her husband with fire in her eyes.

"India, sir? India!" she cried. "I would never see my son again! I have read of India, sir, and to send James to such a place is a death sentence! A death sentence, sir, for both him and me, as I could not live while he did not!! How dare you suggest such a thing! You will leave this room, sir, and you shall never again utter such a vile notion."

*****

Two tense days later Sophia Lockwood stood at her window and watched her husband mount his bay mare and spur the horse into a gallop. She had been raised among horse people, and so knew how heartless it was to force a cold horse into a run. It was typical of him.

She knew he was on his way to Dublin to visit his mistress, as he had stuffed a bottle of wine and a fresh shirt into his saddle bag. Lockwood typically had their coachman, the ancient, chatty Owen McMurtry, drive him the ten miles into Dublin, but he took the mare on any occasion when he did not wish to have the coachman know of his destination. McMurtry was far from a moral compass, but he showed a marked propensity for sharing too much when he was drinking, which was most of the time.

As soon as the sullen mare and her frisky rider disappeared into the woods at the end of their lane, Mrs. Lockwood called for the maid to lay out her yellow gown, and for Mrs. Carney to have McMurtry bring the carriage around as quickly as possible; she was going out. James had gone out early to call on some of his old neighborhood friends, thus sparing the need for Sophia to explain her errand. She was having a good day, and was determined to use it to good effect. Her announcement of imminent travel took the staff by surprise, forcing McMurtry to return the cork to his whiskey jug and set about the work of harnessing his team.

She was intent on speaking to her cousin Edwin. He was ten years her junior, and when the world was young she had bounced him on her knee. He was now a member of the Irish Parliament and Colonel of the Westmeath Militia. They had spoken only rarely over the past twenty years, as Edwin dearly loved her, and had violently protested her marriage to a man he knew to be a rogue and a blackguard. She had ignored Edwin's advice then, and for every one of those twenty years she had regretted not heeding him.

He had grown fat and bald; she had gone half mad. There was some stiffness when he first welcomed her: "I received your note, dear cousin, with some surprise, but I confess with joy...." But the formality melted when they sat companionably before a fire in the elegant hall of St. Edmondsbury House. He offered her a glass of wine to dissipate the chill of her long drive, and she gratefully accepted. After an hour they had finished the first bottle, and nearly the second.

"It is not too late, Sophie. You could leave him today, now, with or without divorce. You would always be welcome here. I remain a bachelor, you know."

She knew that all too well; rumours swirled about Edwin's tastes. She loved him still.

It took her a long moment to gather her wits, her relentless emotions and straying thoughts, before replying, "I have made my choice, Edwin. As you doubtless know, I am not entirely well. On my bad days I am content not to cut my wrists. On my good days I occasionally smile, and on this, what I feel is one of my best days, I come to you, to beg a favor."

He shut his eyes for a moment at the thought of her bad days, surfacing to ask, still with his eyes closed, "How might I serve you, cousin?"

"I desire my James to hold a commission in your regiment."

"James? Goodness, he is the merest boy."

"He is seventeen, dear."

"You astonish me. Seventeen, you say?" He held a finger to his mouth, thinking, then tapped it once, and said, "I do wish I could oblige, but there are barriers. Your family certainly meets the income standards, but any officer's appointment to the militia must be approved by the Lord Lieutenant. You know as well as anyone the disdain Lord Kerr holds for your husband. I would open myself to the stiffest rebuke if I should recommend his son. It is quite impossible."

Some years before, a drunken John Lockwood had very nearly accused Lord Kerr of cheating at cards, not enough to draw a challenge, but enough to earn a lifetime enmity.

In the face of rejection, Sophia's rationality crumbled. She bolted to her feet, twisting her kerchief, eyes wildly blinking. "I must go. There is much... pressing matters... I... requiring my attention at home."

She stalked quickly, nearly desperately, from the room. Edwin Montgomery hated John Lockwood, hated what he had done to his beautiful cousin. He assumed Lockwood's son would be a stupid, mean-spirited brute like his father. The regiment had far too many such men already. Only when the footman was opening the massive front doors for his cousin did Montgomery mutter, "Oh, damn it all, anyway."

He rolled to his feet and hurried after her. She was nearly to her carriage when he called from the front steps, "A volunteer, then!"

She turned, confused, her eyes unfocused.

She stepped unsteadily down the drive. Edwin hurried forward to take her elbow, and as he steered her to the carriage door he spoke in a soothing tone. "Do not concern yourself, Sophie. I shall see to everything. You see, a volunteer can join upon my command without any approval from the Castle. Just have him at Mullingar barracks on the first day of the month, and I shall see what can be made of him. I dare not guarantee his success, dear—not every man makes a soldier, let alone an officer—but I shall give him every opportunity."

She sat in her carriage and clutched his hand with both hers. Blinking back tears she said, "Oh, thank you, thank you, my dear Edwin."

"Now, dear, I must ask: has he any money? There are expenses he must meet: uniforms, weapons, perhaps a horse —assuming he can ride, so few of these pups can sit a horse— and then there are mess bills and such. If need be, I can provide, but there must not be the slightest hint of favoritism, or the other officers shall make his life a misery."

She looked lost, becoming frightened. "Has he any money? Oh, I suppose not. But he must have such things, mustn't he? Oh, his father shall be so angry." But then with a look of shining decision she said, "Oh, course, I know just how to get some money, without begging one shilling from his father."

"Very well, then, I shall see your young gentleman on the first of the month. I shall do my best for him. Rely on me in this, as in all things."

*****

The coachman and the housekeeper had run the very same errand for Mrs. Lockwood several times in the past, but old McMurtry still did not care to see Moira Carney walking some of the most dangerous streets in Dublin. So dangerous, indeed, that McMurtry could not drive the carriage into that maze of crowded narrow streets and expect to come out the other side with carriage, horses or himself, intact. So he would park blocks away, at the comparative safety of the Customs House, and let Moira down to walk into the filthy street bordering the docks.

He would mutter and curse and tell her to be on her guard, but she'd give him a grin and a dismissive pat on the arm and say, "It's kind in you to worry, Owen, *a grah*, but don't concern yourself. I've never had a bit of trouble here. No one cares for an aging woman in a servant's dress. I'll just slip in and slip back, so don't fret, now." Away from the house they could speak in Irish, her Dublin accent confident and clever.

She walked toward Sheriff Street, and though the streets were crowded with every stripe of foul humanity, no one accosted her. To her right, vast customs warehouses lined the River Liffey: The Sugar Store, The Whiskey Store, The Spirit Vault. The pavement was slick with filth, the dense smells of the stored goods competing with the stench of squalor and decay, while rats scampered at every corner. She was not shocked, and she walked those streets as if she had been born there. She guarded her secret closely, but she had indeed been born there, in an alley behind the infamous Newfoundland Street.

She was not a little proud to come back to her old neighborhood, and while she had scoffed at her dress in front of McMurtry it was as fine a gown as could be found on

Sheriff Street. She passed a couple of older men, rough stevedores, who recognized her and tipped their caps in respect. When a drunken sailor bumped her, leering, and said, "Fancy a go, woman?" she growled and pushed past him.

She heard someone yell to the sailor, "Ya feckin eejit! That's Nate Carney's cousin!"

She glanced back over her shoulder and was not displeased to see the sailor running in terror down the street, and at least two men from the crowd pounding in pursuit.

Nate Carney held court in a second-hand shop where the Lockwoods could never go, but where Moira was known and welcome. A huge man with a wicked cudgel stood guard at the door, but he opened it and offered the formal, "*Dhia duit, a* Moira *a grah*," at her approach.

The shop was dim, but warm and neat. Nate Carney, fifty-five years old and the toughest man on Sheriff Street, was playing cards with three hulking brutes when she came in, but he rose to kiss her and say, "The great pleasure of the world it is to see you, Moira. What have you brought me this time?"

They stepped over to the worn counter, where she produced from her pocket a thin diamond bracelet. "My mistress tells me that this would bring a hundred pounds in any shop in Dublin, but you can have it for fifty."

He took it from her hand, looked it over, and said, "I can have it for thirty, only out of respect for you, cousin."

She grimaced, looked at him for a moment, stuck out her hand, and said "Forty, in honour of our mothers."

He sniffed a laugh, shook her hand, and said, "In honour of our mothers, then. It's a pity we can't honour our fathers, but we'd need to find who in the world they might be, and that seems more trouble than they're worth." Dropping the bracelet into a drawer beneath the counter, he produced a roll of bills and counted out Sophia Lockwood's forty pounds. With a sneer he added, "What's your slice of this pie, cousin? Will your rich mistress see even twenty?"

Moira stuffed the bills into her sleeve, stuck a finger into Nate's chest, and defiantly said, "She'll see forty. She's an honest woman, and I'll be straight with her."

With a knowing grin, Nate said, "But not your master, then? Lockwood treats you like a dog, why not serve him back?"

Moira said, "I'll not turn on the family, Nate."

She spun on her heel, but he followed. At the door he caught her arm and softly said, "Time's coming, Moira, *a grah*. The Committee knows the contents of Lockwood's gun room. Every big house will be raided, as we'll be needing guns, shot and powder, and sooner than later. Rebellion! You had best decide right quick if you want to aid the cause, or stand in its way."

Chapter Two

In Cork Town, the roll at Miss McCarthy's School for Young Ladies bore the name Brigid O'Brian, but among her people she was known by her traditional Irish name, one by which she was honored and limited by relationship and history. At home, thirty miles away in Clonakilty, she was Brigid ni Brian, 'Brigid daughter of Brian'. Her mother had died when Brigid was very young, the great beauty Aisling ni Leary. Among her people Brigid spoke only Irish, but at school she spoke an educated English. She was seventeen, at home for the semester break, and determined that when the next semester came, she would return there.

"Ach, Daidi!" she said to her father, not daring to stomp her foot. "Am I not the finest reader in my class? And are not my maths the best in all the school?"

"Aye, but your spelling is awful, isn't it?" offered her older sister, Anne.

"And didn't Miss McCarthy say just last week that your penmanship was no better than the cat's, and him blind?" added her younger sister, Caitlin.

Brigid nearly whirled on her sisters, but her father held up a stern finger in warning, and said, "Brigid, *a grah*, it's great pride I have in you and your great learning, but reading and maths? What use can that be to a young woman, at all?"

Caitlin, nine years old and an inveterate tease, smiled coyly, "She can teach her hundred children how to read after she marries *Ian O'Sullivan*."

"Caitlin ni Brian," Brigid hissed, "I shall knock you on the head and turn you over to the fairies if you don't—"

She was in turn interrupted by Anne, who was nineteen, sweet-natured, but not always quick, who cried, "Wait! I am the eldest, so I am to be married first! Oh, Brigid, how cruel of you to marry Ian O'Sullivan! I shall be humiliated! An old maid! Oh, Brigid, how could you!"

Ann started to cry, and all three girls turned on one another in raging emotion and furious anger. Resigning himself to the role of spectator, Michael O'Brian leaned back in his chair and looked out the window, as if he might find solace there. It was not solace that appeared, but rather the inelegant form of the young hedge poet, Seamus Heaney, who was hurrying down the lane past their cottage.

Michael O'Brian jumped to his feet, rushed to the door, and called, "*Dhia duit*, Seamus Heaney! What news?"

Heaney scarcely paused, half dancing down the lane, waving his cap over his head, and calling, "*Dhia agus Mhaire duit*, Michael O'Brian! McCarthy has taken the Saxon's head from his shoulders! All of Munster is rejoicing!"

O'Brian roared in delight and cut a quick step or two at his door, but then remembering his manners, he called after Heaney, "What of McCarthy?"

Heaney turned and called with one hand cupped to his mouth, "Run through and rather slashed, but still among the living!" The poet gave one last wave of his cap and trotted away to spread the news in Clonakilty, where tradition required he be rewarded with more than a few tots of whiskey.

In his youth O'Brian had been a famous dancer, and even at age forty he still best expressed emotion through his feet. He danced back into his cottage laughing, to be met with the blank expressions of his suddenly silent daughters.

He said gleefully, "Old McCarthy has killed the Saxon! It's a great day for the Irish, sure!" but was disappointed by his daughters' flat looks. He sighed and went on, "Do not one of you young knuckleheads listen to the talk of the county?"

They raised their eyebrows in ignorant innocence until O'Brian sniffed a laugh and said, "Never worry, my lambs, in truth it's not a fit topic for young ladies." He then went on with growing excitement, "The English, you see, were exercising their troops up at Drishane Castle, in the Yeos Field."

Nearly every field in Ireland had a name, most ancient in origin, but Ann looked puzzled at the sound of such a strange name, and she very nearly interrupted her father for an explanation. Sensing her sister's confusion, Brigid whispered, "Yeomanry," to which Ann muttered a disapproving, "Oh," as the Yeomanry was hated by the common people, with good reason.

"Well, then," continued their father, "while the regiments were gathered there, an English officer, a Saxon dog, disrespected an Irishwoman, putting his hands on her and very nearly... well, never mind what very nearly. In the end she fended him off, as she knew how to handle such a fellow." He paused a moment, then said in another tone, "As your dear mother has gone to the angels, it's for me to fill gaps in your elegant educations, so know this: if you need to dissuade a rogue's attentions, give him a quick knee to the stones, and down he'll go, like a hundred of bricks."

They were country girls and long familiar with such matters, but still, Ann and Caitlin winced in miss-ish propriety, though Brigid nodded subtly and made a mental note.

O'Brian continued, "At any rate, the wronged woman's family protested to the English, but they were ignored, weren't they? Her brother then went to the Castle and challenged the man, an honourable measure, but as her brother was a commoner, the officer could refuse him, the coward. But he could not refuse McCarthy Mór!"

"Who is that, please, Father?" asked Caitlin, wide-eyed.

O'Brian looked toward Brigid, who said, "That is the title of the Chieftain of the McCarthy Clan. He is also Prince of Desmond, and Lord of Kerslawny."

"Well said, daughter. I saw the Mór once, you know, with these very eyes. A few years ago he rode through Clonakilty accompanied by a dozen servants and retainers, mounted like kings. By God, he is a most imposing man, though he must be near sixty now. At any rate, as one of our great nobles he is one of the few Irishmen allowed to carry a sword, and when he heard of the outrage offered to his clanswoman he rode up from Blarney and he himself challenged the Saxon dog! Rumour has it the Saxon was still inclined to refuse the challenge, but even the other English thought him a coward, and so in the end he had to fight. They have fought, and the Mór is victorious!"

"Daidi," asked Caitlin, "why can Irishmen not carry swords? Are they too dangerous, so?"

The older girls rolled their eyes and O'Brian barked a laugh. "Irish swords are dangerous indeed, Blossom, in the right hands. That is why the English have banned them, as they know we would overthrow them if ever we could get fucking organized...." He did not correct his slip, only clenched his fist and stared into the wall.

He recovered with a sad smile, and looking back to his three pretty girls, he said, "Forgive me. Now, let me ask you, Anne, to run and tell your Seanathair O'Brian the news of our great victory, and you, Caitlin, run to tell your Seanathair O'Leary. Leave us, now, so that our Brigid might make me a cup of tea and we might chat a bit." There were no hurt feelings over that, as their father regularly spent time alone with each of his daughters. O'Brian had grown up nearly anonymous, as one of eleven children, and upon the death of his wife he vowed to make his children feel loved.

The eldest and youngest grabbed their shawls and bonnets, kissed their father's cheek, and hurried out across the well-worn paths toward their grandparents' homes, hoping to be the first to share the news of the Mór's triumph.

As Brigid prepared their tea, Michael drew his pipe and tobacco pouch from inside his jacket, carefully loaded the pipe, and asked, "So, *a stor*, shall you be attending Father Doherty's dance? The Dear knows Ann is looking forward to it. If nothing else, you might go and break Ian O'Sullivan's heart."

"Oh, pooh, Da. Ian is a nice boy, but so much the *boy*." Then with a droll grin she added, "Shall you be attending, yourself? Father Doherty so wishes that you spend some time with the widow O'Gara."

O'Brian pulled two chairs up to their battered tea table, and as they settled in, he replied, "Edna O'Gara is a fine woman, but after ten years with your mother, the finest woman in all the world, and with all due respect to Edna, now, I'm afraid she'd be a step down from what I knew."

Brigid blew on her tea, and with a mischievous grin she said, "All due respect to Mrs. O'Gara, I'm afraid she'd be a fall down two flights of stairs and a hard landing at the bottom."

They both laughed long and hard, until Michael said, "I shall remain a man alone, but what of you yourself, *a grah*? Will you ever marry? Ann has three suitors I know of, and your turn will come soon enough. You are your mother's daughter, sure, and while your sisters are pretty enough, you are the great beauty of the world."

Brigid blushed deeply and shyly sipped her tea. So very much like her mother: the color rose in the porcelain skin of her cheeks, her chestnut hair cascaded across her shoulders, and the memory of his lost love very nearly caused a check in her father's breath.

He cleared his throat and eyes, and said, "If you wish, I could ask around and find you a suitable fellow, a man of some means."

She was young but, in her heart, very sure of what she wanted in life. "Oh, Father," she said, sounding every bit the dreamer, "let us not talk of money. I shall marry for love, or not at all. I shall lead apes in hell if need be."

"Apes in hell, girl?" cried Michael, "What kind of phrase is that for a Christian to utter?"

Brigid stood her ground. "It's an expression common among the English, Daidi, and I think it rather clever, though perhaps it doesn't translate well into the Irish."

"I know what the foul phrase means, child. Trust the English to invent such gutter talk."

"But it's from the Shakespeare, Da!"

"Ach, I should have known, more vile chatter from that pompous Saxon pretender. No poet is he, Brigid, no matter what your refined Miss McCarthy might say."

She set her cup down and spoke with great purpose. "As we are speaking of Miss McCarthy, Daidi, it is a favor I must ask. She is the great teacher of the world and, as you know, her school is the treasure of all Cork. She has asked me—*me!* —if I should care to teach a class of the new girls in the fall. So I beg you to allow me one last semester at the school, as I must do more on my English literature, mustn't I, but thereafter I shall be on staff, paid fifteen pounds a year! I can live with Miss Reese and Miss Hendricks in the teachers' quarters, what glory!"

O'Brian stared at the wall, pulling at his pipe, until he muttered, "Glory, is it, child?" He slowly stood, walked over to the hearth and pulled an old bench over to a dark corner. He climbed up, reached into the rafters, and pulled down a long, carefully wrapped bundle. O'Brian slowly pulled away the canvas covering and brought forth a musket, shining and deadly. Brigid sat stunned; she had no idea her father kept such a secret, a secret for which the English would happily hang him.

With a flame in his eye, O'Brian put the musket to his shoulder, dry-fired, then held it at arm's length to give it a stare of admiration. "You may remember my cousin Eamonn O'Brian. Ten years ago he was part of an ambush on a sheriff's party bent on burning out the tenants of Castleconnell, long O'Brian lands. The crown men were cut to pieces, and our Eamonn took this musket from the cold hands of a West Cork militiaman. Plenty of powder and shot, as well. He hid it well, as have those who have borne it since, all vowing to carry out Eamonn's wish that an O'Brian might one day employ it against the English."

With his eyes closed, Michael performed the manual of arms, practiced and smooth, finally saying, "Your sisters know nothing of this, and I show you, *mo stor*, knowing that you shall keep our secret, but I desire to make a point. Some very bad days are coming, and we shall be forced to take a side. There will be no shades of grey, only black and white, and woe to those who choose wrong."

"But Da," said his lovely daughter, "can there be any question as to our loyalties? Are we O'Brians not as Irish as the soil?"

As he returned the musket to its hiding place he avoided her eye, saying only, "I think you shall accompany me when I visit the holdings tomorrow, and we shall speak further."

*****

The next day dawned a cool misty October morning, and Brigid threw her shawl over her head as she went out to the pasture behind their cottage to fetch her father's horse. Buían—Marigold in the English—ancient, swaybacked, and sullen, stood in a corner of the pasture and pretended not to notice Brigid's approach. When Brigid gave her an affectionate thump on the flank the horse cracked open her eyes, slowly closed them again, and loosed a low rumbling fart.

Only after considerable exertion did Brigid get Buían out into their yard, walking the old mare around to warm her. Michael O'Brian, shaved and well dressed, readied the trap. As they got the mare harnessed, Brigid asked, "Da, can we not buy a new horse? Poor old Buían needs to retire to the Damsel's Field, and there live out the rest of her days, sleeping and farting."

"No, Miss Heavy Purse, we shall not buy a new horse, and no, Buían will not retire to a life of leisure. When the time comes, I can get two and five for her at the knacker's yard." With a trace of annoyance, he added, "Have some sense, girl."

"Yes, Father," she said quietly, surprised by her father's snappishness. She had pain in her eyes and was especially gentle with Buían as they finished harnessing the old horse to the trap.

O'Brian rarely spoke harshly to his daughters, and as they climbed up into the trap, sitting facing one another in the traditional way, she averted her eyes and did not speak to him. He did not wish to sound apologetic, but still he had a conciliatory tone to his voice when he said, "This is likely to be a difficult day for me, so you'll understand if I am in no mood for sentiment. But, yes, *a grah*, I suppose I could afford a new horse, but today I hope to show some things to you, so you might see why we live as we do."

Buían had taken the same route into the hills above Clonakilty a hundred times or more, and so Michael had only to click his tongue to prompt her to head out of the yard and turn up their lane, past the ruins of Kilgariff Church. As was their practice, the O'Brians went silent and crossed themselves as they passed the church and the crumbling graves of the revered, restless dead.

Buían's plodding pace carried them up into the narrow lanes, dense hedges, and small patchwork fields in the low hills. Eventually Brigid asked, "Why shall today be difficult for you, Da?"

"You know, I think, that I am the only Catholic land agent dealing in Lord Shannon's properties. The other middlemen, Simmons, Bates and Houseworth, all Protestants, hold the leases for nine tenths of the lands, but if they ever came up into these hills to collect rents, they'd likely not see home again. Rather than send a Proddy and a thousand militiamen up here, they let me handle things, and it goes well enough. Shannon's agent trusts me, and as a Catholic and an O'Brian, the tenants know I'll give them a fair shake."

With a daughter's sincerity she said, "I know you do your best for the poor people, Da, everyone says so."

"I'll not be so well thought of after today, *a grah*." The trap, never well sprung, took a hard lurch and several pounding bumps, as Buían had very nearly veered into the ditch. O'Brian pulled her sharply back onto the lane, saying, "God damn that beast. She does that deliberately, just to show her displeasure." To Buían he called, "It's the knacker's yard for you, just you wait and see, you ill-mannered brute!"

Buían tossed her head and snorted in the manner typical of amused horses, and O'Brian muttered, "Insolence, wherever I turn."

Turning back to Brigid, who was doing her best to swallow a laugh, he was serious when he said, "Today I'll speak to Aedan O'Donovan, and tell the fool that he'll be given no further grace, and will be turned off his holding in a week's time. Twelve months behind in his rents; I cannot allow it to go on, or every soul up here will think it's fiddler's green."

"Twelve months, Da? You've shown more patience than would Lord Shannon."

"I let him stay on until October, hoping he'd pull in a good crop and get himself squared away, but he's a lazy fool of a drunk, and he'll harvest a bushel of rocks and little more. The trouble is that he's the brother of Tadg O'Donovan. Tadg's been my friend these many years, and the most well-respected man in Clonakilty, and here I am disgracing his family."

Buían struggled up a hill steeper than most, and from the top of the rise they saw a column of smoke rising from the trees on the next ridge.

"That is no peat fire, sure," said Brigid, peering ahead. "Might someone be clearing a field?"

"It's October, so folks will be busy bringing in their lumpers, and it's so wet... no, there's no need to be burning anything, at all." With a false cheerfulness in his voice, O'Brian said, "It looks as if O'Donovan shall get a reprieve, and our lessons on the state of the county shall have to wait."

He looked anxiously to either side, then up the road. The lane was narrow, with muddy ditches, stone walls and dense thorn hedges lining each side. He had a four-foot trap behind eight feet of horse, and at its best the lane was perhaps ten feet wide.

"Nowhere to turn around here," he said, sounding falsely calm. "Well, in a bit we'll come to McCracken's place, he's one of my tenants, a good fellow, and we can turn around there, and head toward home."

"Turn around, Da?"

"Aye, *a grah*, trouble, I think."

Seconds later they heard two musket shots, from over where the smoke was rising, then two, three, more. Shouting, then, from up ahead, and O'Brian stood on his seat to stare intently ahead, seeing little through the trees.

"Father! Look!" cried Brigid, pointing at the fields to their right. Two men were running away from the firing, scrambling across stone walls and crashing through potato beds.

O'Brian called out to them, and the nearer one veered toward them, breathless. With a shock Brigid saw it was her cousin, Fergal O'Brian, his coat torn and blood on his hands.

"Michael! The Committee is betrayed! Yeoman cavalry caught us at Murphy's! Hurley is taken, Goggin is shot! Christ, is that wee Brigid with you?"

"What of Tadg O'Donovan?!"

"Safe! Now, for God's sake, flee! They're right behind us!"

With that the young man looked back toward his pursuers, and wilding grinning, he bolted back into the fields, running like a hare.

O'Brian threw the reins to Brigid, leapt down, grabbed Buían by the bridle, and tried to turn her around. The firing and yelling had frightened the old mare, and she tossed her head in terror.

Another musket shot, just to their right. Two yeomen, their red coats bright in the morning light, pursued the fugitives on foot across the broken ground. In their heavy coats and heavy boots they were making slow progress. They made no sign of having seen the cart, hidden by the dense hedges and trees.

Again O'Brian pulled on the bridle with all his strength, but the lane was narrow, and the horse frightened, old, and unwilling. Another musket shot from just ahead, the sounds of English voices calling through the trees, horse hooves on the road. Brigid sat frozen, frightened and alert as a doe.

O'Brian once again yanked the horse's head around, but she splayed her legs in locked defiance and pulled against him. With his left hand holding the bridle he pulled back his right and punched the horse, viciously, over and over, a man possessed. The old horse leapt, lashed out and kicked the trap, nearly lifting it into the air, but then she lurched forward, her forelegs in the ditch, her head in the dense brambles, coming around.

The trap nearly overturned, the harness creaking in protest, the rear of the cart buried in the far hedge while the horse had her head tangled in the near one. Again, Buían froze in pain and fear, the brambles tearing her face, but another flurry of blows drove her to complete the turn, her muzzle bloody, her eyes wild, as she stumbled from the ditch. Brigid could hardly hold her, but finally O'Brian leapt back into the trap and the horse carried them away in a wild gallop, in fear and anger and panic, as fast as she had moved in all her life, away from the smoke and the firing and the danger that had nearly swallowed them.

Chapter Three

"A volunteer in the God damned militia!" raged John Lockwood. "Damn it, woman, are you deliberately working to make a fool of me? I gave my word to Youngblood regarding the boy's appointment to the Madras Infantry! In India the boy would be a lieutenant, a reputable and honourable rank. Instead, you circumvent my efforts and see that fool made a *volunteer*, a rank created to employ penniless bastards! In the militia, for God's sake, the least prestigious service! In the infantry, the least prestigious branch! With the damned Westmeaths, the least prestigious regiment in Ireland! God damn it, I wager you've been dealing with that sodomite cousin of yours!"

Sophia said nothing, her face in her hands, cowering on the drawing room settee. Lockwood reeled over to the sideboard, poured himself another brandy, and said to no one, "You have placed me in a most precarious position." Then, as if he'd discovered something of great import, he said, "I need to piss."

Their youngest son stood at the top of the stairs listening, frightened and angry. When he heard his father stumbling to the back of the house, James steeled himself and walked down the elegant oak staircase.

The servants knew to stay well clear of the master when he was in drink, and in the past James had been equally prudent, equally afraid. But after being away from home for so many months, he felt himself no longer the boy he was; he was seventeen, as tall as his father, and he had survived the casual brutality of an English public school. Further, in a way he could not yet explain, he had been marked by the intimacy, however brief, of a beautiful young woman. He came down the stairs with a façade, however thin, of confidence, and stepped into the drawing room.

It was oddly quiet. His mother sat on the silk-embroidered settee, subtly rocking, her eyes vacant, as she compulsively twisted her kerchief round and round her finger. A red welt rose on her cheek; without examination, James could recognize it as a handprint; he averted his eyes, a jolt of pain piercing his heart. His eyes drifted to a sword on the wall, the small sword of a Lockwood who had served under Wolfe at Quebec, and had been killed there.

John Lockwood was a cretin, but still he had equipped both his sons in the trappings of the gentry, at English schools and with elite sword masters. As boys, James and his brother had spent endless hours at a *salle d'armes* in Dublin, and in England James had worked with one of his teachers, an inveterate duelist, perfecting his skills. He wagered he could master any man within twenty miles. He imagined facing his drunken father, but frantically, deliberately, drove the thought from his head.

"Ah!" cried his father, returning, raising his glass in mock salute. "The *casus belli* himself!"

"Father, Mother is unwell." James worked to control his voice; he hated himself for the quiver that often crept into his voice when he was anxious. "You should not speak to her so harshly."

"Ah, so you were listening at the keyhole? Did they teach such sneaking tricks at school, I wonder? Though I suppose there are few notions of honour among schoolboys."

James had been raised in Ireland, and many of his boyhood friends were Irish. He spoke a moderate amount of the language, and had absorbed more of the Irish temper than he perhaps realized. He spoke before considering his course, with an aggressive edge, even with a touch of accent. "I heard you through the closed door of my room, sir. I wager the people down the lane heard you."

Lockwood senior roared and lunged toward his son. Lockwood was a hard drinker, and at heart a coward. He stumbled, realized he was spectacularly drunk, and so caught himself, through both a blurred sense of propriety but also an eye-blink realization of his son's new maturity. He stopped to weave and hiss, "You sail for India in two weeks' time. Until then, you will forget this God damned foolishness regarding militia volunteers."

"My trunk is already packed, sir. McMurtry carries me to Mullingar barracks at dawn. By the time you regain your senses I shall be gone. Come, Mother, allow me to see you to your room."

James gently helped his mother to her feet and gave her his arm. He paused at the sword on the wall and reached out for it with his free hand, hoping his father did not see how it shook. He straightened the sword knot, and quietly said, "I wager this old blade could use some care. I shall see to it when I return. Mullingar is not far away, and when I return to see my mother I shall return a soldier, shan't I?"

James looked toward his father and thought he saw him flinch at the notion of his son as an angry soldier, armed.

As his tall son helped Sophia from the room, Lockwood senior flushed and dropped into a chair. In truth, Mr. Youngblood of the HEIC was desperate to fulfill his recruiting targets, and had paid Lockwood two hundred pounds to secure his son's enlistment, money which Lockwood had quickly lost at the gaming tables. He was in a most precarious position.

*****

Moira Carney crept up the back stair to anxiously stand at her mistress's bedroom door. She had long before trained herself not to hear her employers' conversations, but still to know precisely what was happening in the house. From the drawing room she heard Mister Lockwood's snarling taunts, and Master James's calm young voice. She had known James for many years, and heard the quiver of nerves in his tone, but after a moment of silence she was pleased to see him helping his mother up the stairs and down the hall toward her room.

Moira stepped up and threw a shawl around Mrs. Lockwood's bent shoulders, giving James a quick nod to show that she would see to her mistress. As Moira led her into her room, Sophia gave her son a quick, lost, loving look.

"We'll see to her, sir," said Moira, "don't you concern yourself."

There was pain and panic in his eyes as he said, "I am to go to Mullingar in the morning, but God, how can I leave her here with him?" He stepped to the door of his mother's room and was surprised to see both the other maids and even old McMurtry there as well, looking conspiratorial. They all spoke softly with Sophia Lockwood, the maids all kindness as they helped her to a chair by the window.

Moira took James's arm and gently pulled him back out into the hall, closing the door behind her. "We shall care for her, sir. It's us who run this house, and it's us who have seen enough of your father's cruelties. This house has become the scandal of the neighborhood, and we won't have it. I've written to your brother John, and he is coming home in a few days to set things to rights."

"Ah, Moira, John is—"

Moira scoffed, "Oh, he's no saint; that I know as well as anyone, but he's ambitious and proud as Lucifer, and a family scandal would taint his plans." With real kindness she went on, "So you go on, now, dear James, and we'll ensure your mother is safe and as happy as God will allow. Go on and be a soldier, knowing your mother is cared for."

*****

Colonel Edwin Montgomery of the Westmeath Militia Regiment spent perhaps one day in four at his office at Mullingar Barracks. The colonelcy of a militia regiment was, after all, largely a wealthy gentleman's hobby, but he took his responsibilities more seriously than most, and his days at headquarters were typically busy ones. He spent that morning reading a report from the Secret Committee of the House of Commons regarding the state of unrest across Ireland. It was estimated that, despite a wave of arrests, raids, and patrols, the United Irishmen had successfully merged their efforts with those of the rural Defenders. Open rebellion was a distinct possibility.

Montgomery then turned to review the reams of letters, logbooks, rosters and registers of his regiment's business. The men of his regiment, as well as those of nearly every militia regiment, were scattered in handfuls across Ireland, deployed wherever landowners howled for protection from their tenants. He had little control over how his men were employed while under the orders of the local magistrates, but as that dispersion of strength was Dublin Castle's strategy, Edwin was content to read the reports and return home. The fall race season was winding down, and he was anxious to attend the Downs before its close.

The adjutant tapped at the door, stuck his head in, and said, "Beg pardon, sir, but Lieutenant Barr has arrived from Athlone."

Montgomery did not look up, only saying, "Lieutenant Barr can bloody well wait." The young adjutant nodded with a hint of glee in his eyes, but before he withdrew, Montgomery added, "Oh, before I forget, pray have Sergeant Butcher report to me,"

Sergeant Butcher, the Quartermaster, must have been standing just outside the office, as he reported seconds later, gleaming from head to toe, every inch the professional. He snapped his salute and rigidly stood at attention.

The colonel stood to return the salute; he was in many ways the merest amateur, but he reveled in the army's formalities and courtesies. Returning to his seat, Montgomery said, "Sergeant, tomorrow a new volunteer shall join the regiment—a Mr. James Lockwood, my cousin's son. I am unacquainted with the young gentleman, and while it is my hope that he succeed, I will not populate this regiment with any additional brutes, idiots, or incompetents. I trust I make myself clear, Sergeant?"

"Very clear, sir."

"Pray quarter him with Ensign Mainwaring. Mainwaring is no more a soldier than my cat, but he seems a decent fellow. By the way, I desire an entry to be made in the barrack orders. The sentries are to deny entry to any and all unaccompanied females. There are far too many wantons prowling the barracks in search of Mainwaring. The boy is far too handsome; no good will come of it."

"Yes, sir," said Butcher without a twitch of a smile.

"Lastly, Sergeant, I do not wish it to be widely known that young Lockwood is related to me; I will not have him heckled as a favorite. You will, though, see him properly equipped. He may or may not arrive with the requisite funds, so if he finds himself short I will make up the balance. But just the basics, please. The boy need not be fitted with silks and scimitars, Sergeant. Dismissed."

Montgomery then immersed himself in paperwork for an hour or more before he reached to ring the small brass bell on his desk. When the adjutant stepped in, the Colonel growled, "Pray send in Lieutenant Barr."

The adjutant nodded, retreated, and his place at the door was soon taken by Lieutenant Charles Barr. Of moderate height, perhaps twenty years of age, he had a slim, athletic build, dashing whiskers, and an elegantly tailored uniform that featured more than the regulation amount of gold braid. If he felt ill-used by the long wait outside his colonel's office, his face betrayed no trace. Despite having ridden in that morning from Athlone, thirty miles in the saddle, no mud or dust sullied his appearance.

Colonel Montgomery did not ask him to sit. He left the lieutenant's salute unanswered as Barr stood waiting at attention. The colonel once again read through the report of a recent incident involving the lieutenant. Without looking up, Montgomery eventually asked, "Lieutenant Barr, I assume you realize why you have been summoned to headquarters?"

"Am I to be considered for promotion, sir?" Barr asked with a flicker of amusement.

Montgomery slapped the file closed, and said, "You had best mind your tone, sir. It is my policy to support the men of my regiment in all matters, but based on these letters from a Father Tobin and a Reverend Mason, who witnessed your recent duel in Athlone, you are to be considered for Court Martial. They declare themselves the voice of the town, and demand you be charged with murder! Your opposite number in this duel was, after all, a mere draper. You had best explain yourself, sir."

Barr raised his eyebrows, offered a moderate shrug, and said, "Sink me; he challenged me, sir."

"Of course he challenged you, sir! You insulted his wife in the street."

"Honestly, sir, I merely complimented her on the magnificence of her bosom. Her husband is far too easily provoked, a very prideful fellow, like most of these damned Irish."

"Was the man wearing a sword?"

"A sword, sir? Well, of course not, sir. He is, or rather, he was, an Irishman of the middling sort. When he challenged me I offered to draw, but the poor wretch was unable to oblige, so I called to a passing dragoon to loan the fellow his sword."

Montgomery sighed and leaned back in his chair. "Did you have opportunity to arrange your seconds?"

"Sadly, no, sir. It was a mere *rencontre*, resolved in minutes."

Barr said 'rencontre' with a muddled attempt at a French pronunciation; Montgomery, who spoke beautiful French, winced. With growing frustration, the Colonel said, "And so you did not retreat to private ground? Every soul in town witnessed the affair? Dear God, was his wife present?"

"We retired to a nearby carter's yard, sir, though I suppose we did draw quite a mob of spectators. I do not recall his wife *per se*, though as I sheathed my sword I do recall the sight of a tear-stained bosom."

"And so, Lieutenant," Montgomery said, "the man was obviously not a gentleman. Yet you accepted his challenge, to fight in the street in front of half of Athlone, including the affronted lady. You might have offered this fellow something like an equitable match if you had chosen pistols rather than swords. It was unfortunate, I shall not say self-serving, that you equipped him with a heavy dragoon sword, a massive thing best used for cutting down trees, and he lasted, what? Three passes?"

"Two, sir."

Montgomery hissed a sigh and raised both his hands from his desk, palms forward, and said, "I realize you are English by birth, Lieutenant, so pray allow me to explain just what you have done. My duty, and the essential duty of every rational officer in His Majesty's service based in Ireland, is to keep the peace. The common people of this island are already in a state of great unrest, and now you, sir, have added fuel to that fire by killing an innocent fool, a draper, for God's sake, and by the magistrate's account the only loyalist in central Ireland."

"My dear sir, would you rather His Majesty's officers be accosted in the street by peasants? If this Irish draper puts on the airs of a gentleman, then he must be prepared to conduct himself as one. If he had never held a sword in his life, am I to blame?"

Montgomery shot the dapper young man a look, and said, "Lieutenant, you will consider yourself under arrest, confined to the barracks pending further evidence regarding possible Court Martial."

Barr hissed in obvious surprise, but still he rallied to say, "I beg to remind the Colonel of the vital nature of my service in Athlone. While my natural modesty prevents me from being overly effusive, sir, I might mention how the local gentry rave of my ability to produce results. Lord Cathcart himself has praised my diligence in seeing every trace of rebellion efficiently quenched! Now, sir, if I might return to my post, my presence is critical to the upcoming raid against rebels taking shelter in the wilds of Carrickynagtan Bog. Captain Young has entrusted me with—."

"And I shall remind *you*, Lieutenant, that Captain Young reports to *me*. You will remain here; we will do nothing more to incite the indignation of *hoi polloi* of Athlone." With an absent air, one which might have been interpreted in several ways, Montgomery added, "Perhaps you might recall your youth in Liverpool. As the son of a customs officer you might sympathize with the feelings of the common people."

Barr reeled; he went to great lengths to conceal his modest origins, and for the colonel to throw out Liverpool and Barr's common family cut him deeply. As a customs officer Barr's father held a respectable place in society, but that place was one completely inadequate for the sire of a *beau sabreur*. It was his father's lack of rank and specie that kept Charles Barr from a commission in a line regiment, forcing him to launch his military career in the most humble of settings: a lieutenancy in an Irish infantry militia regiment.

As the full import of that information was transferred, acknowledged and digested, Charles Barr nodded, swallowed awkwardly, and said, "I am at your disposal, sir."

*****

It was a typical fall day in Mullingar, cool, breezy, with a sky indecisive regarding the matter of rain. On the edge of town a tall brick wall lined a muddy road. Halfway down the wall stood an arched gate, where a fading sign declared it the barracks of the Westmeath Militia. The wall made up one side of the central cobbled yard, while the officers' quarters, the enlisted barracks, and the stables made up the other three. It was a large compound, but far from imposing. Many of the bricks were crumbling, windows had been boarded over, and the brooding weather added nothing to the air of general neglect.

The tall wooden gates stood open, guarded by one bored sentry, but his attention was soon piqued by a four-horse carriage that was smartly driven up Barracks Road. When it came to a halt in front of his post the soldier stiffened, but then, seeing a brown coat in the carriage he relaxed, as there was no officer to salute. Instead, he watched a tall, slender young man step down, one obviously ill at ease.

It was October of 1797, and James Faithful Lockwood had begun his military career. James paused at the side of the carriage, looking about, looking lost. McMurtry climbed down from the driver's seat, stiff after their long drive, and as he worked to untie Master James's chest from the rear of the carriage, he spoke quietly but insistently. "Did ya know, sir, I knew your grandfather when I was a boy? A fine gentleman and a bold soldier. Your Da is far different from his Da, isn't he, and so too do you seem a different type of man from your Da. Go on, now, sir, and you show 'em how a thorough gentleman behaves."

McMurtry rarely spoke to James, and the young man turned to say, "Why, thank you, McMurtry, that was most—"

McMurtry interrupted with an emphatic nod toward the gate and a brief, "Company, sir."

A sergeant strode manfully toward them across the cobbled yard, then drew himself up two yards from James to salute smartly. "Sergeant Butcher, Quartermaster Sergeant, sir."

James nearly saluted in response, but thinking that he was not yet privy to such courtesies, he made a formal, but not overly deferential, bow.

Butcher nodded in approval, and said, "Quite right, Mr. Lockwood, no salutes for you until we have you uniformed proper. Now, if you will follow me, sir, I shall see you to your quarters."

The sergeant then spun on his heel and marched off, forcing James to hurry to keep up. They passed a handful of enlisted men loitering around the courtyard, men who made no effort to acknowledge either the sergeant or the new Proddy boy.

"Upon the colonel's orders, sir," continued the sergeant in a crisp, efficient tone, "I have collected for your convenience various necessities. At what I deem a fair price, you might acquire the uniforms of Lieutenant Haythornthwaite; you are both of a size, though of course, we shall need to alter marks of rank. The lieutenant was recently dismissed from the King's service." They reached the steps to the Officers' Quarters where Butcher opened the door, paused, and said in a quieter tone, "Bestiality, sir."

Taken aback, James went wide-eyed, and managed to reply, "How very shocking."

"Oh, yes, indeed, sir. The Westmeaths are no flash guards regiment, but still we do not condone anything in the roaming line." Eyeing the young gentleman, he asked, "I trust that shall not pose an obstacle, sir?"

"No, Sergeant!"

Mollified, the sergeant lead James through the doors and down a hall, past numerous doorways, all standing open and empty, giving the place an air of neglect and abandonment.

"You will understand, sir," said Sergeant Butcher, "that nearly all of the regiment's officers are with their companies in the field, or on leave."

A rat crossed their path, drawing a practiced kick from the sergeant. At the end of the hall they thumped up two narrow, winding sets of stairs to a hallway under the rafters of the old building. Another rat glared at them from the end of a short hallway. On one dingy wall was scrawled the words, '*Finit hic Deo*'.

James had struggled in his Latin classes, so he needed a moment to puzzle over the graffiti before he offered, "'*God ends here,*' Sergeant?"

In the half-light, Butcher looked back and said, "Just Ensign Mainwaring's little joke, sir. He is a great one for talking foreign."

Two attic rooms lay off the dim hall, the doors bearing a plank with the name of its occupants. Chalked on one door was the name, 'Lieut. Barr' while the other said, 'Ensign Mainwaring/Mr. Lockwood.'

The door to the latter room opened and out stepped a man about the same age as James, dressed in simple breeches and shirt, of moderate height, a kind smile, and an unconscious beauty.

Butcher nodded toward the gentlemen in turn, saying, "Ensign Thomas Mainwaring, Mr. James Lockwood. Mr. Lockwood, Ensign Mainwaring."

Brief, polite, noncommittal, mandatory bows were exchanged.

"Your servant, sir."

"Your servant, sir."

The courtesies completed, Tom waved James into their room, saying, "Do come in, won't you? I have so looked forward to you joining, as things can be so very dull here. There are only a few other officers here, and they are all so very old. I must apologize for the room, as the colonel has banished us youngsters to the attic. It is so unfair; one young lady's visit, and I am branded a detriment to the regiment's morals. So I am afraid we shall share this cave, and while it is small, dirty, dark, and cold, it is ours. Our dear Sergeant Butcher has found you a decent bunk, and I have—"

At the mention of his name, Butcher said, "I shall see that Mr. Lockwood's trunk is brought up," and retreated toward the stairs.

Pointing toward a pile on the bunk, Mainwaring asked, "I suppose Butcher mentioned you buying Haythornthwaite's uniforms?"

"Yes," said James, still unsure of his course.

"Haythornthwaite was not as tall as you, but I have a man in my platoon who was a tailor before his enlistment, and he shall set things to right. But, I wonder, did Butcher mention Haythornthwaite's unfortunate... tendencies?"

"He did." James hesitantly poked the pile and said, "I trust such notions are not... well... contagious?"

Mainwaring pondered that for a moment. "I think not. I was in Haythornthwaite's presence for some weeks, and I have yet to have a single romantic thought of a...."

"...of a quadrupedal nature?"

"Precisely! We understand each other, sir."

James finally returned Mainwaring's smile and said, "I wonder, sir, as we shall be in such close quarters, if you might call me James, please?"

Mainwaring beamed and replied, "James it is! It shall be James and Tom from now on."

Earnestly, openly, they shook hands as a new voice came from the door.

"Ah, the new boy has arrived," said Charles Barr, leaning languidly against the door frame. "As I have refused to play the Ganymede, Colonel Molly has sentenced me to this pit of despair. Still, we might make the best of it." Holding aloft a bottle of brandy, he added with a wolfish smile, "What do you gentlemen say to a drink and a few hands of cards?"

Chapter Four

Brigid added a fresh turf log to the hearth fire and put the kettle on. While she could not keep her hands from shaking, she did keep herself from crying. When her father came in he went to the basin to wash his hands, and as he did so he shook his head, and said, "That mare is ruined, sure. I have never seen a horse so spent."

"I confess, I feel spent as well, Father. I have never been so afraid."

"I am so sorry, *mo stor,* for you to be involved in such a thing, a girl seventeen years of age." Michael O'Brian shook his hands in the air to dry them, and then, ignoring Brigid's tea, he went to the cupboard and poured himself a large glass of whiskey. He stalked back and forth across the room, drinking steadily. "That being said, I am glad your sisters are not yet home, so that we might talk." Turning to face his daughter he held up a finger and said emphatically, "You must forget everything you saw today. *Everything.*"

Her hands stopped their shaking and her mood turned from fear to fury in an instant. "Forget, Daidi? Forget what, I wonder? That my good kind father owns a musket which would get him hanged, my cousin Fergal is a rebel pursued by Yeomen, or that my own godfather, Tadg an Astna O'Donovan himself, is a member of some committee, a committee which has been betrayed to the English, the bloody-minded English?"

Her father paused, his finger still in the air, frowned, and said, "Precisely."

"Christ and His nails, Da, what are you involved in?"

"And since when, Brigid ni Brian, am I required to explain myself to my own daughter?"

Brigid raised her own finger in defiance, and said, "Since my mother has gone to heaven! It seems that God has left me to see to my sisters' well-being, and to talk some sense to our father! You have always spoken of your, of *our*, devotion to what is right, for what our people deserve, but *rebellion*, Da? What madness is that!"

He ran his hand through his hair, a gesture Brigid knew was his way of calming himself, and in a more rational voice he said, "Know this, Brigid: I have done nothing to endanger my family. I know some people, I know some things, but I have done nothing to commit myself."

He went to the cupboard and poured himself another glass. "This is the lesson I meant to teach when we left the house this morning. Now, more than ever, you must see how complicated this web of alliance and reputation is, and how some people might see me, a middleman, as a puppet of the Ascendency bastards. So I show my face, quiet and amenable, to the rich men, but I show my heart to men I trust, and that heart is Irish!" He held his glass aloft in salute, and tossed back the rest of his whiskey.

Brigid sighed and pushed both open palms downward, also trying to calm herself. "And so this is why you'll not allow me to return to school, and to teach there? Come, Da, if I am not to teach, would you have me stay at home and spend my life keeping house for you?"

He sat heavily into his old wooden chair and sighed, "Is that so terrible, girl?" Then, in a kinder tone, he went on, "Think of me, Brigid, a man who has the trust, and knows the secrets, of many men, while his daughter is devoted to this 'English Literature' and is to teach at a school attended by English girls...."

"But, Da, there are English and Irish at the school, Catholic and Protestant girls, and we get on well!"

O'Brian made an insistent gesture, cutting the air with the edge of his hand, and with anger returning to his voice he said, "Do I not know that? Do I not know that is the path that in ten generations might save this country? But for now, *now*, girl, the people are frightened, and foolish, quick to point fingers as they forget any notions of fairness, and cling only to one side or the other. This is the world in which we live, and we must adhere to its tenets, no matter how hateful."

*****

Fergal O'Brian crept along a hedge to kneel beside Tadg O'Donovan, where they both peered up a narrow lane in the failing light. The lane was lined with stone walls and dense hedges, behind which hid thirty rebel Irishmen. Fergal and O'Donovan spoke to one another in whispers, their Irish thick with the broad Cork accent.

"Are you certain, then," said Fergal, "that the yeomen will be coming? My men are anxious to avenge poor Goggin, but all this waiting is testing their nerve."

O'Donovan took an apple from his coat pocket, and as he polished it on his lapel he said, "We have a man in the

Clonakilty Barrack stables, and before you ask, no, I will not tell you his name. But this man has told me that two of the Muskerrys have been granted leave to return home on leave. They live in the big house up at Oak Mount, and to get there they need cross the Kilmeen stream here."

More tense minutes passed, until Fergal whispered, "Is it possible, do you think, Tadg *a grah*, that this is a trap? Might we be betrayed?" With a hint of panic in his voice the little fellow went on, "The yeomen took Hurley; might he have talked? Or, Christ, maybe my own cousin, Michael O'Brian! He saw me at the ambush at Murphy's, and he asked about you!"

O'Donovan calmly took a bite from his apple and said, "Don't talk nonsense, Fergal. Hurley would die before telling them the time of day, and I would trust our Michael O'Brian with my mother's own life. These thirty men see you as their leader; you had best start acting like one."

It was not a moment later that the rebels heard the sound of singing coming from the hill above them, a song dear to the loyalists and loathed by the rebels.

> *We'll fight to the last in the honest old cause,*
> *And guard our religion, our freedom and laws;*
> *We'll fight for our country, our King and his crown,*
> *And make all the traitors and croppies lie down.*
> *Down, down, croppies lie down.*

Two mounted men, relaxed and singing, slowly rode down the lane toward Kilmeen Bridge. Their red tunics were unbuttoned, their bicorn hats tilted back on their heads as they passed a bottle between them. They were three miles from home.

Each of the yeomen had a sabre and carbine hanging from his belt, while the rebels held only pikes and pitchforks —laborers, shopkeepers and a handful of men who had nothing to lose. O'Donovan had stressed to them that they stay in cover until he gave the word to attack, and despite their nerves they held their place as the riders approached. O'Donovan had participated in a dozen ambushes, and in the past something had always gone awry, someone jumped or ran or spoke, causing more panic and bloodshed than was necessary. This time he was quietly pleased to see the riders slip unaware into the trap. With a grin of satisfaction he jumped to his feet and screamed, *"Anois, buachaillí!"* Now, boys!

With roars of fear, anger and hatred, the rebels surged from the hedges into the lane—behind, alongside and ahead of the startled horsemen. The yeomen tried to draw their swords, madly spurring their horses to push through the ambush, but the lane was packed with pole weapons and screaming men. A pike pierced one horse's breast, sending it rearing back, and throwing its rider.

As the yeoman fell from the saddle he cried, "Father, help me!"

The other horseman turned to help his son, but then his horse, too, was speared, and then he was stabbed, two, three pikes lifting him screaming from the saddle. In a moment it was over; both redcoats were dead, stabbed and bludgeoned. Both horses were badly wounded, one lying panting in the ditch, the other staggering away, bleeding heavily.

None of the rebels were hurt. As the two dead men lay in the road, torn and bloody, some of the rebels openly rejoiced, a few stalked about nervously, though most stood shocked and pale. O'Donovan ordered them into four groups, having to physically push some to get them to move, and soon all were moving off into the woods, one of the younger men obviously weeping.

O'Donovan and Fergal O'Brian were last to leave the lane.

Looking down at the two shattered bodies, O'Donovan spit at them, and said, "It's you yourselves who are lying down, aren't you, while we Croppies live to fight for *our* cause."

Looking shocked and drained, Fergal said, "And, so, Goggin stands avenged."

"He is avenged, sure. And now, our murderous oppressors shall in turn avenge their dead, and so the game goes on. We must keep the cycle going, and building in ferocity. Honest men like us must stoke this fire and bring this country to a boil. Rebellion, Fergal boy, and a free Ireland!"

*****

Ever since the girls were very young, the O'Brian family had followed the same tradition every Sunday. First, the family would attend mass at St. Brigid's chapel, as the town, like most Irish towns, was not allowed a Catholic church. The British enmity for Catholicism limited Clonakilty to only a modest chapel.

After mass Michael and his daughters would eat a quick dinner before walking across the fields to visit with Seanathair O'Brian, Michael's aged father, who lived alone in a neat but tiny cabin. There he would formally serve tea, whiskey, and a catechism of the wrongs inflicted on the Irish in general, and the O'Brians in particular.

"*Anois, garinionacha,*" now, granddaughters, the bent old man said that next Sunday, "let us speak of important matters. Pray recite some of the insults and shackles placed upon the Irish by the English Penal Laws."

Brigid and her sisters had not learned of such matters at Miss McCarthy's School, but had heard them so often at their grandfather's knee, and from their father as well, that each in turn quickly ticked them off.

As the eldest, Ann was expected to go first. "Catholics barred from public office," she offered.

"Catholics barred from owning firearms," said Brigid, giving her father a subtle glance.

"No Catholic shall own a horse worth more than five pounds," said Caitlin. That law troubled her, as she liked horses, and dreamt of one day learning to ride.

Anne, the memory of their humble chapel fresh in her mind, said, "Catholic churches, when allowed, are to be built of wood, not stone, and away from main roads."

"Marriages between Catholics and Protestants," said Brigid in turn, "*were* illegal, though that law was modified in 1778 to allow such marriages, but only when performed by an Anglican minister."

Seanathair O'Brian spat into the hearth fire and said, "God curse any Catholic, man or woman, who would dirty themselves with a Proddy."

Brigid rolled her eyes and nearly jumped up to argue with her grandfather, but when her father said, "Amen," she kept her seat and held her tongue. She desperately wanted to teach, to live a life that necessarily involved mingling with the Protestants, but she held her tongue in deference to her father, her grandfather, and their ways.

Sipping his whiskey, the harsh poteen of the rural stills, Michael went on, "You three girls could go on for an hour, but there is one Penal Law in particular which comes to my mind. 'No Catholic shall teach school, upon pain of twenty pounds fine and three months in prison for every such offence!'"

"That one was repealed 1782!" cried Brigid, flushing.

"True, Miss Barrister, but the intent of such laws linger. While some of the Penal Laws are repealed or ignored, in the minds of the Ascendency their spirit remains. At every turn the British want to keep us down, in our place, fixed and limited. We co-exist when we must, but we must never trust them. Make no mistake, they are our enemies."

Chapter Five

James woke early the next morning with a start: a new bed, a new room. He was, for a moment, irrationally frightened, only slowly recalling where he was and why. He looked over in relief to see Tom Mainwaring's bed empty; he would have been ashamed to have his new roommate see him so unmanned. He did not have long to enjoy his relief, as the door was slowly pushed open and Tom peeked in.

"Oh, good, you are awake. As it is Sunday there is no drill, and I took the liberty of raiding the mess for breakfast." He came in and set a loaded tray on the room's sole table. "It is not *haute cuisine*, but still, some decent bread, cheese, and an apple. Oh, and I made an odious assumption, entirely self-serving, and I fear I may have guessed wrong... do you prefer coffee, or tea?"

"Oh, I am a tea man, please," said James, but he very nearly added that he would take either, anything, rather than give offence; but before he could sputter his addendum Tom smiled in triumph.

"Tea it is! I guessed correctly! I am quite absurdly pleased."

They spent the morning in their little room, still a bit stiff and very polite, sipping their tea and learning one another's ways. Tom was helpful in showing how best to wear the regulation clothing, belts, and bicorn, as the uniforms of the disgraced Lieutenant Haythornthwaite, happily free of any residual corruption, neatly fit James Lockwood's long frame. Their one difficulty was the bicorn, to be worn side-to-side, but with a rakish angle. As Mrs. Lockwood had mentioned on more than one occasion, James had a large head, while evidently, Lieutenant Haythornthwaite had a rather small one. It required considerable alteration of the bicorn's interior before the black felt and leather headgear sat square on James's head. The brass cap badge needed polishing.

Once fully outfitted, James stood awkwardly in the middle of the room, self-conscious and not a little proud, while Tom dug up a shaving mirror from his trunk. The mirror was not a large one, so he had to stand on his bed at the far wall so that James might see himself, an officer in the King's service.

"Behold the Queen of the May!" said James, finally smiling broadly.

"You do look quite the part, I must say. Now that you have the veneer, might I suggest we start on your education? Major Moon is likely to grill you as soon as he sees you, so perhaps we might get a jump on him." Turning again to his trunk, Tom added, "My father sent me three quite useful books, if you should care to see them."

They spent two hours sitting on their beds, at first reading aloud the duties of a junior officer of militia, but eventually setting the books aside and drifting into friendly conversation. Their chat ended when the door swung open, revealing Lieutenant Barr standing there, looking elegant, tying back his long hair with a black silk ribbon. He was wearing his sword.

"Come along, you two," said Barr casually, "I am taking you to town. There are two new whores at Barnaby's, and I intend to sample their wares. I hear they are quite pretty: Sally and Shannon. And they are sisters! How I love to defile sisters. You two can do as you please in the tap; a cup of milk and some porridge, perhaps. After my dalliance, I shall allow you to ply me with drink, and I shall regale you with tales of my derring-do while battling the foul rebels of Athlone."

Both James and Tom looked at him with faces that would not have been out of place in a boys' choir, and James said, "But, sir, it is not yet noon, on a Sunday."

"Yes, so the slatterns should be *available.* Lesson the First: It is bothersome to locate a decent whore on any evening, to find two is a damned chore, and to get two and pretty sisters! Quite impossible. Sunday mornings, young gentlemen, Sunday mornings! Sink me, you have a great deal to learn."

James nearly agreed to go along, wondering just what was expected of junior officers of militia, when Tom said hurriedly, "*Désolée*, Lieutenant Barr, but sadly Colonel Montgomery has tasked me with seeing Mr. Lockwood properly settled before dinner today, and I have yet to give him his tour of the barracks."

"Yes!" James said, rather too eagerly. "A tour."

Lieutenant Barr accepted the rejection casually, but as he turned from their doorway he muttered, "Fucking puppies."

There is something about loudly thundering down stairs that delights young men. It was odd, but by the time they had rumbled down the creaking wooden steps and out into the yard, James felt a growing attachment to Tom, as if there were some bond in shared male foolishness.

Trading grins, they set out for the first stop in Tom's chatty tour. The officers' mess was primary in their thoughts; as young men, they shared a wolfish interest in meal times. Stepping in, James was impressed: a large room, tall windows, lofty rafters, and surprisingly elegant tables and chairs.

Tom waved an arm into the space and said, "Grand, is it not? The steward tells me it sits sixty or more, but as all our companies are deployed, we have only five officers here, well *six*, now that you have joined, at dinner." Tom paused, thinking, and went on, "Well, perhaps seven? I suppose Lieutenant Barr shall join as a guest, though I am unsure if he can be received."

James was surprised, and said, "Why ever not? Lieutenant Barr seems quite... well... dashing."

In a conspiratorial tone, Tom said, "Oh, he is quite notorious, even if one ignores his fascination for women of... a certain nature. Captain Thompson of Two Company has taken ill—he is the picture of Alcibiades—and so Barr was given command of the company. But Barr is now under arrest! I am unaware of the details, but rumour has it that the Lieutenant duels with unseemly frequency."

James was unfamiliar with Greek history in general, and Alcibiades in particular, though he did manage a creditable nod, as he muttered an educated, "Oh, Alcibiades... oh my, yes."

They strolled back out into the yard, discussing the quality and quantity of mess fare, and had gone only a short way before Sergeant Butcher emerged from the armourer's shop and strode over to them.

It was soon evident that the sergeant took very seriously the Colonel's instruction to equip Mr. Lockwood with the most basic of kit. While Lieutenant Haythornthwaite's uniforms fit Lockwood passably well, the young gentleman was not so fortunate in Butcher's selection of his weapons.

"Ah, gentlemen," said Butcher, "I was just on my way to your quarters." Holding up a pistol and short sword as if they were holy relics, he went on, "I have worked with Sergeant Curran, and have obtained from his stores a pistol and sword suitable for Mister Lockwood's needs, to be had at *no cost*."

It was apparent why the weapons were to be had at no cost, for while some attempt had been made to recover them, both weapons were far from regulation. The pistol was small, old, and of a small bore, and though the flint had been replaced and it had recently been cleaned, the weapon was more suited for a lady's garter than an officer's sash. James, who knew one end of a sword from the other, eyed the blade with sagging hopes. A battered, pitted, naval cutlass from the previous age, when Butcher handed the weapon across, James found his worst fears fulfilled. While it had a new edge, its shape, weight, and balance were anathema to anyone trained as a swordsman. The wide blade and obtuse point rendered it useless as a thrusting weapon, while its short length and odd balance made it suitable for nothing but brutal close-quarters hacking.

James offered a rueful grin and said, "Thank you, Sergeant Butcher. These shall do famously."

"They're not Tower of London work, sir," said Butcher with only a hint of apology, "but in the hands of a determined gentleman, a fair piece of work."

"Might there be a scabbard, Sergeant?" asked James after making a few mock thrusts, trying to find some virtue in the blade, and failing.

"A scabbard, sir? Well, no. But I shall speak with Sergeant Curran. Perhaps he and his mate might find something buried in his stores, sir." Somewhat downcast, Butcher headed back to the armoury, adding over his shoulder, "By the way, sir, you'll need to be choosing a servant soon. Perhaps Ensign Mainwaring might suggest someone."

Turning to Tom, James asked, "Are we truly entitled to a servant?"

As they resumed their stroll across the barracks yard Tom replied, "Oh, my, yes. The true title is 'soldier servant.' Among the enlisted men it is considered a plum assignment, as the servants are exempt from drill, and they typically manage to extract a portion of their officers' food and drink. My man is named O'Mara, quite a decent fellow. He can suggest one of his mates for you, but of course the choice is yours."

"That is most kind of you, sir. Oh, I beg pardon: *Tom.*"

Tom gave him a smile and said, "You shall get accustomed to me soon enough."

James wore the regulation single shoulder belt, which should have held the scabbarded blade at his left hip, but without a scabbard he was rather at a stand. With Tom's help he tucked the pistol into his sash on his right hip, and the bare cutlass blade at his left.

Eying the outrageous bare blade stuck into his sash, James said, "I feel rather more like a pirate than a King's officer."

Tom croaked, "What ho, matey?" sharing a laugh as they continued their stroll across the barracks yard, where a handful of enlisted men idled under the eaves and eyed the two young men.

"I suppose," said Tom, "that duty requires me to share a few facts regarding the state of the regiment." He grinned and went on, "Goodness, I sound like a Field Marshal, do I not? I have been with the regiment for six months, and here I am, topping it the knob."

"Not at all! I appreciate all that you might share with me."

"Well, then. You might notice that we bypassed the enlisted quarters... we'll not visit there, as the men would not take it kindly. They view it as their private kingdom, and we leave it to the sergeants to manage things." Growing more serious, and speaking in a confidential voice, Tom went on, "And, frankly, James, we might not be entirely safe there. The United Irishmen have made inroads among the men, and while most of them might still be relied upon, it is believed that at least some have taken the United oath."

"So, it is true, then!" said James, rather too boyishly. "I had heard rumours of such things happening, though my father said it was all stuff and nonsense."

As if revealing a great secret, Tom said excitedly, "Government does its best to keep it from the public, as they are anxious to maintain the illusion of the military as a loyal monolith, but the United men are working to subvert every militia regiment in Ireland."

They were interrupted by a corporal at the gate. Tasked with changing the guard, the corporal called across the yard toward the barracks, "O'Rourke, you Jacobian bastard, you'll stand your watch, or I'll see you flogged like a dog!"

After a moment, a big man emerged from the barracks, pulling on his coat, sullen and in no hurry. He strolled past Mainwaring and Lockwood with his eyes down, making no effort to acknowledge them.

Tom scowled and roughly told the man, "Private O'Rourke, you had best make your salute, or I shall encourage Corporal McCarthy to follow through on that flogging."

O'Rourke paused, turned back toward the officers with a look of pure hatred, made a vague wave toward the brim of his bicorn, and went on.

James was astonished to hear Tom, this kind young fellow, speak with such harshness and authority, and when he turned to Tom his face betrayed his shock. Tom grinned awkwardly, "It is unpleasant, is it not? I am still not entirely confident in speaking to my brother man in such a manner, but it is part of our role here. Major Moon has impressed that upon me in no uncertain terms. We shall meet him at dinner, and you will understand. He is a most unpleasant man. He has no love for the kind, the weak or the Irish."

James nodded, privately considering Major Moon's opinions. He eventually asked, "I believe you grew up in England, Tom?"

Tom raised his eyebrows wryly and gave his new friend a crooked grin. "Yes, the seventh son of an impoverished Leicester clergyman."

One of James's schoolmates in England had been the son of a clergyman, and an unbearable self-righteous prig. James had yet to hear Tom curse, and wondered if this handsome ensign might prove another such a fellow. Still, in the face of such frankness James could not help but respond in kind. He hesitated, grimaced and said, "And I am the second son of a struggling Anglo-Irish aristocrat who despises me." There was a long silence, not an awkward one. "At any rate," James went on, stronger, "I grew up among the Irish, and unlike the major, I find them an admirable people. Still, I realize they are like the rest of humanity, in that they have their share of fools and felons."

As they stood together watching the corporal berating O'Rourke and three other men at the gate, Tom said in a sad voice, "I wonder if we have more than our share of both gathered here."

James nodded in understanding, and quietly added. "One other thing about the Irish: I have rarely known them to forget a slight."

*****

Most of the Westmeath Militia Regiment was scattered across the west and south of Ireland, sometimes only in platoon or squad strengths, packets of men tasked with aiding the magistrates in enforcing the English king's dictates. Thus, only the depot company occupied the barracks—mostly newly recruited men—men without loyalty to their officers, their NCOs, or one another. Most of the recruits were desperately poor Catholics, drafted by the local magistrates, Protestant gentlemen who were pleased to dispatch their most troublesome tenants to the militia. The men would be taken from their homes and deliberately assigned to a regiment on the far side of the island.

One of those men was named Diarmuid Doolan. He was an unattractive, cursing, muttering, ill-mannered little man, perhaps forty years old, though he was often mistaken for someone far older. For most of his life he had lived alone on a small stony plot in far Donegal, content with his living of potatoes, milk, and poteen. That life abruptly ended when his landlord, in reckless pursuit of a fox, leapt his massive gelding over Doolan's dry stone fence and into his lazy beds. As the fox darted between the fragile potato plants the horse's hooves churned up Doolan's livelihood, and soon a dozen baying hounds followed the horse into the small field. The rest of the fox hunt was not far behind, wildly galloping through other subsistence farmers' fields with horns blaring.

Doolan, who, the night before, had heavily tested the potency of his latest batch of poteen, was jolted awake by the sound of men yelling, dogs barking and huntsmen's blaring horns. He emerged from his tiny sod cabin with pitchfork in hand, and promptly stabbed the nearest dog in the hindquarters. The dog survived, as did the fox, but the next day the name Diarmuid Doolan was on the list of men to be drafted, in fulfillment of Donegal's quota of militiamen.

Three weeks later Doolan was wearing a red coat in Mullingar. For all his unpleasantness he was not a poor comrade, and he was not stupid; after a month those traits were grudgingly recognized and he was assigned to assist the new armoury sergeant, Curran, in organizing the armoury's muddled stores. Eventually Curran tasked Doolan with digging through those stores in search of a scabbard for the new young officer's cutlass.

When Doolan came across something he thought might be suitable, Curran looked it over, shrugged, and said in Irish, "Aye, that'll do. Run it over to the officers' kingdom, will you? Give it to that tall skinny lad... ach, I can never remember those Saxon names... you know, the one who can't find his arse with both hands."

*****

The young gentlemen had opted to take a nap before dinner, and were both deeply asleep at 2:45 when Private O'Mara came and tapped at the door to ask if Ensign Mainwaring would like to have his coat brushed. There followed a blur of activity, as dinner was at 3:00, and as Mr. Lockwood was to be introduced to his new brother officers, it would be exceptionally poor form to be even a minute tardy.

Private O'Mara stood in a corner dutifully brushing both Ensign Mainwaring's and Mr. Lockwood's scarlet broadcloth coats while the two gentlemen scrambled to wash, shave and comb their hair into something less resembling rats' nests. In truth neither of them needed to shave, neither being of a hirsute nature, but they were determined to act the part. As James had earlier noticed that Tom rarely cursed, he made an effort to check his own habit of doing so, though it required a herculean effort to hold his tongue when the razor nicked his chin and the blood threatened the snowy whiteness of his best shirt.

As they threw their clothes on, they had a hustled conversation.

Tom said, "There shall be six at table. Major Moon is senior, a short round little fellow who never smiles. Where has that comb got to?"

"Please God, he won't ask me anything difficult."

"Do hand me my shoes, won't you, O'Mara?" Then to James, "God has little to do with Major Moon, brother."

James was pleased to have Tom refer to him with such familiarity, and with a suppressed grin he asked, "And I believe you mentioned a Captain Rampage?"

"Captain *Ramage* is the tall fellow who is always sad... neither here nor there... he rarely speaks."

"God damn these buttons; I beg pardon. I envy you your sword, brother. A five ball spadroon?"

"Yes," said Tom modestly, hurriedly. "A gift from my uncle. Ready? Off we go. Well done, O'Mara." As the two gleaming young officers hustled down the stairs, Tom went on, "Lieutenants Trafford and Otway, now, are decent fellows, but terribly old. At least thirty, I think."

"And the sixth," said James, ticking off the numbers on his fingers, outside now, nearly running across the wet cobblestones toward the mess door, "is our dear Lieutenant Barr. Christ but I am nervous."

As they stepped into the mess the other officers were already seated, crystal glasses and wine bottles, some already empty, on the table. Their servants stood at attention behind each officers' chair, and a pair of stewards hustled about with trays and bottles. Major Moon, at the head of the table, deliberately pulled his watch from his snug waistcoat, checked it, nodded in approval, and tucked it away.

"Gentleman!" said Tom. James glanced over and for the first time noticed that Tom truly was a handsome fellow. "May I present Mr. Lockwood, recently joined?"

Tom proceeded smoothly with the honours, introducing each gentleman in order of rank, each standing, exchanging a bow, then stepping forward to shake hands and welcome Mr. Lockwood to the regiment. James was by nature a likeable fellow, anxious to please, and so things went well, and while Major Moon was distant, the others were friendly enough. The only sour note came when Lieutenant Barr's turn to stand and bid welcome came and he offered only a vague wave of his glass, and a slurred, "We've already met."

James saw Moon shoot Barr a look, but the major said only, "Gentlemen, before we take our seats, one word of explanation to the newest member of the mess. Mr. Lockwood, typically there are no side arms worn in the mess, a precaution against hastiness if a gentleman falls into a passion when in drink. But in the interest of increased readiness we now stand armed at all times. Do I make myself understood, sir? Eh?"

"You do, sir."

The major then scowled at the bare cutlass blade tucked into James's sash. "Is that how you intend to arm yourself, sir?"

James did his best not to let his embarrassment reach his face, but failed. "Beg pardon, sir. I know it is not regulation, sir."

"No, no, sir," cried Barr from his chair with a scarcely concealed smile, "a cutlass tucked into one's sash is perfectly acceptable. Indeed, in time it may grow quite fashionable, quite *de rigueur*. If nothing else, it must be tolerable cheap, which is an advantage to gentlemen of... limited means."

They took their seats, James red-faced. He managed to survive the dinner by remaining silent, chewing with his mouth closed, and taking very little wine. The conversation was muted, the major silent except for sharp corrections of his subordinates.

"No talking shop in the mess, sir!"

"I say again, Lieutenant Otway, no bawdy at table!"

"Captain Ramage, your sleeve is in the butter, sir! The butter!"

The food was plain, the wine poor, the dinner's one redeeming quality being its brevity. With some relief the officers stood, quietly chatting and brushing crumbs from their coats while the servants and stewards cleared the table.

In the hubbub a private soldier came in the mess door, approached Mr. Lockwood, made his salute, and said, "Private Doolan reporting, sir, with your scabbard."

After his humiliation at table James was delighted, as the scabbard was of reasonable quality, and a good fit for the cutlass blade. In his relief his caution slipped. "*Go raibh maith agat, a Private Doolan a grah.*"

Major Moon was instantly beside him, in a fury, "What are you about there, sir? Eh? Why is an enlisted man come uninvited to the officers' mess? Eh? And what is that gibberish you're speaking? Are you a King's officer, sir, or some peasant off the bog?"

Both James and Doolan snapped to attention as all faces in the room turned to witness their dressing down.

"Beg pardon, sir," said James quickly. "I said 'thank you' to the private, as he had brought me my scabbard, sir. I... had deliberately ordered the private to enter the mess, sir..."

At that falsehood, Doolan raised his eyebrows and glanced at Lockwood, but remained silent.

" ...and was unaware that the private was not allowed entry, sir. It is my fault entirely, sir."

"What do you mean, sir, saying *thank you* to a common soldier! You are here to act as an officer and you shall comport yourself as such! *Orders* are the stuff of armies, not bloody damned courtesies! And I have forbidden the speaking of the Erse in this garrison, sir! Forbidden!"

The major then slapped his bicorn on his bald head and stalked from the room. The tension dropped sharply; there were some murmurs of sympathy for the new man, and before he returned to his duties, Private Doolan passed by Mr. Lockwood and murmured, "Thank you, sir."

*****

While Tom shaved and dressed in the best uniform his very modest budget allowed, James had his nose deep in *The Military Guide for Young Officers*, a handbook for those unfamiliar with the detailed complexities of military life.

"Are you quite certain you'll not come out with us?" asked Tom. He was completely void of vanity, his one nod to style being a determination to get the perfect rakish tilt to his bicorn. "Friday night is our traditional night in town."

"I had best play the schoolboy, thank you. After the drubbing Moon gave me this morning, I shall study. Do tender my apologies to the others, will you? I do not wish to appear singular."

"They, of all men, will understand your efforts to avoid Moon's wrath."

Private O'Mara tapped at the door to see if he was needed. Tom told him to take the evening for himself, but before he left, O'Mara said, "The other gentlemen are all ready for town, aren't they? Excepting Major Moon, of course, he being officer of the day. And it's been raining, hasn't it, so you had best wear your cloak, sir."

O'Mara returned to his evening in the barracks, and Tom departed with a last sympathetic look, as James made a manly dive into the manual. At that morning's drill, Major Moon had questioned Mr. Lockwood's familiarity with the motions of redeploying a brigade. Mr. Lockwood, with all of three weeks of military service under his belt, had confessed he had no idea—indeed there was not a company officer in the regiment who would have known, the motions of brigades being chiefly the concern of brigadier generals—but he had resolved he would not be caught short again. So now he applied himself to the handbook with a will. However, it might just as well have been written in Greek:

> *Marching off from the left of the center in one column will bring the six battalions into their former order; when they may form by the same method to the right flank, or change its position, by ordering a flank battalion to make a half wheel to the right or left, and the rest to dress upon it; in which case they should all march from their center, form that platoon, dressed to the flank battalion, and then double up the rest upon it.*

James spent an hour trying to make sense of that very foreign language until he sighed in frustration and flipped the book closed. He was not typically given to self-deception, but in this instance he lied blatantly to his inner man, assuring himself he had done enough, that he understood it quite well, and that Tom and the others might have been insulted by his refusal to go into town, and that he had best make amends.

Every bit the boy out of school, he leapt up and gleefully pulled on his coat and bicorn, and, as he was going out of the barracks, he attached his sword as well. He trotted downstairs and into the yard, where a thick darkness reigned, and a thin cold rain fell. There was a lantern at the door of the Officers' Quarters, and another at the main gate, but there was a dark, misty void between them. The oppressive atmosphere dampened his spirits, and they dropped further when he observed a dim shape approaching from across the yard.

The shadowy figure's approach had prompted James to reach for his sword, until the shadow saluted, and said, "Private Doolan, please, sir, if you recall me from this afternoon."

"Of course, Private," Lockwood said, trying not to sound relieved. As his hand was already at his sword hilt, he tapped it lightly and added, "The scabbard does quite well." A brief pause before he added, "Thank you."

Doolan paused awkwardly, and the gentleman nearly went on his way, before Doolan held up a cautioning hand, and hoarsely whispered, "Are you going into town, then, sir?"

"Why, yes, Private," said Lockwood, not impolitely, but with a touch of impatience.

Again, Doolan hesitated, and again the young man began to step away, before Doolan took his arm and hurriedly, quietly, said, "Beg pardon, sir, but don't you do it. Not tonight, sir. I'll not say why, as no man can call me informer, but don't you do it."

"Whatever do you mean, man?"

"I'm new to this business of soldiering, sure, but I'll not be party to such things as I've heard in that barracks. The devil will be afoot tonight. One of my mates thinks well of that Lieutenant Otway, and so has gone to warn him and the other gentlemen in town."

"How can your friend get into town, Doolan?" whispered James. "It is a Friday night, and no enlisted men are allowed out of the barracks."

Doolan scoffed and said, "Oh, God love you, Mr. Lockwood, dear, there are more than a few empty beds in the barracks tonight. But I must beg you, now, sir, not to raise the alarm, or cause a fuss, as the others will find me out. If they think me an informer they'll scrag me, sure."

With that Doolan quickly walked away, into the darkness toward the barracks.

James was quiet for a moment, watching the soldier fade into the gloom. He was an innocent, but by nature a good judge of character, and he trusted this fellow Doolan. If nothing else, he knew one other thing about the Irish: they rarely forget a favor.

Indecisive for a moment, he finally decided that Tom and the others would be all right. Even without a warning from Doolan's friend, there was little that four armed officers could not handle. He would rely on Doolan, and stay in.

*****

James undressed and tried to return to his books, but he eventually gave up, to stand in his shirt, keeping watch from their loft window, for what, he was unsure. A half hour later no word had come. He wondered if he had been cowardly in not going after the others, and was on the verge of going into town when he saw a lone figure hurry through the main gate, drawing a salute from the man on guard there: an officer. James tore down the steps to find Barr out of breath, his hair loose and wet, a bloody cut on his cheek.

"There is trouble in town," Barr said, an odd quiver in his voice. "We were assaulted in the street. I am going to call out the guard. Grab your tuck and come along."

Puzzled, James asked, "Tuck?"

"From the French, *estoc*." Again, James heard the odd tone in Barr's voice as the lieutenant added, "It means *sword,* Lockwood."

James raced back upstairs and armed himself with unconscious skill.

Chapter Six

The small stable behind the O'Brian cottage was home to both the old horse Buían and a good-natured black Kerry milk cow. Her name was Noínín, 'Daisy' in the English, and the three O'Brian girls shared the responsibility for the two creatures' care. Buían, recovered from the trauma of the fighting in the hills, still dutifully pulled their father's trap, and Noínín gave the O'Brians all the milk, cream and butter they needed. The family bought their cheese in town, the mark of a household of some means.

The girls were not overly fond of Buían, but they loved Noínín. That love aside, they jealously minded who had what chore, and the manner in which that chore was carried out. Their father, a republican through and through, rotated their assignments every month. When the calendar turned to October of 1797, it came Anne's turn to do the milking, Caitlin the feeding, and to Brigid fell the odious task of mucking the stalls.

That afternoon, as Brigid was not feeling well, Ann and Caitlin left her at home and walked into town to hear the Brothers of the Buttevant Franciscan Friary sing vespers at

St. Brigid's. They did not tarry there, despite Andrew McCarthy's suggestion to Ann that they sit and chat a bit, but dutifully hurried home in the low light of evening. Stepping through their front door they found a bright fire in the hearth and Brigid at the heavy kitchen table, kneading dough in a violent fashion, obviously blinking back tears. She did not look up to greet her sisters. Their father was in his chair at the opposite side of the room, a candle at his elbow, silently, angrily, flipping through the pages of the *Cork Mercury*.

Ann turned to make an exaggerated, tense face at Caitlin, and they scurried into their room to change into their work dresses and aprons. On their way out to the stable Ann paused to say, not without a certain delight, "Come along, Brigid, the pitchfork awaits."

Brigid looked up and said, "Oh, Anne, for pity's sake!" in a tearful voice, with rather more drama than Ann thought necessary.

From his chair their father snapped, "Anne, can you not see your sister is busy? You and Caitlin can see to the beasts."

"But, Father!" cried Anne.

Caitlin howled, "That is *so* unfair!"

"Perhaps," their father growled, "it is time you find life is not fair. Now, out of my sight, the both of you."

The girls hustled out with their heads down, wounded and incensed. From the stable, Noínín mooed in impatience, and as they walked out into the cool air Caitlin asked, "Whatever has made Father so cross?"

Ann sniffed and said, "I am certain that Brigid has done something terrible and has upset Father."

"Oh, whatever can she have done, do you think?"

"You are just nine years of age, and so may be too young to know."

"Oh! Is it very terrible? Has she burned the stew? Has she renounced Christ?"

"Well, if you promise to tell no one... Siobhan Mahoney told me that Mary McCarthy told her that Ian Callahan has made Brigid an offer!"

"But Ian Callahan is terrible and old and ugly!" cried Caitlin. "Brigid would never do such a thing, to you or to herself!"

Her sister plunked the milking stool beside Noínín and said, "Perhaps Brigid has asked Father for permission to marry, but Father has told her no." With emotion trembling in her voice, Ann went on, "Everyone always says how *smart* Brigid is, and how *beautiful* Brigid is, but she is the *second* daughter. It is for *me* to marry first, to whom I please, when I please."

Inside the house Brigid continued to knead the bread dough far more than it needed, until her father could stand it no more, and burst out, "Damn it, child! For the past two weeks it is your hounding me with this talk of teaching at the English school! You think to wear me down, but let me read you this, and tell me that the Irish and English shall ever mix peaceably." Holding the paper to the light he read aloud in English,

"Committed to the County Gaol last Monday, by the Right Hon. Lord Bantry, John M'Cull and John Culnane, charged with feloniously tendering Oaths; also John Sullivan charged with being present at the tendering and administering of an unlawful Oath."

Returning to the Irish, he said, "I know all three of those lads, decent farm boys, and it's likely they'll not see the light of day again, except at the gallows. And here's another:"

"On the thirteenth of August, 1797, Lord Bantry conveyed to the gaol of Cork, four of these Defender culprits, one of whom was the steward of Roger O'Conner, in whose pocket his lordship found the Defenders' oath; the tenor of which was to be true to one another; not to pay rent, tithes or taxes; and to assist the French, soon expected.

"The O'Conners were once one of the great clans, but they have given spawn to a traitor and a heretic, that dog of a Roger O'Connor! And if that was not enough, here is yet another!

"Yesterday our Assizes ended and the following person was found guilty in the County Court: Cornelius M'Innery, for seditious expressions, to be pilloried twice in Bandon and imprisoned three months.

"Daughter, how can you have shite to do with a people who would pillory and imprison old man M'Innery, a man seventy years of age, and him without the wits of a fence post? So, I shall hear no more of this school!"

"You shall hear no more of my future, Father?" said Brigid, flipping the exhausted dough onto the table. "And here I was, thinking just now of how my mother used to take me onto her lap to read with me, and she telling me how bright I was, and how I must make the most of what God gave me. She, the woman who taught that all of us are God's creatures, and to have room in my heart for everyone, no matter them Irish or English or Catholic or Protestant! And, so, you, Michael O'Brian, will have me forget the teachings of Aisling ni Leary, my precious mother, your lost wife, and you having me content myself with mopping your floors for the rest of my days?"

She had deliberately manipulated him, and was ashamed, and remorseless. At the mention of Aisling's name and nature his mood shifted, as she knew, *knew*, it would. She aged a year in an instant.

He coughed awkwardly, set aside his paper, and looked at her, softly now. "Goodness, but you have a keen memory, Brigid ni Brian. As much as your mother loved Ann and Caitlin, she was certain of you going beyond what she knew." He crossed his arms across his chest and sighed heavily. "I had forgotten that."

She thought she saw a mist cross his eyes. He sat silent for a long minute, looking out the window into the darkness, until he spoke again, his eyes still in the darkness, with regret and resignation. "All right, then. I will haggle no more; have it your own way. You shall leave this house, and teach at the English school, and follow your mother's dreams for you, if not your father's."

She went to the hearth and set the dough down on a hot baking stone. "Thank you, Father," she said with a voice that betrayed her shame.

"Just know, girl, that to folks here, Cork seems like the other side of the world. More than that, you will be seen as casting your lot with the English, and if the world turns dark you might find your way back into this house, but you might just find some, perhaps many, of our neighbors' houses dark and closed to you."

*****

My Dear Miss McCarthy,

It is with the greatest honour that I humbly accept your offer to teach at the School for Young Ladies. As you suggest, I shall take up my post on the First Day of January, 1798. I shall also strictly follow your advice to make the most of the time pending that date to study further the works of the great English authors.

Please know me to be your most obedient servant,
Brigid O'Brian

Miss McCarthy received the fourth copy of the letter, as the previous three had been set aside, the words shaken with emotion, the pages marked with tears.

*****

Michael O'Brian returned home from his rent rounds on a cold fall evening and was welcomed by each of his daughters, each of their welcomes varying in tone. Anne, chopping potatoes at the table, sounded sympathetic; Brigid, reading at the fireside, sad and cautious; Caitlin enthusiastic and healing, as she piped, "Do look and see, Father! I have brushed your best coat for little Cousin Fiona's baptism tomorrow! It shall be great fun, don't you think? Oh, will you dance with me there, Father? Will you, please?"

O'Brian managed a fleeting grin for his youngest, and said, "Sadly there is no dancing at a baptism, child. But we might still dance at home, *a stor.*" Then, with an elegance surprising for a man in rough clothes, a man who had that day collected four pounds five and two from people who could ill afford it, a man with a conscience oppressed by reality, he danced his little girl around the room, humming "Maid Behind the Bar", a gentle reel that delighted all three of his daughters.

The autumn night came early, and after a quick supper, the girls left their father sitting by the fire and scuttled off to bed. They undressed quickly in the cold of their little bedroom, then jumped into bed, pulling the covers over their heads, shivering and kicking their legs under the blankets to get warm. Ann was on the left side of the bed, Brigid on the right, and as she was the youngest, Caitlin was warmest, in the middle.

As their familiar warmth mingled, they settled in and grew quiet. Brigid said, "Caitlin, *a grah*, you'll not be disappointed tomorrow if Father doesn't wear his best coat, it being so fine with your brushing. Indeed, we must all dress simply tomorrow, so we do not insult our O'Leary cousins."

"But why, Brigid?" peeped Caitlin from under the blankets. "I wish to show them how pretty my blue dress is, with its bow, and the rose of red."

"We must not put them in shame," said Ann softly. "You must understand that Mother's family is not so fortunate as we; they living simply, and so we must not show away. We shall dress simply, and none of us shall speak of anything grand. You must promise, Caitlin."

"But we are not wealthy, are we, Anne? I do so want to tell them of my lessons!"

"Ach," said Brigid with a sniff of amusement, "We must be especially careful in speaking of schools and lessons. Seanathair O'Leary's notions of education begin and end with the ancient poems, in Irish, and them never written down."

The next afternoon was bright and cool, the four O'Brians bouncing along in the trap, in clothing clean but worn, old

Buían pulling them toward the cluster of O'Leary homes in the hills west of Clonakilty. The parish priest, too, came to the modest little cottage, quietly insisting on his shilling before bestowing the guarantee of God's love. A hat was passed, sixteen pennies at last were gathered, and the child's immortal soul redeemed.

Twenty or more people were packed into the cottage, and there were thirty or more outside, steadily sipping cups of O'Leary poteen. Those outside were soon joined by many of the witnesses who had been indoors, being hustled outside by the godparents in an abrupt fashion.

As a man not to be trifled with, Michael O'Brian was allowed to remain inside to witness the baptism, but his daughters were shooed outside, doing their best to avoid the mud and filth. The three O'Brian sisters stood together for a while, apart from the crowd of aunts, uncles, and cousins, yet still surrounded by the familiar and comforting smells of peat and tobacco smoke, poteen and farm animals.

"Oh, the Murphys are so rude!" hissed Anne. "Old and wicked and shriveled as the winter grass! Why ever did Liam and Saoirse choose them to be godparents to wee baby Kevin, and him just two days of age?"

Brigid shrugged, and said, "It's all about money, isn't it?"

Ann rolled her eyes, and said, "And what money does that baby have, sister? Is his nappy filled with gold?"

"Golden poop, maybe!" Caitlin giggled.

"Yes, Anne," said Brigid, insistently, "it is all about money. Do you not see it? Why else would our cousins choose the mean old Murphys, neighbors but not family? The Murphys hope to inherit O'Brian property, and the O'Brians hope to be in line for what little the Murphys own. No one speaks openly of such things, but believe you me, all concerned understand what they have to lose, or gain, in such an arrangement."

Ann pondered that for a moment, until she said, nearly whispering. "Cousin Saoirse seems so weak, and her baby so tiny, and their cabin so shabby! They have no property to fight over!"

Brigid frowned, not unkindly, and said, "Anne, *a stor*, the only property they're squabbling over is some rough furniture, a crop of potatoes, the cow, and the pig."

Caitlin, not concerned with inheritance and advantage, said, "But why must the baby be baptized when he is so tiny? Could they not wait a while, until the baby and his mother are stronger?"

Brigid said, with some bitterness, "To avoid an eternity in Limbo, *a grah*. A child must be baptized soon after birth, so that the priest might cleanse him of original sin. If Kevin died before baptism he would never see heaven."

Rain came misting down. Standing there in the cold mud, Brigid looked at the tiny cabin, badly thatched, surrounded by perhaps one acre of potatoes. The O'Leary home was not unusual in that the family occupied half the home while their precious cow and pig occupied the other half, separated by only a low wall. Though she would never say it aloud, she thought, *I wonder if God comes to such places as this, for such people as us.*

The ceremony of baptism complete, the priest emerged from the cabin and hurried away to perform another of God's miracles in a hovel down the hill. The Murphys emerged next and walked straight home, having little to say to the O'Learys and their kin. The remainder of the witnesses then came out into the rain, looking glum, but were cheered when cups of poteen were offered, and the conversations usual to such events ensued. The O'Brian girls mingled easily with their extended family, the soothing lilt of Munster Irish mingling with the mist in the cool still air, the men in their caps with cups in their hands. The women all had their shawls over their heads, the older, more confident ones with cups of their own, the younger ones stealing sips from their husbands or brothers.

After an hour or so Michael came to Brigid and said, "Collect your sisters, will you, *a stor*? We should go, before the rain comes in earnest." But then her father's head snapped to a corner of the cabin, and she too looked to see her cousin Fergal O'Brian cautiously step into view. Brigid had last seen Fergal two weeks before, as he had bolted across potato fields, one step ahead of the redcoats.

Her father waved her away, saying, "You do not see him, Brigid. Now, go and gather your sisters. Go, now, child."

Brigid saw her father and a handful of the other men join Fergal behind the cabin. She found Ann and Caitlin, and asked them to bring the trap around. "I'll wait here for Father, shall I? He will join us shortly, him speaking to Seanathair O'Leary."

After a few anxious minutes her father came out from behind the cabin, walking quickly, ignoring the members of his late wife's family who called out to him to share a cup. He took Brigid's arm and steered her toward the road, and the trap. She felt his hands shake at her elbow.

"Oh, Father, what did Fergal say? What has upset you so?"

"You should not know of this, daughter."

Brigid stopped, turned to face him, and said, "But I do know, do I not? Do not think me a fool, Father."

"Ach, very well, we have no time to bicker. Fergal and his pack of fools have ambushed two Yeomanry officers out at Kilmeen Bridge. They pulled them from their horses and killed them both, dead as Judas." Looking about, as if half the British army was stalking them, O'Brian went on, "There shall be hell to pay, now. A few pikes and some houghed cows are one thing, but men dead! and them officers! The Castle will not let that stand. We shall see more redcoats soon, and blood by the bucket."

Chapter Seven

James Lockwood stood indecisive in the darkness of the barracks yard, his sword in his hand and his pistol in his sash. He heard Sergeant Murphy at the front gate calling out the twelve men of the guard, and he saw a few men in the circle of light at the door of the Enlisted Barracks stepping out into the mist to see what the fuss was about. Barr was at the door of the headquarters office, knocking loudly but getting no response.

Lockwood was in a panic of indecision. He dared not confess to either Barr or Moon that he had been warned of the trouble in town and had done nothing. He had Doolan's assurance that Tom and the others had been warned as well, from the Officers' Mess, buttoning up his coat, looking confused. Lockwood wondered if he had been asleep.

"Hell and death!" cried Moon, his rage seemingly forced, an effort to mask his own laxity. "What are you two young fools think you're at, eh? Why is the guard being called? Make your report, Lieutenant Barr, make your report!"

The two young officers snapped to attention, Barr blurting out, "I was attacked in town, Major! Armed men in the street! It may be a general rising, sir!"

For an instant Lockwood saw a look of terror flash across Moon's face, but that quickly passed, and he barked, "Collect yourself, sir! I want a report worthy of a God damned officer, not some hysterical rant!" He then hissed in frustration, "God damned puppies." Turning then to James, Moon barked, "Mr. Lockwood! Report, sir, if you can!"

"Yes, sir! I was in my room, sir, when Lieutenant Barr came to tell me to arm myself, as there was trouble in town." Seeing that was well accepted, James continued, "I believe we three are the only officers remaining in the barracks, sir. Trafford, Otway and Mainwaring are in town. When they left the barracks they mentioned a plan to go to the Red Lion public house. They were all wearing their swords, sir."

Moon nodded, obviously thinking, when Barr added in a calmer voice, "That's right, sir, we had gathered at the Red Lion. We were at table when a bar maid whispered to us that we were in danger, and to be on our guard. Seeing armed men in the street, Lieutenant Otway ordered the doors and shutters to be barricaded. I managed to slip out a back window and made my way back to the barracks, so that I might raise the alarm."

A wave of relief washed over Lockwood, but that relief was quickly swallowed when he saw a sharp, questioning look come to Moon's face. More relief, then, when he saw the question was intended for Barr, as Moon said in a challenging tone, "Tell, me, Lieutenant, what—" But he was interrupted by Sergeant Murphy, who stepped into the circle of lantern light, came to attention, and made his salute. "Sergeant of the Guard reporting, sir! I regret to inform you, sir, that several of the men of the guard are taken ill, and are unable to carry out their duties, sir."

It was a shocking thing to say, men of the guard refusing their duty, but the sergeant reported it without a hint of emotion on his face. Moon stood dumbfounded as Barr shot quick, nervous looks at the guardhouse and the enlisted men's quarters. Lockwood, too, looked over at the enlisted barracks, where twenty or so men had now gathered, and he thought he recognized Doolan in the misty light of the barracks lantern. He wondered how many of those men could be relied upon.

"I am yours to command, Major," offered Murphy, "but most of the guard are unavailable. Perhaps it is something they ate." Then, he added with some significance, "I am not sure of how many men in the barracks might have eaten the same thing, sir."

"Are the gates closed and barred, Sergeant?" asked Moon after a long moment.

"Aye, sir, aye. I still have three men adhering to orders, one at the front gate, one at the rear, and one at the wicket, sir."

Moon quickly nodded, and said, "All right, then, what shall we do next, eh? What to do..." It sounded to Lockwood as if Moon was asking a deliberate question, but when he received no reply, he eventually offered, "Shall we see who might still be relied on? Yes, let's. We shall sound the NCOs' call. Will you see to it, Sergeant?" It struck James as an odd way to couch an order, especially for Moon; more a question than a command.

Murphy said, "Yes, sir!" and trotted off to find the drummer.

James was desperate to know that Tom was safe, but he held his tongue. In the dim lamplight, Moon looked old and unnerved.

There was shouting from the enlisted barracks, and the officers watched as Sergeant Murphy emerged, dragging the drummer by the collar. Murphy pushed the man out into the yard, and James heard the drummer say in Irish, "All right, you great brute, you needn't be so rough." He then beat out the NCOs' call, the drum shattering the misty quiet, the call sharp and martial.

All five of the garrison's sergeants, but only four of the seven corporals, formed up in front of their officers. "Beg pardon, sir, three corporals report sick," Murphy said quietly.

Moon was obviously straining to maintain his composure. A long moment passed, Moon looking around the gloomy yard as if some answers might be found there.

Finally, his voice cracking, he looked at the two young officers and the handful of NCOs, and told them, "We shall muster the garrison." It was not an order; his tone was that of a conspirator, concocting a plan. "The men who stand to, our loyal men, shall be issued a cartouche of ammunition. Oh, and we shall have them fix bayonets. Then, those men who do not form shall be disarmed and confined to the barracks gaol."

"Beg pardon, sir," offered Lockwood, hesitantly, "I wonder if there may not be sufficient room in the gaol."

Shocked by such a notion, Moon quickly turned to rebuke Lockwood, when Murphy, then all the sergeants, agreed, saying, "That's right, sir. Not room enough... perhaps the stables, sir? We can bottle them up nicely in there, the buggers."

"Very well, then," continued Moon after a moment, his confidence slowly returning, "the stables. We shall lock up the scoundrels, man the walls, and wait for dawn. We can then evaluate our situation, and, if need be, send to Dublin for reinforcement." Rubbing his hands together in decision, Moon went on, "Yes, that is what we shall do. The regiment's honour intact! Sergeant Murphy, have the drummer call out the garrison!"

The NCOs hesitated, looked at one another, and after some quick muffled conversation, Murphy said, "Might I suggest, sir, we wait a bit before sounding the Muster? We NCOs might first take a stroll through the barracks to encourage the men before we force them to declare themselves sick, or well enough, sir."

"Well, if you think that best," said Moon, a reply that even Lockwood, an officer of three weeks' service, knew to be weak and indecisive. The NCOs strode off, a heated discussion breaking out between them as they made their way back to their barracks.

"Sir," James asked of Major Moon, "what of the officers in town? Will we make no attempt to recover them?"

Moon made a rueful shake of his head, and said, "We are in no position to go charging into Mullingar. We have one ill-trained company here, and God knows how many of them have been corrupted by the United men. We face an unknown number of rebels; the town is obviously in a state of rebellion. No, sir, those gentlemen must rely on their own wits."

Barr said nothing, only looking at the ground at his feet. Lockwood, aghast at the thought of abandoning Tom and the others, quickly said, "Might I suggest, sir, you see to things here, while Lieutenant Barr and I slip into town to reconnoiter?"

"Certainly not, sir! In the absence of my company officers, I shall rely heavily on Lieutenant Barr in the coming hours. But as you are so concerned with the welfare of those gentlemen, I give you leave to depart the barracks so that you might scout the town. I am certain that you will be unable to get far, and certainly not so far as the Red Lion." Not unkindly, Moon added, "Mind you, Lockwood, you will exercise great caution; you will return at the first sign of trouble. In any event, I will expect you back in, what? An hour, yes, one hour, with your impressions of the rebels' strength and arms. I shall dispatch Sergeant Murphy to assist your exit through the wicket."

Moon turned and marched off into the yard, calling for Lieutenant Barr to join him. Before hurrying away, Barr shot Lockwood a look, the meaning of which Lockwood could not discern.

Lockwood stood there in the cool dim mist for a moment, thoroughly frightened. The thought of going off into the darkness alone, taking God knows what kind of risks, was outrageous to his seventeen year-old mind, but he also felt a thrill of excitement, a thrill that roared through his mind with an unquestionable, undeniable delight. After some thought, he ran up to his room, threw off his bicorn, sword belt, sash, and coat. He put on an old brown coat, stuck his pistol in his pocket, grabbed his cutlass, and ran back downstairs.

At the wicket he found Murphy and several other men, all carrying their muskets, cartouches of ammunition on their hips. Murphy had found at least a few men to answer his call. Lockwood had been in town just a handful of times, so he pulled Murphy aside, and they quickly talked through the streets he would have to travel to reach the Red Lion. His mind racing, Lockwood turned to the wicket door and the men who stood there. The new wicket guard had wisely trimmed back the lantern that burned there, but even in the half-light James recognized Doolan, who took his hand and said, "*Tabhair aire, fear uasal.*" Take care, gentleman.

Murphy pulled the narrow door open and whispered, "If you run into trouble on your way out or on your way back, sir, you just sing out, and we'll come running, sir."

Lockwood stood very still for a moment, then peered out into the darkness. He nervously said, "Well, I suppose I had best be going." When no one said anything in reply, he went.

The wicket door led out into a dark, narrow side street, tall walls black on either side, the sky dimly greyer overhead. He crept a few feet toward the Garrison Street end of the narrow lane, his left hand sliding along the wall for guidance, his right hand clutching his cutlass.

He reached the corner where the alley met Garrison Street, crouched there, and caught the smell of pipe smoke. There were no lights burning in any of the buildings lining Garrison Street, only a light from far to his right, where the barracks gate lantern burned. After a moment of staring his senses grew more accustomed to the silent darkness, and he saw the shadow of a man far to his left, at the town end of the street, the glow and scent of his pipe betraying his position. It made sense; the rebels had posted a sentry to sound the alarm if the soldiers sallied from the barracks.

Lockwood slipped back down the alley, deciding to try the opposite direction and work through the fields and fences behind the barracks. He made a deliberate effort to be silent as he passed the wicket, afraid the men there would think he had returned a coward.

Lockwood hopped the low stone fence at the end of the alley and slipped into the sheep-tended drill field behind the barracks. Ahead and to his left, the ground was open and surprisingly bright in the mist, while on his right the field was bordered by the walled rear yards of the homes and shops that lined Blackwell Street. The windows were all dark; it was well after midnight, and trouble was afoot. Most of the knowing populace of Mullingar went to bed early and did not heed the noises that rose in the darkness outside.

He did not pause long to consider his course. He was thrilled, his heart hammering, his senses wildly alive, and he was certain, *certain*, that he would find his way, that nothing could harm him, that no one could catch him. He was seventeen and immortal. As he moved quietly along the backs of the yards, he jumped when a dog suddenly barked at him. Lockwood could think of nothing more to do than to harshly whisper, "*A bheith ciúin, madra*," be quiet, dog, and he was more than surprised when the dog promptly did as he was told.

Through luck and blunder he found a narrow passage out onto Blackwell Street, where he paused long enough to look up and down the street, seeing everything still quiet. He did, though, hear shouting from ahead and to his left, toward Linen Street, the wide main road where the Red Lion lay. He crept on, using the deep shadows under the eaves of the buildings that lined the road. Trying to work his way toward Linen Street, he turned up an alley, then through a tangle of fences and passages, sometimes finding himself in dead ends, but making steady progress toward the shouting voices.

He thought he was nearly there, following a narrow, pitch-black passage between two buildings, filtered light coming from the street ahead. He was nearing the end of the passage when a voiced roared in Irish, "What the fuck are you playing at!?"

Lockwood jumped and froze, terrified, his shield of invincibility suddenly gone. Still, one corner of his mind operated, as he instinctively raised the tip of his blade, planted his feet in a swordsman's stance, and prepared to defend himself. In the seconds that followed he considered his position; he could flee, but then again, unless the rebels had firearms he could hold off a hundred men in that narrow passage, where the short, thick cutlass might prove its worth.

Lockwood was by no means a master of the Irish language, but he managed to make out most of what the voice from the street continued, "Damn you, McNally! I told you to fetch that bucket of lamp oil from O'Toole's shop, and you had better fucking well do it! If we can't dig those fucking redcoats out of the Lion, we'll have to burn them out! Put that bottle away, and get to it! We don't have all fucking night!" Silence followed, Lockwood still frozen, until a minute later when he heard the same voice calling in English, further down the street, now, "You may as well come out and face us like men, ya cowardly bastards!"

Lockwood crept to the end of the passage and peeked out onto Linen Street. To his right the street was dark and empty, but to his left the street was filled with men, some holding torches, passing around bottles, all armed with pikes, clubs, and a few firearms. They numbered twenty or so, all in front of the Red Lion, pounding on the shutters and doors, drunk, laughing, taunting, promising to kill every one of the English bastards.

His terror bubbled, but so too his excitement returned in an irresistible wave. He dared not wait, as the man with the lamp oil would certainly return, with terrible results.

He had an idea and grinned madly. A flash of memory crossed his mind, from when he was much younger, and a local girl, Caoimhe McNamara, had tried to teach him a decent accent for his Irish. He tapped that memory, his Irish nearly perfect as he screamed out toward the gang of rebels, his voice roaring.

"Run, boys, run! The soldiers are coming! Fifty of the bastards, howling for blood! For Christ's sake, run!" From the shelter of his dark corner he peered out. The rebels stared up the street toward his voice, started to walk slowly backwards, then in a panic dropped their bottles and torches and took to their heels.

Not believing his good fortune, still grinning like a fool, Lockwood crouched low and hurried to the Red Lion's door. He banged the butt of the cutlass on the battered wood and harshly whispered, "It's Lockwood! Let's make a run for it!"

In an instant the door flew open, the three officers shocked and delighted. Tom and James shared a quick thumping embrace, and after quick handshakes they all dashed out into the empty street, swords drawn. As they hurried toward the barracks, eying every shadow and corner, Otway hurriedly asked, "Have you seen Barr? When the trouble started, we were... separated."

"Yes, he returned to the barracks some time ago. It was he who raised the alarm."

Mainwaring, Trafford, and Otway exchanged a look, but said nothing further. When they reached Garrison Street the pipe smoking sentry bolted, and they halted long enough for Lockwood to describe the situation in the barracks.

A few minutes later the four officers hustled through the wicket, greeted with genuine pleasure by the men posted there, Doolan giving Mr. Lockwood a nod and a slap on the back. The four officers then strolled out into the yard with as much nonchalance as they could muster. The sight of the three missing officers took the wind out of the mutiny, and no man dared not form up and adhere to the word of command.

Soon the NCOs had the men well in hand, marching them back into their barracks, when Moon turned to his five officers and said nervously, "Well, that all came to nothing, eh? Much ado about nothing, eh? Rumors and whimsy; stuff and nonsense. The men are all proven reliable, and our lost lambs are returned to the fold after their scuffle in town."

*****

The next day carried at least the façade of business as usual around the barracks, though both the officers and men granted Mr. Lockwood a noticeably greater degree of respect. James especially appreciated the bottle of wine sent up to his room by Lieutenants Trafford and Otway with a very obliging note.

Opening the bottle, Tom was less effusive in his praise. "I suppose it was good of you to come fetch us from the Red Lion, and I do thank you kindly, but pray do not let it go to your head. Your attempts at derring-do are all well and good, but it does not mean I shall ever introduce you to my sisters," which brought a howl of shared laughter.

Two days later Colonel Montgomery returned to the barracks. When James was summoned to the Colonel's office, Tom first gave him some hurried instruction on how to best stand at attention, and how best to comport oneself as an officer. James was frantically trying to recall those points as he stood before the Colonel's desk.

"I wonder, Mr. Lockwood," said the Colonel, sitting in his stiff leather chair with a handful of notes spread across his desk, "if you have mentioned to your new comrades that you are my cousin's son?"

"Why, no, sir."

"Why is that, sir?"

James flushed and said, "Well, sir, I suppose I'd rather not be treated in a manner different from any other new man."

Montgomery nodded approvingly. "Quite so. Quite so. Well, then." Turning to the notes on his desk, he went on, "I trust Sergeant Butcher has seen to your uniforms and weapons?"

"Yes, thank you, sir."

"You have been here, what, a month, or so? Thus far the reports are of a supportive nature... no brutality, a willingness to learn. I do, though, have a note here from Major Moon. Tut, tut. You speak Irish, sir?

"Just the basics, sir." He was wondering if he was about to be sent home. "I was unaware of the Major's wishes regarding the use of Irish in the barracks."

"The Major's wishes are to be adhered to in this, as in all such matters," said the Colonel. He then added with a casual tone, "Still, your skill in the language may prove useful in a regiment such as ours. And in reference to your actions the other night, it does seem that your knowledge of Irish might prove useful in other circumstances. Do not speak it, but do retain it, sir."

"Yes, sir," he said, with the breath of life returned.

Flipping through the other notes, the Colonel went on, "It has further been noted that you may have an unfortunate tendency toward sympathy regarding the Other Ranks, which is concerning. I trust, Mr. Lockwood, you are not of a tender heart?"

"Not that I am aware of, sir," said James with only a hint of falsehood in his voice.

After further flipping of pages, the Colonel said without looking up, but with a surge in his tone, "Still and all, you did well the other night, though it is in the best interest of the regiment not to broadcast the whole of the story. We must not have the populace doubting the military. That being said, I have here a letter praising your diligence and quick thinking, signed by Lieutenants Trafford and Otway, as well as Ensign Mainwaring." Tapping the letter, he was quiet for a moment, then looking up, he added, "I trust you have interest in promotion, sir? In furthering your career in the King's service?"

"Oh, yes, sir," said James, bright-eyed, trying not to smile.

"Sadly, all the positions for Brigadier General have been filled." Opening a folder and pulling forth a few sheets of paper, Montgomery added, "Happily, in light of the recent clashes, our Lieutenant Evans has opted to sell out. It seems he finds the notion of actual combat distasteful, which seems a disqualifying position for someone calling himself a God damned soldier." Collecting himself, the Colonel went on, "Ensign Bishop has in turn purchased his step, thus opening an ensigncy. With your permission, I shall write to the Castle to inform them that Mr. James Lockwood has been promoted Ensign, Westmeath Militia Regiment, without purchase. My heartiest congratulations, sir. When you notify your mother, do tender my very fondest regards."

*****

Tom's father had sent him six shillings to apply toward a good coat for the coming winter, though Tom had, with a sharp, albeit fleeting pang of guilt, instead purchased three bottles of celebratory wine. That evening he sat on his bed, his back against the wall, a tin cup of wine in one hand and a copy of *The Military Guide for Young Officers* in the other. He was steadily quizzing James, asking with only a moderate slur, "What Word of Command follows the command *Fire*?"

James, sitting on his bed, took a long drink from his cup, and said tenuously, "*Handle your Cartridge*?"

"*Half Cock your Firelock.*"

"Damn." James grinned, the most relaxed he had felt at any point in his month-long army career, and said, "But I have always found it best to be at full cock, brother, or no cock at all."

Tom shrieked in laughter, punching his mattress in glee. When he could manage it, he wiped the tears from his eyes, and said, "You are a brute, James Lockwood, and a poor influence on me. Have I mentioned that my father is a minister of the church?"

"Yes, you have. Have I mentioned that my father is an unredeemable ass?"

Both howled with adolescent drunken laughter, trusting and unguarded, devoid of pretense or defense. Sadly, such moments between men are rare, as men are so often hobbled by pride and their brittle self-image, but still, such moments do occur, serving as keystones in friendships that might last a lifetime. James and Tom, however, had no time for lofty notions, as there came a soft knock at their chamber door.

James jumped up and said gleefully, "Perhaps it is our fathers, come to debate our worth!" He flung open the door, where he was wholly stunned to find two quite lovely young women. The taller of the two coyly asked, "I do beg your pardon, sir, but I wonder if Ensign Mainwaring is at leisure?"

James tossed a nod at Tom in the corner, who did not stir, a look of apprehension on his face.

Inspired by the prospect of female company, In a wholly uncharacteristic way, James said, "It does indeed appear that Ensign Mainwaring is at leisure. Indeed, he is in a state resembling sloth."

He awkwardly turned toward Tom, who rose hesitantly, came to the door, bowed, and with only a slight discomfort, said, "Ah, good evening, ladies."

The young ladies, gazing upon the elegant form of Ensign Mainwaring, stood in silent rapture, though the smaller girl managed to whisper, "Apollo."

Tom gestured toward James, who was rarely a quick wit, and who went silent when faced with attractive young women. He said gracefully, "Ladies, may I present Ensign Lockwood of my regiment? Ensign Lockwood, Miss Mason and Miss Cartwright."

Each of the ladies gave the tall, thin boy a brief, appraising glance, the most cursory of curtsies, and instantly returned their rapturous gazes to the embarrassed form of Tom Mainwaring. The young ladies then flicked their eyes toward the bed from which Tom Mainwaring had come, a flash of, if not lust, then certainly wonder, coming into their eyes.

James was doing his best to think of a way to invite the ladies into their room without sounding more than casually lecherous, when they were joined by Lieutenant Barr, who strolled out from his room looking cavalier, and said with a knowing grin, "You boys have such lovely friends. I wonder, might these two be… sisters?"

Tom sighed, and said, "Simply neighbors, I think, sir." Turning to his wide-eyed visitors, "Ladies, Lieutenant Barr. Lieutenant Barr, Miss Mason and Miss Cartwright."

Over the past few days Lockwood and Mainwaring had not seen much of Barr, but there he was, standing very close to the ladies, eyeing them up and down in an obvious way, prompting both girls to draw their shawls tight across their suddenly vulnerable shoulders.

"Mainwaring," said Barr, "you must offer them some wine. Oh, but you are short of glasses! I am certain to have some in my room. Come, Miss Cartwright, won't you help me fetch them?"

Barr took Miss Cartwright by the arm, prompting a look of alarm to cross both the ladies' faces, and causing Mainwaring and Lockwood to look concerned. Thankfully, the encounter ended with the sound of heavy boots coming up the steps, as the corporal of the guard and the gate sentry thumped up in pursuit of the ladies.

"They ran past me like a couple of hares," the exasperated sentry told his stern-faced corporal, as the ladies, still rapturous but somewhat wiser, were escorted downstairs, through the gate and out onto Garrison Street, where a carriage and a red-faced coachman waited.

Tom rolled his eyes and retreated to his bed and his cup of wine, while James stood at the attic window and watched the ladies retreat. Walking back to their room, James asked in wonder, "Do such things happen to you often?"

"Truly, I do not understand it. I do nothing to encourage them. Do you know that two weeks ago a Mrs. Guilford, a naval captain's wife, old enough to be my mother... well, my older sister... wrote to suggest, as her husband has been so long away at sea... well... some exceptionally improper conduct?"

James took a long drink of wine, and said, "I would give ten years of my life for such a letter," with such open longing that he nearly choked.

Tom flopped back into his bed, not spilling a drop of wine, and said, "Oh, do shut up, brother."

James did his best to swallow his laughter, finally saying wistfully, "I thought such things happened only in novels."

*****

Following some negotiation with the candidate, James decided upon his soldier-servant: the grumbling Diarmuid Doolan. Two days later, as James and Tom were dressing for breakfast and morning drill. Doolan came in with a snowy white shirt and suggested to Ensign Lockwood that he might be more careful when eating his damned pudding. Tom barked a quick laugh, and while Lockwood puzzled over how to respond, there came a rap on their door.

Sergeant Butcher handed across two wax-sealed envelopes. "Letters for each of you two gentlemen. New orders."

Ensign Mainwaring was to depart Mullingar Barracks immediately, to take up a post with Seven Company at Athlone. Tom quietly said, "Well, brother, it seems we are to be separated."

Ensign Lockwood, too, was to immediately depart Mullingar Barracks, in company with Lieutenant Barr. Lieutenant Barr was posted to Four Company in lieu of Lieutenant Evans, resigned. Lockwood was to join the same company. They were to travel to Cork Barracks where they would serve under Captain Holister. Due to rebel activity across County Cork, Four Company was to be reinforced with all available officers and men.

James did not look up from his orders, but only sniffed nervously, and said, "Well Doolan, it's Cork Barracks for us."

"Christ, *Cork*, sir?" replied Doolan, incredulous. "I'm a Donegal man! Whatever shall I do down there? I've heard terrible things about those wild-eyed southern folk, sir. My Uncle Lorcan traveled there once and came home with tales of them walking on all fours and howling at the feckin' moon. Cork! Oh, I fear the worst, sir, the very feckin' worst."

Chapter Eight

Twenty years before, Michael O'Brian had given up farming to act as a land agent to Lord Shannon, breaking convention and serving as a topic of gossip across the parish. While his career choice raised some eyebrows, his greatest finger in the eye of tradition was the house he built for his new wife. An Irish family of middling means traditionally lived in a three-room house: a hearth room in the center, flanked by a bedroom at either end. Built with thick stone walls plastered white inside and out, few windows, and a thatched roof, the little houses were the mark of a successful family. When the O'Brian home was built with four rooms, people wondered if Michael had gone quite mad, or turned pretentious, him with his flashy new job and his beautiful new wife.

Their nearest neighbors, Old Cillian and Fineena Ferrigan, stood at the door of their modestly Christian three-room cottage and looked up Ballyduvane Road toward the new house being built.

"Can you believe it, husband," clucked Fineena, "in our own corner of the world, a four room house! A parlour, it is!

Such pretense. We are the new Gomorrah, and us soon pillars of salt, sure! It's the way of these foolish young people and their money. As my mother always said, *Is buaine focal ná toice an tsaoil.*" A word is more lasting than worldly wealth.

Cillian, a lean little man who spent his life hearing his wife and her mother utter many a word—indeed too many for mortal man to count, sure—pulled at his pipe, and said, "If I was married to Aisling ni Leary I believe I, too, should build her a four room house, and buy her a silk dress, and be content," a comment which earned him another sampling of lasting words.

Twenty years later the Ferrigans were still down the road, but Aisling was long passed. Her fleeting presence on this earth was evident only in the abiding sadness in Michael O'Brian's face and in the beauty of her daughters. The three O'Brian sisters, feigning happiness while blinking back tears in the manner which so puzzled their father, were involved in packing Brigid's trunk.

They had packed trunks before, of course. Ann had attended Miss McCarthy's for three years, and when she turned twelve, Caitlin, too, would travel to Cork. But this packing had an air of separation, of true departure, and their bickering was replaced by tears and affection. Caitlin, who had a flair for baking, surprised Brigid with a napkin full of fresh-baked biscuits. Anne, too, surprised Brigid, when she handed her a worn hat box, and said, "You shall take mother's lace bonnet along; it frames your face perfectly, as it did hers. She would have been so proud...."

At the mention of their mother all three girls began to sob, prompting their father to burst into the room, saying, "What, is there a *bean sí* loose it your bedroom, now? What in all the world could cause such wailing?"

"Oh Father, how can you even ask such a thing!" wailed Caitlin, as Brigid sobbed into her shawl.

"Our own sister is to leave us!" cried Ann as she and her sisters formed a weeping pile of feminine grief on the bed they shared.

Their father scoffed, "Ach, you're off with the fairies, the lot of you." He shut the bedroom door with a bang and returned to his chair and pipe by the hearth. The peat fire had burned low, and in that haunting half-light he pondered who he was in this world, and what course he might follow to best protect and support his daughters. Hearing his girls in the next room, crying and talking, he felt their honest love filling the house. He nearly wept himself, with love but also with deep concern.

*****

When Miss McCarthy opened her school for young ladies in 1774 there were already two other schools for young ladies in Cork Town, but they accepted only the daughters of Protestant families. Miss McCarthy's school would accept both Protestant and Catholic girls, not through any egalitarian ideals, but rather that woman's determination to succeed. While girls of all faiths would be accepted, she set the school's tone early. While she was herself an Irishwoman, she made it a practice to hire English women to teach. Some of those English women were born in England, some in Ireland, and while some were Catholic, most were Protestant. The emphasis was firmly on being English, through language, literature, and culture.

Since its founding the school had become the premier school of its kind in County Cork for Catholic families wishing their daughters to polish their manners, acquire a bit of French, perfect their embroidery skills, and acquire the airs of a woman comfortable in a Dublin salon. In short, for most of the girls, the school was a marriage academy, training them to compete for men of means. For a few girls, though, girls born with intelligence and willpower, the school gave them more, something akin to a true education.

While the aging Miss McCarthy recognized the limits of her school, she took great pride in the girls who became truly educated while in her care. In the twenty-three year history of Miss McCarthy's School for Young Ladies she had hired only two Irish women to teach there.

Brigid O'Brian became the third.

*****

The school occupied a great house, one unfortunately past its prime, on Glasheen Road, south and west of Cork Town. The lower floor was converted to classrooms, while the rooms above became the bedrooms of the various classes of girls. A small room at the top of the stairs was reserved for Miss Bloxham, the humorless housemistress. Miss McCarthy lived comfortably in a private suite of rooms built onto the east wing of the school, while she consigned the school's teachers to a rather dreary annex on the west wing.

Miss O'Brian would join three other teachers on staff. They were led by Miss Klug, a tall, elegant, politely aloof, slightly older woman of great education whose past was never discussed. Miss Klug was courteous to Miss O'Brian, but little more. The other two teachers on staff, Miss Reese and Miss Hendricks, were closer to Brigid in age, if not in background. Both those young ladies had grown up as friends and neighbors near Salisbury, the daughters of large families of moderate means. As neither of their fathers could offer much in support or dowry, and as neither was fortunate enough to find love among the few bachelors in the vicinity, and as neither would accept the offers of penniless rogues, they opted to respond to an advertisement to teach in far-away Cork.

They were both slender, pretty girls, Miss Reese fair-haired, Miss Hendricks taller, with dark hair. They had not given up their hopes for marriage and families, but in the meantime they were not unhappy with their lives, and were attentive to their duties. As they lacked the funds to travel back to Salisbury for the term break, the ladies spent several days crafting gowns from a very few yards of silk. The officers of the nearby Cork Barracks had invited the ladies of Miss McCarthy's School to attend a ball, to be held on the evening of New Year's Day, just three weeks hence.

Throughout the 1790s the world was changing at a rapid rate, changes mirrored by rapid shifts in women's fashion. Miss Hendricks's sister in London was a woman of fashion, one who sent her sister sketches of the latest trends, featuring tall feathers in small bonnets, low necklines, and waistlines just under the bosom. These were the trends which the two teachers hoped to duplicate in Cork on a two-pound budget. They sat side by side, their precious silk spread across a dining table, stitching and chatting.

"I wonder," said Miss Reese, "if Brigid will be invited to the Officers' Ball as well? I do not recall her being introduced, but now that she is on the staff, how can she not be included?"

"Yes, I quite agree," said Miss Hendricks. "As Brigid will not return for another week, I shall make inquiries. Perhaps," she added in a disinterested tone, "I shall write to Captain Rzewnicki to ask his advice on the matter."

Miss Reese gave her a look, with a smile on her face and a mischievous glint in her eye, but Miss Hendricks did not bite, so Miss Reese said, "By the way, are we indeed still referring to her as 'Brigid'? As a student, 'Brigid', of course, but now as a colleague I suppose I must refer to her as 'Miss O'Brian'. At any rate, she is so very young, I wonder if she has come out? Indeed, do the Irish have such a custom? I hope to avoid giving offence to Brig... to Miss O'Brian, but I am afraid of misunderstanding on these matters."

"Indeed. No one can doubt her intelligence, but she is young, Catholic, and, I am sorry to say it, but I must: not the daughter of a gentleman." Then in a different tone, Miss Hendricks said, "Now to think of it, would she have anything to wear to such an event?"

"Oh, yes, in last term's sewing class she created quite a lovely gown with Miss Klug. Muslin, of course, and not *au courant*, but with her complexion and figure she could wear a burlap sack and be the envy of every woman there."

"It is so unfair," replied Miss Hendricks with a sniff. "Every officer in the barracks shall want to dance with her."

"Miss Klug has once again offered to chaperone the affair, and won't she have her hands full with those gentlemen."

*****

Brigid offered to take the mail coach back to Cork, but Michael O'Brian had long made a practice of driving his daughters back and forth to school. Miss McCarthy's was thirty miles from their home, a full day's journey, so O'Brian once again rented the two-horse carriage kept at the Shannon Arms. He would spend the night with his aged cousin, Daniel O'Brian in Ballynagrumollia, then finish the drive home the next day. He was long acquainted with the Shannon Arms's horses, and they with him; he did not mistreat them, and they did not fail him.

They left before full dawn, the December day being short and the road long. Her trunk and battered valise were strapped to the rear of the carriage, and Brigid held her mother's hat box in her lap. It was a cold morning, but dry, and Brigid's sisters had ensured she was properly bundled up for the journey. She still had tears in her eyes and the warmth of their kisses on her cheeks as her father snapped the team onto the main road toward Cork Town. Her father played the stoic, but he had made an obvious effort for her: his best coat, and the broad-brimmed top hat he wore on visits to Lord Shannon. His boots were shined, he was freshly shaven, and Brigid was thrilled. Her great adventure was beginning.

They did not speak much as they drove north and east. It was not, however, an awkward silence, as she had long before realized her father was not the most talkative of men. They did chat a bit about the sites along the way; the ruins of Templebryan Church always drew some commentary. "The poor old place," said Brigid. "It must have been quite lovely back in 1300."

"Hardly two stones left standing now," said O'Brian. "It seems the Templars did not take a long term lease on the place."

After two hours they approached Bandon, where O'Brian glared up the hill at Castle Bernard, the home of Viscount Bandon. As was his habit, O'Brian hawked and spat toward the great castle and damned the Viscount to be eaten by his cat, and for the devil to then eat the cat, the Irish language being capable of such elaborate curses. Some years before, the Viscount, acting as magistrate, had ordered a young O'Brian man to death for stealing a lamb to feed his starving family. The Clan O'Brian, indeed most of the families of Cork, did not forget such cruelties.

They fed and watered the horses in Bandon, then pushed on, her father quiet, deep in thought. It thus surprised Brigid when, *a propos* of nothing, he told her in a sharp voice, "Once at school, you must take care, *a stor*. Make certain every door and window is secured, every night. The groundskeeper and his sons, the Monahans, seem likely lads, but can they be trusted?"

"Yes, Father," said Brigid, taken aback. "Mr. Monahan and his sons have always been very protective of the girls and the staff. I do promise to be very careful indeed."

"Very well, then. After I see you to your rooms I shall call on Monahan to pay my respects. I shall arrange for him to look over you if things turn bad."

"Bad, Father? Whatever do you think—might there be trouble? You cannot be thinking of a *rising*? Certainly you cannot think such madness even possible?"

"*Whist*, girl, how can a simple fool like me be certain of such things? But I hear rumors, do I not? So, listen to me, closely, now. If you should receive a letter from me, from your sisters, from the bloody Pope, and it contains the phrase, '*his Aunt Áine is taken poorly*' then look for me to be coming soon to carry you home. If, though, a letter might say, '*his Uncle Ultan is taken poorly*' you must make your way home as soon as you can, as best you can."

"Yes, Father," she said, shaken, afraid, but attentive.

"Say it back to me, now, *a grah*."

"Any letter saying '*Aunt Áine*', you shall come, if '*Uncle Ultan*' then I must make my own way home."

"Aye, God help us if you see Uncle feckin' Ultan," he said, distracted, heedless, worried. "Take the mail coach, beg a ride, steal a bloody horse, but get you home. If things get to the point of Uncle Ultan the world will be in a panic. If it gets that bad and I was to take out toward Cork, our people might think me a traitor, a damned informer, or the Yeomen might take me up as a rebel." Looking over to her with something like pride, some acknowledgement of her capacity, he added, "But somehow I know, my clever daughter, that if need be, you will find a way. Play the English lady or the Irish girl, but I wager you'll travel the miles far more easily than your coarse old Da."

*****

"I do apologize for my father and I being so… emotional… in our parting. We were eight hours on the road, and we are both rather worn." Brigid heard the quiver in her own voice; never before had her father been tearful at their parting. A voice in her head told her she was foolish for leaving home, for trying to force her way into a world dominated by people who looked down on her. That voice droned on, but she pushed it aside and maintained her countenance. She lived her life with a determination to never make a fool of herself.

In their small, gloomy quarters, Miss Reese and Miss Hendricks gave her understanding smiles, but still, Brigid thought, with a touch of condescension. "Oh, pray, do not mention it," said Miss Reese. "It was quite sweet, actually. I wish my father had been so despondent when I left home."

"I, as well; I do believe my own father's primary emotion upon my departure was relief. He still has six children at home, you know, and I think he was pleased to have one less mouth to feed, though perhaps I am being unkind."

"Oh," said Miss Reese, with a burst of enthusiasm, "speaking of feeding! We saved you a bowl of stew from dinner; it's warming on the hob. I imagine you are hungry, so perhaps we might retire to the dining hall, and while you eat we shall show you our attempts at ball gowns."

Brigid was touched by the older girls' thoughtfulness. She was still on edge, but it seemed that they were all three determined to make an effort. Miss O'Brian, Miss Hendricks, and Miss Reese soon built their first bridge by deciding upon Brigid, Nichole, and Gabrielle, and then drifted to the nature of ball gowns, and how material might best be utilized. As a student, Brigid had known of of the Cork Barracks annual New Year's Ball, as it was held less than a mile away. But when Nichole said, "I happened to come across Captain Rzewnicki when out walking the other day, and he said you simply must attend this year's ball." Brigid was taken aback. She had not thought of such an eventuality, and the image of Michael O'Brian's daughter in the midst of a crowd of redcoat officers filled her mind for a long moment. Gabrielle had been speaking for some time before Brigid focused once again.

"At our last meeting, Captain O'Malley was most attentive. He is handsome enough, I suppose, but it is unfortunate that he is a—" with a flick of her eyes toward Brigid she caught herself, then went on with a false note to her voice, for Brigid was as Catholic as Captain O'Malley, "—such a *short* man. You know how I cannot think well of a short man."

Nichole made an effort to cover the gaffe by saying, "Oh, yes, you had mentioned before how you found the captain far too short for your tastes."

Brigid's armor easily deflected such a minor slight, accidental as it most likely was. Determined to make friends, Brigid cheerfully said, "Oh, I quite agree! Short men so often set their sights on the tallest woman of their acquaintance. It is natural for men, I suppose, to task themselves with dreams of conquest."

"He might fancy you, Brigid," said Gabrielle, "though he is so much older. Goodness, he must be nearly thirty." Brigid said nothing, but she found herself intrigued by the notion of a handsome officer paying her attention, and she swallowed a grin when she thought of what her father might say.

"Oh," said Nicolle, excitedly, "I failed to mention that Captain Rzewnicki also said that due to the unrest in the hills, several more officers are due to join the garrison before the ball. He particularly mentioned two coming down from Mullingar, one of whom, a Lieutenant Barr, is reputed to be quite dashing! So many men! How I love balls."

Chapter Nine

After the incident at the Red Lion, Lieutenant Barr had, unless young women were at large, kept to his room, pleading a bad cold. He left it to Ensign Lockwood to arrange their travel to Cork. Thus, morning found James walking into town, this time with considerably more confidence than when he had ventured out a few nights previous. Temperatures had dropped below freezing overnight, and at the top of Barracks Street James very nearly slipped and fell on a patch of misanthropic ice. He preserved both his own pride and the regiment's; while there were few people on the street, doubtless there were some who would have been very pleased to see a redcoat land on his arse.

He was bound for the Post Office on Linen Street. Stepping in, he found it a small, dingy place, mildew on the walls and a miserable little peat fire in the fireplace. There was no one behind the counter, but through the rows of pigeon-hole mailboxes James saw someone moving around in the back. On the counter he found a battered copy of the *Dublin Mail Routes*. He paged through it, eventually finding:

THE MULLINGAR DAY COACH

Starts from this office every morning at Ten o'clock, arrives at Mullingar before dinner. A coach leaves Mullingar every morning at Six o'clock, and arrives in Dublin at Two in the afternoon.

He frowned, then flipped further back to find:

THE CORK AND DUBLIN COACH

Starts from No. 12 Dawson-street, at Seven o'clock on the mornings of Monday, Wednesday, and Friday, passing through Carlow, Kilkenny and Clonmel, halts at Kilkenny for the night, and arrives at Cork the second evening.

It was as he feared; one day to Dublin, a night there, then two further days of misery down to Cork. There were no other options, as renting saddle horses or hiring a chaise would cost twenty pounds or more, and even then, he and Barr would still have to pay for their servants to take the mail coach to Cork. The army allowed them just a few pence per mile; that morning James had called upon the garrison paymaster, presented their orders, and after consulting his *Mail Route Companion* that tightfisted gentleman had paid out the three pounds ten and six he calculated for two officers and two enlisted men to travel those two hundred ten and one half miles.

James had resigned himself to the discomfort of the Mail, but not yet to its discourtesies. There was no bell, so after an additional minute of being ignored he called out in his newly acquired military voice, "Hey, there, the Postmaster!"

A man slunk out from behind the mailboxes, hissing in annoyance, but when he saw the scarlet coat he stopped, startled, and it looked for a moment as if he might bolt out the back. But the ugly little fellow gathered himself and stepped up to the counter, his hands shaking. With a quiver in his voice he said, "I do so apologize for keeping you, sir, as I was sorting this afternoon's post, and so intent I did not hear you enter. The Postmaster is out, sir, but my name is Higgins, sir, if I might serve you."

James had never before experienced someone being afraid of him. His first instinct was to smile and put the man at ease, but another part of him, the boy who had been bullied more than once, rather enjoyed the feeling. He made a deliberate effort to scowl, nearly making himself laugh in doing so.

Trying to sound stern, James said, "Two insides and two outsides for Tuesday's coach to Dublin, if you please."

Higgins, gone quite pale, quickly bent to pull a large leather-bound ledger from beneath the counter, and fumbled to open it. James had a moment to study the fellow, wondering why he would be so nervous, the realization eventually dawning that Higgins might have been one of the men gathered outside the Red Lion, intent on arson and murder. While James could not identify anyone from that dark night, he was privately convinced that this man had been involved.

Higgins finally found the necessary page, and running a finger along the listing he said with quaking relief, "I am pleased to say, sir, we can accommodate your needs. Tuesday morning, two insides and two outsides to Dublin. That will be..." (some frantic calculations with a stubby pencil) "...ten shillings, three, if you please, sir."

James laid the coins on the counter, gave the man the passenger names, and Higgins scribbled the information into the ledger. With his hand still shaking, he handed James a receipt with something like pleading in his eyes.

James gave the little man a nod, and turned to go. He stopped, though, at the doorway, and pulled a pencil and his day-book from his breast pocket. Looking back, he said in the darkest voice he could manage, "Your name is Higgins, you said? What is your Christian name?"

The man swallowed twice, quickly, then choked, "Matthew, please, your honour. Matthew Higgins."

James wrote down the name, tucked the day-book back in his pocket, set his bicorn back on his head, and said, "I make it a habit of jotting down the names of men I meet, in case I happen to meet them again. Shall I ever meet you again, Higgins?"

"Oh, Christ, sir, I think not. Just here at the Post Office, sir, your humble servant, anxious to please, sir. But nowhere else, I think, sir. I lead a very quiet life."

"Do keep it that way, Higgins."

Walking back out into the street he was pleased with the thought that he had done something like his duty. For a moment he felt, too, a boyish glee in having intimidated such a fellow, but he made a deliberate effort to quash it. Such thoughts were unprofessional, but more than that, they were unworthy of a gentleman. His was a young man's mind, his habits of behavior not fully formed, and he had goals of who and what he hoped to become.

*****

Over the next two hours James ran more errands, all on Barr's behalf, including stops at the tailor's shop, the wine merchant, and the apothecary. All three shopkeepers inquired as to when Lt. Barr would honour his accounts, and the tailor in particular looked concerned when James mentioned the lieutenant's posting to Cork.

Wishing he had brought Doolan along to help carry Barr's packages, James eventually returned to Mullingar Barracks with his arms full.

Doolan was in fact waiting for him at the main gate, and with some relief James handed off the packages, telling him, "Run these up to Lieutenant Barr, won't you? I am due to meet Ensign Mainwaring in the mess to study." Doolan's face was habitually drawn up in an ill-tempered grimace, but as he accepted the packages he had an especially gnarled look to him, prompting James to ask, "Whatever is wrong, man?"

"Well, there is no kind way to say it, now, but your Ensign Mainwaring is gone off to Athlone, bag and baggage."

"Whatever do you mean? He is not to leave until next week!"

"Plans and women fail a man as often as not. Sir. It seems the fellow commanding Seven Company was on leave in Dublin, heard of our young Ensign Mainwaring's posting to his company, and so stopped by here to pick him up on his way back to Athlone. A Captain Weston, a little prig in a coach and four, in a great feckin' hurry he was."

Lockwood stood there, quite a boy, a look of crushing disappointment on his face.

Doolan paused for a moment and sniffed, for him a sincere sign of sympathy, before he gruffly added, "I'll tell you, sir, I did not realize that acting as your servant meant me acting as your feckin' postman as well," handing his officer a folded sheet of paper, "but your friend left this with me, didn't he?" Doolan then shuffled off to deliver Barr's packages while James walked over to an empty section of wall, set his back against it, and slid down to read the note.

James,

A hurried note to express my regret in not tending my farewell in person, and for me to confess my regard for you. You had best feel the same, or I shall return to give you a right good thrashing.

Your particular friend,
Tom

James barked a laugh, looked at the note for a long moment, then tucked it carefully into his breast pocket. He muttered, "Damn it all, anyway," stood, and resigned himself to call on Lieutenant Barr.

*****

Diarmuid Doolan had never before ridden in a carriage, and strictly speaking his fare allowed him only to ride *on* the carriage. Doolan, like many of the desperately poor of Donegal, had never, in fact, ridden in any wheeled vehicle, though he would never admit to it. He stood in the cold, dark fog and eyed the massive conveyance with great suspicion.

It was well before dawn in the street outside the Post Office. Two lanterns threw dim circles of light in the mist, the breath of the four carriage horses fogging in the cold air. A half hour before, the coach had arrived from Longford, and now with fresh horses in the traces and a new pair of drivers the coach was due, past due, to leave for Dublin. The two passengers who had come in from Longford were continuing on to Dublin, both insides. They had long before climbed back into their seats and were now irritably calling for the coachman to get moving.

Ensign Lockwood's chest and dunnage were stowed in the rear of the coach, but it was still some time before Barr's servant, Muldoon, emerged from the gloom with his officer's chest over his shoulder. A tough thug of a man, Muldoon was a former bare-knuckle boxer from Belfast. He tossed the chest up into the luggage bay with brute strength, obviously showing away, and said to Doolan. "So, where's your Saxon?"

Doolan tossed his head toward the Post Office door, and said, "Inside, arguing with the coachman, trying to keep him from leaving without your Saxon. Your boy is taking his feckin' time."

Muldoon sneered at Doolan and said, "Go fuck yourself. He'll be here soon enough." Muldoon climbed up he side of the carriage with an ape-like grace and claimed a seat on the hard bench on the roof. Doolan cautiously followed, his caution prompted by his discomfort with heights and wheeled vehicles, not by the likes of Muldoon. Muldoon was a heavy-fisted *mac soith*, sure, but Doolan had ample experience with his kind. He did wonder, though, why any man, *mac soith* or no, would take up for Lieutenant feckin' Barr. He thought of his father, him always saying, "*Aithníonn ciaróg ciaróg eile.*" One cockroach recognizes another cockroach.

A moment later the coachman emerged from the Post Office, pulling on his heavy leather gauntlets, followed by Ensign Lockwood. "We have waited too long already, sir," said the coachman. "Your tardy friend can take tomorrow's coach, and that is that."

The coachman climbed up into his high seat and took up his reins as James took one last look up the dark street. "To hell with him, then."

James had his heavy cape on, and a bundle under his arm. Pulling a thick wool blanket from the bundle, he tossed it up to Doolan, saying, "Do try not to freeze," and was about to tell Muldoon to climb down when Barr appeared, wrapped in a black cape, as silent and pale as a wraith.

Without a word of explanation Barr opened the carriage door and climbed in, where the two other well-bundled passengers, sleepy older men, sat in the seats facing forward, the customary perquisite of being the earliest occupants. Pointing to one of the men, Barr croaked, "You. Move over to the other side; I must sit facing forward."

"Certainly not, sir," huffed the man. "You delay our departure, then order me about like a common hooligan? I think not!"

James was just behind Barr, paying close attention. He went wide-eyed as Barr pulled back his cloak, displaying the hilt of his sword, and snarled, "A hooligan am I, then? You insult me, sir, a King's officer. Will you stand by your words?"

The man, catching sight of the brass hilt and scarlet coat beneath the cloak, blanched. Quickly shifting across to the other bench, dragging his lap quilt, he hurriedly said, "I do beg... your servant, sir... always happy to oblige an officer..."

As Barr gracefully slid in to the empty seat, James caught a glimpse of the reptilian glare in his eyes. James put a foot onto the coach step, and when the other older gentleman caught sight of a looming shadow with a sword on his hip he, too, quickly, awkwardly, crossed to the opposite bench, saying, "Do allow me, sir... no bother at all... most pleased...."

James nearly waved the man back to his seat, not wanting to take advantage, but then Barr pointed insistently to the seat beside him, and said, *"Le droit de guerre."* James took the seat, feeling pleased and ashamed in alternate measure.

*****

A long, cold, jolting ride ensued. Barr slept, evidently immune to even the harshest movement. As the first light of dawn lit the inside of the carriage, James did his best to look aloof, but his true nature eventually found its way to the surface, and he looked at the two older gentlemen with an apologetic face. They sniffed and did their best to sleep as well. The second gentleman, likely embarrassed to have been daunted by the shadow of this good-natured youngster, looked especially put out.

James found himself too excited to sleep, so he contented himself with looking out the grimy window as the fog lifted, revealing a glittering hoarfrost crusting the fields. They changed horses at Cloncurry, after which the road got progressively better, the fields on either hand gave way to clusters of buildings and then to the depths of the city itself. The Dublin mail yard was a bustling operation in the heart of the city. On that afternoon three coaches were drawn up on the street as coachmen, stable boys, and passengers hustled about. Large, hardworking horses came and went; extensive stabling lined the maze of alleys behind, a distinctive smell masking the stink of the city beyond.

Mail passengers typically stayed at The Whip, a large if aging inn, conveniently near the Dawson Street yard. When James suggested it, Barr gave it one look and said, "You must be mad. I shall not spend one minute in such a vile place. It is certainly the haunt of cretins and dullards." With an easy air, he added, "Do book our places in tomorrow's coach, won't you?" Gesturing toward Doolan and Muldoon as they climbed stiffly down from the coach roof, he went on, "The boys can watch our baggage. I shall strike out in search of a more suitable abode."

James, jealous of Barr's ease, confidence, and air of nonchalant lethality, watched him stroll down Dawson Street. Doolan and Muldoon had each found a soft piece of earth in the yard to nap, leaving Ensign Lockwood to pace in front of the mail office, feeling increasingly insulted, as it was nearly two hours before Barr returned. Barr once again offered no explanation, only looking pleased, saying, "I have booked rooms at the Lion's Stones, down on Townsend Street."

"But that is in Temple Bar!" cried James, who, by chance, knew something of Dublin's less reputable environs. He suspected Barr had been drinking. Catching himself, speaking quietly so that Doolan and Muldoon might not hear, James went on, "We'll have to get a cab to get our chests down there, and then pay to get them back up here by seven in the morning. Could we not stay somewhere... more convenient?"

"Calm yourself, brother. The Stones offer such... diversions. Did you obtain our passage for the morn?"

James was now sure Barr was drunk. "They had only one inside and three outsides."

Barr grinned slyly and said, "Then rank shall play its terrible role. *Droit de seigneur* and all that, you know."

"My French is lacking, but I believe that *droit de seigneur* entitles you to First Night privileges with peasants' daughters, not insides on a mail coach."

In his anger and frustration James had spoken harshly, but the lieutenant paid no heed. "Really?" said Barr, genuinely intrigued. "Oh, that is charming. I shall have to remember that the next time I meet a peasant with a comely daughter." Catching the annoyance on James's face, Barr added, not unkindly, "And so you are wounded. Why is that, Lockwood? You feel as though I have taken advantage? Grow up, boy. Learn this lesson: *take* what you want. You cannot sit back and trust the world to *give* you anything worth having. Damn the feelings of the weak and the timid. I happen to quite flush, so cost is no obstacle. Now, *Ensign*, follow your *Lieutenant* as we go in search of amusement. I am in need of a whore or three."

*****

Dearest Mother,

I do apologize for not having written earlier, but as you might understand the Regiment has kept me rather busy. I have two bits of news to share: First, I am made Ensign! ~~It may please Father to know~~ *The promotion came at no cost, as it came not through purchase, but rather through merit, as I managed not to overly disgrace myself during a very minor scrape in Mullingar. Before you ask, Mother, at no time was your Darling Boy at the slightest risk. Thus, you need not send me any further monies; my pay covers my mess bill, if little more—I do not wish to be dependent.*

Now, as to the second bit of news: Please, please, Mother, do not allow this to upset you, but I have been transferred to Cork Barracks. It is not so very far away, and I hope to obtain leave to travel home, though I must wait my turn, and since I am very junior it may take some time.

There was a disturbance in the street below his window on Great George's Street. He rose from his chair and looked down to watch, the scene below like something from the Bible. He had read the notice in that morning's Barracks Orders: a blacksmith named John Walsh, arrested in some tiny village for forging pike heads, was to be flogged, from the old Market House to the Military Barracks and back. The bloody, agonized man was stopped at intervals to see if he would reveal the names of his comrades. As he staggered, scourged, up the streets, he was followed by his sister, who spoke to him urgently in Irish. Evidently the Yeomen tormenting Walsh spoke no Irish, and assumed she urged him to confess and end his torture. She was in fact urging him to keep silent, to protect his friends and comrades, to defend their cause. James understood her, as did most of the people in the street. Where some had been laughing at the peasant's plight, the mood soon changed, people calling for the redcoats to leave the poor bastard alone. Insults were exchanged, and some of the people bent to pick up stones. The sergeant commanding the detail called for reinforcement from the larger party of yeomen who followed, and James decided to do nothing to aid or hinder the merciless spectacle. In disgust James returned to his letter.

Sadly, my friend Tom Mainwaring (I believe I mentioned him in my previous letter; the minister's son, from Leister) was transferred to Athlone, so the only soul I know here is Lt. Barr, a rather dashing figure, who came down from Mullingar with me.

James nearly referred to Barr as "a renowned duelist," but he thought better of it, as his mother would worry. He had a secret desire to have someone refer to him as a renowned duelist, and a thoroughly dangerous man. With a dangerous wag of his eyebrows he returned to his letter.

There are eleven Militia companies packed into the Barracks. The barracks buildings are chock-a-block in the crumbling pile of rocks called Elizabeth Fort, built way back in 1601. The city has since grown up around it, rendering it useless as a fort, so it is now a cold, cramped misery of a barracks.

Happily, as the barracks are so full, we new boys are billeted on the local residents. I have been forced upon a baker who lives alone in a narrow little house. He has converted his drawing room into my chamber, which displeases him mightily, but he is not a bad fellow.

I do thank you, Mother, for your kind assistance in securing me the start to my army career—

He had an impulse to continue with, *and I would now very much like to come home.* He had been with his regiment for two months, and both in the barracks and in the street he had witnessed little more than brutality, betrayal and stupidity. He and Tom had gotten on well, but that was past, and it seemed that his career would require him to become someone he might not admire. He had begun to wonder if perhaps Barr's advice was as wildly selfish as he had first thought.

*****

"Pass the word for Ensign Lockwood!"
"Pass the word for Ensign Lockwood!"
Four Company had been drilling in the fields south of town, and on their return march the calls found Lockwood, the awkward new boy, in a company of grown men. A messenger directed him to join Colonel O'Reilly in the Officers' Mess.

When Lockwood and Barr had arrived at Cork three days before, they had been introduced to O'Reilly, and as James hurried through the Cork Barracks gate, he did his best to brush the dust from his coat and tried to recall that gentleman: Lieutenant Colonel Sir Hugh O'Reilly, a plump, bespectacled, kindly man, perhaps sixty, who looked more a country doctor than a senior officer of King's troops. James had picked up some bits of education at his bitter father's elbow, including the knowledge that in Cromwell's day, a branch of the O'Reillys had opted to take up Protestantism. James assumed Sir Hugh was of that branch.

In the Officers' Mess, O'Reilly was busily directing the white-coated stewards in setting the mess tables. As James entered, he turned to the young gentleman and said, "Ah! Ensign Lockwood! Thank you for joining me. As you doubtless know, I serve as Captain of the Mess. Once you have your feet, as junior you shall assume the traditional duties of Mess Officer. In the meantime, you shall have opportunity to pay your new brother officers a compliment."

Turning to a pair of stewards who were carrying in a case of wine, O'Reilly called, "McKinney, the Madeira before dinner, the Marsala with the yellow seal after, if you please!"

With a smile he returned to James, saying, "I do beg your pardon; today is Captain Wingo's birthday, and there are so many details to attend to. Now, as to why I called you here: you may be unaware that every New Year's Day the officers of Cork Barracks sponsor a Ball in the Great Hall of the Old Barracks building, just across the road. Just two weeks from now! All the officers subscribe one half of their December pay to fund the ball; I do hope you will not find that too great an imposition. The compliment I mention is another tradition we have, in that, as junior officer, you would oblige your elders by assuming an extra turn as Officer of the Day. You'll thus miss the soiree, though I trust it is not too great a sacrifice for you. Certainly you have yet to make acquaintance with any of the local belles, and you will enable your brothers to entertain their favorites. In speaking to your Lieutenant Barr earlier, he was most enthusiastic about the ball, expressing great interest in meeting the fine ladies of Cork."

Chapter Ten

"Rzewnicki?" said Brigid, even her eyes quizzical.

"Yes," said Nichole, perhaps a bit defensively. "He is quite the gentleman, the son of a Polish nobleman, come to Britain to make his fortune. He has his own company ... Four, I think?"

"Six," said Gabriele, who had a knack for military organization.

"Yes, Six, thank you, dear. I suppose such distinctions are important to soldiers, if not to normal people. I shall make a deliberate effort to remember. In any case, Captain Rzewnicki commands Six Company in the Westmeath Militia Regiment, a position of great responsibility."

It was Christmas Day, and Miss McCarthy was hosting the four teachers in her private quarters. She had reached her seventieth year, and, being a rational being, had grown more fond of her ease than the eager pursuit of the pound sterling. She had always been kind to Brigid, but now that Brigid was numbered among the staff, Miss McCarthy had dropped all pretense of formality. The ladies had shared an excellent meal, some informed conversation on the literature of the day, two bottles of a bold Madeira, and the school cook's triumphant Christmas Pudding, complete with sprigs of holly and flaming brandy. After dinner, the drawing room conversation, spurred by more Madeira, while never bawdy, was free and rather more frank, typical of the conversation of women when freed of the presence of men. Brigid, who had little experience with wine, was enjoying herself immensely, and the other ladies were not far behind.

"Oh, Brigid," said Gabrielle, "you will find Captain Rzewnicki such an admirable young man, and I shall make it a point to have you introduced," a notion which Nichole seemed to disapprove. Leaning forward, speaking in a conspiratorial tone, Gabrielle added, "And speaking of officers, I am in possession of a military secret of great import. Captain Mason has come to an understanding with Miss Murray!"

"What lovely news!" said Miss Klug, who was relaxed and smiling, but of all the women there she was most in control of herself. "They shall make a fine match."

Miss McCarthy, who was well aware that at one time Miss Klug had some hopes of Captain Mason, gave her a private smile of condolence and reached over the table to fill that elegant woman's glass.

"Well, I, for one, am not at all pleased with the news," said Miss McCarthy—if she once had a Christian name it was lost to time—"for while young officers make fine husbands, I am loath to lose my teachers, and yet I am loath to see you young ladies disappointed," —Miss McCarthy was also loath to end a sentence when in drink— "so I am determined that each of you ladies, including you, Miss O'Brian, our dear Brigid, might have your pick of that martial litter, but my goodness, I have yet to inquire as to your wardrobe, Brigid, and I might loan you something from my modest, well, perhaps not so modest, armoire, as in my youth we were much of a size, though perhaps you are rather more...." she waved a vague finger at Brigid's bosom, and went on, "My goodness, how long ago that was, when I was the ambition of many young men of Cork and Kerry, and then, too, of Limerick, far away...."

Miss McCarthy wound down to silence in a mix of nostalgia, regret and unrequited lust, allowing Brigid to look around the table and ask, "Are officers really such fine husbands? Are they perhaps not, as a class, rather prone to... violence?" She had reason to inquire, since, as a class, her people had long been oppressed by men in red coats.

"Oh, they are perfectly respectable!" cried both Nichole and Gabrielle, though there followed a modifying discussion, all the ladies chiming in, in which it was agreed that while the officers of Cork Barracks, like the balance of humanity, had their brutes and their saints, some broad categorizations might be attempted. Yeomanry officers were the least desirable, for while some had acceptable incomes, so many of them were prone to volatility in temper. Line officers were much preferred, as many had private means beyond their pay, and they were acceptable, sometimes wildly acceptable, in appearance and manner. Still, the gentlemen of the Line had an unfortunate trait, in that they were subject to foreign service, being gone for months, even years at a time, and having a significant risk of death at sea, by disease, or at the hands of the King's many enemies.

"I have a cousin," offered Miss Klug into the general melee of discussion, and as usual the others gave her preference. Her Christian name was Carolyn, but it was rarely used. "She was young, perhaps nineteen, when she married a cornet of the Royal Dragoons. Soon afterward the regiment was part of the army which sailed to Holland; I believe it was 1793. She followed the regiment, thinking it all terribly romantic, though her friends and family begged her not to do so. Her cornet died there, at the siege of Dunkirk. She came home a widow with a big belly and a pension of fifty pounds a year to live on. Her father will not see her, and she lives in near-poverty in London."

There followed a moment for them to ponder such a fate, until Nichole said, with evident satisfaction, "And so, dear sisters, we conclude that *militia* officers make the best husbands! QED, ladies, QED," emptying her glass with relish, and private thoughts of Captain Rzewnicki.

Miss McCarthy then slapped the table and said, "Let us hear no more of men, and love, and heartbreak! I have long had in my cellar a bottle of Château Lafite—"

"It is made with real feet," said Brigid with a hiccup, drawing howls of laughter.

Miss McCarthy gathered herself, and continued, "—and to demonstrate my admiration for you, dear ladies, I shall have Cummins bring it up, and as women of intellect we shall expound on matters of greater import than hairy beasts. Now, Miss Klug, I wonder if you might tip us a Christmas carol, as your voice is in such good form. And Brigid, dear, pray jump up and pull that notorious new Jane West novel from the... what do you call it? The shelf. I shall read you ladiesh some passages... this West woman, the didactic shrew, desires to hide behind the name 'Prudentia Homespun', for all love. She would have us all act as brainless servile baby machines... oh, it is quite infamous."

They talked and sang the rest of the evening away, friends before their Christmas, dearer friends afterward. In later years they would recall that night, and each other, with the greatest fondness, in the days before the darkness.

*****

Michael O'Brian was as fond of wise sayings as his father, and his father before him. One came to his mind that Christmas morning: "*Nollaig ghlas, reilig mhéith.*" A green Christmas brings a full graveyard." He noticed the green was still on the grass as he walked toward St. Brigit's with Ann and Caitlin. Afterwards they hurried to dinner at his father's home. Michael was distracted and short, and after seeing the girls home he went out. Ann and Caitlin knew not to question his business when he was quiet.

The night was dark and cold as Michael hurried to meet Fergal O'Brian and Tadg O'Donovan behind the hedge at the Pagan's Cross. Fergal was quiet, out of respect for his Uncle Michael and out of his awe for Tadg O'Donovan.

O'Donovan felt no such compunction. In the delightful coarseness of which Irish is capable, he said, "There is little about you that is admirable, Michael O'Brian, but I must say that you're a prompt fucker, sure."

O'Brian sniffed and replied, "That's what your sister said last night."

The three men pulled off their gloves, shook hands, and a gust of wind howled through the bare trees. "A dark night for dirty work," muttered Michael as they headed out across the fields, having known every inch of them since they were boys.

An hour later and three Irish miles from Clonakilty they pelted across a muddy pasture in the dark, twenty other men with him, breathing hard with exertion, excitement and fear. The West Cork Whiteboys were afoot.

Reaching the shadows under the trees of the Auburn House park, they paused to catch their breath and check their bearings. Some of them passed a bottle around. In the moonlight they could see the big house just beyond, with a cluster of smaller buildings behind. O'Donovan directed Fergal and a few men to watch the front and the wicket, while he, Michael, and ten others went to the rear.

Two weeks before, in the draper's shop in Clonakilty, an Auburn House maid had let slip, intentionally or not, the news that her master and his family would be in Dublin for Christmas. A few days later the maid returned to the shop to pick up her bolt of muslin, and an older woman pulled her aside. In a hurried, volatile, hissing conversation, the maid eventually told her the gun room was on the first floor, wasn't it, the second door to the left of the stairs. Threats and promises from the harsh old woman bought the maid's fearful agreement to leave the rear door unlocked on Christmas night.

The silent men crossed the low stone wall that separated the park from the house grounds. The house was dark, the only light coming from a lantern hanging near the stables. Anxious, their eyes darting, the men reached the stout rear door.

"Hell and death," hissed O'Donovan. The door was locked.

"Christ, Michael! You told us it would be open!"

"We are betrayed! It's a trap!" cried Liam Cullum, and he and two others bolted in panic, leaping across the park wall like deer, and were gone.

"What the hell do we do now, Michael? Eh? Do we sprout wings and feckin' fly up to the gunroom?"

There then came an old man's voice coming from behind them, by the stables, calling, "Who's there? What are you lads about, there?" In the dim lantern light an old man came toward them, a pitchfork in his hands.

Several of the Whiteboys charged the old man, beating him to the ground, venting their fear and frustration, yelling, "Traitor! Turncoat!" Michael ran and pulled them away, and in the noise and stupid confusion, the rear door opened, the maid stuck her head out and asked, "Is it you, then, the rebel men?" but then looking out toward the stables she cried, "Oh, what have you done to old Bertie!" She ran out to where the old man lay bleeding and moaning, and O'Donovan paused a moment before hissing, "Come on then, you lot, let's go!"

In an instant the house was pandemonium. The Whiteboys ran yelling through the dark rooms, the most clever finding the stairs and bolting up to loot the gun room. Two others found a sideboard stocked with liquor, and stood gulping brandy. Another, an older man named McGowan, ran up to the second floor and kicked in a door to a small bedroom where two maids slept. He burst in and slapped them about, and was on the verge of rape when Michael O'Brian, roaring like a bull, found McGowan there, his pants around his ankles, dragged him out, and threw him down the stairs.

Eventually O'Donovan and O'Brian got everyone out of the house, and before the moon set, all the men of the raid had rallied back at Conner's crossroads, as instructed. In the usual post-action mixture of shame, remorse, glee, terror and satisfaction, he calmed and instructed them, though Michael O'Brian had to be restrained from murdering McGowan.

In the darkness, O'Donovan drew the men together, and said, "It didn't go to plan, did it? But still we found a way, and now The Cause can count on three rifles, two pistols, and two kegs of powder—guns we didn't have before! That was well done, lads, though we all have lessons to learn before our next raid. Now, off home with you, and hold yourselves ready. Hear me, now: the rising might come at any time! Death to the English, and long live Ireland!"

*****

Low, wind-torn clouds scudded across the sky, allowing occasional bursts of bright sun to cheer Cork Town and then in an instant be gone. It was the type of sky that presaged a drastic shift in the weather, but few people could read such signs. Brigid O'Brian sensed it. As she stepped up into the carriage she glanced upward with a mix of trepidation and wonder, as nature and time churned their courses.

Men of the Westmeath Militia Regiment had long been posted to Cork Barracks, and, as head of the regiment, Colonel Montgomery thus had a history with that crumbling bastion. He was the traditional Master of Ceremonies for the Cork Barracks Ball, and over the years he had become a good friend to Miss McCarthy; it was his invitation that brought that worthy and the ladies of her school to tea. The tea was a ploy, of course, as were so many such functions, in this case a way for the young ladies to be introduced to some of the officers of the garrison prior to the ball.

And so, the ladies of Miss McCarthy's came to call.

As the carriage clattered into the barracks yard, the colonel was there to hand the ladies down. Miss McCarthy introduced them each to the colonel, the ladies polite, if nervous, though the colonel's natural graciousness did a great deal to set them at ease.

The colonel said, "Now, ladies, if you will allow me to show you to our Officers' Mess, we have a modest tea prepared for you, and I trust you will allow me the liberty of introducing some of the finer officers of the garrison. Those gentlemen are most—" He was interrupted by a group of soldiers passing by on their way to change the guard at the gate. The men paid no notice to the colonel, made no salute, speaking among themselves in a loud, bantering Irish.

Colonel Montgomery glared at the men as they passed, eventually turning back to the ladies to say with mounting anger, "I do beg your pardon, ladies, that you should witness such a breech in discipline. Men of my own regiment! They are in desperate need of instruction in military courtesy. More than that, the speaking of the Irish language is forbidden among His Majesty's forces, as it is often used as a secret language of mutiny and rebellion."

Of their party only Brigid understood the men were speaking of nothing more sinister than their tardy dinner, but she was in no position to gainsay the colonel. She was still thinking in Irish as their group approached a corner, a corner around which came the bounding form of a very tall young officer, late for his place in the posting of the guard, and singing a ribald song. He nearly crashed into Miss O'Brian, causing her to cry out, "*Gabh mo leithscéal, a dhuine uasal!*" I beg your pardon, gentleman, before she could catch herself. Blushing very pink, she said hurriedly, "Oh, I do beg your pardon, I meant to say—"

The others turned to Brigid in surprise, a look of disapproval flashing across the face of Miss McCarthy, but Brigid was rescued by the tall young officer who smiled, bowed and said, "*Dia agus Mhaire duit, fear uasal a grah.*" God and Mary be with you, gentlewoman.

She often had difficulty in reading the faces of young men, but in this instance, at least, she read him quite clearly: curiosity, intelligence, humour, but above all an overarching kindness. Ensign Lockwood and Miss O'Brian stood staring at one another for a long moment until Colonel Montgomery shook his head, sighed and said, not unkindly, "Ensign, I believe you are required at your post."

The ensign saluted his colonel without taking his eyes from those of Miss O'Brian, and with a deliberate effort, he forced himself to return to his duty, looking confused.

"Pray, my dear Montgomery," asked Miss McCarthy, "who was that pole-axed young gentleman?"

Montgomery pursed his lips, and said, "That, ma'am, was our Ensign Lockwood, newly joined from Mullingar." He did not mention that Ensign Lockwood was his nephew. "If you like, I shall call him back and make the introductions."

"Do not trouble yourself, my dear," said Miss McCarthy, airily. "Besides, I am not sure if his heart could bear the strain, the poor lamb."

After an amused, kindly glance at Brigid, Gabrielle asked the colonel, "At any rate, sir, I suppose we shall see Ensign Lockwood again soon, at the ball?"

"Sadly, no, Miss Reese. As the junior officer it is his unfortunate duty to remain in the Barracks, as Officer of the Day."

Brigid surprised herself with the bolt of disappointment she felt, but she pressed on as if nothing had happened, as if no one had noticed her gaffe, as if no one sensed her confusion. She forced herself to listen to the Colonel's explanation of the barrack's history, though to her it was all oppression, cold stone and cramped spaces. They reached the Mess, where two soldiers opened the heavy doors for their party. In the foyer more soldiers came and politely took their cloaks, but as one of them passed back into the cloakroom, Brigid heard him say to his comrades, "*Tá na Sasanach ag siamsaíocht ar a striapacha.*" The Saxons are entertaining their harlots.

Brigid was nervous and still oddly upset, oddly disappointed, thinking of the young man in the barracks yard, and she had had quite enough. She stepped over to the cloakroom door, leaned in, and whispered one of her father's sayings to the three soldiers there, *"Is minic a ghearr teanga duine a scornach, ceathrair."* It is often that a person's tongue cut his throat, cousins.

The soldiers went pale and wide eyed; men of the garrison had drawn a flogging for far less. Their shock, too, came from the notion that an Irishwoman, one of their own, was being entertained by the officers, being honored with the best the barracks had to offer.

Seeing her dart had found its mark, Brigid's face softened, she gave them a wink, (her Seanathair O'Brian had taught her how to wink when she was little, and she took an inordinate pride in being able to do so) and returned to her group, feeling a bit more in control of the situation, and herself.

The Officers' Mess was a large hall built into the walls of the old fortress, more cold stone and pillars, dusty flags hanging from the rafters, a gloomy cavern illuminated by candlelight and massive fireplaces blazing at either end. The gloom of the room was in sharp contrast to the dozen or so officers who stood in eager attendance, their coats red and blue, their tight breeches snow white, their gold braid glittering in the dancing light.

Colonel Montgomery played his role to perfection, a smooth mix of formality and friendliness, introducing each of the ladies, each making her curtsy in turn. While she was desperately nervous, Brigid took some solace in seeing a degree of discomfort on her friends' faces as well.

Montgomery then asked each of the gentlemen to step forward to be introduced in turn.

"Ladies, Major McDonald of the Caithness Legion Fencibles. Captain Beard, of the 9th Foot. Captain Barnes-Wallis of the 9th Foot. I believe you know already Captain Mason of my own regiment, the Westmeath Militia." The introductions continued; when his turn came Captain Rzewnicki gave Miss Hendricks an obvious smile.

Lieutenant Barr held back, intent on being the last to be introduced. As was his habit, he took his time, eyeing the women, classifying them, grading the values of their various parts. He mentally made a list of the order in which he would bed them, given the opportunity. He was pleased with the selection, and had at first some difficulty in deciding who would top his list when Brigid O'Brian stepped into the light.

The conquest of women was his greatest pleasure, his primary diversion, and he held himself a prime judge of the female form. As the others were introduced he had opportunity to confirm his opinion. This, *this,* was the most beautiful woman he had seen in a very long time. The perfect skin, the chestnut hair, the sparkling eyes, the surging bosom, the lithe young body, what delights lay there! Two or three pounds of baby fat, but he would have that off her in no time.

"...and finally," said Colonel Montgomery after only a slight pause, "Lieutenant Barr, of my regiment."

The other gentlemen had maintained a polite distance between themselves and their guests, but Barr stepped through the others and, drawing quite near, made an elegant bow to the ladies. While not quite inappropriate, he made it quite clear that his whole attention was focused on Miss O'Brian.

That young lady was obviously flattered by the attention. Miss Reese and Miss Hendricks smiled at the trim, handsome young Lieutenant Barr with open admiration, and Miss Hendricks's evident regard for Lieutenant Barr caused Captain Rzewnicki to look concerned. Miss McCarthy and Miss Klug were of different ages and vastly different backgrounds, but they had evidently developed the same opinion of Lieutenant Barr, for they looked at him with pursed mouths and hard eyes.

The mess stewards came forward with loaded trays, the mood grew more relaxed, and the gentlemen stepped forward to chat with their guests.

Barr stepped up to Miss O'Brian, angling his body so that no other gentleman could address her without an obvious breech of manners.

"Tell me, Miss O'Brian, shall you be attending our ball on New Year's Day? I hear it is to be quite a grand event."

"I have been honored with an invitation," Brigid replied, trying not to sound shy.

"How splendid. I do so look forward to the soirée, as an opportunity to meet some of the area's finer people, as I am new here, without a friend upon whom I might rely." Doing his best to appear modest, (in truth, he was an actor of the first order) he went on, "I wonder.... I trust I am not being overly bold, Miss O'Brian, and I do beg you to correct me if I am making a fool of myself... but I wonder I might be so bold as to ask for the honour of the first dance?"

With a deep blush and a quick curtsey, Miss O'Brian quietly replied, "I should be most pleased, thank you, Lieutenant."

Barr smiled and bowed in return. It was very much his intention to be the first.

Chapter Eleven

James often had difficulty in reading the faces of young women, but in this instance, at least, he read her quite clearly: curiosity, intelligence, humour, but above all an overarching kindness. Despite the brevity of their acquaintance, indeed despite knowing nearly nothing about her, in the coming days he gave Miss O'Brian an inordinate amount of thought. Those thoughts were among his few consolations, as he found his time at Cork Barracks a misery.

His days consisted of drill, meals at the mess, and time alone in his billet. He was still the new boy, an unproven commodity. When his company was dispatched on missions into town or the countryside beyond, he was deemed too green to join them, drawing dismissive looks from both the men and his brother officers.

Neither was his time in the Officers' Mess any consolation. The barracks ensigns were assigned to a table in a separate alcove, where their youthful exuberance might not annoy their elders. That, at least, was of some comfort, as James, who was slow to make friends, had no need to insert himself into tables full of gentlemen who were, at best, distant. James was an officer of militia, and so had only a narrow band of men with whom he might socialize, as among the officers there was great deal of preening for position. The line looked down on the militia, the militia looked down on the yeomanry, and the yeomanry's attitude toward the balance of humanity ranged from dismissal to open loathing. Yet even beyond those hierarchies, James found himself an outcast, and he was for some days puzzled as to why.

*****

He came into the mess on a Sunday evening two days after Christmas in search of a few scraps to take back to his billet. The mess did not serve on Sundays, and the man upon whom James was billeted, a radical Methodist, did not feel obliged to feed him on the Sabbath. As young Ensign Lockwood's purse was nearly empty, and as he was as fond of his dinner as any seventeen year-old, he came hunting anything the mess stewards might not have locked away.

Four militia officers, none of them Westmeaths, sat at a table playing cards, and the several empty bottles scattered around them showed they had been doing so for some time. James had been introduced to them, but he could not recall their names.

They turned to look at him, and the senior, a major of the Cork Militia, asked, "Ensign... Lockwood, is it not?"

"Yes, sir. I beg pardon for interrupting. I was just hoping to find a crust in the larder, sir."

"Acting as an accessory to manslaughter does give one an appetite," a captain of the North Mayo Militia smirked into his glass.

Surprised, James said, "I beg your pardon, sir, but *manslaughter?*"

The major waved away the captain's insult, saying, "Stephenson speaks in jest, of course. He refers to the duel held this afternoon."

James raised both eyebrows, raised his open palms, and said, "Again, gentlemen, you have me at a disadvantage —"

"You are Lieutenant Barr's... how shall I phrase this... his *protégé*, are you not? It is widely known. Did you not today act as that gentleman's second in an affair of honour in The Shrubbery Park?"

"Upon my honour, gentlemen," said James, clearly confused, "I confess my ignorance of any affair involving Lieutenant Barr, or anyone else, in the bushes or anywhere else—"

A captain of the Corks on the far side of the table sniffed in amusement, and said, not unkindly, "The Shrubbery, son, is a park down by the River Lee, one that lies on the boundary between Cork Town and the suburbs. It is the traditional ground on the south side of Cork to resolve such matters, as after the business is seen to, the participants can scatter across the boundaries and so evade any intrusive authorities. Regarding today's activities, as you were of no service to young Barr, I wonder—"

The question went unspoken, but was answered nonetheless, as Captain Wingo of the Westmeaths came unsteadily into the mess, and, seeing the men at the table, said, "For God's sake, Stephenson, pour me a glass. I am fresh from the field of combat, serving as Barr's second, and am in desperate need of bracing." Looking over at James, he added. "And why does young Lockwood stand here dry-throated? A drink for my friend, here! Barr has established the Westmeath's reputation as swaggering duelists and thoroughly dangerous men, so we might just as well abandon all our moral tenets."

James, surprised and pleased, was handed a glass of wine, but was then quickly relegated to the background as the other officers gathered around Wingo and called on him to explain the details of the duel.

"Well, gentlemen," growled the captain as he took a seat and unbuttoned his coat, "it seems that our beloved Lieutenant Barr and a barrister named Nye differed over a seat at the theater. The merest trifle; Nye is an older gentleman, quite ancient, past fifty, I am certain, and I believe that any one of us would have let the difference pass with a wave of the hand. But not our dear Barr, oh, no indeed. Our duelist pressed the issue, giving Nye the lie. Upon my honour, when Barr asked me to act for him I was unaware of these... I do not wish to cast aspersions... but then, perhaps I do... I am in drink...upon the very unsavory aspects of the meeting." Wingo drank again, and went on, "Once on the ground, Barr was confident as a fellow might be, quite the strutting cock, and, I must confess, I have never seen the like. Christ, I am drunk."

Wingo snorted, looked at his glass, waving aside an offer to have it refilled, adding with a note of regret, "Barr would not hear any talk of apology. They set to, and the old barrister fought well, surprising our combative friend, I assure you, but in the end Barr bested him. You know, Barr had it in his power to deliver a much less serious wound, but he deliberately ran the old fellow through the body. You gentlemen have all been out, you know of how one might stay one's hand. Nye was badly wounded, and is despaired of. Meanwhile Barr's reputation soared, in his own estimation, if nowhere else."

Wingo got to his feet with deliberate effort, and added, "I should mention that as I returned to the barracks I came across Lieutenant Colonel O'Reilly. He told me of yet another raid by the rebels in West Cork. We may indeed need to reinforce the Clonakilty garrison, as there are now more firearms in the hands of the rebels." Wingo ran a hand across his face, blinked, and went on, "Without, we face an organized and deliberate enemy. Within, we are fraught with division and the company of God damned *beau sabreurs* and their whims." He made an effort to stand upright, turned to James, and added, "But for now, I seem to require my bed. Lockwood, be a good fellow and help me along, won't you? But stand thee warned: I may need to be sick *en route*. Lead on, MacDuff."

*****

December 29, 1797
My Dear Tom,

I trust this letter finds you thoroughly miserable. As I myself am thoroughly miserable, and as I am familiar with the wisdom, 'misery loves company,' I am unashamed in trusting you remain my companion, even in this.

You will, I hope, also excuse me in my unmanly confession that I am without a friend here. Barr is unknowable, frustrating. At times he confides in me as if I were his only friend, at other times he treats me with an obvious brusqueness, nearly disdain. The other officers here, of every ilk, a God damned Noah's Ark of rank and regiment, want little to do with me, as a new ~~boy~~ man from a different regiment, but it seems that since Barr and I arrived at the same time, everyone here assumes I am his boon companion, lackey and amoral second. Barr has alienated all but a handful of the other officers, and I am shunned in turn. I have, though, made some progress with the men of my company, as Captain Holister has never bothered to even learn their names. They are on the whole a decent lot, requiring only some attention and respect, and most should do very well.

James checked his watch, a gift from his mother when he had left for school in England at age twelve. Every man of the barracks was to witness punishment at four, a flogging of three Cork militiamen corrupted by the United Irishmen. Floggings were standard practice in all branches of the military, but increasingly common in Ireland as the United men whispered promises of equality and wealth. This would be James's first exposure to flogging, and he was not looking forward to the loss of that particular innocence. He had another hour before he was to report, so dipping his pen, he wrote on.

The Barracks Surgeon, Charles Oades is a good fellow, and he has invited me to dine with him next Sunday evening. He is older than me by several years, but in company he carries himself with such meekness that he is not well liked in the mess. Barr in particular takes delight in tormenting the poor fellow. In conversation, though, Oades proves to be quite amiable, and when I happened to mention my enjoyment of choral music, he lit up amazingly, and invited me to a concert to be held at Cork Cathedral on New Year's Day.

He set his pen down to read over what he had written, and was unsure whether he would ever send it to Tom; he had a dread fear of sounding weak and childish. He frowned, set the letter aside, and went on to write a few lines to his mother. In neither letter did he mention Brigid O'Brian. James was a rational being, but he kept several secret games in his head, one of them being a superstitious notion that if he did not mention his feelings for someone, that person might one day have those same feelings for him. And so, he kept his thoughts about her to himself, as he very much hoped that she might one day think of him as something more than the tall boy in a red coat.

*****

Twenty-five years before James Lockwood became a burden to his domineering father, John Lockwood Sr. had been a Pinking Dindie. A gang of dissolute young gentlemen, many of them failed Trinity College students and sons of great families, the Pinking Dindies were notorious drunkards, gamblers, and whore chasers who haunted Dublin's debauched Essex Street through the 1770s. As those young men exhausted their allowances, or were disowned entirely, the members of the gang made it a habit to leave their gambling dens late at night to roam the dark streets to make up their losses, robbing rich gentlemen at sword-point. (As the Pinking Dindies were, without fail, nattily attired, they were thus well acquainted with their tailors, and appropriated the tailors' term for making holes in cloth, even if they did so with smallswords: pinking. And as they spent a great deal of time with fallen women, they expropriated their slang for gents of style: dindies.)

With such a treasured memory of his thoroughly disreputable youth, Lockwood Sr. had both his sons trained with the finest sword masters that Dublin could offer, the dwindling family accounts be damned.

While John Lockwood Jr. was his father's son in this, as in so many other ways, James Lockwood usually showed little natural genius for much of anything. In nearly every field of endeavor James struggled in his brother's shadow, finding middling success only by applying himself with a dogged workman-like resolution

At age ten James's first lessons in swordsmanship seemed to be another such: his first instructor, the grizzled Signore D'Amato, suggested it might take a year or more before Master Lockwood would understand which end of the sword to grasp. One of the few times James had ever made his father laugh was when the boy suggested that Signore D'Amato's visage did little to recommend him; a fellow bearing so many scars might be a swordsman, but perhaps not an especially *skilled* swordsman. Eventually D'Amato refused to work with such a *scemo*, this boy who asked so many questions. James was then passed off to an aged Irish gentleman, John McCabe, in a dim hall in a fading Dublin neighborhood, a man who discovered the skilled swordsman hidden in the slender body of the quiet, awkward, uncertain youngster. When the day came that James bested his elder brother, Lockwood senior roared in surprise, a moment James recalled in later years with muted pleasure. When James came to routinely best his father, there was markedly less celebration in the house.

*****

Deep beneath the bastions of Cork Barracks a senior sergeant acted as Barracks Sword Master. Down a twisting series of granite steps lay Sergeant Prentice's kingdom, the Sword Hall, a long, dim, arched room of dank stone. There he trained the officers of the garrison in swordsmanship, earning a shilling for each sweating, grunting, flashing hour of instruction. Nearly every officer took advantage of his services, as they all knew their lives might one day hinge on their ability to wield a blade. The smallest advantage might be the key between life and death, or, more importantly, between honour and dishonour.

A hundred years of Cork Barracks tradition dictated that on every Monday afternoon the sword master would preside over a series of mock duels. The subalterns were required to attend, their superiors typically attended, and occasionally even the very senior officers came to watch their juniors exercise the gentlemanly art. In that December of 1797 the barracks was full to capacity, so more than seventy officers sat in knots along the walls of the narrow hall. The dueling ground consisted of a path of coarse sand down the center of the room.

The Sword Hall's list of traditions was long and strictly adhered to: the hall would be illuminated by a hundred candles, never less, so that no man might blame gloom for his defeat. The officers of the garrison would present themselves in their shirts, tight breeches, and Hessian boots. No alcohol was allowed in the hall, to prevent any untoward loss of temper. There was to be no wagering, as the matches were to be strictly an exercise in honour.

The sword master would in turn select from the assembled gentlemen four pairs to spar, the duelists using the matched pairs of practice foils kept there. As they were pointed out, the duelists would strip to the waist, and set to. The matches were the best of three touches; each match might last frantic seconds or long sweating, panting minutes. In every instance the gentleman fought with desperate earnestness, men whose self-image was largely based on their honour and their ability to defend it, while the informed opinions of the watching crowd of their brother officers meant nearly as much.

James had spent several sessions with Sergeant Prentice, a considerable investment for an ensign whose purse contained few shillings, but he had yet to be selected to spar. He had spent the previous Mondays on the sidelines, carefully studying the matches, consciously noting the skills, habits and tactics of the men he might one day face.

On that last Monday of 1797, Prentice had hosted three matches, tense affairs that filled the training hall with the smells of sweating men and candle smoke. As the two panting duelists of the third match saluted one another and returned to their friends, Prentice crossed his arms and studied the assembly of officers.

"Captain Rzewnicki, I wonder if you would take up a blade, please, sir." Then turning to James with a raised eyebrow, he went on, "Ensign Lockwood would pose an interesting match for you, I think."

There followed some surprised murmuring, as Rzewnicki had been trained on the continent, and was highly regarded.

James knew he had surprised, and perhaps pleased, the old sergeant in their practice sessions, and when that Monday came he wondered if his turn would come. Still, he jumped when selected, and Dr. Oades, who was sitting beside him, slapped him on the arm and said, "Oh, good for you, James! Go and show them a thing or two, old boy."

Barr was sitting with the flash crowd; when for the fourth time that day he was not chosen to spar he looked put out, and one of the men near him said, "Perhaps next week, old cock. For now, let us be entertained by the sight of your boy being dismembered."

James pulled a foil from the rack and walked to take up his place at the far end of the hall, desperately nervous and doing his best not to let it show. He felt terribly self-conscious as he pulled his shirt off, thin, pale, and hairless in front of so many grown men. Still, if his mother had been there she might have noted how the past year had been good to him, filling out the lean hard frame of the man he would become.

James had to walk past Barr and his stylish acquaintances. Without a smile, Barr looked up from his chair and said, "Die well, but quickly, won't you, Lockwood? There is a new girl at Mrs. Keith's, and I simply must be her first tonight."

One of the other stylish gentlemen sniffed and muttered to his friends, "Christ, he is as nervous as a bridegroom."

James made no reply as he took up his place, his mind and his hands unsteady, the harsh comments buzzing in his head, as Prentice stepped over to formally inspect the button at the tip of the practice blade. Prentice gave him the traditional instructions, "Remember, sir: no hits will be scored above the neck or below the waist. Touches will be awarded solely upon my judgement. The best of three shall be victor." Then, quietly, a muttered, "Mind your third position, sir."

Prentice then stepped down the sanded path to speak to Rzewnicki while James made a few practice thrusts to calm himself, his nerves frayed further by numerous hoots, though he did hear a few welcome cheers of encouragement.

Before he knew it, it had started. Rzewnicki was on him in an instant, viper quick, his blade a blur, but Mr. McCabe's training was deeply ingrained. Defend without giving ground, anticipate the opponent's next assault, stall, frustrate, study, find a gap, and then a lightning riposte. In swordplay James found the physical activity coupled with the need for absolute focus, and every other concern was erased. The nerves were dismissed, utterly forgotten, and he might have been anywhere in the world, alone with this puzzle to be solved, this one man who wished to better him, and James Lockwood had grown tired of being bettered.

For James, swordsmanship was more than reflex and muscle memory; he had a deep understanding of it. During their endless sessions, the aged McCabe had patiently answered the boy's many questions, eventually coming to call him *Ollamh*, Professor. McCabe had taught many men, and he understood that some learned slowly, but deeply. James was one such. Once he combined the basic skills of muscle and reflex with the intellectual understanding of what he was doing, swordsmanship became quite simple for him. Captain Rzewnicki, for example, had a tendency to carry his point a bit low after a parried thrust. That left his sword arm shoulder vulnerable... thus.

"Touch!" cried Sergeant Prentice. "First touch to Ensign Lockwood."

Gasps and roars of surprise from the other gentleman, and the match resumed.

Again, James relied on his defensive skills. He was nothing if not self-aware: he knew that much of his personality, and thus much of his sword skill, was based on protecting himself. He found the physical manifestation of that protection immensely satisfying. Over and over he parried Rzwenicki's point, frustrating and tiring his opponent. Another lesson James had learned from McCabe: if your opponent made a mistake, he was liable to make it again. Eventually Rzewnicki did so, his point again too low, earning him another startling, livid welt on his right shoulder.

"Touch!" again cried Prentice. "The second touch, and the match, to Ensign Lockwood. Thank you, gentlemen, that was well done. We end today's matches with quite a fine display of the art, most gratifying."

The two combatants shook hands, Rzewnicki with a shake of his head and a sigh of frustration. James pulled his shirt back on quickly and returned to his seat, the congratulations of men he respected echoing in his ears, a modest grin growing on his face.

Some of the gentlemen gently teased Rzewnicki, but he spoke loudly, so that every man there might hear. "In Poland my peasants say, *"Nie wywołuj wilka z lasu."* In English, perhaps it might be rendered, "Do not call a wolf out of the woods," much like your "Allow sleeping dogs to lie." With a wry grin he nodded toward James and added, "Do not be deceived by Ensign Lockwood's mild manner. A man would do well to think twice before provoking him. I, for one, should not care to face him in earnest."

Prentice dismissed the officers, and as they stood and gathered their things, several of the gentlemen paused to congratulate Lockwood, all with new respect in their tone.

Barr, however, made an obvious effort to avoid him.

*****

Late that night the hulking Private Muldoon presented a well-worn pass to the Sergeant of the Guard at the gate of Cork Barracks. The Sergeant had been expecting him; Lieutenant Barr had gone out earlier that evening, which typically meant that Muldoon would be required to go out into the cold, dark streets to retrieve his officer.

As the private had few other responsibilities, he did not mind this particular duty, especially as he soon became acquainted with Barr's favorite haunts. That night he found Barr staggering down Sullivan's Quay, drunk, even by army standards.

Muldoon put a massive arm around Barr, propped him up, and began to walk him back up the street. "Come now, sir, it's back to the barracks with you. Be a good gentleman, now." He noticed deep scratches on the lieutenant's face, a woman's nails, sure, and torn gold braid on the elegant coat. Dark stains on the gentleman's hands, blood, likely not his own.

Barr would never explain himself to Muldoon, but still he muttered toward the slick dark cobblestones, "She said I'm poxed." He sang a few bars of a ribald song and then whispered into the darkness as they careened down the street, "She said she wouldn't lie with a poxed bastard like me. A whore! Too good for me!" He held up a bloody hand and hissed, "Now she isn't too good for any man, is she?" He laughed sharply, and even Muldoon, who had seen a great deal of ugliness in his life, had a look of horror on his face.

Chapter Twelve

The first day of 1798 was a Monday, and throughout the day the officers of Cork Barracks busied themselves with the final details of their New Year's ball. The issues were numerous, and varied: the musicians brought down from Dublin had arrived on time, but upon seeing the great hall of the Old Barracks they refused to play, indignantly insisting that the damp and chill of the place would ruin their instruments; the recipe for the hot punch, a fixture of the ball since time immemorial, had been misplaced; the senior officers of the various regiments argued bitterly over the placement of their regimental colours in the rafters, as the gentlemen of the line took offence at their standards being placed so near those of the yeomen; but of greatest concern was the matter of two trusted mess stewards who were found to have United literature in their possession, and were placed under arrest.

Brigid O'Brian was concerned about her bust.

She was as self-conscious as any young woman, likely more so, and after several private test-fittings, and without a mother or her sisters to advise her, she was at a loss. She had

152

been fifteen when Miss Klug had helped her make her gown, but she was now seventeen, and the original bust line, a bit daring for the younger Brigid, had become something which might go unnoticed in Paris or London but would likely convey the wrong impression in a room full of attentive gentlemen in Cork Town.

She was uncomfortable asking the advice of the other ladies of the school, as she had been teased more than once about her burgeoning figure, and she was deeply hesitant to bring attention to herself. Instead, she waited until the other ladies had gone off on a morning walk before she pulled on her gown and hustled down to Miss Klug's classroom to stand before the one full-sized mirror in the school, where her worst fears were confirmed.

When the ladies returned in a fine glow, one which they hoped would last until that evening and so enchant the officers of the barracks, they found Brigid standing at the mirror, tugging and pulling at her gown, slumping her shoulders, and very near tears.

Nichole gasped, "Oh, my dear Brigid, whatever is wrong?"

Brigid whirled to face her friends, stood up straight, and with raised eyebrows she shot her eyes downward.

All four ladies stood in the doorway and followed Brigid's eyes.

"Oh, my," said Gabrielle.

"Oh, my, indeed!" cried Brigid with open palms and a break in her voice. "I look like a tart!"

Miss McCarthy raised an appraising eyebrow, and said, "I am strangely comfortable with it."

Miss McCarthy, however, was quickly shuttled aside, and Brigid was soon reduced to her shift. In a frenzy of stitching, pins, darts, a layer of elegant gauzy silk and then a prudent second layer, Miss O'Brian was, by late morning, lovely, appealing and by no measure a tart.

As the final version of the gown was presented to universal approval, with Brigid's beaming, effusive thanks, the housemaid brought in the mail on a pewter salver—Miss McCarthy's school not being an institution much given to silver. The mail held little of interest, certainly nothing to keep the other ladies from hurrying off to tend to their own preparations for the ball, but one letter addressed to Brigid prompted her to find a quiet corner to read. With a mix of affection and anxiety, she recognized her father's hand. Her sisters had written several times since she left Clonakilty, but this was the first letter from her father.

Brigid a stor,

We are all well here, and we hope you are also well. A quick note to let you know that your Cousin Bronagh may come to visit. That of course should mean little to you, but she says that while your Aunt Áine or Uncle Ultan are not to be expected for some time, come Spring they shall certainly come, and hopefully stay for some time. That is just as well, as the Winter has so far been a wet one, but I wager we have a dry Spring.

Your Most Affectionate Father,
Michael O'Brian

Two messages: the first, she would likely be called home in the spring, in her father's company or her own. A notion quickly flared: she would defy him, she would do as she pleased, but her defiance caught in her throat when she considered the second message, ominous, as she recalled a snippet of the United catechism, often repeated around her father's house.

"A wet winter, a dry spring,
A bloody summer, and no King."

*****

Roaring fires were stoked in both of the great hall's massive fireplaces, warming the air enough to placate the Dublin musicians; the recipe for the hot punch was found, and several gallons were soon blended in great steaming bowls; it was agreed that the colours of the garrison's regiments would be arranged by seniority, guaranteeing the line's precedence; and as there was still suspicion of United men among the servants, the officers attending the ball were asked to hang their swords along the walls of the hall rather than leave them in their quarters.

Colonel Montgomery sent a carriage to fetch the ladies of Miss McCarthy's School. He had earlier sent a note to his old friend, Miss McCarthy, asking her to open the ball with him, a great honour, one which Miss McCarthy accepted with her typical aplomb. Her gown was red silk, made in Dublin itself, her young friends in simpler dresses but possessing the benefit of unconscious beauty. The carriage drew up in front of the school, the horses' breath steaming in the cold, thrilling darkness, and the five ladies hustled out in their cloaks and fur muffs, each in a fine glow. A brief lurching ride in the carriage carried them to the Old Barracks, where they were handed down by stern sergeants into flickering lantern light and a blur of gathering humanity.

In the loud, crowded anteroom, the ladies had left their things with the polite soldiers on duty there, and with Miss

McCarthy at their head, they stepped into the Great Hall of Cork Barracks shining like a handful of diamonds.

The officers of the Westmeath Regiment had planned the interception of their guests with military precision. In the swishing, noisy crowd they were a solid island of red coats, gold lace, and polite, perhaps overly enthusiastic, welcomes. Miss McCarthy gracefully took Colonel Montgomery's arm, sharing the smiles of comfortable old friends. Captain Rzewnicki's attentions were focused upon, and most eagerly received by, Miss Hendricks. Gabrielle and Carolyn were whisked into the hall by two other officers whose name Brigid could not recall, and as other arrivals pushed past them she found herself in the company of Lieutenant Barr.

"It is most kind of you and your brother officers to welcome us with such... precision, Lieutenant."

"You seem displeased, Miss O'Brian." Barr grinned.

"I am not accustomed to the ways of soldiers, as to my innocent eyes this all seems very scripted to the gentlemen's wishes, paired off like so many ewes to the ram, with no thought to the ladies' desires."

"My apologies, Miss O'Brian. It was not our intention to offend, but we wished you to be..." A woman beside them in the crowd laughed uproariously, drawing a furious glance from Barr. "...we wished you to be in the proper company. Several of the gentlemen here are the merest rogues." He offered her his arm; she deliberately waited a beat before accepting it. He went on with a teasing note in his voice, "Please be assured that in the future, I shall make it my most ardent goal to give proper thought to your desires."

She sniffed in derisive response, thinking that if her father were there he would punch Barr for the colour of his coat, then perhaps a second time for speaking to his daughter with such familiarity.

"Tell me, Lieutenant, how is our Ensign Lockwood? He is such a charming gentleman." She glanced over to see her shot had gone home. It had. "I do so wish he were in attendance tonight, though I suppose he must be an officer of great merit to be in command of the barracks while the rest of you gentlemen frolic?"

Barr said nothing, just nodding, though she saw a flash of fury cross his face. Still, she thought Barr was the best-looking man she had ever seen. He had no kindness in his face, but that smooth confidence was very appealing.

Turning away from him, she took a long moment to revel in the glamour of the scene. She had attended many town dances; such fun, but so familiar. Here, she was dazzled; most of the gentlemen were soldiers, in red coats and blue, their gold braid glittering in the light of a thousand candles. Their ladies were not to be outdone, elegant women in their finest, all satin and silk and buoyant skin.

A mustachioed officer of hussars, in a tight blue uniform, his pelisse thrown over his left shoulder, outrageous cadenettes at his temples, saw Brigid and his eyes flared, very much the hawk on the hunt. He took a few steps toward Brigid, was deflected by a fierce glare from Barr. The hussar said nothing as they strolled past him, but he smiled and politely bowed to her. She shook her head, wondering what Michael O'Brian would say if he knew that she was having to do with King's officers. It was all so confusing, but she was enjoying herself immensely.

With military punctuality, at precisely nine o'clock the orchestra struck up a minuet. Barr, who was being most attentive, quietly explained to Brigid that the first dance was for only the most senior of the officers. General Abercromby was the senior officer present, though as Mrs. Abercromby was at home in England—and, in truth, he did not much care for dancing—the general deferred the opening to the next senior couple, Colonel Montgomery and his lady. To act as head couple in front of two hundred other guests was not a post for the faint of heart, but the Colonel and Miss McCarthy performed with unfeigned style.

Lieutenant Barr proved himself intelligent company, another trait which Brigid found attractive. She was growing to like him; but still, when he remarked that the room was warm and offered to take her shawl to the cloak room, she felt a brief chill, declined his offer, and pulled it closer.

Various country dances followed, most with Lieutenant Barr, dances at which she excelled, as did the lieutenant. She was having a wonderful time, and when one dance required the dancers to hold hands for several seconds and he smiled and pressed her hand a bit more firmly, she returned his smile and returned the pressure, if just for a moment.

As the evening progressed it became clear to Brigid that many of the gentlemen present were hesitant to speak to her, and no one beyond the handful of Westmeath officers had asked her to dance. Their hesitation was not of a societal nature, as the invitation had clearly stated that the event was to be considered a private ball, and thus the rules of introduction were much relaxed; tradition held that the roof served as the introduction. Their hesitation, she soon understood, was due to Lieutenant Barr's reputation. The other gentlemen were hesitant to provoke him, and so contented themselves with eyeing Brigid from a distance. Numerous ladies gave them looks as well, appraising, scornful or curious in turn, and Brigid found herself amused by the thought of those glittering British eyes seeing her as the trophy of a renowned *beau sabreur*. She knew she was nothing of the kind, but she stood taller, laugh more loudly, and danced more recklessly, playing the role for an evening.

The whole affair was a play, a sham, as she knew who she truly was, and what the future likely held for them all.

Despite the bubble of reputation surrounding Barr, on several occasions Brigid noticed one officer lingering just beyond their circle, a small, painfully nervous looking officer in a very plain coat. He looked so very out of place that she felt sorry for him, standing awkwardly alone amid the chatter and the dancing.

After a particularly active dance Brigid and Barr stood back and sipped punch while the rest of their friends danced on. Abruptly, the nervous gentleman strode forward and quickly, loudly, awkwardly said, "Charles, old boy, I wonder if you might introduce me to your friend?"

Brigid looked over at Barr, hoping he would not savage the poor little fellow, and she saw a mix of disbelief, amusement, and affront churning on Barr's face. She understood him better, now. She would not put the poor man's dignity at any further risk, quickly saying, "You must excuse the Lieutenant, sir, as he is out of breath after that lovely reel. My name, sir, is Brigid O'Brian."

The gentleman's face was flush with relief and pleasure, and he bowed deeply. Brigid curtsied in response, and Barr finally said, curtly, "Miss O'Brian, Dr. Oades, the barracks surgeon. Oades, Miss O'Brian." Draining his glass of punch, Barr said with just a hint of mockery, "Breaking many hearts tonight, Doctor?"

Oades, however, gave all his attention to Brigid. "I won't keep you but a moment, I promise. I wished only to tender my regards, Miss O'Brian, as well as the regards of our mutual acquaintance Ensign Lockwood, who sadly could not attend tonight's glittering soirée. He particularly desired me to seek you out, to convey his regret in not—"

Barr took her arm and steered her away, saying, "Thank you, Oades." Then, to her, "It is nearly time for the supper break, Brigid," (She nearly pulled away from him at this improper, familiar use of her Christian name, but he smiled at her, and she forgave him.) "and we best queue up now or be consigned to the bitter dregs."

A clutch of older ladies stood in a corner of the hall while their ancient husbands gathered in the opposite corner to drink too much and refight battles of their youth. Those ladies were thus not in a forgiving mood, and spent their time taking critical note of the ball's attendees. One of their topics was the pretty young girl, she stood out like the moon in a dark night, didn't she, but she wasn't truly beautiful, was she, and she was far too young for the glances of so many of those lusting devils. She danced far too often with that young stallion with the tight breeches. One of the old ladies ventured out and returned to the flock to whisper that the girl was named O'Brian, an Irish girl, how could she manage an invitation to a ball of His Majesty's most loyal subjects, and the handsome lieutenant was named Barr, a notorious rogue and duelist, which drew sniffs of derision and secret dusty stirrings among the old hens.

As the night wore on, the sedentary ladies had more fuel for gossip, as the dances grew more frantic, the punch went to many heads. Several of the gentlemen took the opportunity to grow overly confident with the ladies and some of the ladies were not as firm in deflecting those attentions as prudence demanded. There were goings-on which would spark gossip aplenty the following day, but Miss McCarthy, no novice in such matters, herded her charges home before the gentlemen grew indiscreet.

*****

The oldest people in Cork called them the hours when the old gods walked, well after midnight, as Michael O'Brian and his daughters lay sleeping.

They were jolted awake by a hammering at their door, and while at first Michael had feared the Yeomen had come for him, it proved to be only Tadg O'Donovan.

Michael shooed Ann and Caitlin back to bed with, "Never fear, my blossoms, it's just your Uncle Tadg come to call." Then to O'Donovan, he hissed, "What the hell are you about, you mad fool? Tromping about in the freezing black night, scaring the shite out of me and mine?"

O'Donovan was deadly serious when he replied, "Throw some clothes on, Michael. Let's walk a bit."

When Michael came out, pulling his coat on, he could sense other figures in the darkness beyond, crunching the frozen grass. As they walked away from the house, Michael's heart raced with surprise and not a little fear. "What is all this, Tadg? Have you brought half the town out? What the fucking hell are you about?"

Hesitantly, O'Donovan replied, "First, I'll tell you I have no doubts about you. I fought hard in the Committee meeting, but there were others —"

"What!" cried Michael, "That fucker O'Malley still cares to call me traitor, does he?"

O'Donovan wheeled to face him, poked a finger into his chest, and hissed, "It's not just O'Malley, boyo. Other voices question your loyalty. You work for Lord fucking Shannon, his lackey —"

"What man dares calls me a lackey! I collect rents, sure, but am I not as fair as a man can be, giving time to those who are a bit behind? Do I not pay the widow Driscoll's rent from my own pockets?"

"Oh, aye, Michael, you are pure as my sister's arse, sure, but it's the fucking *appearance* of things, isn't it? Can't you get it through your thick skull that the most of the men of the movement are scared shitless of their own shadows? Informants cost us twenty men in Bandon last week, most of those poor fuckers off to the gallows. Our lads wonder if it could happen to them, they look about to see who might turn them in, and one name comes to a many a mind: Michael fucking O'Brian, devoted employee of the great Proddy bastard Shannon, and what else? Oh, O'Brian's daughters go to a Proddy school, and one actually *teaches* there, a willing servant to the oppressors —"

Michael boiled over, lowered his shoulder and tackled O'Donovan, swinging both hard fists as they fell. O'Donovan landed some blows of his own before the shadowy men in the distance rushed to roughly separate them, all of them panting and cursing.

The men of the Clonakilty Defenders shoved O'Brian back toward his house as O'Donovan called after him, "*Appearances*, Michael! Get your house in order, before your friends come to assume the feckin' worst!"

*****

The students would be returning in the coming week, so the day after the ball found the teachers folding away their gowns and turning to their syllabi. They were gathered in the central hall, deciding on the placement of each student, trading memories and gossip from the ball, when they heard a ringing of the bell at the front door.

"I believe it that may be Lieutenant Rzewnicki," said Nichole. Setting aside her pen and trying to sound nonchalant, she added, "He mentioned he might call."

Without looking up from her class roster, Carolyn Klug said with a hint of a smile, "I had wondered why you wore such a lovely dress for a simple day of school work."

The housemaid stepped into the room, and, as predicted, she said, "Lieutenant Rus... Riz... the foreign gentleman... for Miss Hendricks, please."

Miss Hendricks nearly squealed in delight, though as she jumped to her feet the maid added with some significance, "And, a Lieutenant Barr for Miss O'Brian, please."

All eyes went wide and turned to Brigid, who sat blinking in surprise. "Whatever can he want?" she said, then using both hands to quickly tuck back loose strands of hair, she took the moment to calm herself. She also saw Miss McCarthy and Miss Klug exchange a look of concern, but she was caught up in her excitement and quickly walked to the door as Nichole took her hand.

As they walked the short hall toward the front door, Nicole quickly, frantically whispered, "You'll leave Pavel and me alone in the drawing room, won't you? Oh, please do, Brigid, dear. I think he may... well, he might wish to be alone with me. Might you take your beau off to the garden or the woods?"

"The *woods*?" whispered Brigid, but they were then stepping into the hall, formal, polite, and collected.

There followed the requisite courtesies, Lieutenant Rzewnicki and Miss Hendricks tense and preoccupied, until Brigid nervously suggested, "I wonder, Lieutenant Barr, if I might show you... the garden? Even in winter it is quite... well, interesting, I suppose."

"I should be most pleased," said Barr smoothly.

Miss Hendricks and Lieutenant Rzewnicki declined the necessary invitation for them to join the expedition out to the small, frost-ravaged garden, both pleading an oncoming cold. As Barr helped Brigid with her cloak, Nichole gave her a look of deep gratitude, somewhat mollifying Brigid as she and Barr stepped outside into the cold.

"That was adroitly done, Miss O'Brian."

"I do apologize, Lieutenant. I thought that Miss Hendricks and Lieutenant Rzewnicki might... appreciate some time alone."

Barr sniffed in derision or amusement, Brigid could not tell, then said, "Does she truly believe he'll make her an offer? If so, she is to be disappointed."

Brigid's mask slipped as she stopped, placed a hand on Barr's arm, and earnestly asked, "Oh, are you serious? Does he not care for her?"

Barr sniffed again, and said, "Oh, he is mad for her, in his tragic Polish way, but he is a coward. Afraid of his family, of hers, of how she would be received in his little Polish fiefdom, of his own inadequacies. Christ, I wonder if he has even kissed her."

"I think you underestimate him. He seems perfectly gallant, and Miss Hendricks thinks most highly of him."

They walked on and he took her arm, and she did not resist. "You are not a foolish woman, O'Brian; please do not say foolish things. Rzewnicki is a coward, and so is this Hendricks woman. They are attracted to one another, and they ought to act on it."

He looked down at her, daring her to flare at him, perhaps desiring her to do so. She looked into his face, into that look of attraction and predation, and she told herself to have nothing to do with him. But he was wearing those tight breeches, and God! he was handsome.

Chapter Thirteen

James Lockwood had grown up with a boy named Phelan O'Reilly. One afternoon, as the two boys took their leisure in the highest branches of a tall sycamore, Phelan had explained to James the history of his family, including the scandalous story of how a branch of the family had been faced with a Cromwellian choice to either convert to the Anglican church or be exiled from their Cavan lands. Rather than be driven to the wilds of Connaught, that branch of the O'Reillys, the branch that eventually provided the world with Lieutenant Colonel Hugh O'Reilly, had suddenly realized the blessings of the Church of England, and so remained in Cavan with their fortunes intact, if not their reputations.

Lieutenant Colonel O'Reilly was no soldier, but he was an amiable old gentleman, and he gave Ensign Lockwood a smile when that young gentleman reported to the regimental office, a pair of small rooms in a corner of Cork Barracks.

"James! Thank you for reporting so quickly. I shall keep you just a moment. I preface my comments by telling you that every officer of this barracks appreciates your willingness to take the guard while the ball was in progress.

Unfortunately, when General Abercromby this morning learned of such a junior officer being the only officer left in the barracks, he was, well, somewhat put out. He went on rather severely about the island teetering on the edge of rebellion, and us dancing away, and he then threw some rather stinging barbs about fiddling and Rome burning and such. We reminded the general that we were just across the road, but he insisted that I speak to you to determine if you were quite prepared for the task. It is water under the bridge, but the general is not to be assuaged. I do hate to ask, but I wonder if you would recite, please, the special addendum to yesterday's orders of the day?"

The Lieutenant Colonel had a reputation as a kind, if not especially bright, man. James was, at first, startled by a senior officer speaking to him with such familiarity, especially since they had previously rarely spoken outside of duty. He wondered if O'Reilly had heard that he was Colonel Montgomery's nephew. He felt a twinge of anger at the thought, but he had fortunately read through the orders several times before standing the guard, so he could confidently say, "Well, sir, if I might be allowed to summarize: both companies of the 9th Foot are to line Barracks Street so that they might honour the guests and to quell any disturbances which could rise in the street."

O'Reilly held up a hesitant finger and interrupted with, "Oh, regarding the line companies... as an aside... they are so sensitive regarding their seniority. I hope you did not mind awfully their sergeants reporting to their own officers. There was of course not the slightest reflection on your abilities, but there we are..."

"Not at all, sir," said James with all sincerity, since he was privately intimidated by the stern professionals of the line. He went on, "The two yeomanry companies are to stand the guard. The men of the militia companies are to remain in their quarters."

"Yes, we particularly noted that section to General Abercromby, in that, *'the militia companies are to remain in their quarters,'* is not, *'they are confined to the barracks'* as that rings of... well... confinement. We explained to the general our concern that some of the militiamen might turn to mischief should they realize so many of their officers were out of the barracks. They are after all, merely Catholics in red coats, though I am not to prate to you, sir, a brother Westmeath officer."

Even with his understanding of the O'Reilly clan's relationship with religious alliance, James was in no position to gainsay such a senior officer, but he did say with some formality, "In all honesty, sir, I believe the great majority of the men in my company, no matter their faith, can be relied on. There are a few malcontents, of course, but with fair treatment I hope most might be brought around, and the few hard cases kept in line by the sound men."

"Really?" said O'Reilly, genuinely surprised. "Do you truly think so? How very encouraging. Several of the other company commanders claim their men cannot be trusted, though of course they allow their sergeants to run things. I understand you have gone so far as to learn the names of the men in your company, which is quite laudable, laudable indeed. A leader of men, and all that, don't you know." Then, in a conspiratorial tone, he went on, "Just between us, James, there is some possibility of companies of the garrison being detached to remote locations in the spring, so that we might quell disturbances and intimidate the peasantry. The magistrates do cry out so, begging for red coats, no matter the type of men in them, to enforce their edicts." Cheering up, he added, "I may well be tasked with an independent command, and if so, I shall certainly request you and your company be placed under my command. We shall quell rebellion, and make time for some fun along the way. Remind me, which company are we speaking of?"

"Four Company, sir, Captain Holister."

A frown crossed O'Reilly's face. "Oh, dear, Holister. He can be so difficult, he and his endless illness. Still, let us soldier manfully on! I trust, James, we shall certainly accomplish any duties assigned to us, without too much bother."

*****

As barracks surgeon, Dr. Charles Oades had a desirable apartment in the garrison, one quite apart from his surgery. The doctor's late morning Sick Call was a staple of barracks life, as he and his mates diligently tended to the ills, real or imagined, of the hundreds of men of the garrison.

Sick Call was the preserve of the enlisted men. The officers of the barracks were allowed private consultations, and on that January afternoon Lieutenant Barr requested a private session with Dr. Oades, away from the prying eyes and gossiping tongues of the barracks surgery.

In Oades' rooms Barr reluctantly shared his symptoms, and Oades made a quick mental diagnosis, but he kept it to himself until after he had given Lieutenant Barr the courtesy of a full examination.

"Thank you, Lieutenant, I believe we are finished. You may get dressed." In this professional setting Oades was a very different man than the Oades of any other circumstance; it was an unconscious metamorphosis, but one obvious even to Barr, who was nearly civil as he pulled his clothes on and said, "Very well, then, Doctor, what nostrums do you prescribe? This rash is such a nuisance."

Oades bent over his desk, jotted a few notes, and said, "My apologies, Lieutenant, but I can do nothing for you."

"Oh, come, now, Oades. I have teased you once or twice, and you repay me by violating your professional oath? Your reputation is sterling; I had assumed you above such pettiness."

"I do assure you, Lieutenant, there is no animosity in my diagnosis. I take no pleasure in informing you that a lady of your acquaintance has demonstrated her regard in one way, but her animus in another. The Great Masquerader has in this instance openly declared himself; the chancres are unmistakable, every other symptom adding its voice to only one conclusion: you have syphilis, sir. I do wish I could convey better tidings, but my profession often requires a disagreeable candor."

Barr was silent for a long moment, his head down, his face knotted, his fists slowly clenching. "You ignorant little *bastard.*"

"You are upset, sir, your passions inflamed—"

"I have a slight God damned cold and a small sore on my manhood, and you tell me I have the French pox! You are a fool, a petty little prig, and I shall see you damned, Oades!"

"Calm, yourself, sir. The lesions on the *membrum virile* are most pronounced. You yourself are the best witness to the symptoms. You must face the news as best you can. The end result, while inescapable, is of indeterminate timing. You have some time, though you must of course alter your social interactions in accordance with your condition."

Barr pulled on his coat, and as he armored himself in the King's scarlet he hissed, "Damn your impudence, Oades. Damn your incompetence. Damn you to *hell!*" He stalked to the door, but Oades grabbed his sleeve.

"Take time to absorb the news, Lieutenant, but in the end you must come to realize that you must, *must*, withdraw yourself from the company of decent women. Nay, from *all* women."

Barr harshly pushed Oades aside, and with a bark of laughter he added, "No matter what ails me, I'll do as I please, so you can go fuck yourself, you little fool. Oh, does the word 'fuck' offend you? Believe me, Nancy Boy, I will fuck who, and when, I please."

*****

On a cold, wet, foggy morning Captain Holister, slender, coughing, and frail, lead Four Company, Westmeath Militia Regiment, out of the barracks and into the fields south of Cork Town. While the fields were typically policed by sheep, they had also been leased for the garrison's drills. The weather through the fall, and now into the winter, had been cold and wet, and much of the drill ground had been churned into deep mud.

The captain was mounted, wrapped in a heavy cloak, a scarf up to his ears, and his bicorn pulled down low on his head. While Ensign Lockwood had his cloak, and the fifty enlisted men had their greatcoats, they marched in wet boots, and were soon ankle-deep in mud. Lockwood had learned he could bear a great deal of discomfort so long as he distracted his thoughts. That distraction was always at hand, as thoughts of Brigid O'Brian filled his head more often than not. He knew that Barr was calling on Brigid—in his mind he dared call her by her Christian name—and Barr's bragging cut him deeply. James was certain he lacked the confidence, experience, money, wardrobe, and looks to compete with Barr. He slogged through the mud and pined for her.

Holister was a capable officer, and exercised his company in the art of deploying quickly from column of march to line, and then back again. Holister was patient with the men, and kind in explaining to Lockwood how speed, not adherence to drill regulations, was key to success in battle.

After an hour and several evolutions of the exercise, Holister's energy was visibly waning. He reined up at Lockwood's side, and said, "I think that is enough for today, Ensign. I am done in. I trust you don't mind seeing the company back to the barracks? Your first independent command, eh?"

"Yes, sir. Thank you, sir," said Lockwood with a modest smile as a cold rain started to fall.

Holister turned his horse toward home, and as he passed the company, he called out in a reedy voice, "Well done, Four Company!" then spurred away up the muddy road.

Many of the men cheered him in return, but some did not, and Lockwood made a mental list of which men he should keep an eye on. The company was already in column of march, so he needed only to take his place, not without a little pride, at the head of the column, and call out, "Route march! Forward, march!"

A route march did not require the men to march in step, a mercy for mud-caked men with cold, soaked feet. It was two miles back to the barracks, and they set out as it started to rain harder.

They had covered about a mile, just reaching the scattered buildings at the outskirts of town, when a rider came pounding down the road toward them, clods of mud and a spray of water in his wake. Lockwood held his hand up to halt the column as the rider pulled up harshly and franticly called out, "Captain Holister! Captain Holister! You are seconded to me, sir! For God's sake, we must hurry!"

The man on the horse stared down at the cloaked, sodden figure at the head of the column as that man replied, "My name, sir, is Lockwood! Captain Holister has already returned to the barracks."

"I do not care what your name is, sir! Do you command here, or not?"

"I do, sir, but—"

"I am Major White, 34th Foot, seconded to Home Office!" The rain drummed down as the major reached under his cloak, produced a folded sheet of paper, handed it down, and yelled, "I am in desperate need of support! As the only barracks company currently available, you will assist me in apprehending rebel leaders meeting up on Blackrock Road! Follow me! Tally ho!"

The major madly spurred his horse up the road, reined in, and screamed back, "Forward, sir! Forward!"

Lockwood opened the folded orders, trying to shield them under his cloak, and as the rain blurred the ink he detected Colonel Montgomery's signature. From behind him the senior sergeant, Plunkett, stepped up and privately said, "Don't you worry, sir. We're with you."

Lockwood swallowed hard, wiped the rain from his face, and called, "Company! Quick route march! Forward! March!"

A hard, rapid march north, halfway back to the barracks, then the major turned them down a road, a cobbled road at last, that lead east along the south bank of the River Lee. As they followed Blackrock Road, a low dike on their left separated the road from the marshy ground along the river. To their right, small but stylish houses on large wooded parcels lined the road.

Major White urged them on, but soon, men began to fall out, exhausted or lame. Lockwood pointed to a reliable man, and said, "Corporal Malloy, fall out and collect stragglers—round them up and get them back to the barracks. Forward, now, men, forward! Not much further now!"

The rain was drumming heavily, the nightmare pace seemingly endless, as Major White lead them on relentlessly. Lockwood fell in beside Sergeant Plunkett, and panted a question. "Dare we try to load in this rain, Sergeant?"

Plunkett, out of breath and in obvious pain, coughed a laugh and rasped, "No, sir."

White finally reined in, and Lockwood halted the company. Every man bent over, gasping for breath, some men coughing, some retching. The rain did not relent, exhausting, pummeling. White pointed down a narrow path that lead back through trees to a cottage that sat well back from the road.

"There! There, Lockman, is your target! A dozen rebel commanders! Alive or dead! Huzzah!" With that, White drew his sword and spurred his horse down the lane, quite alone.

From behind him Lockwood heard his company, voices calling for, "Rest, please, sir, a fucking minute, eh," and another coughing, "Fuck this!" while another called out, "What are we about, lads, fighting civilians, innocent folk, when—" and Sergeant Plunkett roaring, "Silence there, you pack of God damned moon calves!"

Then the muted sound of shots thumped out from the cottage, three, four. None struck White, but his horse did not care for it, and so disgraced herself, pulling, bucking, and snorting through the trees, back toward the road, White clinging to her neck in desperation.

The last shot whistled through the trees and struck Private Michael McCaughey, one of the best liked men in the company, who collapsed screaming and bleeding.

"Fucking hell!" shouted one man, another crying "They shot Mikey!" while another screamed, "The bastards!"

"Four Company, follow me!" roared their officer, and for the first time as a soldier, James Lockwood was blind with rage, drawing his sword and pelting down the gravel path.

His company followed.

Men poured from the cottage—civilians, some armed, some frantically trying to mount horses tied up by the door, others running madly off into the fields behind, as still the rain hammered down. There was little sound beyond the rain and the pounding of blood in his ears as James reached a man who was trying to mount a dancing horse. Lockwood, trying to strike him with the hilt of his sword, missed and instead struck the horse The horse bolted, giving James the chance to throw the man to the ground, but the man was a fighter and made to rise again, until two men of the company smashed him down with the butts of their muskets.

An old man stepped into the open door of the cottage, a musket in his hands, calmly leveled it, and fired. The ball struck Private Daly, dead in an instant. In seconds Daly's mates avenged him, furiously striking the old man down, the butts of their muskets rising and falling, over and over, and in a flash, Lockwood realized he had forgotten to order the men to fix their bayonets. Still, he saw that some of his men had done so, and any of the rebels who resisted arrest were stabbed or beaten down.

It was over quickly. Seven rebels in the yard were down, alive or dead. Yelling and gunshots echoed from the fields behind the house, and Lockwood called for Plunkett to call back the few men who had gone haring off after the last of the fleeing rebels. A woman's scream from the cottage caught his attention, and as he trotted toward the door a second scream, louder, more terrified, prompted him to run. He leapt over the body of the old man at the door, landing in the gore, his wet boots betraying him, and he fell headlong into the blood, wrenching his knee, dropping his sword, his bicorn flying down the narrow hall.

In the small drawing room he found three men of his company holding four women at bayonet point, one of the women old and weeping, begging for permission to go to her husband, the others frightened, weeping, cowering, their weeping screams drowned by the roars of the enraged redcoats, "You killed our mate! Shut up, shut up! Traitorous bitches! Where are the rest of the them!"

Laying on the floor, covered in blood, his knee an agony, Lockwood had trouble calling the men back. They finally relented, and he sent them to search the rest of the cottage for any remaining rebels. "And no looting, there. We are soldiers, not God damned thieves."

A moment later Major White appeared, having abandoned his horse, running into the cottage, crowing, "Such a bag, Lockfoot! I shall certainly mention you in my report! We have O'Doorly and O'Shea! Ah, and their women as well! The Castle shall be well pleased!"

Eventually the rain ended, and as Lockwood sat on the front steps, Sergeant Plunkett came to share the news that the fight in the hedged fields behind had turned ugly: Private Murray had been killed, and Corporal Cassidy and Private McManus had been wounded. Out in the fields three rebels had been killed; there were no further prisoners taken.

With deep pain in his eyes, Lockwood choked back his shock, whispering only, "Ah, Jesus," unconsciously slipping into an Irish accent. Two of his men dead, more badly hurt, men whom he was responsible for.

Plunkett sat down beside him, and said, "Ah, Jesus, indeed, sir." With that he took a deep pull from his canteen, then handed it to the young officer, kindly saying, "A soldier's only consolation, sir: King George's rum. Fuck all else."

Lockwood took a manly swallow, handed it back, and said, "A fitting summary, Sergeant."

The realities of his profession once again struck him, and he wondered if there was indeed any consolation in a soldier's life beyond indifference. An image of Brigid O'Brian flashed in his mind, and he once again despaired of ever seeing her again.

A troop of Yeoman cavalry arrived to brutally bind the prisoners and march them away. The dead and injured rebels and their women were hauled away in a requisitioned wagon, their weeping echoing in Lockwood's ears as he ordered his own wounded carried to another wagon to lie in the straw, beside the blanketed bodies of Privates Daly and Murray.

James was lifted, wincing, onto a rebel's horse. He had earlier resolved to trust his men, and now they trusted him as well. He ordered the farmer's wagon bearing their dead and wounded to lead the column. He choked back sobs that rose from deep within him as he rode on slowly, and there was weeping and cursing and pride in the column as they marched like soldiers, in step, back to their barracks.

*****

Dr. Oades poured two generous measures of Irish whiskey into the only containers he could find in Ensign Lockwood's larder, a pair of battered tin cups. He was a small man, and so careful of how much whiskey he consumed, though the gangly young Lockwood, sitting grinning upright in his bed, his injured leg propped up on several pillows, felt no such compunction.

"It is my opinion, as a medical man," said Oades as he sat in the room's only chair, "that the healing properties of whiskey, specifically *Irish* whiskey, are remarkable, and unappreciated by the vast majority of medical professionals." He took a sip, sighed, and added, "One day I shall submit a paper to the Royal Society, and make my name."

"I am of your opinion entirely," said James with a sniff and an appreciative swallow. "Indeed," he added, waving an educated, if inebriated, finger in the air, "if I might add, the term 'whiskey' is the bastardized version of the Irish, *uisce beatha*, or, 'the water of life'."

"The very *aqua vitae* of ancient lore, then!" cried Oades, enormously pleased.

"Quite so. I have been quite downhearted since yesterday's fighting, and my knee has been very troublesome, but am now comfortably numb. How very wonderful."

"Oh, I should mention that I have submitted my report to Colonel Montgomery: you shall have three days excused from duty, then seven days of light duty. In ten days you shall be fully bipedal, with the aid of Mr. Jameson's beneficent tincture."

They both sipped more of their whiskey, each separately stretching their eyes at its effects, until Oades asked, "Tell me, James, what are your opinions regarding fornication? I speak of fornication as coupling outside of marriage, rather than copulation, which seems a necessary requirement in the strictures of marriage."

Lockwood tilted his head, considered the question for a moment, and said, "I believe I am in favor. Yes, I can declare with some certainty, I am in favor of fornication." With an affectionate smile, he added, "Whatever prompts you to ask?"

Oades frowned, and seriously said, "I ask out of professional interest, not idle curiosity. I have a patient, an entirely anonymous patient, whose conduct *vis a vis* fornication concerns me."

"You are not saying that fornication is unhealthy, I hope?"

"Oh, no, in the proper circumstances I have nothing against fornication *per se*. Many men seem quite devoted to the practice, and recent studies point to a proportion of women who may indeed enjoy the act, however brief and messy. There are dangers, of course, in undertaking such vigorous, strenuous, activity; there are numerous instances of people dying during the act."

"But usually just on the inside," said James, deadpan, until he erupted in howling laughter, drawing a sniff of amusement from Oades.

While James collected himself, wiping his eyes and muttering, "Just on the inside... oh, my God, that is funny...." confident this was the greatest witticism he had ever managed. Oades returned to his reverie, obviously still mulling over his troublesome patient.

James eventually asked, in an obvious effort to distract Oades, "So, Charles, tell me the latest gossip from the mess. Any news?"

"Well, let me think. Oh, yes, I meant to tell you this, at any rate: today at dinner there was a great deal of conversation regarding your company's action against the rebels, to universal praise. A letter from a Major White was passed around, in which he thanked Colonel Montgomery for allowing him the honour of commanding one of the garrison companies in action against a band of bloodthirsty rebels. Toward the bottom of the letter you were mentioned once—I believe you were referred to as Ensign Lookworth—which our people thought rather shabby."

The names and faces of his dead and wounded came crashing back into Lockwood's mind as Oades nattered on. "We had that excrementitious soup again at dinner; for what we dole out in mess bills, we really ought not be fed such offal. What else... oh, our comrades Rzewnicki and Barr remain great favorites with the ladies at Miss McCarthy's. I know you were as impressed with Miss O'Brian as I. I do not typically choose to sit with those gentlemen, but I did overhear some of their banter, and while the details escaped me there was some talk of an offer being made."

"An offer? So soon?" said James with deep concern.

"Yes. Yes, indeed," said Oades with equal concern.

Chapter Fourteen

Miss O'Brian spent several hours reviewing lesson plans at her desk, still self-conscious with the notion of her own classroom. She had no illusions about her fitness for the position; she was, for example, well aware of her own failings in the application of punctuation, and she was studying a text regarding the proper placement of commas when Gabriele and Nichole came into her room, smiling broadly.

"We do hate to interrupt, Brigid, dear, but we need you to resolve a dispute between us. As English girls we turn to you as our expert in such matters: do the majority of Irish people truly believe in fairies?"

Brigid paused for a moment, hesitant to make herself, or her people, appear foolish in the eyes of her friends, though she was certain that most of her family and neighbors were perfectly comfortable with the concept of fairies. Even Brigid, the rational, educated young woman who would scoff at the suggestion of such foolishness, would discreetly cross herself and give a wide berth to any fairy fort she came across when walking the fields, especially in May, when the fairies were at their worst.

With a laugh, Brigid said only, "Oh, I suppose some of the older country people still believe such things. Whatever would prompt you ask?"

"We overheard Siobhan and Ciara talking as they made up the beds," said Gabriele. "Siobhan was complaining about how hard they had to work, and Ciara told her to just wait, because when spring comes the fairies would come to the school and turn the world upside down."

Brigid's face fell into a mass of confusion and shock. Nichole did not notice, and so she went on, "I told Gabby that they would not really believe such nonsense—oh, dear Brigid, have we said something to offend you?"

A quick, choked laugh, until Brigid managed, "Did they truly say that? No, no... I quite agree, they were talking nonsense... pay them no mind."

There followed an awkward pause as Brigid went pale.

"Well, then, thank you, dear," said Nichole with a note of awkward apology. "We shall leave you to your lesson plans, then. But pray do not forget, Captain Rzewnicki and Lieutenant Barr are coming to tea."

"Yes, of course, thank you."

Brigid waited until she heard their footsteps fade down the hall before she shot to her feet and strode toward the teacher's quarters, her heels striking sharp and quick. She opened and closed several doors, looking for the house maids, finally finding them in Miss Klug's room. She quickly shut the door behind her, and hissed in furious Irish, "What nonsense are you two fools uttering in this school? Your black souls to the devil! The Saxon gentlewomen overheard you talking about fairies in the spring! *Is buan in do thóin mo mhallacht!*"

Miss O'Brian customarily treated the servants with kindness, and her use of the old, 'My curse on your buttocks forever!' visibly shocked the maids. Trained from youth to assume a position of deference when challenged, they both lowered their heads and murmured, "Beg pardon, miss." They spoke in English, though Brigid thought she could detect a note of defiance in their tone.

"Fairies, is it then, you're thinking of?" Brigid went on in Irish. "Are you two keeping company with rebels? You honestly think those ruffians will give two damns about you? Do you know what you're hoping for? No matter your place or faith, men shall be slaughtered, women ravished and houses plundered and burned!"

"Yes, miss," both the maids muttered, their faces closed, their eyes blank.

She tried to collect herself as she studied them. Siobhan was older, probably thirty, and Ciara was well into her twenties. They were small, thin, and plain, and Brigid knew a hundred women like them. They occupied the lowest positions in Irish society: Catholic, women, and achingly poor. They were the lowest rung on a very tall ladder, and though Brigid was much younger she had advantages they would never know. She went on quietly, "Have I not seen both sides of the troubles? Does not my own family in Clonakilty sometimes speak as you do, anxious for change, and for the English to go? And so, too, do I not have friends among the English, even among the English officers themselves? There is good and evil in both houses, mark my words, and if war comes, they shall fight one another with terrible ferocity. For now, for God's sake say nothing; do nothing to compromise yourselves. If the worst happens, stay close to the school, and trust God to see you through."

*****

Lieutenant Barr and Miss O'Brien walked across the frozen grounds of the school, their footsteps crunching the morning hoarfrost in the silent, frigid air.

"It is quite ridiculous, you know," she said, "for us to be forced out of doors every time you and Rzewnicki come to call."

"I cannot disagree. I have mentioned to Rzewnicki more than once that he needs to expedite his attentions toward your friend Hendricks."

Their path led uphill toward a stand of ancient oaks, and as they strode up the hill she said, "They are so sweet together, but I wonder if he might grow more assertive in his affections? She is certain of hers, I know, though of course she cannot act upon them."

"Rzewnicki is an ass. May I kiss you?"

She stopped, paused and said, "No, I think not."

"May I ask why not?" he asked, with the slightest catch in his voice.

Making a dismissive wave at him, she said, "Because you needed to ask. A budding mutual affection should prompt such a step in our relationship, not an awkward *non sequitur* question in the middle of a serious conversation. Really, Lieutenant, have you never been truly fond of someone, where such things happen of their own accord? Is there no spontaneity in your nature?"

He deliberately ignored her questions, replying, "Are you afraid someone should see us? Are you ashamed to show physical affection?"

"I would not be ashamed; I should rather like to be kissed, I think, but not after being addressed with such discourtesy. Shakespeare tells us—"

"You read too much."

They walked on, up into the woods, the trunks like the pillars of a winter cathedral.

"Are you not fond of me?" he eventually asked.

"I am undecided."

"Christ!" he sighed, turning to face her, and she could see anger building in his eyes. "I have called upon you a dozen times, and still I do not warrant a damned *kiss*?"

"*Warrant*, Lieutenant? Is that what you expect, some type of transactional relationship, where after so many visits I am in some way obligated to reimburse you? After ten visits, a kiss? After a hundred visits, am I to grant the final favor? Honestly, sir, one would think you were accustomed to paying for your *amours*."

He said nothing, only hissing in frustration.

They walked on. She was upset with him, in fact she had been dissatisfied with him for some time, but he was handsome, and usually interesting, and so she searched her mind for something neutral to say. She said mildly, "The newspapers are increasingly shrill about the possibility of rebellion. What do the men of the garrison believe? Is there still a chance for peace?"

"Peace!?" he coughed derisively.

"Yes, peace. Some middle ground, where—"

"There can be no peace with these loathsome beasts. The Irish are animals to be tamed or killed. The teagues are—"

He had been slapped more than once, but she punched him, a balled-up fist in the face that sent him reeling. His face was all astonishment, quickly morphing to rage.

"Teagues, are we, you strutting bastard? *Go n-ithe an cat thú is go n-ithe an diabhal an cat!*" It was an old curse, one she rarely used, but she was rarely so very angry.

He had no idea what she had said, but it jolted him, a shock of surprise and flaring excitement.

She snarled, "How dare you use the word *teague* within my hearing! Are you such a fool that you don't know what meaning that word carries, or do you simply not care? Oh, what a fool I've been. I had been warned about you! You are no gentleman!"

For the first time he sneered at her, an open pit of belittling derision. "Don't play coy; you know what you want from me, O'Brian. You desire spontaneity? I could have much more than a kiss, right here. I could take you right here, you little tease—" He suddenly stopped, catching himself, and though she thought she saw a flash of regret cross his face she balled her fist again.

"Go," she ordered. "Leave. I know you now; get out of my sight."

She turned her back on him and stalked back toward the school. Trembling with fear and fury, she expected at any moment that he would grab her from behind. She knew she was terribly vulnerable, but she did not look back.

At the school door she finally looked behind her, to see him standing alone at the edge of the woods, a relentless, shadowy, threatening figure staring at her from the cold distance.

*****

Ann and Caitlin O'Brian, hanging sheets out to dry in the weak afternoon sun, saw Tadg an Astna O'Donovan emerge from the woods at the foot of their hill. They waved to him, and Ann called to her father, "Da, *a grah*! It is Mr. O'Donovan coming up through Nóínín's field, and him looking stern as Pilate on a Sunday!"

Michael O'Brian told his daughters to return to the house in a harsh tone that surprised them. He then walked down into the field, giving his old cow a reassuring thump as he passed. He shook O'Donovan's hand, and asked, "Will you walk up to my house, Tadg?"

"I will not, thank you. I am your friend, but I come today only to convey a message from the committee. I hope I am still your friend when I leave here."

"The fucking committee," Michael said, but with real concern in his voice.

"Do you still refuse to leave Lord Shannon's employ?"

"I do. I have three daughters to support, and I'll not see them sleeping under a hedge."

"That is what I told the committee. Assuming that, then, they voted that you are to be trusted to keep the secrets you hold now, but you are to attend no further meetings, and you are to participate in no further actions against the Saxons."

"So, I can be trusted, but only so far, is it? I'm out?"

"That is so."

The kitchen window opened, Ann stuck her head out, and called out, "Dear Uncle Tadg, would you care for tea?"

"I do not, my dear niece, thank you! I must return home before the rain comes!" Then turning back to Michael, tensely, quietly, he said, "So keep the job, brother; you'll be left in peace. But you may want a wee word with our Brigid, as we hear she is making some unfortunate friends up in Cork."

O'Brian nodded, considering. He then asked, "Tell me one last thing, brother. Will the rising truly come?"

Tadg waited a long moment before saying, not unkindly, "Aye, it's coming. But when the shit starts, stay fuckin' home, Michael."

*****

James sat on the one chair in his room, his bad leg propped up on the bed, carefully running an oiled whetstone along the edge of his sword. Private Doolan hustled about the room, tucking clean clothes away and stuffing the dirty things into a bag, sniffing as he did so. With a sniff, Doolan managed to convey elements of frustration, exasperation and an indefinable air of being put upon—quite a remarkable skill—but James had learned to ignore him when he was in a mood, which was most of the time.

"Oh, there you go, dripping oil on the floor," Doolan muttered as he bent and wiped up the drop with a rag he whipped from his back pocket. "You ought to give your sword to the armourer, shouldn't you? He'd do it right without all this bloody mess..." another sniff of derision, "...sir."

Without looking up, James said, "The armourer is a butcher; his wheel is far too coarse. You saw what he did to Captain Holister's brand new sword; the edge is quite ruined. No, Doolan, I'll do this myself, thank you very much."

"The only feckin' thing you'll do yourself..." muttered Doolan very quietly as he stuffed another soiled shirt into his bag, prompting Lockwood to pause, sigh, and suck his teeth. Doolan quickly said, "Oh, by the way, sir, a package arrived this morning from your mother, the dear woman. Two new shirts, two!" Then more quietly, a sniffed, "And won't you be needing them, with the stains on the sleeve of your best?" Pulling a letter from his jacket pocket, he added more clearly, "There was a letter enclosed, too, so there was. She is a good mother to you, young gentleman, and I trust you shall write to her this very day, thanking her for the shirts, and do include my very best thanks and regards, won't you, now, sir, to the dear woman?"

James sighed, and asked, "I will certainly mention you, as she already thinks very highly of you. Speaking of mothers, did Mrs. Lynch have her baby?"

"No, sir, not yet," Doolan said with his creaking laugh. "But she was pondering on it good and hard when I left the barracks to come tend to you. Dr. Oades was with her, the odd, good-hearted little man. Christ, but that woman can howl! God granted her a pair of lungs, and I wager her baby will be a howler as well, with the blessing." He crossed himself absently with what passed for a kind look on his face.

"Dr. Oades will see her through. Be sure to tell Lynch he's excused from duty for a couple of days. I'll clear it with Captain Holister."

"That's good in you, sure. Lynch will be right pleased, him being so attached to his Missus. Those Mayo lads make good husbands, if not much else. If you'll not mind, sir, I'll stop by the cathedral itself on my way back to the barracks, so that I might light a candle for them, the dears."

James pulled coin from his pocket, handed it to Doolan, and said, "Light a pair for me as well, please, if you would."

"I will indeed, sir, I will indeed." In a thoughtful tone he added, "I believe the Lord accepts Proddy prayers as well as those of the faithful, in times such as these."

*****

Dr. Charles Oades sat at the window of his quarters, steadily looking down into the yard of Cork Barracks. He sipped Irish whiskey at a carefully measured pace; he was a medical man, and his experiments had informed him of the dosages required. He was determined to take only enough to brace his mind, so that he would be capable of following the course he had decided upon. He would not drink to smother grief or worse, to foment self-pity.

As a military surgeon he had limited experience with obstetrics, but he had until that day taken pride in his record of successful deliveries. That confidence, however, was now shattered.

He had lost both Mrs. Lynch and her baby.

He mentally reviewed the steps he had taken, debating with himself over what he might have done differently. In the end he knew no physician of his acquaintance could have dealt with that massive bleeding, though that knowledge was of little consolation. He had left the weeping John Lynch with his friends to return to his quarters and sit by his window.

Oades knew that Lieutenant Barr and Captain Rzewnicki had ridden out earlier that day, and after an hour of watching, he saw Barr return, alone. He watched as Barr slid from the saddle of his heavily sweating horse and walked unsteadily into the Officers' Mess. Two men from the barracks stables came out to see to the horse, shaking their heads and comforting the trembling beast.

Doctor Oades took one last sip from his glass, but no more. This was a medicinal dosage, not some drunkard's license. He walked down his stairs to the yard, not unsteadily, but he was aware of, and intellectually intrigued by, the dull ache at the back of his head and the uncharacteristic confidence surging through his mind.

He stepped into the mess, stopped at the door, and looked over the room. The mess was nearly full; many officers had already gathered for dinner, and several tables were full of gentlemen drinking wine and chatting. The doctor eventually saw Barr, who had taken a seat at a far table with several of his cronies. Oades, resolved and blindly certain, started across the room.

One of the officers at a table he passed, a captain of the 9th Foot, said kindly, "Come, now, Doctor, take a chair with us. You look unwell," but Oades did not veer from his course.

He walked up to Barr, bent to speak privately, and whispered, "Did you call on Miss O'Brian today?"

Barr took a long swallow of brandy, and then replied quietly, "What of it, Nancy Boy? She is mine. Are you jealous that I might have taken her?"

Oades stood upright, and loudly said, "You, sir, are no gentleman." He had not struck another human being in all his life, but he backhanded Charles Barr across the mouth with a blow that would have impressed an accomplished pugilist.

Barr's head snapped back, but his expression did not change. He wiped a hand across his mouth, saw the blood there, and, in the shocked, staring, silent air of the mess he calmly asked, "You'll answer for that, I assume, Oades?"

"I am at your disposal, Lieutenant."

Chapter Fifteen

James Lockwood got to his feet and flexed his leg. It was stiff, but caused him surprisingly little pain; the whiskey had been a good temporary relief, and Charles had left him a small bottle of the alcoholic tincture of laudanum, which had done wonders. The doctor, however, had been insistent in his instructions: James was to take fifteen drops, three times a day, no more, and no less. His knee now scarcely bothered him at all, and so too, the troublesome memories of the fighting along Blackrock Road seemed a distant memory. It was only when he thought of his dead and wounded that clarity returned, a clear jet of pain that jolted him. He exhaled sharply and remembered that Privates Daly and Murray were dead; he thought of them, and was ashamed to realize he could not recall their Christian names.

He hissed in anger and limped over to the rickety table that served as his desk and read aloud from the company roster, "Private *David* Daly and Private *Eamonn* Murray. David Daly and Eamonn Murray, God damn it."

He resolved to never again forget them, and so pulled his Day Book from his jacket pocket, flipped to the blank pages in the back, and carefully wrote across the top of a page, "Killed in the King's Service while Under My Command," and listed there the full names of his two men, his two dead men. The page below those names was blank—his future, his career, mocking him, begging for more names. He felt that if that page was ever full, he would one day run mad. He cursed himself for being such a God damned weepy child. Running a hand across his face, he poured an extra dose of the laudanum, far more than fifteen drops.

He was tossing it down when Doolan came barging in, clucking, "Come along, now, sir, it's time to go, and haven't I secured winged damned Pegasus for you to ride," but he went quickly silent, busying himself with straightening the shirts in his officer's trunk while Lockwood wiped his face.

Doing his best to mask anything resembling emotion, Lockwood strapped on his sword and said in an overloud voice, "Well, then, let us see this Pegasus. It is getting late."

Doolan stepped up to him, keeping his eyes on the coat, brushing away imaginary bits of dust, saying, "The boys will appreciate you dressing in your finest, sir."

"Yes. Yes, of course."

Outside, a truly beautiful dappled strawberry mare was tied to the house post. James was tempted to ask what a horse like that might cost, for even a day, but before he could ask, Doolan waved away his question, saying, "The boys at the George and Patrick owe me a favor, two favors, indeed, and so she'll not cost you a penny." Then, *sotto voce*, "I'll not have my officer limping down the road, will I? No, I will not."

It was Dr. Oades' prescription that spoke when James asked, "Did you not get a mount for yourself?"

Doolan looked at him incredulously, saying sharply, "And what would a Christian Irishman want on the back of a horse, for all love? I am no better and no worse than any of

God's creatures, and so I shall keep my feet on the ground, *go raibh maith agat*, and look into this good horse's eyes like a fellow being of God's creation, not like some...." Doolan's eloquence faded, and so he fell back on his pinched-face annoyance.

Dutifully accepting the reprimand, James said only, "Well, in any case, thank you, Doolan."

The wake of Privates Daly and Murray was held in a dilapidated corner of the old barracks, opposite the great hall which had only days before seen the glittering New Year's Ball. The mourners had been consigned to a crumbling room, its roof collapsed, only cold clouds above. Traditional wakes were not typically tolerated in Cork Barracks, dismissed as Papist superstitious nonsense, but Colonel Montgomery was so appreciative of Four Company's diligence in overrunning the rebel meeting that he gave his men free rein to mourn their dead. The surviving men of the company were thus given leave to cross Barrack Road to the Old Barracks to mourn. Their wounded comrades would not be left back, and so were carried from the hospital across to the old barracks, much to Dr. Oades' annoyance.

Peg O'Connor, the wife of Corporal Kerrigan O'Conner, had been asked to be *caointhe*, the lead keener, and so first to mourn the deceased. Peg's keening was especially valued, as she recited poetry lamenting the loss of the loved one in addition to crying and wailing.

Lighted candles were placed around the bodies. On a rough bench at their feet lay a stopped clock, the hands halted at the moment of their deaths, and a broken mirror, their images removed from this existence. Clay pipes, tobacco and snuff were placed in the room, and every man there was expected to take at least a puff and blow the smoke toward the door, as the smoke kept evil spirits from finding the deceased.

The handful of women sat around the bodies, keening in grief, the dead men's mates in the shadows beyond, trading stories about their lost friends and softly laughing, all while taking long swallows of the true *eischa beatha*.

Ensign Lockwood stood in a dark corner of the cold, open room. He only vaguely recalled his ride to the barracks, the effects of laudanum taking hold, and in the lantern light—he distinctly recalled the details of the battered old lantern—he remembered his men greeting him, helping him down from his horse, though he could not understand why they seemed concerned. He somehow found his way back through the dark passages between crumbling walls to the rear of the barracks. For some reason he had trouble measuring time, but it was of no concern. He had few concerns, only a dream-like view of the world beyond his comfortable inner man. He discovered, too, that his hearing had grown unnaturally sharp; he heard so much more, and the sounds were of great clarity. He stood quietly in the dark and overheard his men discussing him from what seemed a great distance away.

"Not a bad fellow, on the whole, though a Saxon."

"No Irish blood, I think, with a name like Lockwood?"

"It would be 'Glasadhmad', I think, if rendered into God's Irish. Not a bad name, sure, but not traditional, no, not by any measure."

"Have you ever met a man by the name of Glasadhmad, Sean Mooney, *a grah*?"

"Well, then, brother, let a man think on it," said Mooney, evidently the company's expert in matters regarding family lore. "There was, I think, once, a Glasadhmad I once met in the County Clare, but him being—"

Doolan stepped up to Lockwood, looked up at his officer, a look of puzzled concern on his face. "Are you all right, there, sir?"

James stepped forward, moving on before hearing the whole of Mooney's wisdom, Doolan in his wake, to where the candles flickered at the head and feet of the two shrouded corpses. The women there went quiet, expectantly looking up at the young man who stepped into their circle. Ensign Lockwood paid them no mind, winding his way past them to stand glassy-eyed between the two linen-draped bodies.

He knelt on the cold stone floor and prayed in earnest for the first time in many years. He then stood and gently kissed the heads of both the shrouded figures, the practice reserved for the fathers of the dead, drawing hissed angry comments from a few of the mourners, but Diarmuid Doolan angrily waved them down, saying in his sharp Donegal Irish, "He is their *officer*, damn you. It is his place, and theirs, them being so far from home."

A murmur of agreement eventually rose in the room, and as Lockwood returned to his dark corner there were appreciative comments rumbling in his ears. Sergeant Plunkett stepped over to shake his hand, and seeing the ensign unsteady on his feet, he called, "A bench and a blanket, for God's sake."

Lockwood spent most of the cold night there, though in his laudanum dream state it seemed like minutes, or days. He slept, and dreamt, wild, frightening dreams of a demon in black haunting his every step, but he dreamt, too, of Brigid O'Brian, a shining kindness in the dark. When he woke he saw the first gray of dawn in the sky above. The candles had burned low, most of the mourners were quiet, some asleep, others quietly smoking and drinking, though the *cointhe* relentlessly moaned a poem of loss.

As he got to his feet James felt clearheaded, but somehow older, different in some indefinable way. He had a deeper understanding of life, and of its brevity, and so determined to call on Brigid O'Brian. He had been the shy boy for too long. He slowly left the cold, crumbling room, limping badly, as his knee was stiff and painful now, touching a few shoulders as he passed by his men, getting some sad smiles and soft blessings in return.

Out in the cold, silent street, Lockwood found Doolan waiting—dear, old reliable Doolan, holding the reins to the beautiful mare, but Doolan looked upset, an unusual look for him, and, even more incongruous, Charles Oades stood there as well, standing beside a lovely chestnut mare.

James ran a hand across his face, feeling the dried tears on his cheeks, finally feeling the chill that had crept into his frame during the hours in the dark. "Charles," he said, "whatever brings you out at this hour? And why have you brought a horse?" Perhaps it was the last trace of the laudanum that allowed his mind to absorb keen details about the doctor: he looked smaller, more fragile than usual, but he was at peace, steady in his mind, freshly shaven, as alert and cheerful as a songbird.

Oades kindly smiled at him, and said, "Dear James, I hate to trouble you, but I wonder if I might beg a favor."

A bit taken aback, James raised his eyebrows and said, "A favor? Well, of course, Charles. Anything at all; I am yours to command."

The kind smile flickered, broke, and nervously returned. "I am due down in the Shrubbery in a few minutes for an affair of honour, and I wonder if I might beg you stand as my second."

"A duel!" barked James, never more startled in all his life. "What in hell has brought you to a duel?" In a panic, he went on, "No matter; I shall and go and speak on your behalf. There is certainly some misunderstanding... some unintended insult that can be quickly forgiven and forgotten."

"There can be no apology. A blow was delivered."

"A blow!" James gasped, running another hand across his face, trying to absorb this madness. But one certainty rang clear: a blow could never be excused. "Christ, Charles, who struck you? Perhaps it was an accident?"

Oades' smile grew stronger, more determined. "It was I who delivered the blow, brother, quite deliberately. Now, come, we must go. I must not be late, and be thought lacking."

As Oades turned to mount his horse, James grabbed his arm, still in disbelief. "You struck someone, Charles? Who in God's names would you ever strike?"

For a moment James saw the brittle mask of confidence slip from Oades' face, but still Oades managed a grin, and said, "Why, Lieutenant Barr, of course. Now, let us be off."

They had less than a mile to ride, and as Oades' horse was already warm, he could in good conscience put the beast to a trot. James tried to be gentle with his mare in the cold dawn, following Oades slowly through the empty narrow streets, high walls and dark buildings close on either hand, down toward the Lee, and the Shrubbery. Several times James tried to speak with Oades, but the doctor waved him back.

As the streets opened, they passed the ruins of Gill Abbey and the cave of St. Finbarr, a tumble of ancient stones, where a cloaked old man stepped off the narrow street to let them pass. The old man looked up at as Oades passed him by, ignored, but then caught Lockwood's eye, and in that brief moment, James heard the old man call to him, "It is a fell dawn, young master. You must—" but the rest was lost as they rode to their meeting, beyond.

The center of The Shrubbery Park was a large manicured formal garden, but much of the rest of the park straggled along the south bank of the River Lee. Narrow paths wound through dense stretches of trees and bushes. As James guided his horse to follow Oades through the maze of undergrowth, he briefly wondered how Oades knew his way. He sniffed at his own foolishness; of course, Oades had been there many times before, acting as the surgeon required at all proper duels.

The path rounded a massive old beech and suddenly they were on the dueling ground. They tied their horses to some saplings at the edge of the grassy field, level ground about fifty by twenty yards in size, completely cut off from prying eyes. There was no frost, but a cold, dripping dew clung to the grass and the dense foliage that surrounded them.

At the center of the ground the Barracks Sword Master, Sergeant Prentice, stood alone. Off to one side stood Mr. Birch, one of the barracks assistant surgeons. As a neutral party he could not show open favor, but he and Dr. Oades did share a discreet wave, Birch looking terribly concerned.

At the far end of the clearing Barr paced to and fro, a chained tiger. He wore no cloak; indeed, he had already pulled off his fine scarlet coat, his fine white shirt grayed in the misty light. With him stood Captain Fox of the 29th Foot, who had been posted to the barracks just days before. He was not tall, but slender and fit, with dark features; they had been introduced, but Lockwood knew nothing of him.

With the parties on the field, Sergeant Prentice motioned for both the seconds to step forward. They each presented the sergeant with the traditional shining guinea for his services.

"Captain Fox, the offended party chooses smallswords, I believe, sir?"

"He does."

Prentice had a burlap bundle under one arm; he opened it and handed a dueling sword to each of the seconds. The blades had razor-sharp edges and wicked points.

Lockwood broke decorum to say, "Captain Fox, may I say, this is hardly fair; for God's sake, please convince Barr to choose pistols, and allow my man something like a chance."

As a neutral party Sergeant Prentice retained his stony countenance, but he did look expectantly at Captain Fox. Fox looked away, and said, "I have already made that suggestion to my man; he insists upon swords." Then in a human, nearly confessing tone, he quietly added, "When Barr asked me to act for him, I agreed without inquiring who he was to fight. He was a brother officer in need, and so I was honoured to assist him. I confess that as I was new here in Cork, I was... well... anxious to be accommodating. When I heard he was to fight this poor fellow, the *doctor*, for God's sake, I begged Barr to release me from my agreement, but he insisted I carry through for him. This is terribly awkward."

Lockwood again broke etiquette, saying, "Can you convince him to satisfy his honour, at least his notions of honour, with a slight wound? For God's sake, sir, Oades can scarcely hold a sword." When Fox was slow to respond, Lockwood, asked, "Perhaps I can speak to Barr myself? I have known him some time...."

"That would be very improper, as you well know," said Fox, snappish. "On the other hand, it is not too late for your man to refuse the challenge."

"You know he cannot."

"I know," said Fox with a sigh. "Damn this. Whatever possessed your man to strike Barr? Was he in drink? Can there be any grounds by which we can honorably end this?"

Lockwood could only shake his head, and said, "I have suggested that. Oades insists his blow was sober, and deliberate."

"Damn."

Prentice stood silent as the seconds parlayed, but it was obvious he was keenly interested in the discussion. He had fought or presided over a hundred duels, and was well aware of what was at stake.

"Captain," said Lockwood urgently, "If Barr still insists on carrying through with this, please press upon him the need for a drawing of blood, but no more. If he truly harms Oades, every man in the barracks shall loath him; he shall certainly be hissed from the garrison."

"I shall do my best to convince him, Lockwood, but I guarantee nothing."

Fox paused, then leaned in closer, and went on, "Pardon me for saying so, Lockwood, but you are very young for such responsibility. Would you prefer one of the other officers to step in? I could send for—"

"I am perfectly comfortable, thank you," said Lockwood, stiffly. Then, his voice cracking, he added, "Doctor Oades is my friend."

In the cold misty half-light, Fox nodded. They bowed to one another, then turned and returned to their ends of the field, leaving Prentice standing alone, the model of tradition, if not justice.

Lockwood returned to Oades and handed him the sword, and he noticed the doctor flinched a bit before taking the grip. The doctor said, "I trust, James, that you will not think poorly of me if I confess that I am terribly frightened."

Lockwood urgently said, "You need not carry through with this. You are on the ground; that is enough. You have made your point."

"I must do this. It is... necessary." As he pulled off his coat, Oades quietly added, "Are you familiar with the concept of a sin offering?"

"Oh, for God's sake, Charles, do not speak nonsense. If you are to do this, you must concentrate. At all costs you must keep your point up. You must in turn focus on his point; your point stays still, and you break your wrist in either direction to... oh for God's sake, Charles, you must not do this." Lockwood did not add that by ignoring Barr's edge the doctor invited a cut by Barr, but any wound he would suffer from the edge, while painful and bloody, would typically not be serious. Oades could survive this.

Prentice called, "Gentlemen! Pray step forward!"

From his post at the edge of the trees Lockwood watched Oades walk slowly forward. His steps were steady, but James saw his hands shaking.

It was just seconds later that Prentice said, *"En garde."* The points went up as the sword master retreated a few steps. He then said, "Begin."

With one deadly-quick motion, Barr beat aside Oades' guard, then with a flick of his wrist he made a quick slash that laid open the side of Oades' face. A great deal then happened very quickly: Charles Oades' right hand kept his grip on his sword, though his point dropped to the ground. His left hand instinctively reached up to grab his face; he did not cry out. From their various posts around the field, Lockwood, Fox, and Prentice all took a step forward, threw a hand up, and called out for the duelists to halt. Charles Barr fell back half a step then lunged again, a cobra uncoiling, a terrible satisfaction on his face as he ran Oades through.

Lockwood and Birch reached Oades in just seconds. While the doctor tried, and failed, to give Lockwood a reassuring smile. Birch pulled back the shirt and nervously, awkwardly pressed a thick bandage to the heavily bleeding chest wound.

"The lung, colleague," said Oades softly, looking at Birch with some reproach.

"A *circus quadruplex*, then, doctor?"

"Please," said Oades with a sharp intake of agonized breath.

"I have the requisite materials in my saddlebag. I won't be a minute." With that Birch ran off, leaving Lockwood pressing down on the bandages, but still the blood poured. Lockwood quickly Birch was a fool, and that Oades was lost. He choked back a sob.

"*Circumforaneous*," gasped Oades with some satisfaction. A fresh jet of pain roared through him, but still he managed, "James. James." Reaching up, he took his friend's hand. "You must seek out Miss O'Brian. She must be warned." Oades winced and gasped, writhing in pain. "Christ I am so afraid, James, so afraid."

"Oh God, oh God. Charles, what can I do?"

Oades went pale, a ghastly ivory, but more at ease as he faded. "Dying," he whispered. As Lockwood leaned in close, Oades gasped, "Warn her. Barr has *syphilis*. Understand? Tell her. Seek her out."

"Yes, Charles, I understand. *Jesus*. I shall tell her. Oh, look, now, here comes Birch with your bandage. You shall certainly—"

Oades coughed, blood gurgling up into his mouth. He gave his friend a flickering scarlet smile, and died.

Chapter Sixteen

Major General Sir John Moore was commander of His Majesty's forces in Ireland's six southern counties. Stiff in his scarlet and gold, he sat stiffly in a cold anteroom, waiting for an audience with John Jeffreys Pratt, 1st Marquess Camden, Lord Lieutenant of Ireland. Moore had been waiting for nearly two hours, likely a deliberate insult. Moore possessed one of the best minds in the British army, and used those hours to mull over his plans for training his light troops. Moore was also rather prideful, and so swallowed the urge to check his pocket watch; he would not give Camden's secretary, who sat smugly by a fire in the inner office, the satisfaction.

General Moore was a cultured, experienced officer, and like many of the senior military advisors to Lord Camden he was new to the staff. Like Major General Abercromby, the newly appointed commander of His Majesty's forces in Ireland, Moore was a Scot, and so, too, like Abercromby, he held the Lord Lieutenant and his Ascendency cronies in considerable contempt.

Moore was there to inform and persuade Lord Camden, but cherished little hope of being able to fulfill either goal. Eventually he was ushered through the dim halls of Dublin Castle and into a gilded office.

The interview was a formal one; Lord Camden came forth from behind his desk, a massive mahogany affair, only for a moment to greet General Moore, after which he retreated to his seat of authority and waved Moore to sit on the plain, narrow, thoroughly uncomfortable chair that sat before his desk. In a corner of the office a silent secretary sat ready to record their conversation.

"I trust," said Camden as he flipped through his notes, "you shall pardon the brevity, the wholly necessary brevity, of this interview, General Moore, but the weight of the responsibilities placed upon me by the King allow no time for unctuous chatter. You soldiers insist upon these endless reports, sir, so pray do proceed, but *succinctly*."

"As you wish, my Lord. The news from the south is not good. Many of the regiments under my command have been scattered in small pockets across Munster, and only the larger towns and cities are held in force. If the rebels manage a rise in any concerted manner, those small outposts shall be defeated in detail before they can unite, and the—"

Camden waved Moore's concerns aside, saying, "Yes, yes, that topic has been discussed *ad nauseam* with your General Abercromby. I am surprised at the need to remind you, sir, that the protection of the lives and property of the gentry is our prime consideration. I have personally ordered the positioning of these troops to ensure the safety of our gentlemen and their property. If the gentlemen were to be put in jeopardy, this island of ape-men would be doomed beyond redemption. Pray, sir, move on."

"Point the second: The United Irishmen continue to make inroads in the militia regiments. The commander of the North Down Regiment, for example, has ordered six of his men hanged for sedition, and reports that he is unsure if his regiment can be relied on. Even in the most rural counties, the White Boys and the Defenders, typically more concerned with local agrarian grievances, have allied themselves with the urban United men. Should the organization and leadership of the United men be fully joined with the raw numbers of Defenders —"

"Yes, yes, next."

"Third: our agents in France relay further evidence of a possible French expedition to aid the rebels. My Lord, if French arms and expertise were to combine with the raw numbers of Irishmen who might rally to the rebellion, only a war of massive scale might preserve Ireland for the King."

"I am convinced," sniffed Camden, "that His Majesty's Navy, God knows they cost us enough, shall keep the French at bay. The likelihood, the wildly improbable likelihood, of a French expedition aside, surely, General Moore, you overestimate both the number of rebels and their capacity for evil? I am certain a more determined effort by you gentlemen of the military—vigorous searches for arms, thorough interrogations of the peasantry, and so forth—shall snuff out these handfuls of malcontents in short order. Firmness, sir, firmness, is called for."

"My Lord, torture, rapine and rape are not tools of honourable soldiers—"

"Oh, come now, sir, this is no time for delicate scruples! The lives and property of gentlemen are at stake!"

"Begging your pardon, my Lord, but I contend that moderate treatment by the military, and preventing the troops from pillaging and molesting the people, would soon restore tranquility. The people would certainly be quiet if the gentlemen and yeomen would only behave with tolerable decency, and not indulgetheir ill humours and revenges upon the poor."

Camden coughed, sniffed, and said, "Enough. I am to assume, then, the advice offered by His Majesty's senior officers is that this government should follow a course of weakness and pusillanimous submission? Do I have that quite right, sir?"

"Justice and humanity are not derogatory to power, my Lord."

The Lord Lieutenant rang a small bell that sat on his desk, and another secretary immediately opened the towering walnut doors. Camden returned to the files on his desk, dismissively flicked two fingers, and said, "Thank you, General Moore. Mr. Whitby, please show the General out."

*****

In a Connaught shebeen, fifty men of the Defender movement, proud, desperately poor, landless, assembled to hear a fellow from Galway itself, one Daniel Skerritt, who had come up to talk a little treason. The place with close with pipe and peat smoke, the sharp smell of untaxed whiskey, and the sharp stink of unwashed men. The Galway man in his tweed coat, white breeches and half boots looked sadly out of place. The Defenders were not quickly impressed by this *piteog*.

"A Skerritt, are ye?" asked one of the older local men. "There're no Skerritts hereabouts. Who are your people?"

"I was born in Clare, but that doesn't matter, does it? What matters is—"

There were roars of derision, and the old man loudly said, "Oh, it matters a great deal, boyo, when you ask me to put the lives of me and mine into your hands."

Christopher Boyle, the village blacksmith and leader of the local Defenders, stood at Skerritt's side at the head of the room, waved down the chattering crowd, and said, "Come now, lads, let's give Mr. Skerritt here a chance. He's one of the United men, ya see, and his comrades in Galway, hell, in Dublin itself, are offering to join up with us men in the hills, and kick some English arse."

"Precisely!" crowed Skerritt. "The English can be thrown down! They have stolen our lands, and it is high time we took it back! Do you know, men, that the English own ninety-five percent of the land, while we Irish, the native people of this land, hold only five percent?"

A number of the men looked puzzled, Liam Cullum eventually asking, "What the fuck is a *percent*?" A dozen voices tried to loudly explain it to him, many incorrectly.

In the back, Niall Malone stood and called out, "You bring us weapons, city man, and then we'll show the yeomen a thing or two!"

From the bar, Quinlan O'Conghailes roared, "Shite, boys, as soon as I get a musket in my hands I'm going up to Hampton House, kick in the front door, kill old man Brown, and have my way with that wee daughter of his!" There quickly followed roars of disapproval, laughter, and derision, and only after Boyle roared at them to shut the fuck up did the crowd settle back to listen to more of Skerritt's proposal. His talk of a general rising and a new republic were met with only moderate interest, but when Finn O'Hare, one of their own, was asked to step forward to tell them of how the yeomen came to search his home for weapons did they sit and listen in rapt attention.

"I was away," O'Hare told them, "gone to Cregmore to sell a pig, as fine a beast as a man could want. But while I was away, lads, the yeomen came, didn't they, the bastards? They treated my family rough, but then they found my father's old pike hidden up in the rafters. Hell, I had nearly forgotten it was up there, hadn't I?" He ran a hand across his rough face and went on, grief building in his voice. "Oh, they found that toothpick of a pike and they went mad. My wife, my daughter! Used! Some of you lads know my brother, him as simple as a wee child, but the English thought him some mastermind of rebellion, and they tortured him to death! Flogged at the triangle, then a cap of hot pitch!"

The men of Lackagh Township leapt to their feet and swore their devotion to the cause, and death to any man not baptized as a true Catholic. David Skerritt, a Methodist, quietly snuck out to ride home to Galway, wondering just to whom he was now allied.

*****

Still, across Ireland, normal life went on. The new school year was scheduled to begin, and so students began to return to Miss McCarthy's School for Young Ladies. Over several days the girls arrived, their families parting with their daughters, granddaughters, nieces, and wards with a mix of relief and reluctance, a mix determined by the various temperaments involved. The older girls and their families parted with the practiced air of public school veterans, but the first-year girls, those who were to be Miss O'Brian's charges, often parted with a clinging tearful reluctance that, while touching, was painful to Miss O'Brian, who had hoped her girls would be excited to be in her class.

The ladies of the school had been concerned for Brigid, for she and Lieutenant Barr had parted brass rags—much to the relief of Miss McCarthy and Miss Klug. Nichole and Gabriele did their best to console their young friend, though Brigid was not in much need of their sympathy. They found her more disgusted and angry than saddened.

It was noted, too, among the staff that the number of girls attending school was markedly down, a trend worrying to Miss McCarthy, always the keen businesswoman. Concern over what the spring might bring had caused several families, both Protestant and Catholic, to keep their daughters at home.

On the afternoon when the staff were at their busiest, settling in new girls and settling squabbles as to who was to sleep near who, Captain Rzewnicki spurred up to the school, his horse, a chestnut gelding he dearly loved, in a muck sweat. Rzewnicki leapt from the saddle and did not wait for Jimmy Scanlon, who came hurrying out to hold the horse, but instead quickly bounced up the steps to loudly pound at the door.

The rattled maid ran to call for Miss Hendricks, who was upstairs settling her restless students, a young woman in no mood for company. As she came down the stairs—she was unaware that she was particularly lovely when in a passion— she was clearly annoyed by the captain's arrival. Rzewnicki paid no mind to her mood, taking her by the elbow and pulling her into the drawing room and closing, with not a little violence, the heavy double doors.

Miss O'Brian and Miss Reese happened to be passing by, and by the merest chance heard Miss Hendricks began to berate her beau, but that gentlemen, in a wholly uncharacteristic furor, overrode her and spoke with considerable force. Those two young ladies then had the decency to retreat from the door, standing down the hall all aflutter until Rzewnicki emerged. He offered them both an elegant, oddly significant bow, then strode back outside where he called, "Chodź, mój koniu!"

Sadly, Jimmy Scanlon spoke no Polish, but the horse evidently did, as he pulled free and came to his master as faithfully as a dog. With a pleased, determined air, Rzewnicki rode away.

Brigid noticed that Rzewnicki was wearing his sword; it was typically a rule of society that gentlemen did not wear a sword when making a social call, and she wondered briefly if there was trouble in town. But then Nichole, relaxed, happy, if still a bit unnerved, stepped out of the drawing room, looking thoroughly kissed. She smiled at her friends, and tearfully gasped, "I am to be married!"

Among the wild shrieks, hugs, and requisite jumping about, the few doubts still circling Brigid O'Brian dispersed like a summer fog. Barr was once again proven wrong: Rzewnicki had proven his affection for Miss Hendricks, Barr's cynical shite be damned. She was well past him.

*****

The good news soon spread through the school. The students were atwitter, and the cooks made a special effort for supper. Still, the next day was a school day, so the staff ensured the celebrations were limited. Miss Bloxham, the housemistress, herded her charges to bed with little concern for the girls' romantic musings.

The teachers, however, were discreetly invited to Miss McCarthy's rooms to carry on the festivities, where she once again proved her cellar equal to any challenge, producing several bottles of champagne. It was wine of surpassing quality, an elegant contribution to the celebration of the engagement of a penniless young teacher to a Polish officer of unknown fortune.

When Brigid unsteadily returned to her room, happy but with her head spinning, she found that a maid had left a letter from the second post on her bedside table: a letter from her father, containing the words '*Aunt Áine is taken poorly, and will come see us come spring.*' She sat heavily on her bed; it would not be long before her father would soon come to take her home to Clonakilty.

That was it, then. Rebellion was coming.

<h1 style="text-align:center">Chapter Seventeen</h1>

On that chill January afternoon it was Lieutenant Athelstan Throckmorton's turn to act as Officer of the Day for Cork Barracks. Throckmorton, a fat, indolent young man, had been an officer of the North Cork Militia for four years, during which time he had spent perhaps three months with the regiment. Sitting in the chill damp of the guard house he was in a foul humour, primarily because he had been recalled to the regiment from his family's comfortable Dublin townhouse. It was bad enough that rumours of discontent among the troublesome peasants had prompted the end of his extensive leave; now he had to spend twenty-four hours at the beck and call of the sullen enlisted men of the guard, men who were little better than the rebel peasants. The lieutenant did not speak to the men; he left their supervision to the sergeant of the guard. In truth, if any issue of real import had been brought to his attention, Throckmorton would have been at a complete loss as how to address it. The men of the guard, indeed the great majority of the enlisted men of the barracks, loathed Throckmorton and the officers of his ilk.

Sitting in the gloomy officers' chamber of the guard room, Throckmorton busied himself with compiling a report regarding the readiness of the various units that made up the garrison. He intended to present it to Colonel Montgomery, who he hoped would, in turn, pass it on to Major General Clinton. His arrogance had not rendered Throckmorton a complete fool; it was his opinion that the companies of the line were of the greatest readiness, and two of the companies of the Westmeath Militia had made some progress toward military proficiency. The companies of the other militia regiments were of varying quality, from barely competent to nearly mutinous. The yeomanry, both foot and horse, remained a loyal but unskilled and wildly undisciplined force. It was Throckmorton's informed opinion that the excesses committed on their forays into the surrounding towns and villages were creating rebels at an exponential rate.

Throckmorton's attention was soon diverted by the unannounced, impolite and wholly undisciplined entrance of Ensign Lockwood, who burst into his office, quite interrupting his train of thought. The ensign made no salute, only crashing in to roar, "Sir, I must speak with Lieutenant Barr. He is not in his quarters, and it seems he is nowhere in the fort."

"Ensign, you are in a passion. You will address me only after you have gathered your senses—"

"Beg pardon, sir," said Lockwood, seething with rage, "but Lieutenant Barr has committed murder, and I intend for him to stand for it."

"Murder!" cried Throckmorton. "That is a bold charge, sir."

"Cloaked in the guise of a duel, Lieutenant, but murder in the eye of any man who would call himself a gentleman. Barr fled the scene, but by God, I shall see him taken up by the Prevost, or I shall I have his blood on my sword."

"You shall have neither, sir, and you shall calm yourself, or I shall call the sergeant and have you placed under arrest." Throckmorton looked down at his report and silently mouthed, "God damned puppy."

Lockwood fell silent, panting, wide-eyed and agonized.

Throckmorton then recalled recent discussions in the mess praising Ensign Lockwood's qualities as a promising young officer. Throckmorton, who was not a promising young officer, thus said more carefully, "At any rate, Lockwood, Lieutenant Barr is quite gone." Searching for a sheet of paper buried on his desk, he pulled one out, and said, "Yes, here it is. Yesterday Lieutenant Barr applied for emergency leave so that he might tend his ailing father in Liverpool or some such place. Lieutenant Colonel O'Reilly approved the leave, and I saw the lieutenant spur out the front gate perhaps twenty minutes ago. I wondered at his paternal devotion, him seeming not a gentleman of a particularly affectionate nature, but it now seems that his departure, I will not say flight, was perhaps instead inspired by a less noble motivation."

"Gone? England?" gasped Lockwood, at a loss. In a wondering tone, he whispered to himself, "He applied for leave even before the duel... he planned this from the first."

"Thus, Lieutenant Barr is quite removed from your notions of justice, Ensign. The lieutenant colonel granted the lieutenant three months' leave, with a codicil for additional months upon application in writing."

Lockwood's hand fell from the handle of his sword.

"So, tell me, Ensign Lockwood, just who has Lieutenant Barr *murdered*, by your reckoning?"

"Doctor Oades, sir."

"The doctor? That meek little fellow?" said Throckmorton. "In a duel with Lieutenant Barr, you say? Goodness, whatever could have prompted such a lunatic match as that? My, I suppose that will pose a loss to the garrison." Seeing that Lockwood was in no mood for banter, Throckmorton went on, "So, Lockwood, I suggest you content yourself with seeing to the doctor's affairs." Looking up at the tall young officer, he said more kindly, "He was your friend, I suppose? My condolences, then. But, life goes on, sir." Consulting another sheet of paper, he sniffed and added, "I see here you have the guard after me. By tomorrow dawn you had best gather yourself."

*****

James and the staff of the hospital saw that Charles Oades was carefully laid out in the garrison hospital, covered in a white sheet. All his goodness, his gentle nature, was gone, wasted. "We'll see to him, now, sir," said the assistant surgeon, Birch. "All of us down here thought the world of him... we'll see to him right proper."

"Yes, yes, of course," said Lockwood, at a loss as to what to do next. He had never before experienced the death of a friend, and was unsure as to what emotions should rule his mind, let alone his actions.

In the end it was left to Doolan, who saw him back to his billet, and who went out to get his officer something to eat. When he returned he also bore the post: a letter from Charles Oades.

James sat holding the letter for a long moment, his hands shaking. After an awkward pat on his officer's shoulder, Doolan slipped out, and Lockwood unsteadily broke the seal.

My Dear James,

A quick note before I see to this fellow Barr. I find myself in a unique humour: the outer man quakes at the thought of the quite certain pain, and the possible, perhaps even the likely, extinguishing of the flame; but the inner man, oh, the inner man, my dear James, is content to the point of near rapture.

I should mention that I have contracted consumption. Only a medical man would detect it at this, its earliest stages, and as such I am intimately aware of its inevitable course. It will kill me soon enough. Being a coward of the first order, I am determined to avoid its decidedly unpleasant finale.

Now, as to the main aim of this letter: you should know that Charles Barr has syphilis. As a medical man I cannot betray my oath and expose him, but my death will certainly render such a vow moot. I cannot allow Barr to continue to carry on as he does, so I had best do my bit to put an end to it.

James turned away from the letter and choked out, "Ah, damn, Charles." He glanced at the bottle of laudanum on his bedside table, denied himself that escape, and read on.

If things end badly, pray do not mourn me. The fate of consumption aside, I have a debt to resolve on a separate matter, as I am convinced that I was in some way responsible for the loss of Private and Mrs. Lynch's baby.

They had named her Niamh, the dear lost soul. I grieve deeply, though my profession and my demeanor do not allow such a display. I believe that if I should die today, it is God's will (what a fellow He is, don't you think?) that I am to go and tend to young Niamh. She had (has?) fair hair. Pray pardon my wild musings; I share them only with you.

Miss O'Brian should in no way feel obligated to me; what I do, I do for my own reasons, though if she takes some benefit, so much the better. My life has been blessed with few close companions, but I trust, I pray, you shall remember me, despite the brevity of our acquaintance, as your most devoted friend—

Charles

P.S. Now, I beg you to go and seek out Miss O'Brian. Shall I refer here to her as <u>Brigid</u>? Oh, how very daring of me! I am such a rascal.

P.P.S. I think you and she would make a grand match; your souls seem to me both of such a fine character, though of course she is far too pretty for you. Be happy. Have babies. Laugh.

Farewell.

Over the past weeks James Lockwood had wept more than at any time since he was a very young boy; his father would not have his sons crying like women. But now, as a young man, James decided he had wept enough. He did not weep for Charles Oades, but rather sat and reread the doctor's letter a dozen times, eventually coming to smile, to laugh, at the memory of his friend, his dear friend.

*****

"Beg pardon, ladies, but a gentleman is at the door, asking for Miss O'Brian."

It was tea time, but a Tuesday, and the ladies were certainly not expecting visitors. They were wearing their worn, old school dresses, as they had counted on nothing more than a few minutes sipping their tea and enjoying a brief respite from the demands of fifty girls.

For an instant Brigid pictured Lieutenant Barr returning, a dark shadow crossing her soul, but she sniffed that phantom aside and asked the maid, "Did he give his name, Siobhan?"

"No, ma'am, he did not." Brigid stood and tried to gather herself while the other ladies gleefully wondered who might the gentleman might be. Siobhan stepped over to Brigid to say quietly, "A very tall young gentleman, Miss, a redcoat, the poor man. He is terribly nervous, but he seems a good sort, if you take my meaning."

Her heart jumped. Her heart was completely foolish, of course, but it jumped of its own volition. James Lockwood had come calling, sure, there could be no other man of such a description.

*****

Miss O'Brian and Ensign Lockwood sat in the school's drawing room for some minutes, awkwardly discussing the weather. Irish weather, a study in cool, damp consistency, provided little fodder, but after a self-conscious pause, Miss O'Brian attempted, "I believe, sir, you are a friend to Lieutenant Barr?"

To Brigid's immense satisfaction, James bristled and replied. "The lieutenant and I were, at one time, acquaintances, but our association is at an end."

To James's immense satisfaction, Brigid then grinned and replied, "The lieutenant and I were also, at one time, acquainted, but so, too, is our association at an end."

They shared a shy, satisfied smile. James then grew serious, and said, "I wonder, Miss O'Brian, if you recall Doctor Oades of the garrison?"

"I do; we were briefly introduced at the ball. He seemed a very kind gentleman."

"He was. He was indeed." James struggled to go on. "Unfortunately, Doctor Oades and Lieutenant Barr had a disagreement."

"Oh, please, sir, do not tell me..." said Miss O'Brian, suddenly clenching her hands.

"The news is evidently not yet well known, so I am saddened that it falls to me to tell you that Doctor Oades is dead."

Miss O'Brian looked out the window toward the cold Irish afternoon. She eventually said, "He was a dear man." Crossing herself, she went on, *"Ar dheis Dé go raibh a anam."*

"Amen," said James quietly. He had no need to ask Miss O'Brian what she had said, as the expression was often used in Ireland, a land long haunted by untimely death. 'May he sit at God's right hand.'

After a long pause, James went on, "Lieutenant Barr has fled the country; he will certainly not face any consequences. The magistrates will soon forget the affair." Then, attempting a more positive note, James added, "Still there is hope for some measure of justice. Doctor Oades was my friend, and despite his... eccentricities... he was respected by the men of the garrison. When Barr returns, and some day he must return or resign his commission, he is certain to be shunned by every officer of Cork Barracks."

"Pardon my ignorance of such matters, but is that a very terrible punishment?"

"Oh, yes, very terrible indeed," said James, doing his best to sound a seasoned veteran. "Honour is important to every gentleman, but it is everything to an officer. To be shunned is to be silently informed at every turn that you have no honour, you are not an officer, and worst of all, no gentleman."

"His shame would be immense," she said, her eyes wide.

They sat quietly for a while, both of them absorbing the news and one another's reactions to such tidings.

Then, with a hollow laugh, he took a very great chance, and said, "You know, one of the doctor's other requests was that I... we..."

But then Brigid saw Gabby discreetly, if urgently, wave to her from the door. "Oh, my," said Brigid, in a panic, "I must go. My students are waiting for me, and we have semi-colons to discuss."

"Semi-colons!" cried James, standing to go. "I beg pardon, Miss, for delaying a topic of such pressing importance. I wonder, though," he said, switching quickly from strained wit to grinding awkwardness, "if I might call again soon?"

Brigid gave him a playful smile, raised her eyebrows, and said, "Tomorrow afternoon is convenient, sir, if you are quite free."

His heart jumped. His heart was completely foolish, of course, but it jumped of its own volition. "Until tomorrow, then," said the ensign, grinning like a fool.

*****

That same day, a troop of yeomen cavalry sortied from Clonakilty Barracks to ride the eleven miles to search Dunmanway for weapons, a village long rumoured to be a stronghold of rebel sentiment. The yeomen were well mounted, in tight white breeches, tight blue coats, and stylish round caps with bear fur crests.

After suffering the torture of the village smith and threats to hang the priest, the people turned over a dozen pikes and two stolen firearms. Satisfied that they had every weapon Dunmanway could offer, the yeomen amused themselves by beating the priest and burning the smith's forge to the ground.

The next night, twenty Dunmanway men left their homes and slipped into the cold darkness, intent on houghing their landlord's cattle and burning his barn. Their landlord, who held hundreds of acres in Cork, had never set foot in Ireland. He lived in indebted luxury in England, though his agent lived in Laurel Mount, a fine, if small, house nestled in the woods east of the village. That aged gentleman, who had nothing to do with the yeomen and who wanted nothing more than to be left alone to study his butterfly collection, made the mistake of going outside when his dog began to bark. The infuriated villagers, their knives wet with cattle blood, turned on him, surging through the darkness to brutally beat him to the ground. They killed the dog, ransacked the house, and stole three firearms before returning to their homes as full-fledged rebels.

*****

Diarmuid Doolan was rumoured to possess several virtues; an ability to choose wine was not one of them; he chose the wine for Ensign Lockwood's table solely by price. When James returned to his billet, he found a fire in the hearth, a tidy supper, and a bottle waiting for him. He poured himself a glass, winced at the smell, then with a shrug took a healthy swallow, quickly deciding the vile concoction was a mixture of grain alcohol, lead, and cochineal. He did not feel overly poisoned, so pulled the table in front of the fire, lit a candle, and as he ate his supper he read through the serial letter he had been writing to Tom Mainwaring. He added a paragraph or two every few days, and once a month he mailed the accumulated pages. Tom was equally prolific, their friendship unconsciously growing stronger with each letter. With his glass in one hand, he took up his pen with the other, and set to.

Tuesday 23 January

I have called on Miss O'Brian! Well might you laugh at my sense of triumph, Lothario, but I, for one, must seek out the company of young ladies, as I lack the luxury of being pursued by buxom Amazons at every turn.

She was very kind, and seemed quite pleased with me coming to call. Indeed she has asked me to call again tomorrow! I must find a way to arrange the time with Captain Holister. I rode the local inn's stable mare today, but as I cannot afford that expense on a regular basis I shall have to walk the three miles to the school, but if need be, I believe I could fly the distance.

James went on to relay the details of Dr. Oades' death, slowly, painfully, reliving the duel and his anguish, but he stopped at sharing the detail of Barr's syphilis. He wondered at his hesitancy, eventually deciding it was born of a tumbled sense of propriety, affection, and loyalty for Charles Oades and Brigid O'Brian, and a grudging memory of the admiration he once held for Barr. There lingered another motive, one which tested his notions of honour, but it flickered nonetheless: to hold the secret of Barr's syphilis might one day prove of value. He would keep the secret; he was not finished with Charles Barr.

Chapter Eighteen

"It's scandalous, isn't it?" said Ciara as she knelt and built the fire in Miss McCarthy's drawing room. "That redcoat is here near every day, and our Brigid O'Brian is only too glad to walk with him come rain or shine, with no chaperone at all, at all." They were speaking softly in Irish, recalling Miss O'Brian's scolding from a few weeks previous.

"Oh, you are grown hard in your heart," said Siobhan as she made the bed. "They are so happy with one another."

"But a redcoat! A bloody officer! And a Proddy! A trinity of evil, if you ask me. If her family knew what she was about, I wager they would drag her home by the ear and spank her bottom like a Kilkenny bodhrán."

Siobhan, who had met a nice young militiaman (a Catholic boy, but a redcoat from Donegal, which seemed wildly foreign to a Cork girl) at Cronin's Pub after Mass on Sunday, only smiled a bit as she fluffed the pillows.

Ciara sniffed and went on, "Her beau had an umbrella with him the other day! An umbrella! Have you heard of such a thing? And her hanging on his arm under that wee tiny thing, talking close and laughing like... well, I mustn't say, her being good to us, on the whole, but still, it's scandalous."

"Oh, say what you will, but if that tall good man called on me, I'd walk with him, sure, umbrella or no."

"Sure and it's a wanton slut you are, Siobhan Barry," Ciara said, not unkindly.

*****

The world spun on at an increasing pace. In Paris, for instance, the five men known as the Directory ruled revolutionary France. They were regularly harried by a Belfast barrister named Theobald Wolfe Tone, who had been dispatched to Paris by the United Irishmen, to make urgent requests for French troops to intervene in Ireland. The aborted French invasion of Ireland in 1796 had been an abject failure, sure, England's luckiest escape since the Armada, but Tone begged for another attempt, pledging a quarter million Irishmen who would rally to join a French invasion force, even one of moderate strength.

*****

They laughed together a great deal. She teased him, and he teased her in turn. They grew so very comfortable with one another that one afternoon, as they walked in a cold rain, the first buds of spring just starting to show, he took a deep breath, leaned over, and kissed her in a wholly inappropriate, wildly welcome manner. He would have broken it off after a moment, content to be the happiest man alive, but she laid a hand on his arm, drawing him closer, and in a few seconds they were both quite sure that they would spend the rest of their lives together.

*****

In Clonakilty, Tadg at Astna O'Donovan worked in his carpentry shop, building everything from furniture to farm carts. Government's brutal searches and widespread arrests had claimed most of the movement's firearms and leaders, but so too had those tactics hardened the resolve of hundreds of local men. On occasion some of those men would drift by his shop to sell a bit of timber or perhaps order a new bench for their home, and would be quietly told to stay strong, to lay low, and give no cause for the redcoats to suspect them, as the day of reckoning was coming.

New men, too, would be brought by the shop to be questioned by O'Donovan. Only after he was convinced they were not traitors or spies, the bane of countless rebel organizations in Ireland's long and bloody history, would he swear them in, and so too would they be taught the same catechism Michael O'Brian had taught his daughters. It now rang as a prediction coming to fruition:

> *"A wet winter, a dry spring,*
> *A bloody summer, and no King."*

*****

Five officers of Cork Barracks pooled their resources and invited the ladies of the Miss McCarthy's to a concert of choral music at St. Anne's church. In truth, once word of the evening spread in the mess, the five gentlemen struggled to keep any other gentlemen from insinuating themselves into their party; Ensign Lockwood and Captain Rzewnicki were especially intent on spending the evening with Miss O'Brian and Miss Hendricks without more that the necessary number of chaperons and extraneous hangers-on.

In the cold, foggy darkness of a February evening, the gentlemen arrived in two carriages to carry the ladies to St.

Anne's, a beautiful Church of Ireland edifice which had stood since 1726 on Cork's burgeoning north side. There was a bit of a scramble in determining just who was to ride in which carriage, as the two courting couples slyly attempted to have the smaller carriages to themselves. Miss McCarthy, a woman of a liberal disposition and no prude, nonetheless took her responsibilities seriously, and so when she realized what they were about, she hurried back to place herself firmly between one couple, with both eyes firmly on the other.

Even in the cold air, the smells of the crowded city grew worse where the North Bridge crossed the River Lee; the waste, both real and human, of the city settled there. The carriage stalled in traffic as the coachman waited for his turn to cross the bridge, and a handful of filthy children, dressed in rags, their feet bare on the cold pavers, went from wagon to dray to carriage begging for scraps. Nearly every vehicle had a lantern burning beside the driver, and in the flickering light and shadow the children, darting between the wheels and the legs of stamping horses, looked like the spirits of humanity's shame.

Times and hearts were hard, and the children had little luck, being cursed away from farm wagons, tradesmen's carts, and gentlemen's carriages in turn, until they happened to tap at one carriage window, where a beautiful young woman turned to smile down on them. Brigid handed out the few pennies she had in her bag; when her fortune was exhausted, Ensign Lockwood gave her what little he had, until the carriage began to move again, and Brigid called out her blessings and Lockwood called, "Watch your toes, there, *leanaí!*"

Miss McCarthy, Miss Hendricks, and Captain Rzewnicki watched their young friends with some amusement, and as the carriage rattled over the bridge Rzewnicki asked, "You speak the Erse, James? What is this *leanaí*? It is a curse, I wager? I find it is best to first learn to curse in one's newer language, as it proves so useful."

With not a little pride Brigid said, "*Leanai* means 'children' in Irish, Captain. Ensign Lockwood is one of the few military gentlemen of my acquaintance who has endeavored to learn Irish." She gave James a look which made him blush.

Rzewnicki gave them a sad smile, and said, "In Poland there are such children as well, in the thousands, countless. It is useless to empty one's purse to them; a handful of sand into a tide."

As their carriage passed through the pack of beggar children who haunted the north end of the bridge, James looked out at them, and said sadly, "It is a prodigious tide."

Brigid nodded knowingly, and said, "Do not despair, gentlemen. In the end, goodness shall win the day, I am quite certain."

Captain Rzewnicki and Miss Hendricks subtly rolled their eyes, Miss McCarthy smiled softly, and James was entranced.

They soon arrived at St. Anne's, and as James handed Brigid down, she looked up at the brightly lit building and said, "Goodness, what a lovely church."

In a private, playful tone he asked, "I trust you do not mind setting foot in an Anglican church?"

"Certainly not, sir. I believe the same God dwells here as at my little church at home." As she took his arm, she leaned over and added, "But pray never mention it to my father."

He looked at her with raised eyebrows and asked, "I wonder if I shall ever have occasion to speak to your father?"

She did not reply, only sticking a sharp surreptitious finger into his side as they walked up the worn stone steps to join their friends.

The concert was well attended, for the choir was well known throughout Munster. As the party found their seats, Captain Rzewnicki, by happy coincidence, happened to sit beside Miss Hendricks, and Ensign Lockwood chanced to sit close beside Miss O'Brian. Both couples discreetly held hands and, while polite to the other members of their party, they were obviously there only for one another.

The choral group featured twelve singers, men and women, singing beautifully crafted ancient music. Their "Media Vita" was deeply moving, though when it was over Brigid leaned over and whispered to James, "It is beautiful, but I do so wish I knew what it meant, don't I?"

James, whose Public School education included extensive course work in Latin, in truth understood perhaps one word in ten, whispered in return, "I do believe it was about God, and us begging for help, and, I think, us being already dead?"

Brigid sat up straight, whispering, "Perhaps then I'd rather not know what it means...."

Later, the singers treated then to a stirring rendition of "Sí do Mhaimeo Í," which allowed Brigid to show off a bit. "It is a perfectly silly song," she whispered to him, "about a handsome young man in love with a pretty young woman, but he instead chooses to marry a rich old hag."

James raised an eyebrow, and seriously said, "It is not silly at all, I think. That seems a perfectly sensible course for the gentlemen, a very practical decision—" She ended his tease with another sharp finger in his side, and a playful sniff of anger.

He barked a satisfied laugh, drawing a scolding "Shush!" from behind, causing them both to make a face and shrink into their chairs.

Miss McCarthy leaned forward to look over at them, sat back up, and whispered to Miss Klug, "Foolish as new colts, the both of them." Then, sighing, she added, "I should give all I own to be like that, once again."

Miss Klug gave her kind, understanding smile, and reached over to hold the old woman's hand as the last song, "Jerusalem," a deeply moving, ethereal piece, was sung by the women of the choral group, who had placed themselves about the old church, carrying candles, the most beautiful thing they had ever heard.

As the carriages carried them home, James thought Brigid seemed unhappy, and he wondered if he had done or said something to upset her. He was unaware that two days before, she had received another letter from her father, but had not yet opened it. She carried it in her bag, where she could not forget it, its weight immense.

*****

Lord Edward Fitzgerald was the son of one of the finest aristocratic families in Ireland. He was young and handsome, a Protestant, a former officer in the British army, a gentleman who had traveled extensively in America and Europe. He was also one of the key leaders of the United Irish movement, and in the spring of 1798 he was largely responsible for planning the coming rebellion. As more and more United Irish leaders were being arrested, Fitzgerald was one of the few who remained at liberty, as the Castle was hesitant to issue a warrant for one of their own. Fitzgerald was a proponent of an immediate and violent rising, refusing to wait for French support. He was married to Stéphanie

Caroline Anne Syms, known as Pamela, a woman of beauty and ability, and they were parents to three young children.

He lived the life of an outlaw, rarely spending two nights under the same roof, steadily issuing orders, actively advocating the violent overthrow of his own class.

*****

James thought of Brigid constantly, well aware of, and completely delighted with, being the cliché of a young man in love.

Every St. Patrick's Day the officers of the Cork Barracks staged a raucous party. Numerous traditions, some not entirely gentlemanly, were adhered to, including the practice of every ensign being required to drink a bottle of wine as quickly as possible, dash out to the courtyard where he would mount a horse, then ride up the steps of the mess, rein in at the head table and sing a ribald soldiers' song.

Of the eight young gentlemen participating, Ensign Lockwood was doing well until, riding into the mess, he struck his head on the lintel, rendering himself insensible, but endearing himself to the roaring older gentlemen. Lockwood did, however, recover in time to participate in another long-standing tradition, in which a secret ballot was held to determine their choice of the most beautiful woman in Cork. Most of the officers had met Miss O'Brian only briefly at the New Year's Ball, but still, she carried the day by a wide margin. Lockwood, somewhat addled with both wine and concussion, was unsure just how to take such open admiration of his sweetheart, but kind comments from a number of the gentlemen convinced him of their genuine regard for her.

The next morning found most of the officers of the barracks indisposed, though Lieutenant Colonel O'Reilly was at his desk, applying himself to the prodigious stack of paperwork which lay there, regimental business which was badly in arrears. O'Reilly, happily long immune to any of alcohol's aftereffects, applied himself to the regiment's business with uncharacteristic diligence, as word had come that Colonel Montgomery was en route to inspect his companies in Cork.

O'Reilly's clerk, a humpback named Fernsby, hurried in to present him with the pay records, records which Fernsby had long been corrupting to his considerable benefit. O'Reilly had specifically asked to review them, so as he laid them on the desk the clerk was happy to say, "By the way, sir, I should mention that Ensign Lockwood is outside, hoping for a word."

O'Reilly looked at the mountain of paper yet to be addressed, slapped the pay roster closed in exasperation, and said, "Do see to the pay again this month, won't you, Fernsby? That's a good fellow. Also, do look into what we spend on coal and candles, as the men are crying out about cold and dark. I tell them this is not St. James, but they are forever crying about their comforts." Straightening his coat, he went on, "And do send Lockwood in, if you please."

Ensign Lockwood looked somewhat the worse for wear, so O'Reilly had him sit. "Now, what brings you in to see me, James?"

"You might recall my interest in Lieutenant Barr's return to the regiment, sir. Today marks the date when his leave is due to end, and I wonder if you have heard of when we might anticipate his return."

"Lieutenant Barr?" O'Reilly turned and dug into a pile of paper, and said, "Oh, yes, I seem to recall you and the lieutenant had a falling out over... what was it, a game of cards?"

"The death of Doctor Oades, sir."

"Yes, yes, pity, that," said O'Reilly absently. "Oh, yes, here it is." He pulled out a letter and in an instant James recognized Barr's hand, the script sharp and angular, the pen cutting deep into the paper. O'Reilly looked it over and went on, "This came in last week. He applied for a ninety-day extension due to his father's poor health. It was granted, of course, our service being of a beneficent nature."

Lockwood clenched both hands into fists, the colour quickly returning to his face as he hurriedly said, "Come now, sir, certainly in must be clear to the meanest understanding that this alleged illness is simply Barr's invention to avoid investigation of the doctor's murder."

"Now, now, son, let us not toss about such harsh language. 'Murder,' for goodness sake. I, for one, understood the affair was conducted according to form; let us not hold grudges. Brother officers and all that, you see? A united face toward the enemy, what? What?"

*****

They had come to love a stand of ancient birch trees that stood on the hill overlooking the school. The trees were just coming into leaf, with a promise of comfort and strength to come. They sat together on a smooth old fallen trunk, their treasured place. It was there that he made her an offer, tearfully accepted, and they had time and privacy to talk and to plan and to dream.

In the manner of young people in love, they soon lay entwined, disheveled and terribly happy, wrapped in his cloak in a private corner of the grove. He ran his fingers through her hair, amazed and delighted, and though a loving smile had not left her face the whole time they were together, eventually a shadow passed over her face, and she said, "Shall you speak with my father, *a grah*?"

I was the first time she had called him *a grah*, love, and his heart leapt. "Must I?" he asked with a laugh.

"Of course you must, sir," she replied, trying to sound serious, but failing. But then the shadow returned, rendering her quite serious, as she added, "I hesitate to say anything which might hinder our happiness, but I must tell you that my father has written to request my immediate return home. He will bring our trap to carry me home very soon, and I am unsure as to how long I shall be away; it is a family matter."

Aunt Áine is taken poorly and is due very soon indeed.

"Oh," he stammered, nonplussed. "You must go, of course, pray do not concern yourself. As to your father... I shall be required to remain in the barracks for several days, as the colonel is due at any time, and there shall be reviews and inspections and such, and so many of our officers are away on leave. But then I shall certainly rent that lovely gray mare from the Red Lion and ride out to Clonakilty to see you, and to speak to your father. So, this Mr. O'Brian of yours; is he very terrible?"

"He is very... traditional, but he does have a good heart, and he treasures an honest man."

"I am not much, but I am that, I think."

"You are indeed, James, and so much more." She kissed him again, but then firmly said, "I fear that there shall be trouble, terrible trouble, soon, and I beg you to take great care. The garrison here in Cork is very strong, is it not? You are quite safe here in your great strong fort?"

"Oh, do not worry for me; it would take five thousand men and a great train of artillery to dig us out of that old pile of stones. Have no fear, my love. We shall be married, Brigid, and that knowledge, that certainty shall sustain us both, no matter what comes."

*****

Colonel Montgomery returned to Cork with new orders from Dublin Castle crinkling in his breast pocket. He called every officer in Cork Barracks into the Mess to hear it read aloud.

"Gentlemen!" he called. "Your complete attention, if you please. I have here a new General Order, issued by the Commander in Chief of His Majesty's forces in Ireland, General Abercromby himself." He read it word for word.

No. VIII
ADJUTANT GENERAL'S OFFICE
GENERAL ORDERS
Dublin, 26ᵗʰ February, 1798

THE very disgraceful frequency of courts-martial, and the many complaints of irregularities in the conduct of the troops of this kingdom, having unfortunately proved the army to be in a state of licentiousness, which must render it formidable to everyone but the enemy....

There followed a general howl of disbelief and rage, including some very pointed comments regarding General Abercromby. Colonel Montgomery, calling them back to order in no uncertain terms, went on with some satisfaction, giving particular emphasis to a portion late in the order:

A very culpable remissness having also appeared on the part of officers, respecting the necessary inspection of barracks, quarters, messes, &c. as well as attendance at roll calls, and other hours, commanding officers must enforce the attention of those under their command to those points, and the general regulations, for all which the strictest responsibility will be expected for themselves.

Montgomery then went on to read orders detailing a massive redeployment of His Majesty's forces in Munster. Many of the rural detachments were to be recalled to Cork Barracks to instill something like discipline. Most of the garrison, some of whom still behaved like soldiers, would in turn be deployed to aid the magistrates in the suppression of rebellion.

Through the long reading of the orders, James listened closely for the one that which most concerned him: "Westmeath Militia, Four Company, Captain Holister, Ensign Lockwood, to Limerick."

Limerick was more than sixty miles to the north, and a hundred miles from Clonakilty.

Nearly every officer of the garrison subsequently tried to schedule an appointment to speak to the Colonel, and only very late in the day, as Montgomery was walking across the wet courtyard to his quarters, did Lockwood finally approach him.

"I beg your pardon, sir, but I wonder if I might trouble you with a request?"

Montgomery, pale and drawn, stopped to look at Lockwood with exasperation. "I am bombarded with requests, Ensign. Know there shall be no thought given to leave for any officer under my command, and any man who makes such a request after hearing such an order from the Commander in Chief shall be judged accordingly, my nephew not excepted."

"Oh, pray do not misunderstand me, sir!" said Lockwood hurriedly. "It is only that my company is to move to Limerick, while Five Company is to transfer to Clonakilty. I ask only that I be allowed to transfer to Five Company, and serve under Lt. Colonel O'Reilly in Clonakilty. I know his company is shorthanded, Ensign Andrews being on leave in England."

Montgomery sniffed and said, "I beg your pardon, James. I had assumed you would be as self-serving as these fools with whom the Castle saddles me. Clonakilty, eh? Are you quite prepared for such a posting?" he asked with some concern. "Things in the smaller towns are quite different from the fortified cities, you know. Whatever would prompt you to request such a transfer?"

Lockwood coloured, stammering, "It is a personal matter, sir."

"I see. That young woman you have been calling on, then? I believe she is a lady of the Catholic faith; I can only imagine your father's reaction to such a relationship." With a hint of a nostalgic smile, Montgomery went on, "Though I imagine my sister would be pleased to hear that her son has found love. Is it indeed love, James? That seems very hurried; are you quite certain of your affections?"

"Oh, yes, sir, quite certain. But my affections aside, sir, I am determined to do my duty. I may be of some use to Lt. Colonel O'Reilly."

Colonel Montgomery stood silent as the cold rain grew heavier, his eyes on the pavers, considering his options. Without looking up, he asked, "You are well acquainted with O'Reilly, James?"

"Oh, yes, sir. He seems a most... capable... gentleman."

"You are your mother's son, James, and no fool, so you know O'Reilly is... oh, he is a good fellow, but the man has no bottom. I speak frankly, placing my trust in you; I can count the officers whose judgement I value on one hand. You are one. Against my better judgement, I shall allow you to go to Clonakilty, and I shall trust you to serve as... well, a bridge, I suppose, between O'Reilly and his company. There are some men in that company who are devoted to the rebel cause, but most might still be convinced to stay with the colours. Make no mistake, nephew, you shall be near your sweetheart, but so too you shall you be placed in a difficult position, one likely to grow damned hot before summer comes."

*****

Diarmuid Doolan was tidying his officer's quarters, a duty that included stoking up the little fireplace (using most of the ensign's remaining peat), drinking the last inch or two from a bottle of the ensign's wine, and sitting in the little apartment's only chair while staring out the window at the pouring rain.

A carriage came up the street, no unusual occurrence, but it stopped in front of Mr. Easton's house, where Ensign Lockwood was billeted. Mr. Easton lived quietly and had few visitors, so it was more unusual still when the carriage door opened and three cloaked women emerged, and, judging by the grace with which all three leapt over the torrent of water at the gutter, they were young women.

The front door knocker clacked, and Doolan heard Margie, the housemaid, hurry down the hall to open the door. There followed the gentle, oddly reassuring, murmurs of female voices, and then a further surprise for Doolan, as there came a soft knock at the room's door. Doolan hid the bottle, buttoned up his coat, and opened the door to see Margie widen her eyes, discreetly toss her head toward the hall, and say, "Three young ladies to see you, Private Doolan."

The loveliest young woman that Diarmuid Doolan had ever seen stepped forward, the colour high in her cheeks, and she said, "I do beg your pardon, sir, for disturbing you, but my friends and I were out calling on friends, and I, we, had hoped to find Ensign Lockwood at home." The other two young ladies stood near the street door, looking uncomfortable, as the maid, at a loss, beat a retreat back toward the kitchen.

"Oh, no, Miss," said Doolan, trying to sound kind, "it's Field Day, isn't it, and the ensign and most of the rest of the garrison will be out drilling in that fec—er, most unfortunate mud." Then, mostly to himself, but still aloud, he added with a satisfied grin, "And won't they be having a time of it."

"Oh," said the young woman, disappointment written in her face. "Well, I wonder if you might tell the ensign that Miss O'Brian, Miss Hendricks, and Miss Reese called."

"I will, indeed, Miss. I am the ensign's soldier servant, if you please, Doolan, private, Westmeath Militia, late of County Donegal. Ensign Lockwood shall be right disappointed to have missed you."

Miss O'Brian glanced back toward her friends, both of whom were edging closer to the door, then nervously added, "We typically do not make calls upon single gentlemen, of course, but I had very much wished to tell him something...."

"Well, Miss," Doolan said with real kindness, the gnarled fellow wholly taken by the young woman's obvious goodness, "if you ladies would care to step inside, you might maybe write him a quick note?"

Miss Hendricks and Miss Reese both gave Miss O'Brian a wild look and a subtle, frantic shake of the head; they had no notion of exploring a single gentleman's apartment, where they might actually see a man's bed. In truth, Brigid and her friends had set out in the King's Inn carriage only after Brigid had begged their help; if she had visited Ensign Lockwood alone, she would have been the talk of the neighborhood.

Looking back at her friends with a bit of defiance, she turned to Doolan and said, "Yes, thank you, Private Doolan, that would be most helpful, *go raibh maith agat.*" May good things come to you. The Irish courtesy was a card she played quietly.

Her play was successful. Doolan paused a moment, and with what grace he could muster, be bowed, and said, "*Tá fáilte romhat, bean uasal óg.*" You are welcome, young gentlewoman.

With that, she followed the redcoat into the small room. It was fortunate that Doolan had been cleaning up, as things were well stowed, the gentleman's laundry was no longer scattered across the floor, and the bed, which the young lady studiously ignored, was neatly made nonetheless.

Doolan quickly realized that he could not recall where, indeed if, his ensign kept pen and paper, the private being unacquainted with the written word. As he hustled to check the few places Lockwood might have stowed such things, he saw Miss O'Brian examining the better of his officer's two coats, scarlet broadcloth, draped across the back of a chair.

Running her hand along the sleeve, she fondly said, "This is the coat Ensign Lockwood wears when he calls on me. He always looks so very dashing."

"Oh," said Doolan, sighing and giving up on his search, "that is my doing, entirely, Miss, my doing entirely. He's an unmade bed by nature, isn't he, but I tidy him up good and proper, and in my care he's as fine a gentleman on the outside as he is, by nature, on the inside."

"You seem very fond of him, Private?" she ventured to ask in Irish, with a curious, tentative smile.

Doolan was incapable of blushing, but by miracle the slightest tinge rose in his cheeks, and raising one corner of his mouth, he replied in his sharp Ulster Irish, "I should never admit it to himself, would I, such things not coming to me naturally, but yes, Miss, to your private ear I confess I have developed a liking for him. You, as well, I think?"

"Oh, very much so, sir, very much so." Allies, now, in language and shared affection, Brigid continued in Irish, "Now, bother yourself no more with the pen and paper— please, may I ask your Christian name, Private Doolan?"

"Diarmuid, please, Miss," said Doolan, enchanted.

"I am called Brigid, daughter of O'Brian. And so, Diarmuid, I shall trust you with this: please tell our friend that I must tomorrow leave for Clonakilty, much against my will, and I shall cling with all my heart to the... agreement... James and I have made, and I place every hope of him finding me in Clonakilty someday very soon." She blushed to the tips of her ears.

"Clonakilty!" cried Doolan. "Why, Miss O'Brian, it was he himself just this morning who told me he had seen fit to join a company marching to Clonakilty itself! With the blessing, we shall be there in a week or two!"

"Oh, has it truly been arranged?" cried Brigid, clasping her hands, and Doolan could have sworn a bright light emanated from every inch of her frame. "Oh, what very good news that is! A thousand thanks! May God place a flower on your head, *a Diarmuid a grah!*" She might have hugged him, but that would have crossed one boundary too many, and her thoughts returning to propriety she went on, "I must go! Pray, give Ensign Lockwood my very, very, fondest regards, won't you?" With that she nearly danced out the door, hurrying away to join her friends.

Chapter Nineteen

Michael O'Brian snapped the reins, startling his cousin Jimmy's two horses. On the trip up from Clonakilty the pair had come to believe the driver to be of a gentle nature, but after picking up a young woman and beginning the pull back toward home they had come to believe otherwise.

The rattled team lost their heads, nearly veering into the ditch, causing O'Brian to pull them over hard, roaring, "*Go dtachta an Diabhal thú!*" The horses, neither of whom wished the devil to choke them, returned to their duty, but remained as upset as the driver.

O'Brian gritted his teeth and growled to his middle daughter, "Brigid, you are stubborn, ill-tempered, and you will not speak to me in such a manner! You are the most willful girl God ever placed on this miserable island. Would either of your sisters say such things to their own father? No, Miss Sassy, they would not. I tell you that rebellion, death, and destruction are coming, and all you can say is, '*Oh, no, Da, things are fine, you worry too much.*' You would rather teach idiots, listen to poofs sing, and go to fancy dances! I have come to save your *life*, girl. You shall be safe at home, with me. Can you not stop your selfish childish mewling and *think*?"

Brigid had been calm enough when her father had come to fetch her, not wishing a scene in front of Miss McCarthy and her friends, but she had loosed her temper as soon as the school was out of view.

She stuck a finger in her father's face, (a gesture she had inherited from her mother, which Michael might have noted, had he been in anything short of a blind fury) and said, "Da, you had best learn I am a full-grown woman, capable of my own damned—"

"My own daughter cursing! And her speaking to her own father! Christ, the things they teach girls in English schools!"

"— *damned* decisions," she continued, raging, her finger never flinching, the colour high in her cheeks, "and it is you, Michael O'Brian, and no other, who taught me to curse!"

"Curse away, child, but rebellion is coming, and know that a young woman alone would be an easy target for rogues of every stripe, once the wolves are loosed!"

A farm cart loaded with cut peat heading toward Cork Town passed them going the other way, and the aged driver shook his head at the young woman haranguing her father, pointed his pipe stem at her, and called over, "You mind your Da, there, young hussy!"

For a moment Brigid had a look of astonishment on her face, gasping, "A hussy, he calls me! And him a stranger to me!" Nonetheless the insult had gone home, and she made an effort to moderate her tone as she told her father, "I am not alone at the school, you know, Da. Miss McCarthy and the other teachers are always there."

"Oh, so your life and honour will be defended by that old bird and a handful of English dainties? Sure, Satan's minions must be shitting themselves."

"More than that, Daidi, we ladies of the school have made some good friends among the soldiers of the garrison, gentlemen who would—"

"Ach!" roared Michael in triumphant exasperation. "Now, that, girl, is another subject I had planned to explore! We might just as well speak of it now as later. Is there some young scoundrel in a soldier's coat who has talked sweet to you, telling you to defy your own father?"

"I shall never lie to you, Daidi, and so, I shall tell you… well, yes, I am… involved with someone." The anger in her tone was gone, replaced by a hesitation, if one toned by pride, and perhaps a bit of wonder.

"Ach, I knew it! Some devil has turned my good girl into this willful harpy. What is the name of this hound, so that I might seek him out and beat the ways of a decent Irish gentleman into his wee frame?"

There followed a long pause, one in which Brigid hesitated, also one in which Michael remained insistently silent, not allowing his daughter to take an easy path. "His name is James Lockwood," she said finally. She was proud of the strength with which she announced him. "He is an officer of the Westmeath Militia Regiment."

"A redcoat *officer*?" cried Michael, pulling the team to a sharp halt. He did not look at his daughter, only crying his disbelief to the muddy road ahead. "*Lockwood*? A Proddy, then! And an Englishman! Jesus, Brigid!"

Brigid, trying to stay calm, trying not to cry, said, "Yes, he is a Protestant, Daidi, but he was born in Malahide…."

"Oh, that makes all the difference, sure! A local oppressor of us and ours, rather than one of the more distant sort. A real catch, him. *Fuck!*"

"Daidi, James and I love one another, and—"

"Love! Jesus. *Love*, girl, is the tool of cads and charlatans."

"You loved Mamaí...."

Michael threw his own finger up in warning, hissing, "You will not foul your mother's memory when speaking of this boy, this *Sassenach* puppy."

Brigid looked down, her hands clenched in her lap, and said, "He is so very kind to me, so very thoughtful...."

"Oh, I'm sure he is, the dog." Michael sighed heavily, then in a tone of disbelief and anger he said, "What the *fuck*, girl, were you *thinking*? I heard the rumors going about, of some redcoat calling on you and all, but I thought him some militiaman, an Irishman and a Catholic, and I thought maybe I'd allow it, but now I see I have been far too easy on you, a fucking doormat, me. You spit on all that I believe, all that I am." In an exhausted, disbelieving tone he added, "God damn it, Brigid. You've brought shame to us all."

They did not exchange another word as Michael pushed the horses hard to carry them the final thirty cold miles back to Clonakilty.

*****

Throughout April, the King's troops scoured Ireland, searching for arms and rebels, terrorizing the common people and burning the homes of anyone suspected of sympathy with rebels. In the south, General Moore, for all his protestations of humanity, reported to the Lord Lieutenant that it was his intention that the moment a single redcoat would appear, the people would flee in terror.

A patrol of the Cumber Yeoman Cavalry had been assigned to work their way up Ballyduvane Road, an Irish mile west of Clonakilty. That troop of the Cumbers, three officers and forty troopers, had been based in Clonakilty for some months, and had grown notorious for their callous brutality.

At the first sight of the Cumbers, the McNamara family at the foot of the road sent their son Paul running up the hill to warn their neighbors. The McNamara family was the first to abandon their home and run out into the fields with their most prized possessions, and they were soon followed by every family up the road in turn. Many of the panicked families pulled their cows behind them, though Matthew Callaghan, inordinately proud of his hog, would not abandon his dear Luch, 'Mouse' in the English, and he tried madly to pull the massive beast up into the hedges.

The O'Brians owned the finest house on the road, and Catholics who put on airs were first to draw the Camber's attentions. Nonetheless, of all the families on the road it was only Michael O'Brian who stood steadfast in front of his home, drawn up to his full height, his arms crossed across his chest, his green caubeen pulled down at a rakish angle, and no trace of fear on his face. When an officer and four troopers reined in and looked down at him in derision, he did not flinch, him offering them only a slight nod and a "Good afternoon, gentlemen."

The fat young officer stretched, yawned, and said, "I am Lieutenant Ross. My men shall search your home and outbuildings. If any contraband is discovered, you shall be, etcetera, etcetera." Looking back toward his eager troopers, he flicked two fingers toward the O'Brian house and said, "Have at it, then."

O'Brian shook his head, pulled a paper from his coat pocket, and, holding it up, he said, "I am a long trusted employee of Lord Shannon, and I hold here proof of his protection—." The troopers, who had begun to swing down from their horses, slowly settled back into their saddles. In

West Cork, Lord Shannon's word was second to only to God's, and typically more discernable.

Lieutenant Ross's demeanor changed, and he reached down to accept the letter from O'Brian with tentative courtesy. By the time he returned it, the courtesy was not feigned. He nodded, and said, "Your servant, sir." Then turning to his men, he said, "Move on."

The troopers were slow to follow Ross up the road. One, a pimple faced boy, spoke to the others, loudly enough for O'Brian to hear. "Have you seen this Papist's daughters? The middle one is the finest, and I hear she's back from school. Lord Shannon or no, given a half a chance, I'd fuck some of that learning out of her, I can tell you."

O'Brian could only slowly exhale and glare.

With insolent smirks the Cambers turned their horses and rode on.

*****

On a typically chill, damp, April Irish morning, Lt. Colonel O'Reilly and Ensign Lockwood rode slowly south out of Cork Town. Lockwood rode a tall chestnut mare. He reached over to pat her neck, and said, "I thank you again, sir, for the loan of your horse, particularly one so lovely as this."

"Oh, pray do not mention it," said O'Reilly, beaming. "My family maintains quite a good stable, so it was nothing for me to send for an extra mount. God, this is all quite exciting, is it not? An independent command, at last! Glory awaits, James, and I assure you that there is honour enough for us both! I do hope, though, that this new company is not composed of sullen brutes... it will make things so unpleasant if they do not spring to command as they ought."

"Regarding that subject, sir," said Lockwood, "I took the liberty of calling on Lieutenant Hazelton, who had been with Five Company, and who is now confined to hospital in very poor health. He has been ill for some months now, but he kindly gave me a summary of the company's state, if you should care to hear it, sir."

"Oh well, yes, that would be useful, I suppose."

"Well, sir, it looks as if we shall have our hands full. For some months the men of Five Company have been scattered across the forts, guarding the Cobh of Cork. That type of dispersion is, I'm sure you'd agree, sir, detrimental to morale and discipline."

"Oh, yes, quite... well, unfortunate, as it were."

James sighed, not for the first time that morning, and went on, "Yes, sir. Twenty men were at Cove Fort, living in a miserable basement barracks. Forty others had been sent out to Spike Island Fort, which is a cold, wet, lonely posting. Forty others were sent down to Fort Camden, that is the battery on the harbour's south side, sir, where they served under Captain Gabriel of the Royal Artillery." He spoke the name with some significance, hoping to draw a response from the colonel.

"Yes, yes," chirped O'Reilly. "I have heard that name mentioned in company. Is he not known... well, for something?"

"Yes, sir, he is a renowned officer of the Orange Order, and a rabid enemy of the Catholics."

"Oh, my." After a long pause, O'Reilly added, "I wager many men of the company are of the Catholic faith, are they not, James?"

"Well, yes, sir, likely all of them."

For all his odd ways, O'Reilly was a fine horseman. Like Lockwood, the Colonel handled his reins only in his left hand, the military man's way to ride, leaving his sword hand free. A stylish carriage on the way into town passed them, the prosperous family waving, the children crying, "Oh, hello, soldiers! Huzzah! Huzzah!"

Lockwood touched his hat. O'Reilly took his off and waved it in enthusiastic response, then turned to tell Lockwood, "That's why I'm a soldier, sir. Did you see how they loved us? God, what glory it is to wear the King's coat. But you were speaking of service matters, and I do not wish to interrupt. My orders state that I am to relieve a Captain..."

"Maxwell, sir."

"Yes, that's the fellow. What of him?

"Evidently, sir, the captain seldom deemed it necessary to spend time with his company, and having been granted leave to visit his fiancée in Dorset, he has not bothered to return."

"So, I take it, these men we are to command might not be in the best of spirits."

"Quite right, sir." A patient pause. "There have been several instances of misbehavior. Several men have been flogged for drunkenness, insubordination, theft and fighting. One was hanged for murder. Two others were found guilty of Republican sympathies, and so were hanged. It seems, sir, that our company is in rather a shambles."

"Oh, let us not fret over details. We shall lead Five Company to glory! This posting to Clonakilty might seem a small step, but it shall lead to great things for us both, my boy, just you wait and see."

*****

Royal Navy barges gathered the seventy men of Five Company from around Cobh Harbour and rowed them across to Ringaskiddy of the harbour's west side. There the company was joined by a nervous young lieutenant named

Melinydd of the regiment's depot company, who had brought a draft of thirty new recruits to bring the company up to full strength. The draft had been brought down from Dublin by sea, as the new men were prone to desertion.

Lieutenant Melinydd and the company NCOs were hard pressed to march the hundred men the fifteen miles west to Ballinhassig, where the company's new officers were to join them. At one point two young men tried to run, and were dragged by their sergeants and thumped back into place. Their names were marked for flogging when the company reached Clonakilty Barracks.

The company spent the night in a barn in Ballinhassig, and as they formed to march the second leg of their route, O'Reilly and Lockwood rode into sight. Melinydd was only too pleased to be relieved. As he mounted and rode off, he called out to the men, "Best of luck, Five Company! All the best!"

A few men called out a farewell, but by and large the men of the company looked sullen and ill-tempered. Lockwood thought the colonel would address them, try to build some type of bond, but he only called out, "Company! March!" and so with the two horsemen at their head, the column began its match toward Bandon Barracks, another fifteen miles off.

The men of the company might have been ill-tempered and grumbling, but most of them were soldiers. They fell into the ancient ways of infantry: marching beside their mates, weapons on their shoulders; steady footsteps mingling with the sounds of rattling equipment; mostly silent, heads down, going about the business of putting miles behind them.

The day was fine, the route reasonably short, and Bandon Barracks was expecting them. The company was given an unexpectedly good meal and decent quarters, and only the best for its officers.

The next morning, however, cold rain and howling winds delayed their departure. It was after noon before they set out, fifteen miles from Clonakilty. O'Reilly checked his pocket watch several times. After a few miles, he pulled his bicorn down against the cold rain, turned to Lockwood, and said, "You know, James, I believe I shall ride ahead and ensure the barracks is up to snuff. Good of the men, and all that, you know. You can manage, can you not, James?"

"I suppose so, sir, if you think that best," said Lockwood with some surprise.

"Yes, and in truth, I should be loath to be late for dinner there, as there was to be a bit of a welcome dinner for me... us... and one hates to disappoint one's new comrades, eh? Eh?" With that he spurred his mount into a trot, calling out, "I shall see you there!"

The Colonel had insisted that he and Lockwood ride at the head of the column, but as he was now his own boss, James pulled his horse aside to let the company pass him. He studied them, and many of them studied him, their faces a mix of curiosity, mistrust and some flashes of enmity.

At the rear of the column their drummer hobbled painfully, one of his friends carrying his drum, two others trying to help him along. Lockwood was ashamed not to have noticed earlier. He quickly called a halt and learned the man's name was O'Malley.

While most of the men tried to find a dry spot along the road to sit, O'Malley dropped to the ground, wincing. Crouching beside him, Lockwood asked, "What ails you, Drummer O'Malley?"

"Beg pardon, sir. It was the dear Doctor Oades, God rest him, who told me I have the rheumatism. It was he himself who showed me how to make a poultice to treat the worst of it, but this cold and wet has fucked me, sure."

There were a few buildings scattered about, but Lockwood could see nowhere he could safely leave the man. Shrugging, he said, "Well, then, Drummer, there is nothing for it. You shall ride, and I shall walk."

"A horse, sir?" asked O'Malley, astonished. "Whatever would I do on the back of a horse, Your Honour? The lads'll say it's me playing the favorite. No, that won't do at all, at all."

"Well, O'Malley, unless you can sprout wings, we shall have to leave you here in the ditch. And those fellows at the door of the shebeen down the road look as if they would be pleased to come over here and cut a man's throat for tuppence."

O'Malley made a pained grin, and said, "I could always tell those shebeen boys I'm a deserter, and come to rally to the Republic, sir." Then, sniffing in dark amusement, he added, "Though that lot would likely be more pleased with tuppence than any fool cause. And these days a man in a red coat has a hard time making new friends, doesn't he?"

With an amused sniff of his own, Lockwood replied, "I have found that to be very true, Drummer."

"Well, then, sir, I had best get up on that beast's back, if she'll have me."

The ensign was pleased to see O'Malley's friends hustle over to help him to his feet. As the drummer limped past the horse's head he paused and spoke softly to her in his melodic Irish. O'Malley was in such pain that he could not use the stirrup, and so his friends had to lift him up into the saddle. O'Malley looked thoroughly uncomfortable, and as Lockwood handed him the reins he asked, "What was it you said to the horse, Drummer?"

"Well, sir, I humbly begged her pardon for taking advantage, but as she is an amiable creature, she offered me a wee ride."

One of the men who had helped hoist O'Malley into the saddle barked a laugh and howled, "That's the only female, on two legs or four, that has ever offered a ride to Seamus O'Malley!"

It was the first general laughter of the day, and Lockwood took advantage of it, walking up the column before it faded, calling with a tone of authority, but not an unkind one, "On your feet, there, men. We're off. On your feet. You, soldier, what's your name? Private Dougherty, then, you seem to be one of the stronger men. Do what you can for your mates, will you? Good man. You, sir, for God's sake don't leave your musket in the mud. On your feet, there." At age seventeen, falling into a new role.

One of the men the ensign passed tossed his head back toward O'Malley and quietly offered, "That was good in ya, sir."

Looking up and down the column, sensing more energy, perhaps even a trace of good will, Ensign Lockwood called, "All ready, then? Company! Route march... march!"

They headed down the darkening road.

Chapter Twenty

"You know," said Tadg O'Donovan, staring into the fading embers of his hearth fire, "in the end, you are the only man I can speak to of such things. Some of the men of the movement look to me as some sort of pope, writ small." Taking a long drink of *uisce beatha,* he went on, "When I am, in fact, merely a carpenter with a bad back and an affinity for wayward barmaids. Oh, and a hatred for the English, of course, which I suppose is my most laudable attribute."

"Oh, believe me, brother, I am all too familiar with your faults," said Michael O'Brian. "In addition to your confessed failings, I might add that you are far too willing to drink a friend's whiskey, and I know for a fact that you fart far more often than the average Christian."

Slumping in his chair, O'Donovan sniffed in amusement, and said, "Kiss my pink arse, O'Brian."

A long, comfortable silence, until O'Brian said, "Did you know, Tadg, I saw you at Donal Quincy's wake last week?"

"I saw you as well. It is well that we did not speak, as there were a great number of my men there."

"Shit, your house is always cold," said O'Brian, and he leaned forward and tossed another peat log onto the fire, its smoke instantly filling the room with the sharp smell of Irish home life. "The widow Quincy," he said, "God, what an awful woman, but she did manage to hire a fine fiddler for the wake. Did you hear him playing 'Galway Rambler'? If I should die tomorrow, you must find that fiddler and have him play that tune at my wake. God, what a master. That's a tune a man might dance to!"

O'Donovan sniffed, took a long drink, and with a stifled smile said, "Dancing? Christ, there shall be dancing at your wake in any case. I dare say it could not be repressed, not to mention the general merriment."

O'Brian laughed, tossed back the last of his glass, and said, "It's late. I should go home."

In the dim light of his hearth, the leader of the West Cork United Irishmen waved O'Brian back into his seat, poured him another drink, and said, "I promise, this shall be the last glass. Just allow me a few minutes more to bemoan my fate, and then I shall send you home to your girls."

"If your men knew I was here, many... well, some... of them would think you guilty of keeping company with a traitor."

"Fuck them. They are afraid of their own shadows. Rebellion is a nasty business, and some of those boys need to grow a pair." O'Donohue hissed in frustration, and went on, "Did you hear, Michael, that in Dublin most of the Central Committee is arrested? Feckin' informers again. A meeting at Bond's house was betrayed, and most of the Committee was swept up like yesterday's dust. All save Neilson and Fitzgerald, who were late. Imagine that, saved from the gallows by a lack of punc... ah fuck, what is the word?

"Punctuality."

"Just so. So, now the Central Committee consists of two men: Nielson, a Presbyterian newspaperman with the military experience of a schoolgirl, and Lord Edward feckin' Fitzgerald, a Proddy enthusiast, a fancy one-time officer with a pretty wife, an aristocrat who lacks the sense God grants a rabbit." O'Donovan exhaled sharply, and said, "Christ, I am drunk."

They sat together some minutes in silence as the fire burned down, and they heard a stoat take a rabbit just outside O'Donovan's door, the rabbit screaming in the pure voice of agony.

O'Brian poured himself two fingers more, tossed them back, and asked in steady voice, "When will it begin?"

"Soon, or never. Before the whole of the country is thrown in gaol, someone, God knows who, shall give the word and the Dublin lads will stop the mail coaches. That will be the signal."

"I tell you, brother," said O'Brian, steadily growing more angry, "the whole world is crumbling around us. Did you know that my daughter, *my* daughter, is in love with an Englishman?"

"Humph. That upsets you, I suppose?"

"Of course it does, ya ignorant prick."

O'Donovan was silent for several minutes, and O'Brian wondered if he had gone to sleep, until he muttered, "I wonder if we have poisoned our people, forcing them into one side or the other, white or black, and naught but hatred for the other." He abruptly sat up, rubbed his face with both hands, and quickly added, "Maybe we should shut the fuck up and let them find what happiness they may."

In a voice tainted with real pain, O'Brian said, "Happiness, Tadg? You make a poor revolutionary, brother."

"If I should cause harm to this Proddy boy, and so bring your daughter grief, I would regret it all the days of my life."

*****

Her second day at home, and hardly a word spoken to her, Brigid put on her bonnet, and said in a muted tone, "I am going into town for salt."

The stony silence that was now the norm in that typically gregarious house was shattered by Caitlin, the younger sister, who suddenly cried out, "But, Da! You said we weren't to go out alone! Why does Brigid get to go to town, and Ann and I not?"

Michael O'Brian, sitting in his usual place by the window, said from behind his newspaper, "She has nothing to fear from redcoats, does she?"

"Oh!" gasped Brigid in angry hurt, and so she walked quickly, blindly, to the door and slammed it closed behind her. As she stalked down the road toward town, not bothering to preserve her boots or hems from the mud, she held her basket in one hand and ran the back of the other across her eyes, determined not to cry.

She had expected her father's fury, but had not anticipated how deeply it would hurt her. She had expected, too, that her sisters might show her some resentment, for she had left them for the glories of Cork Town. She had, however, clung to the hope that they might support her in her love for James. That hope had proved vain. Her father had announced Brigid's choice of man the moment they walked in the door, in sullen shame, telling Ann and Caitlin that, "All that is lacking is for her to marry the *Sassenach*, and our humiliation shall be complete."

Caitlin had immediately taken her father's side, and when Ann had hissed her usual, "Oh Brigid! How could you!"

Brigid knew she had lost her last hope of an ally. She wondered if Ann was more upset about Brigid's connection to a Protestant redcoat officer or the thought of a younger sister usurping her place as the first to find love.

As Brigid passed the McNamara farm at the bottom of the road, she saw the whole family out tending their lazy beds. As she expected, they studiously ignored her, though their two dogs, Bréagh and Amadán, Dummy and Stupid, came out with tails wildly wagging to say hello. They had long been friends with Brigid, and as she bent to scratch behind their ears she took some comfort in knowing that Mr. McNamara had allowed them to come out to see her.

She had the rest of the long walk into town to calm herself, and to consider her options. All her plans, though, still revolved around James Lockwood. For him, she would throw away all she held dear.

The closer she got to town the friendlier people became. It interested her to see how news of her downfall—it amused her to think of herself as fallen—had yet to travel as far as Clonakilty proper, though she was certain that the stories would arrive soon enough. Several people offered her polite greetings, and a few folks with whom she was acquainted asked her about her work in wildly exotic Cork Town.

The shopkeeper at McGivney's was particularly kind to her, and after selling her a pound of salt he gave her a bit of taffy as a welcome home gift. She allowed herself the luxury of wandering past the village shops for a while, certain she would not be missed at home.

She paused to look in the window of Mrs. Sheehan's dress shop, staring at a blue silk gown with a daring neckline, wondering if she would ever own such a beautiful dress, when she felt someone come up close behind her, too close, a tall, somehow threatening shadow, and then the terrible, familiar voice.

"You know, O'Brian, I could buy that dress for you. You could dress up to entertain me, my pet. You could do —"

She whirled to face him, trying to back away but she was pinned to the wall. It could not be, but it was he, Charles Barr grinning down at her. Stunned and deathly afraid, she quickly crossed herself and whispered, *"Dia eadrainn agus olc,"* God between us and evil. She tried to gather herself, feeling so very small, so very weak. "Captain Barr, how did... Jesus... I thought myself done with you, sir," pushing past him into the street, "and yet you haunt me still. I do not wish to speak with you, sir."

She pulled her shawl up over her head, both hands pulling it down, a shelter, as he called after her, "Come, now, O'Brian, can we not be friends?" but she did not respond, did not pause, drawing stares from the people there, the poor girl hurrying away as the redcoat roared in harsh laughter.

It seemed impossibly far down Patrick Street to the stables at the corner, but finally reaching Sovereign Street and turning toward home she began to run, running like the girl she had been, the tears flowing freely, not caring who saw her or what they thought of her.

*****

It was twilight as Five Company drew near to Clonakilty. A rider came trotting up the road toward them, and Lockwood recognized the blue coat and crested helmet of the yeoman cavalry. He did not much care for yeomen. Still, the trooper was polite, saluting and saying, "Corporal McAndrew, Camber Yeomanry, please, sir, dispatched to escort you to the barracks."

Pleased that he would not have to stumble around in the dark in an unfamiliar town full of people who may or may not wish to see him dead, Lockwood exhaled in relief and happily said, "Lead on, MacDuff."

"McAndrew, please, sir," said the man with some irritation.

Lockwood shrugged and waved him on. Most of those final miles were downhill, the smell of the sea in their noses, the knowledge of a warm meal ahead giving some spring to their steps.

The Clonakilty Barracks were small, but new. The buildings and their perimeter wall stood on the north side the of town, and as the weary company neared their new home Lockwood saw that the other men of the garrison, a company of the Galway Militia and a troop of the Camber Yeomanry, were drawn up in the yard to salute their new comrades. It was a handsome compliment, and Lockwood ordered the company to halt and form up into something resembling a military column. There was discernable grumbling, some of it intentionally loud enough for the young officer to hear, but a few of the men still had a soldier's sense of ceremony, and Lockwood heard one man say to his neighbors, "Oh, shut up, you ignorant bastard. Act the part for a few minutes, won't you? Jesus."

Drummer O'Malley insisted on dismounting, and with his mates' help he slid down and hobbled over to take his place near the head of the column. With their gentleman back on horseback, as God intended, O'Malley tapped out the step as the company made its entrance. Their performance was not discreditable, and after the requisite salutes and introductions the men were dismissed to their dinner, while the other officers returned to their quarters, leaving O'Reilly and Lockwood to talk in the dark cobbled yard.

"Now, James," said O'Reilly with a hand on the young man's shoulder, "I have a rather difficult task with which to task you, but I have every confidence that you shall comport yourself as an honorable gentleman, a young officer destined for great things. Pray, follow me into the mess." Curious, James followed him through the doors. In the anteroom O'Reilly unbuckled his sword belt and hung it on the pegs lining the walls, and Lockwood followed his example. "There are no swords allowed in the mess here, a tradition I believe you shall find in all well run barracks." Leading James into the officer's mess, he nodded significantly toward a man sitting at the far side of the room.

James would not have been more surprised if the devil himself had been sitting at table, and perhaps there was small difference, for it was Charles Barr behind one of the long mess tables, his feet up, sipping wine, completely at his ease. Barr, however, had evidently not been informed of mess traditions, as he had his sword on his hip. Either O'Reilly did not notice, or he chose not to challenge him on the point.

"God damn it," whispered Lockwood, instinctively reaching for the sword that he had set aside.

"Now, then," said O'Reilly, reassuringly. "You gentlemen are well acquainted. I ask that you both comport yourselves like King's officers. I shall step out of the room, and trust you to resolve your differences without passion, in the spirit of Christian gentlemen. But duty does require me to remind you both of two rules which must not be trespassed upon, not that gentlemen such as yourselves would ever forget such precepts. One: duels between officers of differing rank are forbidden. Two: dueling in time of war is forbidden, and it is war we are involved in, gentlemen; do not mistake." With that, O'Reilly spun on his heel, and hurried out.

Lockwood's shock morphed into rage, and he strode across the room, crying out, "You bastard! You made out to be my friend, but you are nothing but a poxed murderer! Oades never had a chance!"

The long heavy table separated them. Lockwood kept himself from lunging across the table, but thumped both fists on to the wood, leaning heavily toward Barr, while the lean lieutenant sat at his ease, nonchalant, perhaps even slightly amused.

"Goodness, James, what a sniff you are in. Your words are most hurtful, but in honour of our former, much lamented, friendship, I shall let it pass." He sipped his wine, set the glass down, and went on, "And, of course, as you and O'Brian know, as *only* you two know, I perhaps deserve that first moniker, even if 'poxed' is such an unkind term. 'Murderer', though? Hardly. I have fought many duels, and if the other party was not as skillful as I, that is surely not my fault."

At the mention of Brigid's name, the realities of the situation began folding in on Lockwood, and he gasped, "But how... why... the hell did you come here, of all places?"

"Oh, that is a charming tale," said Barr with a sudden, slightly mad, cheerfulness. "Your uncle, that raging poof, saw to it that I had no future with the Westmeaths—which is just as well, as the regiment is populated with idiots, pederasts, weaklings and, as I mentioned, damned poofs—so I exchanged into the Galways." Holding up his elegantly tailored scarlet sleeve, he went on, "Besides, I rather like the black facings. *Très gothique, non*? At any rate, the Galways were pleased to have me, having been given an account, however exaggerated, of my spectacular martial exploits."

"But you murdered a brother officer! Christ, you were hissed out of one of His Majesty's regiments!"

"Oh, what stuff and nonsense. Fighting is frowned on, but boys will be boys. Besides, certain allowances are offered to officers of experience in these troubled times. The Galways were having rather a hard time keeping their men in line, and were frankly elated to have me join. How very charming of them."

James pulled out a chair, and sat down hard. He took a moment to study Barr: thinner now, pale, unwell. The mad gleam in his eye was even more pronounced, like light dancing on a knife's edge.

Barr set aside his glass, plucked an apple from a nearby bowl, sighed, and after a deliberate bite, he said, "No hearty congratulations on my return to active service, James? You will not wish me joy? You are not in a forgiving mood, are you? Well, then, I shall sum up my happy tale: the Galways had thought to post me to their company in Cork, but I think both you and I know that Cork might have proven a tad *warm* for me. They then suggested that I join one of their companies in Clare—can you imagine *me* in Clare, for God's sake?—but when I saw they had a company in Clonakilty—a most happy coincidence, don't you think?—I simply insisted on coming down here."

Aghast and pale, Lockwood sat up straight. "You are *posted* here, then? Jesus."

"I had wondered if our lovely mutual friend might scurry home to Clonakilty when things got messy, and I was right! How clever I am. I saw her in the street today, and she was so pleased to see me. She was in looks, I can tell you, and I nearly dragged her into the alley to—"

James lunged across the table. In a blur, Barr was on his feet and his sword halfway out of the sheath.

"Now, now," said Barr as they each froze in place. "Remember, we mustn't fight. We both want to keep our commissions. And we both want to give O'Brian—"

O'Reilly burst back into the mess hall, booming, "I trust fences are mended, gentlemen, brother officers once more?" He then saw James, still halfway across the table, and Barr, coiled behind it, his hand on his sword hilt. As Lockwood and Barr straightened and backed away from one another, he nervously went on, "Well, that is all settled, then. Come, Ensign Lockwood, let us see to our quarters." With false bonhomie he added, "These rascals from the Galways and Cambers have taken most of the prime rooms, but I hear there are two officer's rooms together on the north wall which are yet available. Come, now, sir, glory awaits!"

Lockwood gave Barr one last look of hatred, then turned to leave. At the door, O'Reilly turned to study Barr for a moment, a puzzled look in his eyes.

"Never fear, Colonel O'Reilly," said Barr in a reassuring tone. "Young James and I shall be fast friends soon enough. After all, we have so many interests in common."

<h1 style="text-align:center">Chapter Twenty-One</h1>

"You had best wear your brown coat. It is a fine old coat, and less likely to attract lead," said Diarmuid Doolan, as he watched his officer dress.

"No, I think not," said Ensign Lockwood. "I shall present myself as the man I am."

"Well, then," Doolan fussed, "don't go alone. Take a friend, for all love. I hear there are rebels behind every hedge down here, bloodthirsty savages, these southerners." Then muttering to himself, "Oh, but you have no friends, do ya?" He then added, louder, "Perhaps that false Irishman... your Colonel O'Reilly... ask him to ride with you. He can draw some of their fire, at least."

Lockwood sighed, pulled on his coat, his scarlet coat, and said, "You are of no help whatsoever."

Doolan, wounded, howled, "What, is your shirt not the cleanest in all this God-forsaken wilderness?"

"This is West Cork, not the Congo." As he straightened his stock he quietly added, "The colonel has given his permission for me to make this call, but he made it clear he does not care to venture out of town without the entire company at his back."

Doolan had arrived a day before the company, in a hired cart with O'Reilly's two servants. The ensign's baggage consisted of one chest, while the colonel traveled with six. Lockwood's quarters in Clonakilty barracks were spacious, at least by military standards, as they had been intended for more senior officers. O'Reilly, however, had kindly insisted the ensign reside there, deliberately as far from Lieutenant Barr's quarters as possible.

Lockwood placed his bicorn on his head, at the jaunty angle Tom Mainwaring had taught him back at Mullingar barracks. The first time James had put on the uniform he'd felt he was play-acting, but now the bicorn, the uniform, the role, unconsciously fit him.

Doolan took up a brush to get the last of the dust from the scarlet broadcloth, and relentless, he went on, "Well, even as much as a Christian loathes the yeomen, why not take a few of those brutes with you, as an escort, like?"

"I am going to call on a young lady's father, Doolan, not galloping off on an arms raid," said Lockwood casually, trying to ignore the knot of anxiety that kept trying to make itself fully known. "Though I will bend one rule of etiquette, in that I shall wear my sword, despite this being a social call."

"Well, do you at least know where you'll be going? Or shall you tell your horse to find the prettiest girl in Ireland, and trust it to find the way?"

"She lives on Ballyduvane Road," said Lockwood with just a hint of uncertainty. "It is on the west side of town. I shall ride out that way, and then... ask for directions."

Doolan rolled his eyes, and as he put away the last of the ensign's things, he muttered to himself, "Jesus. I can see it now: 'Beg pardon, my good sir, but after you and your friends have stopped shooting at me, might I ask the way to Ballyduvane Road?'"

Lockwood had long before learned to ignore Doolan's muttering. Instead, he studied himself in the mirror, fully accoutered, nodded, and said, "I know this isn't the best coat in the kingdom, but you have made it look quite fine. Well done, Doolan."

"I brushed and brushed, didn't I?" said Doolan, brightening. "And I polished those old brass buttons until the angels themselves might see their reflections, then sewed them on double-strength. Our Miss O'Brian deserves the best, does she not?"

"She does, indeed, Private." Then with a voice that betrayed some of his anxiety, he added, "I had best be off."

In the yard, Lockwood found the stable boy had brought his mare around, but five men of Five Company stood there as well, muskets on their shoulders. "Whatever are you men doing turned out? You were to have the whole of the day to rest. Surely you have not been called out for guard duty? I shall speak to the colonel —"

"Oh, never you worry, sir," said one of the men, a corporal. "It's just that me and a few of the lads here, why, we enjoyed the past few days so much, walking about, and were talking to Private Doolan, here, that we tossed in for a wee walk today as well." Then, as Doolan came down the steps behind Lockwood, he asked him, "Where are we bound, then, Diarmuid?"

"West of town, lads. Just a few miles, I'd think."

Each of the men carried his musket, cartouche, stuffed haversack and canteen, and more equipment had been stacked besides the officers' quarters steps. Doolan quickly threw on his pack and slung his musket, and when the surprised ensign caught his eye, Doolan sniffed, and in an irritated tone he said, "It's just as I predicted, you being stubborn, going out alone with all these rebels about, and we can't be having that. Our Miss might be unhappy if you was found full of holes by the side of the road. Besides, my every joint is stiff after riding all the way from Cork in that damned cart, bouncing and jolting, and I need a bit of a stroll to work out these pains, don't I?" A deliberate pause ticked away before he added, "Sir."

"Well," said Lockwood, blushing in an unmilitary fashion, "this is quite good in you men. I thank you." Looking over at his tall mare, he went on, "But I should look rather foolish, I think, mounted while the six of you march behind. Perhaps it would be best if I went on foot as well."

"Yes, sir," said Doolan. "We were thinking that as well. The local folk might take it better, so, as being somewhat less... ah what was the fine word you were saying earlier, John Coleman?"

"Provocative," said one of the men, with a knowing look.

"Very well, then," said the ensign. "I should not wish to appear provocative. On foot I shall go." He dismissed the stable boy, though the horse gave Lockwood a quite discernable look of disappointment. The ensign then looked over his little command, and said, "I ask your pardon, men, but as we are new together, I am still hesitant on names. Corporal... Nugent, is it not? Pray, remind me."

The corporal nodded, and said, "Nugent, yes, sir." Then pointing out the others, he went on, "Privates Murtagh, Brady, Coleman, and O'Hea. Sinners of a moderate bent, each one, but good lads in a pinch, and not quick to take offence, if you take my meaning, sir."

"I do indeed, Corporal. All right, off we go, then."

The two Galways who had the guard saluted as the tall young Westmeath officer and his men approached the gate.

One of the Galways nervously spoke up, "Beg pardon, sir, but standing orders state that sorties consist of fifty men or more, sir."

Barely pausing to reply, Lockwood, feeling wildly reckless, waved him aside and said, "Do not concern yourself, Private. The other forty-three shall be coming along shortly."

Sharing grins like boys out of school, the seven men walked into town. Redcoats were not an uncommon sight, though such a small group was rare. With the recent spate of harsh steps enacted by the military, the men who had had once been tolerated, accepted as a necessary inconvenience, were now widely hated. Most of the people on the streets of Clonakilty thus went out of their way to avoid the seven Westmeaths, eying them with suspicion, or worse.

It was somewhat disconcerting, then, when Private O'Hea stopped a man on the street to ask about the sheep he was leading up the road. The man, Patrick Cronin, was leading his prize Belclare ewe, Fonn, across town to be bred with Nevan Murphy's ram. When the soldiers started to ask Cronin about Fonn, he was at first afraid they intended to make stew of her, but Private O'Hea had been raised a on a sheep farm, and in Meath was once renowned for his knowledge of Summer Mastitis. The other four Meath men, too, knew one end of a sheep from another, and the soldiers had a brief, informed and amicable discussion with Cronin.

Lockwood and Doolan, further up the road, thus had a moment to talk quietly. "So, tell me," asked Lockwood, "just how did you convince these fellows to come along on this little adventure? They scarcely know me... and they have just met you."

Doolan said, "Irishmen adore a love story, don't they? And of the men of the company, these five are the ones who have decided they like you. Sir."

Lockwood sighed and said, "So, you took a poll, Doolan? Five out of a hundred?"

"You're doing better than O'Reilly. Null out of a hundred, him."

Lockwood mouthed a curse and looked back toward his men, who took the hint. O'Hea shook Cronin's hand, they wished one another God's blessings, and the redcoats walked further up Sovereign Street. There were plenty of shops, but few people shopping, and a general air of poverty and unhappiness haunted the place. Still, after a long, wet winter, the town had been blessed by a warm spring, holding a promise of a good harvest come fall, with a farm town's flickering hope of better days ahead.

As the soldiers left town and passed into the rolling hills, there were some casual insults shouted at them, sometimes openly, sometimes from behind a hedge, but, as Corporal Nugent had predicted, the men of the patrol took no offence, only good-naturedly suggesting that the other fellow go lie across himself.

On only one occasion was there a chance of real trouble. Lockwood and his men passed a roadside shebeen, a common feature of rural Ireland, and at the announcement of a handful of redcoats coming up the road the patrons tumbled out the door to have some fun, emboldened by liberal application of poteen. They numbered twenty or more, with stout *bata*, Irish fighting sticks, in their hands.

One of the younger local men stepped out into the road, pointed out the young officer with his cudgel, and said, "You should have brought more men."

Private Coleman loudly replied, "That's what your sister told us last night, mate," with unfeigned confidence, long the mark of tough men.

Coleman's witticism drew barks of laughter from both the soldiers and the shebeen men. The redcoats did not hesitate, walking past the shebeen with scarcely a glance. One of the biggest of the toughs, grinning, tossed a thumb after them and said, "They're all right, aren't they?" and that was the end of it. The soldiers went on their way, and the locals returned to their cups, still laughing at the insulted youngster.

The redcoats were a mile west of town when Lockwood finally decided to ask directions. That was easier said than done, as the road was scarcely populated, and anyone coming down the road toward them quickly took to the fields, giving the redcoats a wide berth.

It was only when Lockwood and his men crested a hill did they come upon an old two-wheeled cart, pulled by an ancient horse, driven by an even older man, at last finding someone unable to flee them, someone who might be pressed for directions.

"I beg your pardon, sir—" began Lockwood.

"*Gan aon Bhéarla*," no English, said the old man from up on his seat, who despite his obvious fear was as obviously defiant.

Private Doolan rolled his eyes, stepped forward, and said in Irish, "Oh, don't be an ass, brother. Where lies the road of the fort of Duvane? We mean no harm to you, or those who live on that dear road."

The cartman, despite the outrageous accent of this Donegal fellow, recognized he was being addressed as an honest man, by an honest man, and so shrugged and pointed out the way, and as he had some conscience, he added, "But know, soldier, they are good folks up there, and would not hurt a fly, would they? You'll not burn and turn to foul rapine?"

"No worries, brother, as it's on a social call we are, we being as harmless as Saint Kevin, and as poor."

And so further up into the low hills they went, the narrow road, lined with hedges, low stone walls, and small, meager homes abandoned at their approach. At the foot of Dunleavy Road itself they passed a small but tidy farm where an older woman came out into her yard, saw the redcoats, dropped her bucket and gave a squeak of alarm.

Ensign Lockwood, who had grown increasingly withdrawn and pale as they came nearer the O'Brian house, had nothing to say to the woman, and so once again it was Doolan who spoke, saying, "Don't concern yourself, sister, at all, at all, as it is not the devil's business we're on, but Christian visiting. Now, pray, might you point out the door of one Michael O'Brian, the fine man he is?"

She eyed them suspiciously, and seemed to have a wicked reply at the tip of her tongue, but then her face changed, and to the anguished young man she said, in English, "You're Brigid's sweetheart, then?"

Surprised, concerned, but also a bit flattered, Lockwood flushed, and said, "Yes, ma'am."

She studied him for a moment, seemed satisfied, and so nodded, and pointed up the road. "The third house on the left." Lockwood thanked her, and as the soldiers turned to go, she added matter-of-factly, "Brigid's mother, Aisling Bean Uí Brian, was a friend of mine, young *Sassenach*, so just know that if you break her heart, Caoimhe Uí McNamara shall come for you. You'll not be wanting that, son."

"No, ma'am. Thank you, ma'am."

That exchange drew furtive grins from the other men of the party, but when Doolan looked over at his officer, he saw the young man had gone quite still, staring up the hill toward the O'Brian house. Seeing the poor man ashen, a gleam of sweat on his brow, Doolan leaned over to say, "Don't forget, now, sir, this Michael O'Brian shall be there, but with any luck you'll catch a glimpse of herself, and won't that make it all worthwhile?"

*****

Michael O'Brian had noticed that Brigid had been staying close to the house, following her brief foray into town. He took it as a gesture of apology, and it further weakened his resolve on the matter of this *Sassenach*. Brigid's devotion to the boy reminded him of how passionately he and Aisling Ni Leary had loved one another back when the world was young. But the world was a different place now, changing far too quickly for his liking, and he pondered at some length the question that perhaps might there be a respectable love between people of such wildly different backgrounds.

Still, O'Brian and Brigid had not discussed anything about the Proddy interloper, not since that shocking revelation she shared on the trip home from that damned school. But after his discussion with O'Donovan, his resolution had been quietly shaken, and when he went to bed at night, in the very bed with which he had lain with Aisling, he further questioned himself. Despite his conscious efforts to restore it, his resolve was privately crumbling.

He spent that morning rebuilding the stone wall that lined the rear of their property, as Dunleavy's bull had been trying to get at their Noínín again. He typically found solace in hard physical labour, but when he returned to the house he was as unsure as when he had left it. He cleaned up and was sitting down to a bowl of Ann's stew when Caitlin came running in from hanging the laundry, crying out, "Redcoats!"

"Damn it," muttered her father, "and no alarm from McNamara's? They must all be asleep down there." Pausing, then deliberately returning to his meal, he went on, "Ann, *a grah*, take a look, will you... how many are there?" As she hurried to the window, he added, stressed, "Be sure, now. Not yeomen, child, but redcoats?

"Yes, father, redcoats, but just a few, walking up the road."

"Regulars?" he asked with a mouth full of stew.

"How do I tell?"

Brigid came bolting from her room to join her sister at the window, quickly saying, "Oh, there are no regulars based near here! There are only two militia regiments, they in their red coats." She stood close beside Ann, and clutching her hand, she added with a tremor in her voice, "The Galways have black facings, and the Westmeaths yellow."

"Westmeaths, then!" cried Ann, realization dawning as she turned to Brigid with a nervous smile.

Brigid stared at the approaching men for a long moment, until she cried out, "It is James! Oh, God, my dear James!" Then, catching herself, she turned to her father with pleading eyes, she said, "Daidi, *a grah,* I believe it is Ensign James Lockwood of the Westmeath Militia who is coming to call, please. Oh, please, Daidi, *please*," she added in a half whisper, so earnestly, her eyes her mother's, and Michael remembered his Aisling, and how he felt for her when he called on old man O'Leary a thousand years before.

O'Brian sniffed, and grudgingly said, "I suppose courtesy requires me to see him, redcoat or no."

Brigid immediately gave a little scream and began to hop about the room with her hands to her face. Her sisters, too, given the opportunity to go to pieces, did so, shrieking and crying and hugging their sister, all trace of any previous enmity gone.

Michael O'Brian, though, was a cool head in a crisis, and despite his own, quite real, emotional turmoil, he soon restored order to this suddenly wild, weepy household. "Very well, then. Caitlin, fetch my good coat, if you please. No, you do not have time to put on your new dress. Ann, wipe your eyes, child... yes, I am so happy as well... gather yourself, daughter, put on the kettle, and set out the things for tea in the parlour, please. Brigid, stoke the fire in the parlour, two logs of peat, I think, then hurry and set out some of those biscuits you baked; pray use your grandmother Mary's own elegant plate, and then you shall retire to your room. Yes, Miss Sassy, to your *room*. Today is the province of gentlemen. Ann, Caitlin, when he comes to the door, you shall gather yourselves, answer the door, greet our guest, then you, too, shall retire to your room. And, mind you, if that bedroom door opens one wee bit while this... fellow... is here, I shall beat him out onto the road, and that shall be the end of it."

*****

The O'Brian house with its four rooms was the finest house on the road, but at that juncture it posed a great problem for Brigid Ni Brian, as the hearth room lay between the girls' bedroom and the parlour, making it exceedingly difficult to overhear the conversation there. She was nearly forced to physical violence to get her excited sisters to hush, and even with her ear to the door, the voices from the parlour were achingly faint.

"Pray, sit, Ensign Lockwood."

"Thank you, sir," she heard her James say. "May I say, please, sir, it is most kind of you see me, unannounced." She could hear the break in his voice, the quaking nervousness, and she knew her father would notice it as well.

"Pray do not mention it. My Brigid, who is most dear to me, sir, most dear, mentioned her... acquaintance... and has spoken of you in the most flattering terms."

Her heart leapt to hear her father say that, and she too felt a surge of pride, as her father was so well spoken, the picture of an Irish gentleman.

It was at that moment that Margie, their oldest hen, an overbearing, humorless bird, began to squawk loudly from beneath their window, crying out that she had laid an egg! An egg! Brigid took her ear from the door, frantically thinking of some way to quickly strangle Margie, when Ann and Caitlin, who had been standing on the bed on tenterhooks, silently hysterical, took the opportunity to burst out, "Oh, God, Brigid, what are they saying?! Is father beating the poor man, so?"

After what seemed an eternity Margie was quiet, Brigid managed to silence her sisters, and putting her ear once again to the door she could make out her father speaking.

"You have stated your case, sir, so pray allow me to state mine. You must know that if I allow my daughter to leave my home on your arm, she paints herself as an outcast from her family, from her people. So, too, shall she be viewed by your your people, as... what? An adventuress, a common wanton? And you, sir, surely your family would see you in a far different light, if you should marry a commoner, an Irish Catholic girl—"

Noínín, long a cow of some passion, chose that moment to begin to moo loudly, evidently calling for the attentions of Dunleavy's bull, an understandable sentiment, but one which once drowned out any sound of anything but bovine romance.

Caitlin ran to look out their sole window, and cried out, "Oh, Dunleavy's bull is across the wall!" That was just as well, as the mooing ceased, replaced only by the occasional contented grunt. The ear once again to the door, Brigid could hear her father.

"I am unsure if I care to consign my daughter to such a life. Indeed, sir—"

The cows' antics had drawn the attentions of Bréagh and Amadán from down the road, living down to their names, who came running to investigate, barking like fools, and once again Brigid lost any chance of hearing anything useful. It was only after several minutes that Ann managed to call the dogs to their window, her leaning far out to scratch them, both dogs being slaves to pleasure. Finally Brigid could hear her James speaking, in a more confident voice now, and she nearly burst with pride.

"Now, one last point I must raise. I hesitate to mention it, sir, as I thought it unfair... perhaps dishonorable... to even mention it during our discussions, but I find I must speak to you about one further complication. There is an officer, a rogue formerly of my regiment, a man hissed from the garrison... who has intentions toward Miss O'Brian which are, frankly, less than honorable."

"Bring him here, then, so that I shall beat his arse!"

"I think that might prove unwise, sir. Should he come, he would have a hundred men at his back, and looking for any excuse to kill you, burn this house, and... behave monstrously. He is an exceptionally violent, evil man, sir. Even if you would deny me, sir, I beg you to—"

Ann had been standing close beside Brigid, her ear, too, to the door. With wide eyes she drew back, and gasped out,

"Oh, he must be speaking of the Black Galway! I have heard he is a very wicked man."

Brigid's attention instantly turned to her sister, and with an anger and fear in her voice, she said, "What do you know of this man?" When Ann hesitated to say more, Brigid hissed, "For God's sake, Ann, tell me!"

In a conspiratorial tone, Ann leaned forward and said, "The Black Galway, they call him, because the Galways had been decent enough to the people, weren't they, but in the few days since this new officer came to town they have done some terrible things. I heard that at Ardfield they beat Mr. Condon most cruelly, and set a hot pitch cap on the head of the poor blacksmith at Ring Arundel. And it's the Black Galway behind it, and yesterday I heard Mr. Barry tell Daidi... well, he told Daidi that the evil fellow was asking about you, and where we might be living."

"Jesus," gasped Brigid. She abandoned the door to quietly sit on the bed, her sisters joining her there, the three of them holding hands. After more long minutes they could hear the rumble of men's voices in the hearth room just beyond, but then the voices faded and the house was quiet. Brigid collected herself, and after a long embrace from her sisters, she stepped out her bedroom door.

Her father was standing at the front door, his arms folded across his chest, watching the redcoats heading back down the hill.

Brigid stepped closer to him, and tremulously asked, "Daidi?"

He turned to her, his arms still crossed, and said with resignation, "Tomorrow morning, you, Brigid Ni Brian, shall be married."

Brigid's eyes grew wide, pouring tears, and one trembling hand went to her face.

He held up a hand of caution, and added, not unkindly, "Mind you, it shall be a Catholic ceremony, *mo mheile stor*, to be held at St. Brigid's. Your Ensign Lockwood agreed to that; it is the least he can do to appease this family's honour. I shall go into town now to arrange it with Father Sheeran."

With that, he gently embraced her, and raising her face he bent to kiss her forehead, then each cheek, just as he did when she was young. As he got his coat and hat, he said, "You and your sisters should go into your mother's chest and fetch her wedding dress. She would have been pleased to see it worn again, at her own daughter's wedding."

And then he was gone, down the hill toward town, and for the first time, Brigid saw him walking like an old man.

Chapter Twenty-Two

St. Brigid's was a small parish, and so merited only one priest, Father Sheeran, who had shepherded that flock for twenty years and more. When Michael O'Brian came to call, the priest was putting on his coat and broad-brimmed black clerical hat, as he had been called out to the widow McLaughlin's home to deliver last rites. But O'Brian was a prominent parishioner, so Sheeran invited him back to the drawing room of the parochial house, and as they made themselves as comfortable as was possible in that austere room, the priest said, "Birdie McLaughlin has been busily dying for some days now, so I can likely spare you a few minutes, my son. But, before you tell me of the purpose of your visit, Michael, I require you, as I require all my parishioners, to solemnly vow to honour the position of the Holy Church, and so denounce the sins of violence and rebellion, the vile resort of Satan's legions."

"Of course, Father," said O'Brian with a clear conscience, but a private smile.

"I expected nothing less." Sheeran had, like his flock, grown up speaking Irish, but now he insisted on only English being spoken in his presence.

O'Brian studied the old priest's face, and recognized *áirse scothaosta,* the *arcus senilis,* in those fading eyes. For a moment O'Brian was tempted to raise the issue of the church's role in Ireland, but held his tongue, determined in the purpose of his visit, and so said, "I am come to beg a favor, Father."

"I am here to serve, my son."

"Father, I'm asking after you performing a wedding tomorrow, here at the church, for my daughter Brigid."

The priest sniffed, raised an eyebrow, and said in in a slightly scolding tone, "You surprise me, Michael O'Brian. I know you as a man of some means; will you not host the wedding at your own home, and extend hospitality to your friends and neighbors? And, so, too, will you ignore the traditional banns?" With a slight shrug and a knowing air, he added, "I saw your Brigid at Mass this Sunday last, and she seemed in no need of an immediate wedding. Sure, she is not so far gone that you cannot wait three weeks, for propriety's sake?"

Like nearly every person of common birth in Ireland, O'Brian had long since learned to control his emotions in the face of authority, authority of any stripe, and so he could reply mildly, "Pray, do not mistake me, Father. My Brigid is in no trouble. But she and her groom both agree with me that in this instance a simple ceremony here at the church would be the best course, as she is to wed a Protestant gentleman, an officer of the garrison."

With a sharp intake of breath, the priest sat back, absently tapping his lower lip with the tip of his finger. He sat staring at O'Brian for a long moment, hoping to make him uncomfortable, in which effort he failed. Eventually, the priest said, "And you have agreed to this, O'Brian? You willingly allow a heretical son of perdition into your family? And you know, of course, that by her choice of husband Brigid sunders all ties with those of her kind, of *our* kind. She must acknowledge that as well?"

"She does, Father. This has all been discussed at length." O'Brian did not wish to debate the priest. Neither would he tell the sneering old bastard about the threat posed by the Black Galway, this Lieutenant Barr, nor would O'Brian bring up his certainty that rebellion was imminent, and his belief that in the end, his Brigid would be safer with her soldier. Thus, O'Brian said only, "It might all be summed up, Father, by saying that she loves him, and, after speaking to Ensign Lockwood, I am convinced of his love for her."

"Love," sniffed the priest. "The refuge of the foolish and the weak."

"Christ himself could not have said it better, Father."

The shot went home, and the priest flared, waved a finger at O'Brian, but found no cogent reply at hand. He instead leaned forward in his chair, and said, "All right, then, I shall officiate the ceremony. But as a sin offering, Michael O'Brian, you shall pay one pound, no, a full guinea, to Mother Church for the service, as you are the man allowing this unnatural union."

"And this, Sheeran, the same ceremony that you'd perform for two shillings for any other soul in the parish?"

The priest smirked and watched as the father of the bride stood and slowly counted out the twenty-one shillings, nearly the entire contents of his purse, but then, before O'Brian could turn to go, the priest added, "And of course, O'Brian, you should know no adherent of the heretic faith can be allowed in my church. It is only through a sense of Christian charity that I perform the service at all, but not the full rite, mind you, and certainly not in our revered church. I say Mass at eight o'clock tomorrow morning, so let us have our little wedding at dawn. But... where? Oh, I know... the Shannon Arms! A common pub for a common union." O'Brian opened the door and turned away, and to that broad back the priest added, "They are doomed to hell, you know, O'Brian, both of them, violating the most basic of God's tenets. The walls between good and evil must stand inviolate." O'Brian was gone as the priest finished his thought: 'Inviolate, I say, unless one pays,' contentedly smiling at the coins on his desk, 'one's indulgence.'

*****

Upon his return home Michael O'Brian took refuge in his chair, behind his newspaper, in a high state of irritability. He was a man who valued peace and quiet, and so his mood was not improved by the tumult of activity in his house as his three daughters, well aware that this was to be their last day together, exercised the full range of emotions available to them, in endless combination, all while laughing, crying, packing trunks, and taking in dresses.

When James Lockwood came to speak with their father, Ann and Caitlin had caught glimpses of the tall, young man in the elegant uniform, and they showered Brigid with any number of questions about him. When talking about her prospective husband, Brigid made it a point to speak loudly, and at length, hoping her father might be listening from behind his paper. She noticed, but did not mention, that at one point he spent nearly a full hour on a single page of the *Cork Mercury*.

After their supper, their strength and emotions spent, well aware they would need to rise early, the sisters agreed that their preparations were as complete as one day allowed. For the first time since her return home, Brigid did not dread crawling into the bed she shared with her sisters. It was April, and though the days were growing warmer, the nights remained cold, and the girls undressed and burrowed under the quilts with frantic energy. At the foot of the bed sat Brigid's trunk, packed, reminding them this would be their last night together.

After they had been under the covers for some minutes came the muted, dreamy voice of Caitlin. "Brigid?"

"Yes, *a grah*?"

"I must know, does our new brother—I am so thrilled to have a brother!—keep his hair long? I think so, but I saw him so briefly."

"Oh, yes. Some fashionable men, silly, prating brutes, are cutting their hair short in the French fashion, but my James has long, thick hair."

In her best big-sister voice, Ann said, "His hair aside, Brigid, I do wish you would reconsider and have your banns read from the altar. Sister Immaculata says that the banns must be read on three Sundays in a row so that there can later be no questions of the legitimacy of a marriage."

"Ach, the banns are so old-fashioned, aren't they?"

"But such a hurry, Brigid," Ann went on, in a voice that sounded nearly unkind. "People will talk, gossiping beasts, saying that you *had* to marry."

"Whatever do you mean that she *has* to marry?" urgently whispered Caitlin, who, even at age nine, was a country girl, and as some of that knowledge of carnal nature came to mind, she gasped, "Oh, you don't mean... oh, what a terrible thing to say, Anne, of our own sister!"

From her warm, comfortable burrow of blankets, once again content in her sisters' esteem and affection, perhaps indeed envy, Brigid said with a smile in her voice, "Oh, let them say what they will. But what Irish woman would marry without first knowing the worth of her man?"

"Oh, Brigid," said Ann with an edge of jealousy, "you *didn't?*"

From beneath her blankets Brigid smiled.

"Oh, you are very bad," said Ann without conviction. After a moment, she asked, "How... was it so very wonderful as they say?"

After a brief, contented, silence, in a smiling voice, she whispered, "Oh, yes, every bit that wonderful, and more."

*****

"No, no, sir, *we* shall genuflect, but you mustn't," said Private Diarmuid Doolan as he and his officer hurried down Sovereign Street toward the Shannon Arms in the dawn light, by God's grace a perfectly lovely spring morning.

An anxious Ensign Lockwood replied, "Well, it shall be my first... appearance... in a Catholic ceremony, and I do not wish to appear singular." He then waved a hand in vague motions across his chest, and added, "When I was a boy, Jimmy Brady tried to teach me to cross myself... what is the old saying? Nose, toes... and then is it left, or right?"

"Ah, Jesus!" said Doolan, his usual whine brought to a fevered pitch by the importance of the day, their terrible tardiness, and the fact that his officer seemed determined to step in every mud puddle they came across. "That is likely how the Jesuits teach it, the blasphemous hounds, but you mustn't cross yourself, and why? Because it's the *Catholics* who will be doing such things, not the *Anglican*, which is you, sir."

"Colonel Sykes said he would come by, to serve as a witness. He is also a Protestant, so perhaps I won't stand out quite so badly." A note from Brigid's father crinkled in his breast pocket, one which had been delivered to the barracks late the night before, which explained, in scrupulously polite but tense terms, the nature of the upcoming nuptials. It was the contents of that note which made Lockwood and Doolan so tardy, as they had been up very late, and then well before dawn, knocking on doors in an attempt to secure an affordable apartment for the newlyweds. They had that morning woken an irritable but ultimately agreeable woman who owned a storefront on a narrow street from the barracks, and who was willing, indeed eager, to lease a small room in the rear of her first story.

Secure in where he might carry his new bride, but now tired and irritable, James was hoping the whole affair might soon be over, where he and Brigid might be together and alone at last, but Doolan was relentless. As they neared the Shannon Arms his servant said, "Now, sir, you promised, you bloody *promised*, that you would write your sainted mother to tell her of your nuptials. Is it done, then?"

"Well, no, but I started a—"

"Ah, Jesus, I knew it! Did I not tell you how I lost my own mother in my early days, and how a man fortunate enough to have his mother alive might write to her every once in a while, if only to tell her that he is to be feckin' *married*?"

"Oh, *shut up*, Doolan, won't you?" snapped Lockwood, prompting the gnarled little fellow, privately but deeply wounded, to pinch his face closed and look off to the distance.

They walked in tense silence for a few minutes, until they saw the Shannon Arms down the street, and Lockwood stopped, and though he did not look at Doolan, he said, "I shall write a letter to my parents later today, after the ceremony, a *fait accompli*, as it were. Brigid has already told me how she would like to write a letter to my mother, and so I can include that in the same cover, which will please my mother."

Doolan paused, and still looking down the road he grunted, nodded, and muttered, "That'll do, sure."

They both sniffed, the spat resolved, and then, unconsciously in step, they marched away the last yards of James Lockwood's boyhood.

The innkeeper met them at the door, a fat, kindly man, long acquainted with the O'Brians, telling Lockwood, "It's all arranged, young master, I trust to your satisfaction. The bride's party is all here, as is our good Father Sheeran." James wondered if he caught a note of irony in the innkeeper's voice, but the man went on, "My Missus so loves a wedding, and has decorated the room, no matter the short notice, at only a modest cost, sir, as we are always at your service, sir."

Ushered inside, James was unsure of just how his wedding would play out. He had of course attended weddings in the past, but in a disinterested role, and had paid little attention to the intricacies of the event. Bracing himself, determined to play the role of the confident young man, his first challenge was the imposing edifice that was Michael O'Brian, and another man standing beside O'Brian who eyed Lockwood with great interest. Distant nods were exchanged between the groom and the father of the bride, though O'Brian pulled a pocket watch from his vest, eyed it with a raised eyebrow, and as he returned it to his pocket he gave Lockwood a sharp look.

Most of the pub room tables had been pushed off to one side; the flagstone floor, though freshly mopped, still carried a scent of stale beer. Mrs. Innkeeper, glowing by the stairs, had indeed decorated: sheets were artfully draped over the beer taps, and bows tied here and there, genuinely brightening the otherwise worn room.

A side door opened and the priest stepped in, fully accoutered. He said nothing as he took up his place at the head of the room. James's mask slipped accordingly. Two extremely pretty girls then came down the stairs, with not a little grace: Brigid's sisters. O'Brian stepped over to make the introductions. Ann and Caitlin were obviously excited and very pleased to meet their new brother-in-law, and Lockwood, anxious to please, was hoping to make allies of his new sisters.

"Are you prepared to proceed, sir?" asked O'Brian. "I am certain Brigid is growing anxious upstairs." Nodding toward Doolan, who hung in the background, he added, "Is this the extent of your party?"

Rallying at the thought of seeing Brigid, Lockwood said, "I expect my colonel to arrive shortly, sir. This is Private Diarmuid Doolan of my company, my—" the word 'servant' stuck in his throat, as both insufficient and unkind, and so Lockwood ended up saying, "—well, comrade."

That made Doolan swell, and he stepped forward, made his salute, and said in Irish, "God, Mary and Patrick to you, Michael O'Brian. May God bless all here, on this joyous day."

That, at least, went over well. The man who had been standing by O'Brian, oddly not yet introduced, took the opportunity to step forward, made his leg, and with a grin, Tadg an Astna O'Donovan said, "My name, sir, is Smith, long a friend of the family, and our Brigid's godfather."

The tardy, beaming, breathless, gold-braided form of Colonel Sykes then burst through the front door. "I am here at last, dear friends! What a busy, glorious morning... such a happy day!" He then busily introduced himself to everyone in the room, including the pensive priest, for Sykes was immune to social restraint, and so he was helpful in filling the time while the final arrangements were made.

The mood in the room grew tense, as the unfamiliar and possibly unfriendly faces surreptitiously measured one another. But then Brigid O'Brian came down the stairs, carrying a bundle of spring flowers, more flowers in her hair, wearing her mother's sprigged muslin dress, embroidered overall with tiny leaves and flower heads, the puffed sleeves edged in, a breathtaking beauty that recalled them to their duty and the spirit of the day.

The ceremony itself was a blur to Lockwood, though he recalled being allowed to hold Brigid's hand, and that his mind reeled, on several levels, when the priest significantly said, "Wilt thou, with her, accept lovingly from God the children with which he will deign to bless you and nurture and educate them in accordance with the law of God and of his Holy Church?"

He said, "I will," after only the slightest pause, and he glanced over to see Brigid make a face, and he gave her hand a squeeze, which made them both stifle a giggle. He was prompted to say, "I will," on two or three other points, not much caring what he agreed to, only knowing she was his all, until he was finally told he might kiss his wife, his wife! And there were tears and applause, and honest, open, hearty congratulations, handshakes and embraces.

The front door swung open and Charles Barr stepped into the pub.

"*Voila*, my surprise guest arrives at last!" cried Colonel Sykes with a wave of his arm and a broad smile.

Nearly everyone in the room had a reason to hate Charles Barr, and a nearly discernable wall of loathing kept him very near the door. Ann and Caitlin looked puzzled for a moment, until their father hissed, "The Black Galway," and they, too, went pale with fear and hatred.

Barr sniffed, leaned against the door post, crossed his arms, and said, "My, what a somber wedding. I trust there have no last-minute disagreements over the... unusual... nature of the union?" Then with a grin he went on, "All that aside, I see my attendance comes as a surprise, and so perhaps that might lend a special emphasis to my congratulations to the happy couple. I must say, Brigid, that I have rarely seen—"

Brigid flared and hissed, "If you really must address me, sir, you will please refer to me as Mrs. Lockwood."

Brigid was pale, clutching James's arm, as her husband went scarlet and said with a voice of trembling fury, "Get out, Barr."

"Now, now," cried Sykes, stepping between Barr and the tense, staring bridal party. "This is my doing entirely, Ensign Lockwood. You know how I have hope that you and our Lieutenant Barr might make amends, and as the lieutenant is the Officer of the Day. I thought he might shirk his duty for a moment or two so that he might drop by and act as witness and sign the register as a brother officer, mending fences, eh? Eh?"

"He must leave here, Colonel Sykes," O'Brian said flatly. "Or I shall not answer for the consequences."

"Come, now, gentlemen," cried Sykes, alarmed, when Lockwood, O'Brian, and O'Donovan all took half a step toward Barr.

Barr held up both hands in mock surrender, though Brigid, who perhaps knew him best, saw a flash of genuine fear in his eyes. Barr bent to quickly sign the register that stood on a table by the door and then with the slightest bow he turned to go. But he caught himself, and slowly turning back, with a tilt of his head he looked at O'Donovan, and asked, "Do I know you, sir?"

O'Donovan made no reply, but slid a hand inside his coat. With a raised eyebrow and a slight nod of his head, Barr left without another word.

Aware at last of the enormity of his *faux pas*, Sykes rendered his congratulations and apologies, and, pleading urgent business, he left hurriedly. It took the rest of the party some time to recover their spirits, though a bowl of punch produced by the Shannon Arms played a role. There was, however, none of the dancing, splendid food, infinite bottles, and endless friends and family that marked traditional Irish weddings, and they all soon realized it was time to go.

Michael O'Brian kept in the background during the tearful moments as his daughters parted. But he eventually stepped up to James and Brigid, reached out to take both their right hands, and clasping his over theirs, with a choking voice he said, "May God be with you and bless you. May you see your children's children. May you be poor in misfortunes and rich in blessings. May you know nothing but happiness from this day forward."

Michael O'Brian had meant to say more, much more, but before he could calm his heart they were gone, out into the bright sunshine of the new day.

Chapter Twenty-Three

The wedding service complete, the innkeepers scurried about, dragging the furniture back into place and pulling down the ribbons and bows, quickly reestablishing the Shannon Arms's usual atmosphere of dim dissipation. Ensign and Mrs. Lockwood had been successfully launched into the world, and so Michael O'Brian, his role played, leaned against the bar, absently sipping whiskey. Father Sheeran joined him, and taking his stole from his shoulders, the priest reverently kissed it. As he wrapped it in its silk case, he quietly said, "I am disappointed that it is hardly dawn itself, my son, and yet you imbibe strong liquor? More than that, I am astonished, Michael O'Brian, that you allowed that rogue Tadg O'Donovan to attend your daughter's wedding, the man who leads the forces of rebellion in our own town. He has been seduced by Satan's own lies, and blatantly ignores direct orders from Mother Church."

"He is her godfather; it is tradition," O'Brian said dismissively. But he then went on with more energy, "Speaking of the position of the Holy Church, Father, *a grah,*

I wonder if you are acquainted with Father McKinnon up at Drinagh West?"

"I believe I have had the honour once or twice, at the Bishop's Palace. The Father is one of those wild young fellows, but he shall heed the bishop's crozier soon enough."

"McKinnon is young, perhaps, Father, but active, oh, my, active. I'm hearing that two of his flock, a father and son, were accused of the murder of their landlord. A terrible thing, murder, especially when the two accused men are well known, and well liked, in their community. Ya know, though, Father, it seems that both these fellows proclaimed their innocence, saying they had been with Father McKinnon, and so their very own priest could vouch for them. But the priest denied them, didn't he, and so the boy and his Da were sent to the gallows this Monday last. The people of North Cork are enraged, their hatred of the crown brought to a rolling boil."

"A sad tale, O'Brian, but what is the fate of two North Cork wastrels to me?"

"The point, Father, is that the man and his son had indeed been with the priest, but Father McKinnon sacrificed them, sending them to their deaths, just so that the people of North Cork would be enraged, and easily lead to rebellion when the time comes. For every priest like you, spouting the Church's weak drivel about meekness and restraint, there is a mad zealot like McKinnon, who would see innocent men hanged rather than have the English lord over us one more day. Do not mistake it, Sheeran, rebellion is coming, and all hell is coming with it."

Sheeran looked straight ahead, his visage locked, until his face broke and he hissed, "Get out of my sight, thou foul son of filth. *Vade retro, Satana!*"

O'Brian coughed a laugh, tossed back the last of his drink, and said, "Leaving your beloved English now, are we? Well, then, *Go n-ithe an cat thú is go n-ithe an Diabhal an cat, David Sheeran.*" May the cat eat you, and may the devil eat the cat. An odd curse to English ears, but among the Irish it was deeply cutting.

****

From the refuge of a shadowed alley, Charles Barr stood silently watching the newly minted Ensign and Mrs. Lockwood as they walked, laughing, arm in arm down Sovereign Street. Barr's body tortured him, as a new wave of syphilitic sores had flared in his groin, an endless torment. Even so, his eyes were active, glistening with a malicious pleasure. The Lockwoods—Christ, how he hated them—were laughing and chatting, obviously without a care in the world, but Barr knew they had feet of clay. He knew the Penal Laws, whereas they evidently did not.

"Sweet Christ!" he nearly said aloud, the realization growing. "They had a priest, but no Anglican minister! The marriage is illegal. Illegal! He's made a whore of her... God knows she merits the title. I could not have planned this better myself. I needn't have worried... I shall come out of this without a scratch."

He had already taken some preliminary measures. Within the next few days both General Moore and Colonel Montgomery would receive letters from Barr's dying father in England. The letter would beg those gentlemen to grant leave to Lieutenant Charles Barr, so that Barr, the model of the affectionate, devoted son, might fly to his father's side before death's cold hand closed over his humble heart. Barr was certain the letter would have the requisite impact, as he had paid a dissolute Dublin scrivener four shillings to write them.

It was Barr's intention to be out of Ireland before the powder keg blew; in particular, to be out of Clonakilty. He knew   that the peasantry hated him—he reveled in his moniker, the Black Galway—and suspected that the first stroke of any local rising would have a decidedly personal edge, in that it would fall on him. More than that, his servant, the massive Private Muldoon, had relayed the current barracks gossip: several men of Barr's company were intent on scragging their officer at the first opportunity.

Barr had taken those steps to preserve his professional honour, but he now needed to seal the one danger to his societal reputation. He did his best to restrain a mad smile that came to his face as he watched Lockwood and O'Brian continue down the street, deliriously happy, and he considered the many options before him.

*****

Michael O'Brian sat at the long low bench that sat in front of the Shannon Arms, his legs stretched out before him, crossed at the ankles, his eyes closed, his arms folded across his chest. Tadg O'Donovan joined him there and assumed the same posture. After a moment Tadg muttered, "A wedding at my favorite pub, at dawn itself, and the Black Galway in attendance? You always throw the best parties, O'Brian."

"Oh, that's not the whole of it, brother. I just cursed a priest, so my chances at heaven have likely dropped a peg or two."

"They may have improved; Sheeran's a shite priest."

They basked a moment in the rare minutes of Irish sunshine, until O'Brian sighed, "Jesus, Tadg, what more can this day bring? It'll be angels flying out me arse, next."

More quiet sunlit moments passed, well spent. O'Donovan eventually stirred enough to ask, "Shall we get pissed?"

After a sharp exhale and a brief consideration, O'Brian said, "Shite, why not? You're buying, though, it being my daughter's day."

"God, how I love weddings," O'Donovan said as they got to their feet. He threw an arm around his friend as they strode back into the pub.

*****

"I still cannot believe that we are at last married! I am so very happy." She looked up at him with such joy that his heart skipped a beat.

"How beautiful you are, my Brigid, my dear wife! I shall never tire of saying your name, or seeing your face." With a playful tone he quietly added, "I suppose it would be terribly indiscreet if I were to kiss you here in the street?"

She teased, "Oh yes, sir, quite indiscreet, even if there are so few people about...."

He pulled her into a quiet doorway and kissed her, and there was, quite nearly, some very indiscreet conduct, until she pulled away and stepped back into the street, trying to keep a straight face, as she smoothed the front of her dress. Grinning like a fool, he dutifully took his place beside her, though as they resumed their stroll she felt the need to swat away a hand that wandered.

Still, it was only another few yards further down the street before she pulled him into another doorway to kiss him in return. Eventually the homeowner, an old lady who had forgotten what it was to kiss and be kissed with such fervor, opened her door to shoo them away, cackling in Irish, "Away with you, you two young alley cats! This is a Christian home! And you, Miss Tart, rubbing such a fine dress against a red coat, for shame!"

They both put on exaggerated grimaces and ran holding hands back into the street. At that time in the morning there were few people out, though in those dense, older streets of Clonakilty a couple of the aproned shopkeepers were opening for business in the horizontal sunlight. Some townspeople recognized the newly married couple and called out their blessings, while others paid them little attention. Some deliberately turned their backs.

It was not a large town, but still there were sufficient winding streets for them to stroll. As they wandered up George Street, she asked, "How shall we spend the rest of our day, our first day as a married couple, dear husband?"

"I confess our home won't be quite ready yet. I have secured us a neat little set of rooms near the barracks, though—"

"Oh yes, Aideen, the maid at the Arms, told me all about it. The rooms at Mrs. Blackburn's shall be lovely, dear. Our first home!"

"However do you know that? I only secured them last night!"

"It is a small town, sir, and news travels fast. You are evidently unaware that you and I are the topic of endless gossip. We are in turn treasonous, tragic or romantic, depending on the whim of one's heart, or one's politics."

"Well, then," he said, a bit deflated, "I suppose you already know that I have given Doolan my purse and some close instructions as to what to purchase to finish the place. He has this notion that married gentlemen should have a potted plant, so I fear we shall return to find a massive potted palm, and little else."

"Oh, we need only a few sticks of furniture, sure." With wide eyes and a coy smile, she added, "But there shall be a bed, my dear husband, shall there not?"

He barked a laugh and said, "Oh, do not concern yourself on that count, young lady. I have ordered Doolan to stretch my credit to its limits and secure the largest, softest bed in all Cork."

"We shall spend days and days there!"

"Oh, what a splendid thought. We shall take all our meals in bed, without a stitch of clothing!"

"On that point you take a great deal for granted, sir!" she said with a sparkling laugh. "But while dear Doolan does his shopping, let us walk up McCurtain Hill Road and I will show you the standing stones of Templebryan, where fairies are known to dance in the light of a full moon. And beyond that, down to the vale of the Shannon, where there is a lovely pub owned by my cousin's cousin—a Hurley, but one of the good ones—where we can get a bottle and a loaf, and picnic in the sun. It is such a lovely day!"

*****

In Dublin, Lord Edward Fitzgerald, the last member of the original central committee, had been arrested and badly wounded. The men hurriedly appointed to fill the empty seats on the committees, central and provincial, scarcely familiar with one another, met in fearful secret, to bitterly debate the next steps. A few argued for an end to violent rebellion, some argued for a delay, and of those, some still spoke of a possible French intervention. Others, most, cried out for immediate rebellion before the organization collapsed entirely, but differed in a dozen ways as to how the rebellion should be carried out. One member of the Leinster Provincial Directory, Thomas Reynolds, a Catholic silk merchant and a traitor, reported every word to Dublin Castle.

*****

The ground floor room of Clonakilty Barracks was crowded, noisy, and thick with the smells of unwashed men, pipe smoke, and peat logs burning in the two fireplaces. Rough tables and benches ran down the middle of the long, white-washed room, and wooden double bunk-beds lined the walls. Two men were assigned to each bed, where they would sleep head to foot on a straw-filled mattress, each man issued a bolster and two thin blankets. The rest of the room's furnishings consisted of racks for the muskets, and shelves and pegs from which to hang knapsacks and uniforms. There were no boxes or cupboards where the men might keep their possessions, as the army did not encourage personal belongings. The company was not to be encumbered by excess baggage, and the men should have no interests outside their confined world.

In honour of Ensign Lockwood's marriage, Colonel Sykes had ordered that the day's drill be cancelled, and that the men should be given double their usual rum allowance. The men thus had reason to take some pleasure in Lockwood's marriage, though in one circle of rum-sipping men, Conor Kelly huffed, "He had the sense to marry a pretty Irishwoman; that does not render him Saint fucking Patrick."

Another member of that mess, the young Ian Cheevers, wistfully said, "I wish that Brigid O'Brian would marry me. By God, I'd—"

"You keep a respectful tone, now, Ian. She's a proper lady, our Miss," said Corporal Hanahan, an older man and a regular church-goer, looking up from under his stern eyebrows.

"I wasn't speaking improper," said Cheevers, turning back to his brass work with uncharacteristic zeal. "It's just... well..."

"Well, you never mind, young man. As for you, Kelly, Lockwood begged Robert Daly off his flogging, which brings him some credit in my book, even if it does not bring it in yours."

"I had the guard that day," said Ian O'Mullhollan, "how did Daly get off?"

"Well," said the Hanahan, assuming his role of mess story-teller, "O'Malley already had the cat out of the bag, there never being a man so consistent in his duty as O'Malley. Sykes was going to order two dozen for Daly, him being absent without leave, but Lockwood spoke up, and asked Daly why he was out, giving him his chance, ya see, and Daly tells how he and his Missus were out looking for their Jaimie, him being just three years of age and being lost in this new town, and how Daly hustled back to the barracks as soon as they found the boy down in the woods."

"Never was a boy for wandering like wee Jaimie."

"Aye, a few swats on the bottom and being confined to barracks for two days won't break that urge to roam," said Owen McCawley, looking over to the far corner of the long room, where the young ne'er-do-well tormented his pet mouse.

Conor Kelly huffed in his usual way and said, "That being said, Lockwood's still an Englishman, and our sworn enemy."

"He was born up in Malahide..." offered O'Mullhollan.

Another huff, and, "Just because a man is born in a bakery doesn't mean he's a baker, boyo."

"Oh, will you not shut up, Kelly? Lockwood's all right, and if I hear you or one of your rotten mates say the word 'scrag' again, the men of this mess shall beat you like a Connacht bodhrán."

Meekly, looking down, but still fighting, Kelly muttered, "Man? More a boy, him."

"He's married to Miss Brigid ni Brian, and that's a man's role, and honour. Between the United Men and our Miss, I wager there'll soon be none of the boy left in young James Lockwood. For now, we'll do things up proper."

*****

It was a splendid day, warm and sunny throughout, and in later years recalled as one of the best days of their lives. When they returned to town they came down Barracks Road toward their new home and found the company drawn up, bayonets fixed, but with spring flowers stuck in the barrels of the muskets. All eyes were locked straight ahead, but some gave them broad smiles, and at the sight of the beaming young Irish bride more smiles broke out, sharing in the joy of the young Irishwoman.

It was his company.

From the top of the steps of their new home, the beautiful young woman, fairly glowing with happiness, curtsied to them, and waving to them, she called out her thanks and blessings. *"Go raibh mheile maith agat, saighdiúirí a grah! Dia dhaoibh go léir!"* she cried, and perhaps they were now hers as well.

Chapter Twenty-Four

General Moore insisted that every man in his Cork city headquarters, from his senior aides down to the sentries, be a veteran of at least one campaign. His military secretary, Major Monson, was painfully qualified, and walked with a distinct limp as he stepped into Moore's office to say, "Beg pardon, sir, but a delegation of gentlemen has arrived from Macroom, and are insistent upon being granted an audience."

"Ach," growled the aging, balding Moore from behind a desk loaded with maps and files, "if I speak to one more of these howling apes that passes for a gentleman in Ireland I shall be driven to coarse murder. It seems that every rascal in England has been sent over here, granted a hundred acres and an Irish title. Brutal, strutting, cowardly brutes; they would not last a day in Scotland. If I were an Irish peasant I would revolt as well, and be damned to these so-called gentlemen."

"I believe I have heard you say so, sir," Monson replied with a twisted grin.

302

"But before I face those fools, let us discuss two matters of import. The first... you may tell that fellow Barr that his leave is granted, and that as far as I am concerned, he might stay in England until the century is complete. That damned brutal whelp causes no end of trouble wherever he is assigned, and now proves himself a coward as well, insisting upon leave, even with the island in crisis. I hear he has quite ruined his company."

"If I may, sir, remind you that the Castle has forbidden any leave, in light of the state of emergency..."

"Ach, the Castle may kiss my ripe pink arse. Never mind it. I shall speak with Abercrombie. Our chances against the rebels are better without Barr than with him." Moore paused to take the slightest sip of the glass of whisky that was by his side at all waking hours.

The secretary scribbled a note on his pocket book, as Moore continued, "Secondly, this note from Montgomery, requesting that his companies be shifted closer to Cork. He desires his companies to be within a two days' march of one another, so that the Westmeaths might act as a regiment should the need arise, which seems bloody likely. It is a soldierly request, but can we accommodate him?"

With a grunt, Moore got to his feet and went to join his secretary, standing over a large map of the south of Ireland, where colored blocks noted the dispositions of Moore's scattered troops. Moore folded his arms across his chest, sighed, and said, "We are spread so thin, Monson. A great deal of bread, and a wee pat of butter." Finally he tapped a spot on the southern coast and said, "Here, in Clonakilty; who has the Westmeath's Five Company?"

"Lt. Colonel Sykes, sir."

"Ah, yes, our likeable ninny. Did I not see a note go past my desk, in which one of Sykes's officers was married?

Ensign ...." Moore was renowned for reading everything he could get his hands on.

"Lockwood, sir. He is in Clonakilty, with Sykes and Five Company. The ensign married a local girl, an O'Brian."

"A good match, I trust. There is some comfort in hearing there is yet a bit of normal life somewhere on this bloody island. Remind me to write a note to wish them joy."

"I can craft something for your signature, sir," offered Monson.

"Nae, thankee," said Moore, taking a stronger pull from his whisky than he typically allowed. "I wish it to come from my own pen. I recall Montgomery mentioning this Lockwood fellow. Young, but capable. Hopefully he shall deliver Sykes from evil."

"Amen."

"All right, then, you will please issue orders for those moves: Caithness Legion will move from Bandon to Clonakilty, trading locations with Five Company, Westmeaths, who move from Clonakilty to Bandon. That should please Montgomery, his company much closer to Cork Town. Oh, and Bandon is still short of guns; have Sykes escort a pair of six-pounders up to Bandon when he leaves Clonakilty."

Weston jotted down a few last notes and turned to go, halting as Moore held up his hand. "One last thing, please, man. Tell them these moves are to be executed within two days' time. We need the men in position before the world goes dark."

*****

From beneath a mass of tumbled blankets the muffled voice of a young man said, "I wonder what time it is."

A young woman's slender arm emerged from under the covers, paused, and after a moment she quickly pulled the sheets back over her head, and wistfully muttered, "Daytime." Soon thereafter, however, she added with more firmness, "I am hungry."

"For what, I wonder?" came the smiling voice of her young husband. "Is it time for breakfast, luncheon, or dinner?"

"Food of any kind, my dear James, my *husband*! But food!"

They tumbled out of bed, hurriedly dressing, laughing, and she was the first to open the door. But as she took the first step down the dim, narrow, stairs she stopped with a choked shriek. Charles Barr sat on the lower landing, using an oiled whetstone to slowly sharpen a long, slender dagger. An empty green bottle lay at his feet.

James, instantly in a rage, came up behind Brigid and she whirled to face him, using both hands to hold him as he tried to push past to protect her, and she stood her ground to protect him.

"Mind your manners, Lockwood," said Barr mildly, absently. "I went by your room at the barracks, and it seems you left your sword there."

"What in hell's name do you want here?" said Lockwood in a voice hissing of hatred and disbelief.

With a sniff of weak amusement, Barr said, "I have been sitting here an hour or more. Goodness, what a racket you two newlyweds make. You are quite the eager wanton, O'Brian, though I had long guessed that."

"Oh, you *bastard!*" she cried, and both she and her husband took a step down toward Barr, but they froze as he held up the dagger, a sheen of oiled menace in the shadowed staircase.

"Tut, tut, let us have no unpleasantness," said the immaculately uniformed Black Galway. He dreamily waved a finger at them and rolled on, "But as you insist, I shall proceed to business. My horse is outside, and I am off to England for a glorious holiday away from this dreadful island. I take ship in Dublin, as I first have a personal matter to attend to there. So, I shall be brief. Before I go... I offer a bargain. You two shall speak to no one... *no one*... about my... unfortunate... medical condition." Despite the veil of drink he felt a bolt of pain from his groin, a lightning flash that exploded in his head, and he nearly gasped aloud. "I, in return," he said as the pain receded, "shall speak to no one about the illegal nature of your marriage."

"Whatever do you mean, you dog?" James said sharply, but with the slightest quiver of fear in his voice.

"Really, must I explain?" sighed Barr, the fog of alcohol rolling back into place. "You are both fools of the first order, but surely you are familiar with the Penal Laws?"

"Stuff and nonsense, sir," said Brigid. "Those old laws have not been enforced for years and years."

Addressing the walls around him, he said, "Enforced on the occasional whim, perhaps, but think of the glorious times in which we currently live, dark passions brought to a round boil! The Protestants hate and fear the Catholics, the Catholics hate and fear the Protestants—our present company excepted, of course, to an awkwardly obvious degree—and all it would take to destroy you would be for one honourable, conscientious, correspondent—myself, for example—to incite the nation against you."

Barr pulled himself to his feet, blinked hard several times, whistled softly, and gesturing toward the empty bottle, he went on, "I am currently acting as my own physician, and have prescribed Absinthe for any slight discomfort I may experience." He giggled and added, "You may understand that I have had an unfortunate history with physicians."

From above, Lockwood quietly said, "Oades wanted only to help you."

Barr was unfocused, teetering, and he muttered, "I concede only that he died well. Surprising. Mousey little poof... Christ, how he bled." Rubbing a hand harshly across his face, the edge returning, Barr went on, "Returning to your marriage. A handful of letters to the press, and think of the scandal I could generate! The word would be loudly proclaimed, so that every Catholic peasant would hear that Brigid O'Brian has whored herself to a redcoat. The private shame of the O'Brians will be spread to every hovel in Ireland. And Lockwood, but think of your family and their ilk, pillars of the Ascendency—Christ, how I delight in the laurels which brutes place upon their own heads—imagine the prim, proper, genteel brutality. And do not believe for a moment that the service would stand by you, the fickle bastards."

James turned to Brigid and offered, "We might still go see an Anglican minister...."

She looked at him in disappointed surprise, and said, "But, James, we promised my father!"

"Oh, goodness, her delightful father, the rough-hewn *paterfamilias*!" howled Barr.

Brigid, furious, determined, was clinging to her husband, as James said, "Very well, then: Barr, fight me! Play the gentleman once more, and we shall resolve this once—"

With all her strength she pounded a fist on her husband's chest, crying out, "You must not fight him! I will not risk losing you!"

"Damn it, Brigid, there is no risk! I can take that bastard in three passes! Two!"

Still she frantically clung to him, as from the darkness below came the wheedling voice, "I have no time for debate! Yay or nay? Do we have an agreement?"

"Yes!" she screamed, looking down at Barr as she clutched her husband's shirtfront with both hands. "Upon our scared honour, we shall say nothing so long as you hold your tongue. Now, for God's sake, go, and never trouble us again!"

"Lockwood? Your word of honour, now."

To his wife he said quietly, "I do not fear him; I would certainly..." But as he studied her face he went on, loudly, to Barr, "Yes! Upon my honour."

"Well, then, that seen to, I shall be on my way." Barr straightened his coat, and casually added, "Oh, and by the way; if in future days you think of betraying me, do remember that any children you might produce—and goodness knows that appears likely, the way you two couple with such astounding frequency—"

James did not raise a hand, only hissing in pained frustration, as Brigid held him, her eyes clenched shut, desperate for Barr to go.

Barr grinned, and went on, "I can see them now, the Lockwood spawn, row upon row of pink, pumpkin-headed little dullards—well, goodness, they would each be branded a bastard. How very horrible. Pray, keep that in mind." Snapping his bicorn onto his head, he turned to leave, and waving two fingers over his head, he called back over his shoulder, "Ta! Do enjoy the rebellion!"

And so Barr was gone, leaving the Lockwoods gasping at the top of the stairs.

*****

Caitlin O'Brian anxiously sat atop the low stone fence that ran in front of her grandfather's modest home. She had been waiting there for what she was quite certain was an eternity, until she finally saw her father's trap come up that remote, deeply hedged, lane. She stood atop the wall to call out, "Oh, Da! Da! You are at last come to carry us home! Ann is napping, sad she is without Brigid. I baked bread with my own hands alone today! Seanathair O'Leary is unhappy with you, Da, as he said that you allowed Brigid to marry a heretic!"

Michael O'Brian pulled his old horse to a halt, shook his head, and stepped down to get his kiss. "Do not be over concerned, *a grah*; your Seanathair O'Leary is unhappy about a great many things. Since your Seanmathair O'Leary fled to the angels, the clever woman, he is unhappy about the birds singing too loudly, and the sun setting without his leave."

He walked to the rear of the trap and pulled down an old valise, causing Caitlin's face to fall, and she said, "I was hoping it was you coming to take us home, Da."

"You'll need to stay here, daughter, the sorrow and the woe, for a while longer."

"Oh, Da! You yourself said it was just for a handful of days that Ann and I would stay far from home! It is very cross I am with you, Da!"

"A few days more, only, *mo mheile stor*." Holding open the lid of the valise, he added, "Have I not carried to you more of your own clothes?"

After a quick glance and a dismissive sniff, Caitlin said, "It is like a clurichaun you pack, Da."

"A clurichaun, am I? You mind your tone, now, young Miss. Just you know this: word has it that the Black Galway is gone from here, but bad days are still hard upon us, and you shall stay here, deep in the country, and be safe, whether it please you or no."

Caitlin crossed her arms and stomped her foot in silent disapprobation, just as her mother had done many years before. With a start O'Brian recalled that Caitlin had known her mother for just days. She had learned the gestures from her sisters, and while his Ann was safe there with her grandfather, a sob caught in his throat for his Brigid, another man's love and charge.

"You are a clurichaun, and a tardy one, Daidi. Cousin Fergal was here this morning, asking after you, and he told me that I was to tell you he was going off with Uncle Tadg, and I would next see him when Ireland was free. Will Ireland soon be free, Da? May I stop going to school?"

O'Brian's hand was visibly shaking as he turned to touch Caitlin's upturned face. "You will be returning to school as soon as this madness is over, *mo stor*. But whether you'll be studying English or Irish, I suppose that remains to be seen."

*****

The second night of their marriage was a somber one. The Lockwoods were asleep when a thunderous banging at their door jolted them awake.

Brigid, instantly alert, screamed, "Oh, is it Barr?"

"Who the devil is it?!" roared James, sleep still thick in his voice.

"It's Doolan, sir! Colonel Sykes's compliments sir, and you are to report immediately! He's in a right fit, him."

James jumped out of bed, struck a flame to a candle, and hurriedly threw on his uniform.

Brigid sat up in their bed, blankets to her chin, and through a mix of fear and disappointment, blinked hard, and said, "But I thought you were to have three days?"

"I am very sorry, my love, but it seems that some foolishness has come up. I am sure it is nothing."

She frowned, growing awake, and said, "You did not marry a fool, James Lockwood. Is the rebellion come?"

He raised both palms in uninformed frustration, and said, "I should be back in an hour, but if not, I shall send word. Now, pray bolt the door behind me."

As Lockwood stepped onto the landing, he paused to hear the bolt sliding into place. He turned to Doolan, who told him, "I brought your sword, sir, thinking you might need it presently, if these fucking rumours are true." The private was fully turned out, his musket in his hands, his bayonet fixed.

They quickly clattered down the stairs, and as they stepped out the door, Doolan looked carefully up and down the dark, wet street. For the first time, James thought the private seemed shaken. Doolan pointed to the horizon where a bright fire danced on a distant hilltop. "Look there, sir. The devil is afoot this night." A moment later another blaze jumped into life on a hilltop few miles further west.

"Doolan," said Lockwood, trying to sound calm, "perhaps it would be best if you kept watch here, until we know what's on."

"I shall watch over her as my own daughter."

The slick cobbled streets were deserted, and it was only when Lockwood approached Clonakilty Barracks that he saw another soul, where three blue-coated yeomen stood at the gate, fully turned out with their carbines in their hands, loudly debating the likelihood of a rebel attack. Lockwood had never before seen yeomen assigned to stand guard; typically the pampered horsemen were allowed to sleep the night while the Galways or Westmeaths stood watch. Sykes had obviously lost confidence in the militiamen.

It was only when Lockwood had approached to within a few yards of the gate that one of the yeomen noticed him, and wildly swinging his carbine to his shoulder, he cried, "Halt!"

Held at gun-point for the first time, James pleased himself by being more insulted than afraid. He sighed, and said, "Ensign Lockwood, Westmeaths. What the devil are you men about?"

"Beg pardon, sir," said the trooper, lowering his weapon. "But those bloodthirsty rebels are about, and we've been told to expect an attack at any time."

"Then you had best stand your guard like soldiers instead of standing about haggling like a pack of fishwives. You might live longer. Now open the gate, for God's sake."

The barracks yard was a study in disorganization. Westmeaths, Galways, and yeomen tumbled half-dressed out of their barracks, forming up in the flickering lamp light, their officers and NCOs roaring orders, some contradictory.

Lockwood found two more yeomen standing guard at the door of the barracks headquarters. These two at least knew their duty, and raised their carbines in a proper salute.

He strode into the headquarters to find Sykes alone, his uniform coat open over a bare chest, sitting behind his desk, feverishly flipping through a handful of scattered papers.

Sykes paused, looked up at Lockwood, and giving him a smile of relief and genuine affection, he said, "Oh, James, I do so apologize for pulling you from the arms of your charming bride, but it seems as if the walls of the world are crashing in on us. A dragoon from Cork brought in this handful of pages from Moore's headquarters, stuffed into his sabretache like yesterday's laundry. These are all back-up copies; God knows what happened to the originals. It seems there has been some trouble with the mail coaches, and some dispatch riders have gone missing."

Sykes glanced down to see his bare belly, and hurriedly standing and buttoning up his coat, he laughed weakly and went on, "You may understand that things are in a bit of a tizzy. The dragoon said men tried to stop him at several points on the roads into town, even in the dark. He was fired upon up near Shannonvale. Just think, a King's dragoon, shot at! But, still, he found a path across the fields, the brave fellow."

"May I ask, sir, what news the dragoon carried?"

Throwing up one finger, Sykes dug through the papers with his other hand, eventually pulling out one battered page, crying, "Here it is... look at this! We are to immediately march to Bandon!"

"With no notice?" said Lockwood, stunned. "You may recall, sir, that Mrs. Lockwood is here in town...."

"Oh, yes, yes, of course. Mrs. Lockwood... well, of course, she will be most welcome here in the garrison, safe in your quarters until arrangements might be made for her to join you in Bandon. Yes, of course."

A quick rap at the door, and a yeoman sergeant entered, snapped a professional salute, and said, "Sergeant Youngblood, sir. Captain Mason orders me to report sir, that the roll has been called. The Camber Yeomen are all present. Of the Westmeaths, I beg to report six men have deserted, sir. Of the Galways, fifteen men have deserted."

With a look of shock on his face, Sykes managed to say, "You are dismissed, thank you, Sergeant." He was stock-steady until the yeoman was gone, and then muttering, "I must visit the chamber of ease..." Sykes bolted from the room.

James took the opportunity to pick up a page from the pile, and holding it to the faint candlelight he read a few scribbled lines, barely legible, the pen of a man in a mad hurry, or a mad panic.

Secret. Dublin is to be the key to the rising. The rebels intend to seize the city and trigger a message to the rest of the country by stopping the mail coaches. While mail coaches have been stopped in some areas, other areas had no notice of the planned insurrection and with the United Irish leadership mostly in prison or in exile, the rising has flared up in in a localized and uncoordinated manner.

Lockwood picked up another crumpled page.

The news of the rising spreads. The Kildare Committee was the first of the outlying regions to recognize the start of the rebellion. Shortly thereafter a yeomanry sergeant in Kildare named George Crawford and his fourteen year old granddaughter were murdered by a party of rebels. The same band of rebels then stopped the Limerick mail coach, which they drunkenly plundered. One of the passengers, Lieutenant William Gifford, aged seventeen, of the 82nd Regiment, was shot and piked to death when he refused to join the rebels.

Sykes reappeared, wiping his mouth with a silk handkerchief. Lockwood made no secret of having gone through the scattered pages. The ensign looked at Sykes, exhaled sharply, and said, "It appears, sir, that we're stuck in."

*****

Five Company was drawn up in the chill, damp, darkness, as Company Sergeant Major Ahern stood at their head. He was the only soldier of any real experience in the company, and so was by nature not prone to wild swings of mood. The company had been there for some time, formed in their ranks between the Galways. Ahern considered them sloppy bastards, and the yeomen feckin' prima donnas, standing at their horses' heads, eyeing the militia with suspicion.

An anonymous voice came from the ranks behind Ahern, quietly saying in Irish, "These posh officers can stuff it up their arses. Let's say we all take off through the rear gate, boys, and shed these fucking red coats?"

Ahern growled but did not turn around, only loudly saying, also in Irish, "I can hear you, Private McGrath. You are not fooling anyone, I know it's you. One more word and I shall have you on report. Now, silence in the ranks, like good lads."

Soon thereafter Ensign Lockwood came hurrying down the steps from the headquarters building, and, striding up to Ahern, the young officer said, "Sergeant Major, we have new orders. Colonel Sykes orders the company to march, once morning comes. We are to reinforce the garrison at Bandon. For now, have the men stand down and see to their packs. I'll stir up the kitchens and ensure a good breakfast is prepared before we set out."

Lockwood turned to go, but then paused, and turned back to Ahern. "I had forgotten... the company wives and children shall remain here. We will send for them in a few days. And, Sergeant Major, pray ensure that every musket is clean, the flints keen, and cartouches full. I shall inspect every man's kit before we set out."

More than pleased to leave the yeomen and the Galways standing in the misting rain, the Westmeaths fell out and returned to their quarters, harried by their sergeants to pack up. The married men had to explain the departure to their families, and the reason for their new orders was widely debated across the company.

Corporal Hanahan said, "There is great wisdom yet to be gleaned from the ancients, lads. We've all heard, *"Íarus fis, túathus cath, airthius bláth, teissius séis."* Knowledge in the west, battle in the north, prosperity in the east, music in the south.

The men of the mess all looked over to nod in agreement, and Callahan went on, "And, Ian Cheevers, in which direction lies Bandon?"

"Why, in the north itself, Corporal *a grah.*"

Chapter Twenty-Five

It had been many years since Diarmuid Doolan had seen the need to remain awake all night, but he stood watch, steadfast, at the front door of the Lockwood's lodgings throughout the long hours after Ensign Lockwood had been called to Clonakilty Barracks. Doolan, never one to shy away from the ways of a curmudgeon, thus felt entitled to a foul mood when morning came. There was no sign of Lockwood's return, only, with the rising of the sun, a wizened boy came trotting down the street. He stopped at Doolan's post, and chirped, "A letter for Miss O'Brian, please, sir."

"Have some respect, boyo. It's Mrs. Lockwood, now." The boy handed the letter across, and Doolan eyed the blank cover, closed with green wax, but with no seal. "Who sent this?"

"I'm told to say, 'a friend'."

"I'll take it up to her, then. Off with ya."

"But you'll not be forgetting me, please, sir? It's a hardworking boy I am, and poor."

"It's a tip you're wanting? I'll give you this, then: take that sprig of green from your cap, you mad pup, before some yeoman thinks you're a grown rebel and skewers you."

The boy muttered a surprisingly vicious curse, and as he headed back up the street he called back over his shoulder, "Long live the Republic!"

As he headed through the door Doolan shook his head and said to himself, "He'll be a corpse by the end of the week, that one. Feckin' eejit."

Doolan found Brigid Lockwood standing at the top of the stairs, clutching the rail. "I heard voices; is my husband come home, Diarmuid?"

"My apologies, Missus, but, no, he is not. But a letter is come for you." As he brought it up, he added, "Even a man as unfamiliar with the written word as your devoted servant, Missus, can see the cover is blank, though the boy said it was from a friend."

She examined it, curious, then broke the seal and unwrapped the cover to find a sealed letter within. She studied the address, and though she had never met the sender, she went quiet, as she recognized the hand.

"Whoever is it from, Missus?" whispered Doolan, sensing her anxiety, but then, hearing heavy footsteps outside, he whirled to bring his musket to bear on the door.

The door flew open and there stood Lockwood, who said, "Pray, do not shoot me, Doolan. I'm having a bad day already, and I imagine it shall grow worse." Lockwood then took the stairs two at a time, and Brigid rushed past Doolan to embrace him. As eager as he was to hold and kiss her, he noticed the letter she held. "Whatever is that, my dear?"

She handed it to him, and softly said, "A letter from your father."

As they walked up to their little apartment, he studied the cover, puzzled, saying, "But how could this ever get to us? The mail coaches were stopped by the rebels days ago."

"A boy brought it a few minutes ago, sir," said Doolan, eyeing the room, wondering if there was anything to eat.

"It came in a plain wrapper," said Brigid, hesitantly. "All I can guess is that when the mail coach was stopped, one of the men there... perhaps a friend of my father... went through the mail bag, recognized your name, and knowing of our marriage had it sent here." She sighed, and added, mostly to herself, "Out of a sense of humour, I wonder, or was he trying to be kind?"

James flipped the letter over, and said, "Your father's friends may be rebels, but remarkably considerate rebels; the seal is intact."

Doolan said, "I'll return to my post out front, then, I suppose, ever the faithful servant." As he thumped down the stairs, he grumbled, "No bed, no breakfast... Christ, what a life."

James sat on the bed, and, taking Brigid's hand, he pulled her down to sit next to him. He opened the letter, and together they read,

> *26 May, 1798*
> *James:*
>
> *I am in possession of your letter of the 21st instant. My riposte shall be brief. As your wholly ill-considered marriage to this person—a person of no family or fortune, a person of a faith and a people in direct and violent opposition to our own—is contrary to every requirement and desire of this family, it is*

my duty to inform you that you will receive no further support, of any nature, from this family.

You have long taken perverse pleasure in defying me at every turn, and in consideration of your irresponsible union—an insult to all we cherish!—it is my fervent hope that we shall have no cause to communicate upon any instance in the future. Further, you will favor me by having no further contact with <u>any</u> member of this family.

In closing, I might mention that your mother has been consigned to the care of Dr. Moore's Hospital. It is my opinion that it was news of your unfortunate marriage which tipped her already fragile health to her current state of delusion.

It is my desire that you now bear the full weight of your willful, impulsive, and selfish marriage to a person of such low birth and dubious morals, one that has destroyed your future. It has also destroyed the relationship with your father, the relationship that your previous behaviors had so severely strained, to the point where it now stands unrecoverable.

John Lockwood, esq.

She began to cry softly, saying, "Oh, James, I have ruined you."

He wadded up the letter and tossed it into a corner. Trying to sound cheerful, he said, "Oh, do not be silly, my dear. It is what I expected, what *we* expected, from him. Indeed, it is all for the best. We now have that seen to, and we no longer need concern ourselves with John Lockwood, Senior."

"But what of your dear mother?"

His forced veneer cracked a bit as he replied, "I shall write to her as soon as I get two minutes. I confess, I worry for her. But for now, my dear, we have a great deal to discuss."

*****

For the rural poor, the arrival of the month of June marked the start of the hungry months. It was in June when the previous year's potatoes became inedible, and the new crop could not be dug until August. Even in years promising great bounty, for those summer months the untold millions of Irish who had no form of sustenance beyond potatoes hovered on the edge of starvation.

It was the middle of June when Tadg O'Donovan, the prosperous carpenter from town, strode down the Bandon Road, a handful of his men in his wake, bound for a remote crossroads three miles north of Clonakilty. The weather that morning, in fact all that year, had been glorious, and he took a deep, if temporary, joy in the morning sun.

O'Donovan had been told that no one lived near the crossroads, but upon arrival he found a cottier's cabin built in a roadside ditch, wretched and filthy. O'Donovan the carpenter had a notion as to how a proper home should be built, and as he drew closer to the cabin he felt a keen discontent. In the ditch, two rough stone walls had been thrown up to form the sides of the cabin, and sticks and thatch ran from the hedge to the edge of the road as a rough roof. When the rains came the place would be fairly awash. The family could not lay claim to a true field, but alongside the hedges and beside the road they had planted potatoes. A thousand such lean-to hovels stood within a few miles of

Clonakilty, and many of those desperate families had contributed a father or son to the United Irish forces.

As he walked closer O'Donovan saw several pale, gaunt faces watching him from the cabin door, a gap in in the rough stone wall. Soon a little man, thin and dirty, who might have been twenty years of age or fifty, emerged to cautiously say, *"Dhia agus Mhaire duit, chòire."* God and Mary be with you, sir.

"Dhia, Mhaire, agus Padraig duit, deartháir." God, Mary and Patrick to you, brother. Tadg went on, "The Year of Liberty is come. My men and I are here to throw down the English."

The little man coughed a laugh of dark disbelief, his mask of civility dissolving, and as he looked O'Donovan up and down, he sniffed and said, "You're it, then? I had expected Saint Padraig and a hundred angels, them on white steeds with blazing swords, not a dozen rogues with sharp sticks on their shoulders. It's a great disappointment you are, boyo."

"Ah, go lie across yourself, ya feckin' eejit," said O'Donovan, walking past the man, looking over the crossroad with a what he hoped was a soldier's eye.

The little man skipped alongside O'Donovan, pointing a sharp finger, he said, "You're not fooling anyone, General! You and your 'Year of Liberty' shite! You'll be putting Irish bosses in place of English bosses, when all we need is feckin' food! Fuck your grand notions, give us some unspoiled taters!"

"Just you wait. There will be land for every man, once the English are driven out."

"Don't spout horseshit to me, General. The rich man will always step on the poor man, no matter they speak Irish, English, French, or the language of the fucking fairies."

O'Donovan cursed, and as more of the United men joined him, he turned away from the cottier and ordered, "Sergeant O'Cronin, post pickets a half mile to the south, east, and west. Have the rest of the lads build an abattis—"

"A *what*, please, Tadg, *a grah*?" asked his sergeant.

Secretly pleased to get a chance to use the term he'd read in a military manual the night before, O'Donovan paused, considering a translation to the Irish, then went on, "A fence of logs and brush, man, across the south face of the crossroad. No one comes up this road without our leave."

As the rebels set to work, the cottier realized the rebels had come to stay, and as they brusquely took to the hedges to cut trees and scrub, he followed after them, ranting, "Will you not get out of there, you rebel bastards? You, there, you clumsy bastards, stay out of my feckin' taters! Oh, be damned to you Croppy boys! You know the *Sassenach* shall come and burn my cabin, and while it's shite to you, it's all in the world to me, you trouble-making pricks! I have four kids and me missus here, her with a baby on each teat! Oh, Christ, I hope the *Sassenach* kill the lot of ya!"

O'Donovan walked up into a field above the crossroads to check lines of sight, and as the little cottier continued to squawk a few of the United men took the opportunity to kick his arse, and so convinced him of the righteous nature of their cause.

*****

That night, in a hedge above the crossroads, O'Donovan squatted by a low fire, trying to poke damp peat into something like a Christian blaze. He was pleased that the men of several more parish committees had rallied to the call to arms, and now he had nearly three hundred men gathered around him, their fires like stars on the hillsides.

One of the sentries, a shadow looming in his wake, stepped into O'Donovan's small circle of light. The sentry jerked a thumb over his shoulder, and said, "Michael O'Brian to see you, please, Captain."

O'Donovan grinned and waved the shadow to join him.

O'Brian grunted as he took a seat on the ground by the fire, shaking his head and saying, "Can your revolution not afford a couple of fucking chairs?"

"You're old and fat, Michael O'Brian."

"Fuck off. Now, even though you abuse me so cruelly, as friend to the new republic I might mention that on my way here I passed Ailill O'Reilly and his lads at Garranecore. They were well formed, and looked damned sharp when they drove off a yeoman patrol. But then I walked by Garraneishal, where that wee Davy Walsh, a dozen Owenahincha gowls at his back, stopped me and said I needed a pass to get past his checkpoint. Cheeky little fucker. Wasn't it me who taught him the catechism and brought him into the movement as a favor to his uncle, and yet there he stood, asking me for a fucking pass?"

"I suppose you corrected the lad's poor manners?"

"I did. But Christ and His nails, Tadg... *Captain* Davy Walsh?"

"I'm sorry for your trouble, you poor delicate blossom, but I had to make Walsh a captain, didn't I? Otherwise his men said they wouldn't muster when the day came."

"Uneasy lies the head that wears a crown, boyo." Reaching over to poke the weak fire, O'Brian added in another tone, "Is the day come, then, Tadg?"

"Aye. There has been no mail coach since Tuesday, and a rider from Wexford came in yesterday to say all the southeast is aflame, if he can be believed. I'm convinced it's on, and you, Michael, should be at home. Some of my lads are far worse than Davy Walsh, and some of them suspect you, thinking of your daughter, her Proddy friends, and her new husband, your son-in-law, him with his red coat and an officer's gold epaulette."

After a significant pause, O'Brian quietly said, "Ya know, I never thought I would ever see such a day, but God does enjoy feckin' about. Before I go, let me ask you this: I met my nephew Fergal down on the road. He's in it as well, then?"

"You mean Lieutenant Fergal O'Brian? One of my aides-de-camp."

"Ah, fuck, Tadg. That wee boy?'

"He'll not be a boy when this work done."

"I hope he's *anything* after this, above a rotting corpse."

O'Donovan was silent for another long moment until, without looking away from the fire, he quietly said, "Go home, Michael."

"I will." O'Brian got to his feet, but as he turned to go he added with the slightest quiver in his voice, "God bless you, brother."

Later O'Donovan wished that he might have kept O'Brian there, perhaps to discuss some of the dispositions he had made, but instead, O'Donovan sat alone by the little fire. He then wished he had a drink, but he had ordered that there was to be no drunkenness until their victory was secure. He was well aware that many of the men gathered in the fields around him carried jugs of liquor, and nervous men tended to drink.

For weeks he had studied and planned, torn over how best to isolate and destroy the government forces in Clonakilty. In the end he had ordered the majority of his men to join him, to block the main road from Clonakilty to Bandon and Cork Town beyond. He had detachments on nearly every road, full companies at Timoleague, Lyre,

Bealad Cross and Lisavaird, all in an attempt to isolate the government garrison. In the end, though, all of O'Donovan's dispositions meant nothing if every other chapter of United Irishmen did not in turn rise up and isolate or attack the garrisons of every city and town. And he held no illusions regarding the capabilities of the United Irishmen as a whole, or of his own nervous, willful, and wholly inexperienced men.

Early that morning an additional hundred men had joined the crossroad forces, sending the little army's morale soaring. His army was of a mercurial temper; real doubts sprang up when word spread that the Ahiohill men had decided to sit this one out, as their crops needed tending, but then roared back when the thirty Ballygurteen men came striding down from Crusheennalanniy with pikes on their shoulders, six of them carrying desperately needed muskets.

*****

Michael O'Brian returned to an empty house, as Ann and Caitlin were still staying with their grandfather at his remote home. He was content in knowing that his girls were safe, but, still, he felt a pang of loneliness when he opened the door to silent rooms and a cold hearth.

He scribbled a note for his third daughter: "Brigid, stay close to the barracks; no matter how the rebellion grows, the local men are not strong enough to storm it. And for God's sake, tell your boy to stay there as well."

He resolved to take the note himself; he would not send one of the local boys out into a countryside full of armed men, with a note which might see the boy branded as a traitor to any one of a number of causes. Michael folded the note and stuck it into his pocket, then thinking again, slipped off his coat and put on another, one with a hidden pocket cleverly sown into the lining. He had carried incriminating letters before, but this one would see him hung, not just by the crown but his own friends as well.

He was calm but his mind was active as he strode away from his house. The roads would be blocked by men of both sides, and many of the fields would be within sight of those roadblocks. But he knew of a path that was screened nearly the entire way into town. He hopped across the stone wall around Owen McNamara's south field and confidently headed down the hills into Clonakilty.

It was yet another beautiful morning of a beautiful spring; the apple trees in Mrs. Crawley's orchard were losing the last of their blossoms, but the air was still rich with their scent. He was nearly to town, and knew that two nearby roads were sure to be held by men who, no matter their politics, would be pleased to shoot anyone they might not care for. He would thus need to be especially careful, as that part of the path followed deep hedges along the top of a low ridge between the two roads. The path seemed to end at some points, but he knew just where to squeeze through a hedge or hop a wall to keep heading toward town. One hedge was particularly tall and thick, and he had to climb like a boy to get over and through. He jumped the last few feet down into the next field, and was startled to find himself standing next to a man pissing into the hedge. In an instant he noticed the man had a white coat, poorly made, but then realized it was a uniform coat turned inside-out, a turncoat, a deserter from the crown. In any case, he didn't know him, and so he was no friend of his.

O'Brian was a man who could throw a punch, and the pissing man was in no position to defend himself. Still, the turncoat managed to call for help before O'Brian could silence him, and as Michael frantically scrambled back up into the hedge, ignoring the branches scratching his face and tearing his clothes, he saw several other white coats running toward him, some of them carrying muskets.

As in a nightmare, O'Brian could not find a way through the green hell of branches and leaves, trapped as the deserters ran closer. One of them, a man O'Brian might have kissed, called out, "Don't fire, lads, it'll draw the yeomen!" But then another called out, "He's a spy!" and a third, "Get the bastard!" A second's pause, and then came the crack of the muskets, and four or five balls ripped through the hedge; they might have been deserters, but they could shoot, and the leaves and branches all around Michael were flailed. He finally tumbled out of the hedge, and by some miracle he felt only a tearing pain on his hand, a musket ball blowing a groove across the top of his left hand, burning like a hot poker.

He ran hard, knowing the sound of gunfire would stir the countryside. He had gone perhaps two hundred yards when he came across a large party of Irishmen, a few muskets, mostly pikes, looking frightened, and they called out for him to halt. Thank God, they must have been from far to the west, as he recognized no one, and no one called out his name. But he dared not speak to them, and so tore past, pointing back, and calling out, "Soldiers!"

The rebels paused, and then ran as well, like an anthill stirred, and in a few minutes O'Brian was clear. A mile away he stopped for a few minutes, panting like a dog, to wrap a handkerchief around his bloody hand. He then took a long swing south to ensure that no one was following him, and after two hours more he was at home, exhausted.

He started a small fire to bring some cheer to the house, and perhaps to himself. Going to the little well house at the back of the kitchen, he cranked up the bucket with his good hand. Pulling the handkerchief from his hand, he held it up for a moment to allow it to bleed clean, then poured some of the pure cold water across the wound. He tied one of the tea towels hanging there around his hand, and smiled at how his girls would have scolded him for ruining a good towel. He then poured the rest of the water into the tea pot, and back at the hearth he hung it on the iron and swung it over the keen little fire.

He opened his coat to dig out the note from the hidden pocket, and found the lining had been torn open in his scramble through the hedge. The note hung in his coat by a thread; his second miracle of the day,

"God, let there be a third upon the head of my dear Brigid this day," he said, as he placed the note on the fire, and he prayed for her, and that boy of hers.

*****

Private Doolan stood outside the Lockwood lodgings, drawing more and more attention from the locals as the morning went on and news of rebellion spread. From the corner of his eye he watched as some boys gathered stones at the end of the street, the pups growing bolder, occasionally calling out insults at the loan redcoat. Being a man who valued his privacy, his sleep, and his belly, Diarmuid did not much care for his lot, but he stood his post nonetheless. He was growing increasingly angry, taking long looks back at the door, for Lockwood to come downstairs and tell him what was to happen next, though he was grimly certain the near future did not involve his bed or his breakfast.

Finally, Lockwood came bolting outside, hurriedly saying, "I am away. The company is marching to Bandon. As soon as Mrs. Lockwood has packed a few things, get her to the barracks." Looking up and down the street, he went on,

"Christ. You had best get upstairs. I'll have an escort sent from the barracks. But in any case, you'll need to hurry."

"Right, then. What of your things, sir?"

Lockwood was nearly hopping in frustration and hurry, quickly saying as he headed off, "You can throw them into my trunk, and we'll retrieve them whenever opportunity arises." Then, pausing, he added in a very human tone, "I am sorry to rely on you so heavily, Doolan, but you'll see to her, won't you?"

Doolan sniffed, and gruffly said, "Don't you worry, sir, I'll have her tucked into her new quarters by dinner. Off you go, now, and see you your duty. You need not worry about us, at all, at all."

With a last look and a lingering wave to Brigid, who watched from the upstairs window, Lockwood was off. Doolan thumped upstairs, and without ceremony he hurriedly began to pack his officer's belongings. Looking over his shoulder he tensely said, "The ensign orders that I stay with you, Missus. Please pack your valise, and we'll get over to the barracks. It'll be a good place to take refuge, sure, the Rock of Cashel writ small."

She was kneeling by her trunk, tending her things, and she did not look up as she answered with a shaking voice. "Refuge, Diarmuid? You make it sound as if I am fleeing, hiding like a frightened child. The barracks is certainly not my only option. I could stay here. I could go to my own father's home. I could go where I please."

"Miss, it is time for you to do as your husband orders, whether you like it or no—"

She got to her feet and spun on him with raised eyebrows and a raised finger, flaring, "Is it Brigid ni Brian, bean o' Lockwood to whom you are speaking, Diarmuid Doolan? Am I not a daughter of one of the great families of Ireland? Do you mistake me for a field ewe, mated and fenced? Or am I an honest Irishwoman, and so a person of spirit? I will hear no more about anyone's *orders*, sir." Winding down, she went on, "The ensign and I discussed what is to be done, and so I do what we agreed is the best course of action. You can stuff that talk of orders, for all love. I shall have angels flying... well, no matter."

"Beg pardon, please, Missus," said Doolan, unoffended, with renewed affection. His late mother had dearly loved her boy Diarmuid Doolan, with a graciousness which would have surprised anyone who knew the man, and that worthy woman had managed to instill the smallest touch of her graciousness into his mulish frame. Remembering that worthy woman, he managed a small bow and politely asked, "Missus, *a grah*, is it your desire to be traveling to the barracks, or your father's home, or elsewhere, please?"

"The barracks, please, Diarmuid, *a grah*," she said with a firm nod, then added, "as that seems our best option. My husband must do as he must, and so, then, shall I. I suppose that we all have no choice now, but to do what we must, whether we like it or no, and God help the innocent."

Chapter Twenty-Six

Ensign Lockwood did not wish to be seen doing something as unofficerly as running in the open street, and so kept his pace to nothing more manic than a determined stride as he returned to the barracks. He had been away from his company for two hours, doubting himself, wondering if he had been remiss in his duty, in turn knowing that Brigid needed him as well. It was yet another painful step in his indoctrination to a soldier's life, though he took comfort in knowing that Doolan would die before allowing harm to come to her.

Lockwood found himself, not for the first time, wishing he could speak with Tom Mainwaring. He could discuss anything with Brigid, but he yearned for a friend, not one of his school friends, but a fellow soldier, in whom he could confide the doubts common to very junior subalterns. He allowed himself the remainder of his hurried walk, four full minutes, to wallow in self-pity. Nearing the gate, his soldier's mind returned; it was a part of his mind still forming, but he found himself relishing the prospect of action. He was not a bloody-minded man, but he loved a challenge, and the day ahead was rife with challenge.

Men of the Camber Yeomanry had the guard, as both the Westmeath companies, long relied upon for such onerous duty, had been ordered to prepare to march to Bandon. As Lockwood approached the yeomen at the gate, the typically cocksure brutes looked unsettled as they brought their carbines up in salute. As a red-coated officer and thus a superior being, James gave them only a glance and a casual touch of his jaunty bicorn in return.

Once in the yard, Lockwood was struck by the difference between the two Westmeath companies. At the north end, Captain Barleycorn's One Company sat at their ease, chatting and dozing, unburdened by the presence of their officers or NCOs. At the south end, where his Five Company was assembled, the men tended to their weapons and gear with something resembling a professional air, as they had some idea of what was expected of them by their superiors and, just as importantly, what was expected by their mates.

Between the two infantry companies, the center of the yard was taken up by the men of the Royal Irish Artillery, where they harnessed the battery horses into their traces with their usual dour competence. Lockwood paused for a moment to study them: two brass guns shining in the muted morning light, the carriages, limbers and wagons painted the same moderate grey as every gun in Britain, and the fifty-odd gunners, drivers, and officers in bicorns and red-faced blue coats. Despite the brevity of his service, James had become a thorough-going infantryman, and so thought artillery useful in some rare instances, but a damned nuisance otherwise.

Consigning the artillery to the least of his concerns, Lockwood quickly moved on to where his company was gathered, seeking out his senior NCO. "How do things, stand, Sergeant?"

"Beg pardon, sir," said Sergeant Bourne, coming to attention with his typically formal air. "I beg leave to report, sir, that six men are absent without leave: Privates Farrell, Kelly, Brien, Daly, Maguire and Brady."

"Very well, Sergeant," said Lockwood, swallowing hard. "Good riddance to them. Still, I trust their muskets remain in the barracks?"

"Oh, aye, sir, aye," said Bourne, allowing himself a rare grin. "Those dogs have run, with naught but their coats and a few biscuits. They'll soon be missing their warm beds, sleeping in the hedges with their new friends." In a consoling tone, he added, "I might mention that One Company had fourteen men desert, sir."

"From what I hear, we may run into some of those men and their friends between here and Bandon. Are we quite ready to march, Sergeant Major, and to fight every foot of the way?"

The young officer spoke with such certainty that Bourne was taken aback, eventually managing, "Shall I have the men fall in for inspection, sir?"

"No, no," said Lockwood, shaking his head, "there is no sense in having them standing about when we have a long day ahead of us. But until Colonel O'Reilly calls on us to march, I shall see how they do. By the way, Bourne, I trust you saw to their breakfast?"

"Oh, yes, sir. As you ordered, they are fattened like prime bulls, prepared for anything from..." said Bourne, stumbling to a halt.

"From mahjong to manslaughter, Sergeant?" said Lockwood with a flash of boyish excitement, and with the sergeant-major in his wake, he passed through the company, speaking with each man, relaxed, but not overly familiar. He liked most people, and was disappointed when people did not like him in return. There were men in the company who eyed him with dislike, or worse, men who might not have deserted but still deeply resented their officers. But the excitement building in his heart buoyed Lockwood, and he stepped up to question the few sullen brutes of the company without hesitation. Lockwood ensured that each man had a sparking flint, a cartouche full of dry cartridges, and a knowledge that they were likely to employ them before the day was out.

The Westmeath Militia's Five Company, like most every other company in the British army, was divided into two sub-divisions, and each sub-division into two sections. The sections were then, more informally, split into squads of five to seven men, and even an officer as junior as James Lockwood recognized that the bonds between the men of the squads were critical to any army, from Caesar's legions to his company of redcoats. As he worked his way through the company, he came to the squad best known to him, familiar and fondly remembered, the men who had escorted him to his call on the O'Brians just a few days before.

Corporal Nugent looked up to give his officer a grin and to ask, "All well with your missus, sir?" with the familiarity of a man who had seen his officer as a nervous suitor.

"Well enough, thank you, Corporal. Doolan is with her."

"That Doolan is a mean old shite, but he's right fond of your bride, sir, and will see her settled, without a worry."

"Yes, that is so. Now, let us see to your mates. O'Hea, your flint seems askew."

O'Hea, a short stocky fellow with a scarred complexion, dry-fired his musket, then held up his hands in surrender as the flint in the jaws of his musket once again failed to spark.

Ensign Lockwood took a turn with the stone, but having cracked the flint, he sighed in frustration, stood upright, and called out, "Pass the word for John Coleman!" The man could knap sodden peat to a sparking edge. "Here, Coleman! Be a good fellow and take a look at this flint, would you? I've made a cock of it."

Several of the enlisted men within hearing grinned, for hearing an officer admit to making a cock of anything was a great rarity, and they privately took a greater liking to the earnest young man. One of those men was the gruff Drummer O'Malley, the man who had ridden the ensign's horse for part of the march to Clonakilty and who had since come to develop a grudging liking for Lockwood. So, when the ensign reached him, O'Malley asked Lockwood over to examine the condition of his drumhead. When Lockwood knelt over the drum, O'Malley leaned close to his officer's ear, and hurriedly whispered, "Do you know Eamonn O'Rourke in first platoon?"

"The big fellow with the dark eyes?"

"Do not turn your back on him."

Lockwood nodded and quickly moved on. He desperately wanted to know more, but he could not ask and risk compromising O'Malley. He had only a moment to consider the warning before the headquarters' drummer snapped out the sharp notes of the Officers' Call.

A few moments later, Lockwood sat in the Officers' Mess, one of the nine officers gathered there. He had been introduced to them all, but he scarcely knew them. He was equally certain that Colonel O'Reilly had no idea of who they were, as men or as officers.

The three officers of the Cambers took their seats in braided coats not buttoned up, dapper, wealthy, and brutal. They were not part of the column heading to Bandon, and so contented themselves with sitting off to one side and snapping their fingers for the mess stewards to bring them tea and scones. First Lieutenant Brown and Second Lieutenant Birch of the artillery sat silent and erect, capable and stone-faced.

Next to the artillerymen sat Captain Barleycorn and Lieutenant Salt of the Westmeath's One Company, typical of the men Lockwood had met in militia regiments: inexperienced and disinterested. Lockwood had come to suspect that such men were privately afraid of their men. Some of their disinterest, that studied, distant, feigned nonchalance typical of many of their class, was in fact the fear that any Irishmen might cut their throats if they came too close. It was class guilt, a subconscious acknowledgment of the injustice of their place in Irish society.

James Lockwood, too, was a son of the Ascendancy, but one whose focus was the welfare of the men, the Irish men, under his command.

As he sat at Lieutenant Colonel O'Reilly's side he grew increasingly concerned. O'Reilly addressed his officers in an excited tone, but as Lockwood had now known him for some weeks, he detected the nervous tone in O'Reilly's voice, indeed the quiver of a man who might not be in complete control.

"Gentlemen," began O'Reilly, much more loudly that the small gathering called for, "we prepare to march, perhaps, indeed, to glory itself! I shall take only a few moments of your time. First, pray allow me thank you gentlemen of the Camber Yeomanry for your professionalism during my brief time in command here. I am confident that when the men of the Caithness Legion arrive, you shall accord their Colonel Sutherland the same level of support."

The senior officer of the Cambers waved a scone in thanks, swallowed, and said, "By the way, sir, might I ask when we might expect the arrival of the Legion? I hear they are Scots," turning to his snickering fellows, "and I suppose we should lie in a supply of whiskey and skirts!"

Most of the men in the room laughed aloud; Lockwood did not, and he noticed the artillerymen looked displeased as well. His opinion of them rose.

It took some time before the laughter and murmuring subsided to the point where O'Reilly could proceed, perhaps even more excited. "It is deuced awkward, I know, but as we have received no communication since our initial orders, I know only that we are to march to Bandon and the Legion is to come here."

Getting another wave of scone in acknowledgment, O'Reilly returned to his agenda. "Item the second: the order of march. Captain Barleycorn and One Company shall lead, followed by Lieutenant Brown's guns, and then my Five Company. As overall commander I shall ride at the head of the column, the tip of the spear!"

"Well said, sir! Well said!" cried several of the officers, further lighting up O'Reilly's now beaming countenance.

"Lastly, gentlemen: there have been parties of rebels encountered at several points around town. Few carry firearms, of course, but in one or two instances they resisted the advance of our patrols with some spirit. In the event we meet an enemy force—"

"I hope the peasants attempt to face us!" cried Barleycorn. "We shall drive them back to their hovels, those few that survive the experience! More than two hundred of His Majesty's muskets, supported by two six pounders? By God, we could march to Dublin and back and not suffer a scratch."

"That's the spirit!" replied O'Reilly. Lockwood's ear caught a note of hysteria. "If we encounter those rebels, we shall deploy across the width of the road—"

"Sir, if I may," inserted Lockwood tentatively, "it is a narrow road, sir, lined by hedges, stone walls, and trees along most of its length."

Barleycorn turned to face the young ensign, and said, "Thank you for your remarks, Ensign Lockwood, but I believe all of us have ridden that road more than once. Your Colonel knows best, and if the hedges hinder our deployment, we shall push through them and deploy in the fields beyond. Once in the open, we can demonstrate to the rebels the power of disciplined musketry."

"If I may, sir... I have walked some of those fields, sir, and most are small, with soft earth easily churned to mud. The hedges are thick, and high, and I cannot imagine formed troops crossing them in any sort of order. It is a dense country meant for defense, and in some instances high ground dominates—"

"It seems our young friend is now a military genius," sniffed Barleycorn. "Pray, Ensign, how did you come to know these fields so intimately?"

"Beg pardon, sir. I did not wish to speak out of turn, but I did notice the ground... well, while strolling with Mrs. Lockwood, sir."

O'Reilly said nothing, ceding control to Barleycorn, who went on, "How very charming. Now, if we might turn our thoughts away from romantic wanderings, and once more to the hard business of military affairs."

Lockwood flared, knowing it was unwise, but he had his men in mind, and so forged ahead. "Sir, on such a narrow road our column shall be very stretched out. And the artillery will separate our two companies, by, what, fifty yards?"

Lieutenant Brown held up a knowing finger, and said, "Two limbered light six pounders at fifty-nine feet each, two ammunition wagons and one baggage wagon, each at forty-eight feet, with regulation intervals... one hundred seventeen yards, one foot, precisely."

"Thank you, sir," said Lockwood with an appreciative, impressed nod of his head. Turning to O'Reilly, he went on, "With such a great distance between the two companies, sir, perhaps we might march with skirmishers in front and on each flank? I am thinking of Colonel Smith's predicament at Lexington twenty-three years ago—" Lockwood looked up to see he had gone too far; most of the others looked at him in surprise, derision, and not a little anger. He muttered, "I beg your pardon, gentlemen," and went mute.

In the ensuing oppressive silence, Lieutenant Brown did say, "Propriety aside gentlemen, our young friend has raised a valid concern." Lockwood could have kissed him. "It is indeed a narrow, heavily hedged road for many miles, and my guns will have no room to deploy. And even if we could reach a field to unlimber, if the fields are as small and muddy as Ensign Lakemore suggests, we shall serve as nothing more than targets for the rebels. And while the American rebels possessed a far greater number of forearms than these Irish rebels, his comparison, I think, is not without merit."

Another painful silence ensued. Lockwood resolved to say nothing more, and would do as he was told. Though he thought the march was being mismanaged he took some consolation in knowing that O'Reilly would ride at the head of the column, and so James would essentially be in command of the company. Through the remainder of the meeting he sat thinking of what the day might bring, and of how the men, his men, might behave under fire. He wondered, too, why O'Malley had warned him of Eamonn O'Rourke.

*****

"Let's ambush the bastards!" cried an aging blacksmith named Mahon. In the sprawling rebel camp north of Clonakilty, Mahon commanded only the twenty men from Maulnagearagh, but they had appointed him as their colonel, and so Colonel Mahon insisted upon being considered second only to Tadg O'Donovan, in fact a very close second.

O'Donovan had seventeen officers gathered around him at the crossroads. He knew them all, from the secretive meetings of White Boys and United Irishmen in the long years before Dublin had finally declared open rebellion. Some of the officers were steady, rational men, to be relied upon, but several others were nervous and likely to flee at the first setback, while at least three others were so willful that O'Donovan doubted they would heed his orders.

One of these, a tall, spindly schoolmaster named Riordan, waved a finger at the other officers, and said, "There is no honour in ambush, gentlemen. We must instead charge *en masse* before the *Sassenach* can offer up a single volley. That is how best to harness the native genius of our Celtic natures. The famous Highland charge was initially known as the Irish charge, due to its first being implemented in Ireland, by Montrose's Irish brigade, before the Irish used it in Scotland again under Montrose."

"Jesus," sighed O'Donovan to himself. He was deeply disappointed in them. Arguing like a pack of fishwives was bad enough, but they looked like fools as well. He had asked that the officers mark their status by putting a sprig of evergreen or a green ribbon in their caps, and a green sash around their waists if they could afford it. Perhaps half of them had done so. A few had done nothing, wearing the same coats they wore to harvest potatoes or to man the bar at the shebeen. Others, though, had donned uniforms of their own making. One of his most reliable men had shown up with a bright blue coat and a cluster of long feathers stuck in his cap. The schoolmaster, Riordan, had proven his lunacy by wearing bright green from head to toe, and a gold epaulette on each shoulder. To complete the ensemble he had an ancient, heavy cavalry sword on his belt, a massive thing with a straight blade a yard long, the end of the scabbard dragging in the earth behind him, an outlandish thing for a man on foot to carry.

In the months before the rebellion the officers of all the companies around Clonakilty had acknowledged O'Donovan as their leader, but with actual fighting pending they often ignored him, instead standing about to chat and argue. O'Donovan heard one of them say, "Oh, my goodness, no! There are some good Irishmen among the enemy forces... no, we must confront them with an overwhelming show of force, explain the goals of the rebellion, so that some men of the Westmeaths might join us, and only then might their officers and the handful of loyalists be escorted to a civilized internment until they can be repatriated to England."

O'Donovan cursed softly and stalked past them, catching snippets of their conversation.

"Of course my men can be relied upon, but they must be fed. We require whiskey as well."

"I wonder when the French will come? I hope to get a commission in their army."

"Any man, no matter his birth, who wears a red coat, shall get my pike in his guts this day."

O'Donovan pushed past the knot of officers and climbed through a hedge to reach the field where the bulk of his army was gathered. At last count he had three hundred fifty men, and while some other companies had come in since the count, he was sure that some men had drifted away. Those three hundred fifty faces, expectant, nervous, fearful, and doubtful, looked up at him as he dropped into the field. Old faces and young, all faces of common men.

He inhaled deeply, and roared out in the Irish tongue they shared, "The English will be coming! I will make my stand here and kill as many as God allows! Who will stand with me?"

Those common men jumped to their feet and roared their allegiance, some more enthusiastically than others, holding aloft their pikes and scythes, knowing they were to face muskets and cannon. They cheered their general, and themselves, and their desperate hopes for what changes their rebellion might bring.

*****

O'Donovan had posted a party of his most reliable men on the hill above Clonakilty Barracks. One of them had a horse, a rare and valuable commodity in the rag-tag army, while one of the other men had a decent glass, and it was he who anxiously studied the King's men mustering below. It was mid-morning when the English officers mounted their horses, the drums spoke, the gates were thrown open, and the column of redcoats and cannon snaked out onto Barracks Road.

The man with the horse galloped back to report to O'Donovan with an exact count of the approaching enemy, as well as the disposition of the column. As their spies and the deserting soldiers had told them, the English were marching north toward Bandon, and the rebel crossroads lay in their path.

Chapter Twenty-Seven

The gates of Clonakilty Barracks opened and the head of the column marched out. As they made up the rear of the column, Five Company stood in their anxious ranks while One Company and the string of guns and wagons that were to separate the two companies slowly cleared the yard ahead of them.

Lockwood stood at the head of Five, his sword on his shoulder. He had at first expected to ride to Bandon on the horse he had ridden from Cork to Clonakilty, the lovely mare loaned to him by Lieutenant Colonel O'Reilly. But that morning, just after the officers' call, O'Reilly, effusively apologetic, had hurried over to explain that he had sold the mare to one of the yeomanry officers. And so Lockwood, like the ninety men of his company, departed Clonakilty on foot.

He had long minutes of inactivity as his mind churned—time to fret, to worry about Brigid, about Doolan, to remember he hadn't written to his mother, and for scolding himself for not updating the damned pay roster. He told himself not to think such thoughts and to address the present. He had long possessed the ability to control his mind and emotions, and he mused for a moment on how he had developed the skill. When he was a boy, his father took delight in teasing and demeaning his sensitive son, and he now wondered if perhaps he had learned that skill to avoid any lingering oppression by Lockwood senior. He sniffed in amused self-awareness, then looked about him, trying to concentrate.

Over the barracks rooftops he saw columns of smoke in the air, in the distance. He bent his head to listen closely, and over the noise raised by the men, horses and wheels in the yard he heard a distant musket shot, then two more. He was increasingly certain that the march would be opposed; he swallowed the urge to hurry forward to speak with O'Reilly, to urge him to be better prepared. But that time was past. Instead, he turned from his post and strode halfway down the column of tense, nervous men, to speak to the only man there who was not obviously either. "Sergeant Bourne, the company will load."

Surprised, Bourne said, "Sir, typically we do not go loaded on a route march, as to prevent—"

For the first time the sergeant felt Lockwood's ire, as the young officer snapped, "Have them *load*, Sergeant. While we still have time."

As Bourne gave the necessary orders, Lockwood trotted over to where the yeomanry officers sat on the steps of the officers' mess, smoking and laughing.

"I beg your pardon, gentlemen, but I must ask a favor." He was not nervous in speaking to them, as he was in a hurry, and he despised them. "Mrs. Lockwood and my servant Private Doolan shall be coming to the barracks shortly—Colonel O'Reilly has approved her sheltering here— and I wonder if I might ask you gentlemen to dispatch an escort, to see them in safely? Number Six, Patrick Street. I confess that I now regret having agreed to her remaining at our apartments, but she needed to attend to some personal matters before coming here."

The senior yeoman officer, a Captain Louis, sniffed, and said, "Goodness, sir, are you referring to your O'Brian girl? I hear she is a beauty, but you'll forgive me for wondering if perhaps she might prefer to return to her own people in such times as these? Birds of a feather flocking together, and such, eh?"

There was a change in Lockwood's demeanor, a subtle stiffening of the countenance, quickly recognized by the yeomanry officers. All three drew back from the young man. Lockwood's hand twitched near the hilt of his sword, and he said steadily, "Gentlemen, do not mistake me. I expect Mrs. Lockwood to be escorted here, and that she be received with the utmost courtesy and respect."

Louis sighed heavily, rolled his eyes, and said, "Oh, very well, sir. As you wish. You had best hurry, now, before your company marches without you." He then watched to ensure Lockwood was well out of earshot before he quietly said, "This Mrs. Lockwood might have her charms—I believe we have all heard how wildly expressive these Irish women are with their passions, their wholly wanton passions—but I doubt we find this spawn of the O'Brians to be much elevated above the usual potato-rooting *hoi polloi*. Honestly, we should not be expected to mingle with such persons."

The three yeomen watched Five Company march out, and as the gates were pulled closed behind them, Louis rolled to his feet and muttered, "Oh, damn it all, anyway." He then called out, "Sergeant Morton! A corporal's guard, *a pied*, and right quick, if you know what's good for you."

*****

Private Doolan discreetly pulled back the thin curtains hanging across the apartment's front window, looked down into the street, and whined, "Ah, shite, Missus, there are folks dashing about like it's the end of the world, St. Patrick's Day and my feckin' birthday all rolled into one."

Brigid Lockwood sighed, and said, not unkindly, "Diarmuid, this is not a roadside shebeen, or your regimental guard room, if you please."

"Beg pardon, Missus."

She was sitting on the bed with her hands folded in her lap, her dark hair pulled back with a black silk bow, dressed in a simple work dress. She was strikingly beautiful. Down in the street below, she heard someone shout drunkenly, "The year of liberty is come! Death to the English and their dogs!" She ignored the voice. Brushing a nonexistent speck of dust from her dress, she said, "If things are so bad in the street, it is all the more reason for us to stay here, Diarmuid *a grah*, safe and sound." She had a great love of language, both Irish and English, and the word 'affectation' popped into her mind.

"Ach," said Doolan, turning to her, "did I not promise himself that I'd have you to the barracks by noon? And yet here we sit, and every rebel devil within a hundred miles knowing the wife, the *Irish Catholic* wife, of a redcoat officer sits here as vulnerable as a newborn lamb. Christ, what a life."

She patted her bag, and said with a nervous smile, "Ensign Lockwood and I have said our farewells, and he left me his pistol. More than that, I have you, Diarmuid, *a grah*, the great soldier of the world, do I not?"

"Oh, sure, it's me, isn't it, Nessa Doolan's own son, a handful of sand against this tide of howling fiends. You know as well as I, Missus, that as many madmen as men of conscience are part of this rising, and those black thieves are capable of any evil. With no sign of an escort from the barracks, we may have to chance it"

Her face softened, and she said, "Just another hour or two, *le te thoil*? My family may yet try to contact me, and once I am in the barracks I may as well be on the moon, to them."

It was nearly another anxious hour later before they were startled by the sounds of footsteps bounding up the stairs, and though Doolan reached for his musket and called for her to wait, Brigid bolted to the door, threw it open, and cried out, in delighted surprise, "Ach, Fergal, God and Mary be with you!"

The young man at the door was short and slender, perhaps eighteen years old, though his slight frame might easily have had him mistaken for someone much younger. As he stepped into the room Fergal went wide-eyed, as Private Doolan, every inch the snarling redcoat, his musket raised, challenged him. Fergal relaxed a bit when Brigid embraced him, then a bit more when she happily turned to the soldier and said, "Diarmuid, this is my cousin, Fergal O'Brian. Fergal, this is Private Doolan of my husband's company, who has been kind enough to watch over me while my husband tends to his duties."

The two men gave one another a barely civil nod, and it was a long moment before Doolan slowly lowered his weapon. An awkward moment followed, broken by Doolan eventually surrendering with, "I shall step outside for a moment, then, Missus?"

She gave Doolan a nod of thanks, and when the door closed, she hurriedly asked, "Oh, Fergal, might you be bringing a letter from my family?"

His courage returning, Fergal said, "A letter, cousin? Oh, Christ, no! If the *Sassenach* should stop me and find an incriminating letter in my pocket they would have me hanging from the nearest tree, and no priest at hand, at all, at all. No, honey, I am far too wise for such foolishness."

They were of course speaking in Irish, though in English or Irish Fergal spoke with an accent unique to Skibbereen watermen, a dense accent that required even his Clonakilty cousin to listen with close attention. Accents aside, she had long before categorized him as an irredeemable boy, but she was determined not to show it, and with only a small amount of annoyance in her voice, she said, "Do you bring me any news at all, then, Fergal?"

In a secretive tone he told her, "I have been acting as aide de camp to Colonel O'Donovan. He has entrusted me with several important missions."

"Oh, I am so proud of you, Fergal. But do tell me, have you happened to come across my father, your own uncle? I so worry about him, and my sisters."

"They worry about you as well, *a grah*." Basking in the moment of Brigid's hopeful smile, he went on, "You see, I had a message to deliver to Captain Noonan down on the Lisavaird Road, so I, at no small risk to myself, mind you, stopped by your father's own house. I am to say they are all quite well, and your sisters send their dearest love. Your father, the fine man, says that you must take refuge with your soldier at the barracks."

"Is he at home, then? He is not out with the rising?"

Fergal sniffed in amusement, and said, "Of course he is at home. Did not Colonel O'Donovan strip him of his place on the Clonakilty Committee of the United Irishmen?"

She gasped in surprise, and after thinking for a moment, she softly said, "I had not heard that. That must have been a hard blow, sure. But why ever would Tadg O'Donovan do such a thing?"

"Shite, cousin! Do you think we can trust the secrets of the great rising with the father of a woman, you yourself it is, when that woman is married to a vicious redcoat officer and the oppressor of our people?"

"My husband is the best of men," she said, flaring, "and a friend to the poor and the weak, but no friend of sneaking little shits like you, Fergal."

"I did you this favor, conveying this message, and this is the thanks I get? Ach, to hell with you, *colleen*. I leave now, to do the people's business. We are to attack the redcoat column, and I must hurry if I am to join in the great victory!"

As he turned toward the door she lunged forward and grabbed the sleeve of his coat with both hands. "What do you say, you fool? Do you not know that my own husband is one of those soldiers?"

"You married by your heart rather than your mind; what concern is it to me if you play the tart, and not the patriot?"

She slapped him, hard, hissing, "Out with you, you ugly streak of misery!" He flinched under her assault as she cried and shrieked and slapped his arms, his head, anything she could reach, and drove him to the door. Doolan burst in, his bayonet lowered, glaring at the rebel boy.

"Let me pass, traitor," said Fergal with a break in his voice, as Brigid backed away from him in disgust.

Brigid exhaled sharply, and gave a back-handed wave. Doolan turned his point away and made room at the narrow door. Still, he was indeed Nessa Doolan's own son, and as the boy passed he gave him a shove and growled, "Go lie across yourself, ya gobeshite puppy."

Brigid rushed around the room to gather her bonnet and shawl, hands shaking, calling to Doolan, "We must hurry to the barracks! The column is to be attacked. We must get word to them."

It took only a few minutes to pack the last of her things. Doolan slung his musket over one shoulder and her small chest over the other, and he followed her as she clattered down the stairs.

In the street they found six blue coated yeomen, carbines in their hands. The corporal at their head made no salute, and said only, "You are the O'Brian girl, the wife of Lockwood of the Westmeaths, then? You are to come with us."

Diarmuid Doolan was by most measures a small man, but he was in no mood for that shite, and he swelled menacingly, swinging the chest to the ground and bringing his musket to bear.

The corporal swallowed, eyed the redcoat, and deemed it prudent to turn back to Brigid and add, "If you please, of course, Mrs. Lockwood, we would be honored to escort you the barracks, ma'am."

****

The redcoated infantry companies were formed in columns roughly four men wide and some twenty-five men deep. It was the column of march, right in front, that O'Reilly had ordered, but it was not a fighting formation, and to form into the prescribed three rank line would take considerable time, time Lockwood was sure would not be allowed them. Lieutenant Colonel O'Reilly, who was well aware that many of the men under his command disliked him, or worse, sought to curry their good will by allowing them to fall into route step, a relaxed, unformed pace, despite the proximity of the enemy.

Lockwood would typically do all he could to make the lives of his men easier, but he would not have them approach their enemies as a disordered mob. He thus strode up and down his company, and in a tone they had never before heard from their officer, he cursed them, to quit their fucking slacking, for Christ's sake to close up like soldiers, and to step out like God damned Christians.

Up ahead, Lieutenant Salt, mounted on a bay gelding beside One Company's column, seemed to have been of the same mind, calling similar orders to his men. At the head of the column, O'Reilly and Barleycorn seemed oblivious. At one point Salt looked back at Lockwood, past the guns and wagons between them; their eyes met, and each recognized in the other the frustration of being stuck in an impossible position. The column marched on, approaching the crossroads known as the Big Cross.

*****

It was a beautiful day, the 19th of June. The family who owned the small farm to the east of the crossroad, just beyond the dense hedge, kept a small apple orchard. The blossoms had just recently fallen.

Hundreds of years earlier, a wealthy man had paid for a tall Celtic cross to be raised there, for some reason long lost to history. In truth it was a minor little crossroad, where just one lane from the hills to the west led down to the main road. A hundred years or more before, the cross itself had fallen, and the stone broken up to add to the walls of some crofter's cottage. Still, the name of the place remained. The Big Cross.

*****

Lockwood was certain that an attack was coming, but when it came he was, like nearly every other man in the column, frozen in open-mouthed shock. He could only mutter, "Sweet buggering Jesus," as he watched a mass of rebels break cover from a woods on a height above the road, to left of One Company. He quickly saw it for what it was: a perfect place for such an attack. On the right side of the road, stone walls and a dense hedge locked the redcoats in place, while on the left the ground rose steeply, the area above the slope dominated by dense woods, the woods from which the rebels now poured in a dense mass. One Company was disordered, surprised, and pinned in place; a determined attack would crush them.

*****

Tadg O'Donovan ordered his men, unprofessional, numerous, terrified, courageous and disorganized, to advance out of the woods above the road. Fifty yards of steep green hillside was all that lay between the trees and the road below, between the rebels and the redcoats. He could not have attested to the number of men who advanced with him, as some stout men froze or ran off, while others who hung in the rear unexpectedly ran forward, but likely they numbered between three and four hundred, armed with pikes and achingly few firearms.

In a frenzy of frustration O'Donovan urged them to charge down the hill, at last to engage and destroy the hated redcoats, but some, too many, hesitated. Some would not, could not, kill fellow Irishmen, fellow Catholics, and only stepped from the trees to call for the militiamen to surrender, to join the holy cause. Others, those few with stolen or inherited firearms, contented themselves with firing at the redcoats. O'Donovan saw one fool steadily firing and reloading an ancient pistol; even at fifty yards, the man might as well have been firing at the fucking moon.

No matter the reason why, many of his men hesitated, and only knots of men followed O'Donovan as he rushed down the hill, his grandfather's sword in his hand. Even as he did so, O'Donovan knew they weren't enough, that their advantage in surprise and position was squandered.

*****

Lockwood ordered Five Company to halt, though they had done so already, stunned at the sudden appearance of the rebels. He leapt atop the stone wall that bordered the right side of the road, then climbed up into the hedge above, trying to see what the hell was happening forward. He could see One Company in chaos. O'Reilly, Barleycorn, and Salt called out frantic orders while struggling to control their terrified mounts. A few of their men fired muskets in mad panic, though a few steady hands fired well-aimed shots into the mass of men running down at them. Other One Company men turned and ran off in terror, climbing the stone walls, clawing their way through the dense hedge, Lockwood saw a few of the fleeing men were laughing, pleased with the thought of a rebel victory. More chaos in the ranks of One, as a handful of Barleycorn's men threw their muskets to the ground and called for their fellows to do the same, to join the rebel movement. Officers and sergeants hurried to silence them, to strike them down or drive them off.

While no disciplined volleys were ever managed, and no officer organized a real defense, in the end, more men of One Company chose to fight than not, and their fire broke the impetus of the rebel attack. Still, perhaps fifty of the madly galloping rebels charged the final downhill yards to the low wall held by the redcoats. In a fierce battle of pikes and bayonets, the rebels, unused to such horrors, were first to break back up the hill, but it was not a total rout, and they left many redcoats bloodied.

Lockwood was mad with frustration, craving orders from O'Reilly, knowing he needed to do something, but at a complete loss as to what. Through the roiling smoke he saw more men of One, at least some of them, still firing into the woods above them.

He would wait no longer. Dropping from the hedge, he called out, "The Company will form line!" The familiar order, one they had executed a hundred times on the parade ground, gave the men something to do, a known task, regardless of the madness and noise and smoke ahead. As they had marched in column with right in front, the men formed line facing to the left side of the road.

Lockwood's place was at the far right of the line, and he, too, took some comfort in standing with the men who formed near him, observing their hurry and murmured conversation. Drummer O'Malley was as steady as ever, standing next to his officer, ready to rap out orders to the company. The firing from ahead slowed, but the smoke hung over the road, masking the state of the fighting.

From far down the line one of the men roared, "You get your arse back here, Eamon O'Rourke, or I'll do for you, you cowardly bastard!" Lockwood stepped out of line to look to his left. He saw a flurry of activity and O'Rourke madly trying to flee, caught up in the hedge, clawing at the branches with terror in his eyes. Sergeant Kells of his section was trying to pull him back down, threatening to put his pike to work. But O'Rourke was the only man who broke; Lockwood saw all the other men in place, many hissing, booing, catcalling the coward who was failing his mates when things were getting bad.

"Let him, go, Sergeant!" roared Lockwood. "We don't need such a fellow in Five Company!"

The men roared out a cheer, and as Lockwood returned to him place in line, O'Malley said, "Well, now, sir, that's one rebel bastard seen to."

"So, now another thousand or so yet to go?"

"Thereabouts. But I didn't have much planned for today, did I?"

Both O'Malley and Lockwood spoke loudly, so that the others might hear, and some gentle laughter followed. Even Ensign Lockwood allowed himself a flicker of a smile, but then the rate of firing from up the road quickened, now paced with a desperate edge, and he knew he would have to act, and quickly.

*****

O'Donovan ran panting back up the steep grade and into the trees, where his men regrouped, looking to him for answers. It was the carpenter's first experience of any type of battle, and the noise and smoke, the screaming and the dying, had nearly unnerved him, had nearly unnerved them all. But they looked to him, and he gathered himself to call out, "It's no good to go at them across that damned field, boys! Those muskets are hell itself!" Gesturing toward the deeply sunken lane, the *bealach slogtha* in the Irish, on their right, the one which cut down the hill to form the Big Cross crossroad, he yelled, "But let's rush down that wee lane and have a go at those great bloody cannon! Stuck down there on the road the guns have no bite, and we'll cut the column in two! Come on, boys, once more for Ireland, for liberty and for glory!"

*****

Five Company advanced across the hedge at their front, then swung to the right, where they came to face one last hedged fence that barred them from the sunken lane. It was not the studied wheel of the parade ground, only the rushing of frightened men, men determined not to play the coward in front of their friends. And so, they trotted across the muddy field, the sounds of musketry and roaring voices ahead, clouds of grey, acrid powder smoke, dense along the road to their front right, stagnant in the warm, still air. At every step Lockwood feared a wave of musketry from the hedge ahead, fire which would butcher their advance across the open field. But it did not come, and when they reached the blessed cover they could peer ahead and see that the rebels had made no effort to guard their right. Five Company saw only knots of men, twenty yards from their front, all rebels charging down the lane to attack the guns on the road below. Judging by the firing and powder smoke and roaring there, Lockwood guessed the gunners were defending their pieces in the ferocious manner typical of artillerymen.

Hoping, praying their luck would hold, Lockwood waved his men to cross that last hedge, and as they landed on the far side, he pointed his sword toward the sunken lane ahead and screamed, "Charge!" in a voice he had never before managed.

*****

O'Donovan was in the midst of the guns, swinging his heavy old sword, cutting at the stubborn blue-coated gunners. All about him was chaos, noise, smoke and screaming; his men and the King's men at one another's throats like demons. A redcoat officer, gold epaulettes on his shoulders, spurred his horse into the fray, slashing left and right, but without any obvious skill. O'Donovan grabbed the horse's bridle and ordered the redcoat to surrender, but then a musket, fired from nearby, from behind, and Tadg at Astna O'Donovan fell dead in front of Lieutenant Colonel O'Reilly.

Many of the rebels, enraged, fought to revenge O'Donovan, but some took to their heels and found the lane behind filled by redcoats, firing with deadly intent, their bayonets gleaming in the smoke and gloom. "They're behind us!" came the cry, and every rebel capable of running did so, up into the field, up the hill, striving for the shelter of the woods, craving the open roads beyond, and perhaps a safe road home, the homes which now took on a special, nearly mystical, significance to every man who had woken that morning with the dream, however ill-formed, of a free Ireland.

*****

James Lockwood dropped down into the sunken lane. It was a longer drop than he anticipated, and he felt the awkward landing in his spine, but he was seventeen, and indestructible. There were few rebels left in the lane, and those few were quickly dealt with by his men, their bloodlust merciless.

Lockwood and a few of the men, unstoppable, clambered up the far side of the lane, and up into the field beyond. They found a hundred or more rebels fleeing across the field, some few stout souls turning to hold back the redcoats, allowing their fellows to escape the carnage.

A small young man deliberately turned from his flight to charge Lockwood, deliberately singling him out in the furious melee that surrounded the handful of Westmeaths in the field. Lockwood, himself only seventeen, saw the rebel as a boy, but he charged Lockwood with such fury, such intent, armed with a pike etched with One Company blood, that

Lockwood did not hesitate to defend himself. With a quick flick of his wrist, he deflected the pike's point to his right, and with a lightning recovery of his point he reposted into the boy's chest. The boy's impetus carried him far up the sword, until, gasping, he slid to the ground. James felt no remorse; his reaction was more one of surprise that anyone would be so foolish, so clumsy, as to deliberately attack a trained opponent.

The issue was essentially resolved. The rebels' fury seemed to be broken, but their defeat was turned into a rout by a volley of musketry from the far left of the rebel line, a deliberate fire that came as a staggering surprise to rebels and the redcoats alike. Through that rolling cloud of gun smoke, there came bounding a mass of howling men in red coats and tartan trews, blue Highland bonnets with diced edging on their heads—Scots in full throat. The Caithness men had marched down from Bandon.

The Scots cleared the field in minutes. In the wake of the leading ranks ran a fat little man, trying to keep up, gold epaulettes marking him as their colonel. Breathless, a claymore in his hand, he trotted over to Lockwood, offered his hand, and said, "Sutherland, Caithness Legion!" Then turning back to his men, men who required little further inspiration, he yelled shrilly, "Forward, there! Forward, ye thrawn, ill-feckit gaberlunzies!"

James found his throat constricted, and it took him a moment before he could offer a slight bow and mutter, "Lockwood, sir, Westmeath Militia."

"You fight well, lad."

Lockwood found he still had his bloodied sword raised. Slowly, shakily, he cleaned and sheathed it, then said, "You are a welcome sight, sir."

Sutherland pulled a silver flask from his pocket, took a long drink, and regaining his breath, he said, "You and your men might stand down, now, laddie. My bucks will drive those rebels for miles yet, like hounds after a fox."

The Scottish colonel turned to offer the flask to the ensign, but the young fellow had turned to tend to one of his men. Private Shannon had taken a pike wound deep in the thigh, bright blood arching high. Lockwood worked feverishly to fashion a tourniquet, pulling off his coat and tearing off his shirt sleeve, calling for O'Malley to cut a branch from the hawthorn overhead. The hawthorn was long sacred to the Irish, symbolizing love and protection, but magic carries only so far, and the young officer worked to stem the wound long after the man had died.

Chapter Twenty-Eight

Every ear in Clonakilty Barracks strained to make out the sounds of the fighting that rumbled from up the Bandon Road. Doolan had called Brigid outside when the first smattering of shots were heard, and no matter how she prayed, the firing did not stop, going on and on, the pace building. She stood at Doolan's side at the top of the steps to the Officers' Mess, very near tears.

"That firing is maybe two miles off," said Doolan, his ear cocked. "Our lads didn't get far before running into trouble. And you'll note, too, missus, there is only musketry, no cannon fire. Those rebels won't have many firearms, so that's the sound of our lads, giving them hell. Naught to worry about, missus, at all, at all."

Captain Louis of the yeomanry, in a muck sweat, his coat badly buttoned, emerged from the officers' mess and stepped over to speak to Mrs. Lockwood, but before he could say a word she sharply asked, "Sir, may I ask why you are not sending men to aid the men of the column? Up that road men are fighting for their lives, but here you sit!"

"My dear Mrs. Lockwood!" he said, taken aback. "I beseech you, ma'am, I am ordered to hold this barracks, and I have only fifty men to do so! What more can I do! In fact, I came to ask if you might spare your man. If those devils storm our walls we shall need every man we can lay our hands on."

She hissed in fear and frustration, then glanced at Doolan. He gave her a quick nod, and after a sniff of annoyance directed at Lewis, Doolan slung his musket over his shoulder and walked over to join the handful of yeomen frantically working to loophole the front wall.

Lewis leaned close to her, liquor on his breath, fear and panic in his eyes. Quickly, quietly, he said, "I did not want to say this in front of your man, but I have received intelligence that the rebels number in their thousands. In their thousands, ma'am! After they destroy the column, the rebels then plan to overrun us here, an unstoppable horde! They are the personification of evil, ma'am! I had hoped to defend you and the other ladies, but my troops may be forced to retreat, and regroup... elsewhere. In that event, I am afraid all I can suggest, Mrs. Lockwood, is that you do not allow yourself to be taken alive."

It took all of her self-control not to slap him. Instead she drew back, repulsed, and said, "How dare you, sir! Good God, get hold of yourself! My husband is up that road fighting, and you must be prepared to do your duty as well!"

The insults missed their mark; Lewis just looked wildly around the barracks yard, his men scattered and panicked, as he muttered, "I must return to my headquarters to compile my strategy." He trotted away, leaving her alone. The firing built to a crescendo in the distance, and she nearly gave in to the worst of her fears. She caught, then, a sympathetic look from one of the company wives, one of perhaps a dozen women and their children who had gathered outside the enlisted barracks. The woman who had looked at her nudged a young woman beside her, and they both now looked over at the officer's wife, and offered tenuous, nervous, frightened, smiles.

She found herself craving the company of other women. She walked over quickly, dissolving the distance between them. She was embarrassed when several of the soldiers' wives, women well beyond her in years and experience, some of the them mothers, curtsied at her approach. She curtsied in return, deliberately lower than they had saluted her.

An older woman stepped out to greet her in English. "Good day, ma'am. My name is Caitlin McMahon, wife of Andrew McMahon, of your husband's company."

"Dhia agus Mhaire duit, a Caitlin McMahon. Te me Brigid, ni O'Brian, bean o Lockwood." A formal, polite response in Irish; God and Mary be with you, Caitlin McMahon. I am Brigid, daughter of O'Brian, wife of Lockwood. Receiving soft Irish greetings in return, Brigid passed among the other women, introducing herself, admiring their children, and exchanging hopeful, supportive comments. A few of the wives were unreceptive, but most quickly relaxed with her, united and equaled by gender, language and their shared anxiety.

She found herself standing beside Caitlin McMahon, who gestured toward the lines of saddled horses and said, "See, young woman, how the yeomen have their cloaks behind their saddles, and slung forage bags? That means they're ready for a road march, a coward's flight the moment they first spot an Irishman with a pike in his hands. You mark my words, if the news from the column is bad, this lot will be out the gate in a Dublin minute, and they'll take their supper in Cork Town, bragging of their feckin' bravery."

"Right bastards, that lot," suggested a young mother nearby. Several other women, and two little boys spat on the ground in loathing.

The echoing sounds of firing from up the road suddenly dwindled and died. Still, it was a full thirty minutes before Louis unsteadily emerged from the headquarters building to dispatch a five-man patrol to ride up the road and reconnoiter. From their post at the gates and along the walls, every one of the remaining yeomen eyed his horse, and on more than one occasion their officers and NCOs had to drive them away from their mounts and attempting a dash for safety. The yeomen had long dealt brutality to the native Irish, and were well aware of the terrible retribution due them if they fell into the hands of those people.

An achingly long time passed before the patrol came galloping back, waving their caps, calling out, "Victory! The rebels are running! A glorious victory!"

The gates were thrown open and the gleeful patrol galloped into the yard. Louis buttoned up his tunic, wiped his face, and in response to the fierce cheering, he called, "Silence, there! Sergeant Morton, take that man's name! Damn fools, to doubt the power of His Majesty's sinews! Now, Corporal Lovett, you will make a proper report, or I shall have the hide off you!"

Lovett leapt from his saddle, saluted, and barked, "Sir, Colonel Sutherland of the Caithness Fencibles orders that I report the rebels are on the run after taking heavy casualties. He will have one of his companies pursue the rebels, while a second shall remain on the field, collecting the rebel dead and wounded and destroying the captured pikes and firearms. He orders that two wagons be sent at once to collect the column's dead and wounded, and he and his third company shall then escort the wagons back to the barracks."

At the mention of dead and wounded men, several of the wives cried out in fear for their men, and it was only after they had done so that Brigid realized what the wagons might carry. She had not cried aloud, but as the officers gathered, she ran forward to speak to the patrol's leader, taking hold of his stirrup and asking frantically, "Corporal, did you see an Ensign Lockwood of the Westmeaths? Please, corporal, did you see my husband, my James, is he unhurt? Oh, please, Corporal, please."

The yeoman looked down with a surprisingly human face, and replied, "That tall, thin lad, ma'am? A gorget but no epaulette, and a red coat?"

"Yes, yes, that is he! Oh, please, Corporal, is he well?"

"I can report the gentleman to be quite well, ma'am," he replied, with all the formality a corporal could muster. Then, quietly, he added, "As an aside, like, ma'am, I might mention that his men think very highly of him. He did very well."

Both hands to her face, she doubled over in relief, choking back sobs, until Caitlin McMahon hurried over to help her back to the other women, saying, "He's all right, child, he's all right. You'll see him soon."

Nearly two hours passed before Highland pipes could be heard coming down the road. Brigid did not know the tune; she had no use for war pipes.

The gates were thrown open. The yeomen were formed in ranks to salute Colonel Sutherland, who rode in at the head of his company, who were followed in turn by the wagons bearing the column's casualties. The women of the barracks did not stand on ceremony, but surged forward to learn the fate of their men. None of the wives lost a husband, but two of their men had been wounded. None of the yeomen had been tasked with aiding the wounded, and when the barracks surgeon and his mate waved the wagons over to the small hospital building, the women, Brigid Lockwood included, hurried beside the wagon to help the wounded inside and to tend to the sacred dead.

Sutherland dismounted, and Lewis stepped forward to introduce himself and to explain the state of the barracks defense. After some minutes of conversation, Sutherland eyed the lines of saddled horses in the yard, and with a wry smile, he said, "It seems, sir, that you were prepared for the battle to have gone in either direction. Happily, you can now employ yon mounts to pursue His Majesty's enemies," Holding up a stern Highland finger, he added, "but only His Majesty's enemies, sir. I am new to Ireland, but I am all too familiar with the reputation of the yeomanry. You'll nae torment the innocent, or Dublin Castle shall hear of it."

A gleeful Lewis then leapt into his saddle, and waving his sword over his head he called to his troopers, "For revenge and glory, troop, at the trot, forward!" He was quite familiar with Dublin Castle's attitude toward the peasantry, and in the midst of violent rebellion he was quite sure he could do as he pleased.

*****

James took little pleasure in the back-slapping congratulations offered by the officers of Bandon Barracks. After the elaborate dinner they had given the officers of the column, he retired as soon as courtesy allowed, indeed perhaps a bit earlier. He found the quarters to which he had been assigned to be a cold, cramped, windowless cave with a few sticks of old furniture. He was soon hissing in frustration as he went through his valise, finding he had forgotten to include a blanket when he had packed early that morning. His first, wholly childish, impulse was to blame Doolan, but he then sighed, ashamed of himself.

He was exhausted, but he was certain he would not be able to sleep. He resolved instead to make himself busy, shivering or not, to be productive and not to dwell on that long day. He resolved to consign the day to memory, and no more.

He had killed a man.

In the feeble light of his lone candle he wrote a letter to his mother. He addressed it to her, in care of Dr. Moore's Hospital, Dublin; he could only hope that she would receive it, and could only pray that her health allowed her to understand that it was from him. He promised himself to seek her out as soon as he might be granted leave. He very much wanted his mother and Brigid to become acquainted. He hoped they would like one another, secretly cherishing the notion that they would come to love one another, as he loved them.

The rebel boy at the crossroads could have escaped, but the fool had turned and sought him out, of that James was certain. Whoever the fool was, he had deliberately attacked, and the blame was his. To hell with him. He had been very young, that rebel boy, the scrawny little shit. The rebel had not spent a hundred hours, hell, two hundred hours, with old Mr. O'Reilly in that decrepit Dublin *salle d'armes*. The fool had wielded his crude pike with the skill of a child. He was dead.

James spent an hour updating his pay rosters. Exhaling sharply, satisfied with his progress, he pulled a fresh sheet of paper from his chest to begin a letter to Brigid. Earlier that morning, when the fighting was over and he could spare a moment from his men, he had scribbled a quick note to assure Brigid he was unhurt, that she was not to worry, a note which Colonel Sutherland had kindly agreed to deliver upon the Caithness's arrival at Clonakilty Barracks.

Staring at the blank sheet of paper, his mind was equally empty. What could he say to her? Could he confess to what he had become? Her husband, a killer of fools.

Thinking of the pay roster offered little refuge: Private Benjamin Shannon had died two shillings three pence in debt to his company. James tapped the tip of his finger on the desktop with increasing force, until he swore in quiet fury. It was preposterous that the sum of a man's life could end in a negative balance. Surely Shannon's worth as a soldier, as a man, was more than the rudimentary maths of his pay? He had been a quiet man, a steady if unremarkable member of the company, and yet had done his duty without hesitation. James had scarcely known him, and he felt a bolt of guilt, knowing he had led a man he had scarcely known to his death.

Doubt, regret, guilt, self-recrimination. He longed for one of the bottles of wine still being hoisted in the Bandon Barracks mess. Instead he bolted to kneel by the chamber pot in the dark corner, and was quietly sick.

*****

In a room at the opposite end of the hall, Lieutenant Colonel O'Reilly was in a great flow of spirits. Upon their arrival at Bandon Barracks he and the men of his battered column had been cheered from the rafters, heralded as heroes and saviors of the established order, and by midnight his elation had not subsided. In light of the great victory, the garrison commander had assigned O'Reilly the finest quarters in those expansive barracks, and after that rousing dinner, the victorious colonel had retired to his quarters to script his dispatch, his account of the recent action between his column and the rebels. With a special flourish, O'Reilly addressed the dispatch to Lord Charles Cornwallis, 1st Marquess Cornwallis; O'Reilly had been given a copy of the latest *Dublin Gazette*, which announced the appointment of Cornwallis as both Lord Lieutenant of Ireland and Commander-in-Chief of His Majesty's forces in Ireland. In face of widespread rebellion, the desperate government had granted Cornwallis both offices, and with a stroke of a pen had rendered him the most powerful man in Ireland.

O'Reilly took a long drink of the garrison's claret, a sadly disappointing vintage. He knew he had caught the Bandon officers back-footed, unprepared to provide a suitable dinner for victorious warriors, but surely to God they had something better than this watery swill to offer the heroes of the day? Still, he had to admit, he loved the lift it gave him. He leapt to his feet, threw open the door, and told the sentry there, "Guard, pray step down to Ensign Lockwood's quarters, tender my compliments, and if he is quite at his at leisure, ask if he might me join me here for a moment."

Lockwood appeared, the dear boy, buttoning up his coat, looking ashen, unwell, doubtless exhausted, the poor lad. "Come in, my dear James!" O'Reilly cried, pouring two more glasses, handing one to Lockwood and the other to the astonished sentry, who carried it out to his post, a man who had never before tasted claret, or any of its poorer cousins. "Did I not promise you glory, James? Did I not promise you laurels and the praise of the great? My God, we have done it! Now, pray, sit... no, stand... this prose is best taken on one's feet, a stance of the soldier. I shall not trouble you with the first bits, but I mention you at this turn, and I thought you should like to hear it, first hand, as it were. By God, such thumping prose I am putting to paper! Hear this, now: 'Duty, indeed, honour, requires me to mention, indeed, laud, the role played by Ensign James Lockwood of my regiment, who organized a charge by the men of my own Third Company, as I was engaged with the command of the other elements in repulsing the main rebel assault. Ensign Lockwood distinguished himself by leading his men in retaking the artillery of the column, which had been briefly overwhelmed by a number of rebels.' Is that not the most finite, conclusive, soldierly summary of your exploits, my young friend? You are mentioned in dispatches, James! Surely glory and renown await you! Lord Cornwallis himself shall know of you!"

"Thank you, sir. I am conscious of the honour you do me, but I wonder if I might beg one further favor?"

"You are mentioned in dispatches, man! What more could a soldier desire?"

"Well, sir, I wonder if I could get a letter to Mrs. Lockwood, sir. It would mean a great deal to me, sir."

"Of course, of course, my boy. As a matter of fact, orders have been issued, calling for escorts be provided to reestablish the mail. No doubt you wish to relay to your bride the details of our victory. Her husband, the hero, the slayer of rebels! I heard how you ran that man through this afternoon, young man! You are blooded, a warrior—but are you quite well, James? You have gone quite pale...."

"Oh, pray, do not concern yourself," said James with a wan smile. "A few hours of sleep will set me up, though I shall first write a few lines to Brigid." As he turned to go, he softly said, "How I wish she were here."

Chapter Twenty-Nine

The next morning in Bandon dawned late. For the first time in weeks, dark clouds scudded across the sky, lashing rain. The mail coach from Cork made its Bandon stop at the barracks, with two bleeding horses and a bullet hole in the left door, despite being escorted from Cork Town by a troop of fencible cavalry. The coach carried only the West Cork mail, ranging from military correspondence to the most mundane personal letters. No passengers were allowed, if anyone was so ill-advised as to attempt to transit that fragmented, polarized, island.

The arrival of the mail coach was lost on James Lockwood, who had slept very late, and spent much of the day in his quarters. Courtesy, however, required his presence at dinner at three o'clock. He made his way to the mess at two, where he handed the chief steward a letter addressed to Mrs. Lockwood, and asked him to see it safely in the next post going south. Thereafter he sat alone in the shadows at the rear of the well-appointed room, steadily drinking bad wine on an empty stomach. Earlier that day he had discovered that his left hand tended to shake if he did not clench it into a fist. He intended to determine if claret would quiet it.

From his shadowed corner of the mess James heard the headquarters drummer snap out the officers' call, and he watched the other officers, twenty or so, gather and settle in two obviously distinct groups. The men who had long been part of the Bandon garrison arrived quickly, obvious friends, excited about hearing the news from their new senior officer, eagerly chatting about the prospect of engaging and crushing the rebels. James watched, in sullen understanding, as the officers who had fought their way through the rebel ambush responded slowly, even hesitantly, to the drum's call. They sat off to one side, quiet and serious. The artillery officer, Lieutenant Brown, gave Lockwood a polite nod and sent over a glass of wine with his compliments.

O'Reilly soon strode into the mess, waving a sheaf of papers over his head. "Gentlemen, we are at last in receipt of orders from Dublin Castle, and news from the rest of the island! I am of course newly arrived, but I felt it my duty, indeed my great honour, to call this Council of War."

Immaculately turned out, O'Reilly paused for effect, and then called out, "I shall first offer you gentlemen the latest news. Everything I read points to atrocity, gentlemen, atrocity! I have here, for example, a clipping from the *Gazette*, which cites a massacre of innocent royalists at Wexford! 'Prisoners taken by the rebels were quartered in a large barn. The prisoners' guards twice prevented a gathering mob from harming them, but eventually gave in to the crowd, allowing the executions by musket-shot of over a dozen particularly hated individuals. However, all semblance of control was lost and the barn was torched. People trying to escape the barn were shot, stabbed, beaten to death, or forced back into the flames!' We are fighting beasts, gentlemen, and stand as the sole barrier between order and anarchy, between bestiality and civility!"

The colonel went on at length, reading from newspapers and updates from Dublin Castle, while James finished his glass, then his bottle, and lost focus. He eventually looked about, but could not catch the eye of a steward. "Damned rogues, to leave a man dry-throated." His eyes ached, and he laid his head down on the table for just a moment, fully intending to rise up and argue a point or two, particularly those regarding which aspects of bestiality O'Reilly objected to. Instead, he found only the depths of sleep, allowed to young men who have drunk and seen too much.

*****

The mail coach left Bandon with fresh drivers, horses, and an escort of yeoman cavalry. It proceeded south through a countryside devoid of humanity, silent, abandoned and afraid. Approaching Clonakilty, they passed the Big Cross battlefield, where the cavalrymen loudly hallooed their brother yeomen, busily policing the field. When the coach clattered into the yard of Clonakilty barracks, the bag tossed down onto the cobblestones included the letter addressed to Mrs. Brigid Lockwood.

The quartermaster sergeant brought the letter to Brigid when she was with the other wives in the barracks hospital. She was not so in control of her emotions that she could prevent a squeal of delight when she was given the letter, and saw the familiar bold slope of her husband's hand. She tore open the seal and read it standing there, as the wounded men and the women caring for them traded quiet looks, some smiling, some glaring, some rolling their eyes.

My dear Brigid,

Colonel O'Reilly says that the mail coach will run tomorrow, so I put pen to paper, though this letter is the merest shadow of what it would be like to talk to you in person.

I am reminded of a letter my mother once showed me, written by her cousin in 1777, an ensign in the 17th Foot who served in America. He wrote, "I have long yearned to see my first battle, and my wish was recently fulfilled, to a wholly satisfying degree, in our fight with the Americans. Now that my wish for my first battle has been seen to, I am in no hurry to see my second."

At the time I thought the fellow was just being wry, but I now see the truth of it. The few brief little-runs I have had with the rebels were nothing compared to this. The fighting was all so very uncontrolled, and loud, but above all else, so very confusing, and overall quite unpleasant.

That being said, pray, my dear, do not be anxious for me! I was never in any danger, as my company was all about me, such good fellows, and we were at the rear of the column while all the unpleasantness was resolved up at the front. I thus managed to witness the fighting without ever having to be much involved in it, which is certainly the best course of action in such events.

That reminds me of yet another instance: on one occasion Doolan (early in his role as my servant, and long before he or I came to know you, my dear. You know how he dotes on you) told me, "Weddings are like knife fights; you might enjoy watching them, but you certainly do not want to be in one." Battles, as far as I am concerned, might be added to the list. Which reminds me of a question I had for you: the fellow who stood with your father at our wedding, your godfather, remind me of his name? It is of no great import, but the image of his face recently crossed my mind, and I was merely curious.

As I try to sleep, I find the memories of the fighting have left me oddly unsettled. I had best get past it, as I am a soldier, and so must grow accustomed to such things if I am ever to make my way. Still, I do so look forward to seeing you again, so that I might explain myself in person, and benefit from your wisdom, and your endless kindness.

We newly arrived officers have been invited to join the officers' mess here, though the cost has not yet been mentioned. I now intend to take advantage of that privilege and go and have a glass of wine, and think of you.

I remain your most affectionate, devoted husband,
James Lockwood

P.S. I forgot to mention that Colonel O'Reilly has mentioned me in his dispatch to Lord Cornwallis. It will likely amount to nothing, as Cornwallis has an island full of people to look after, and my name is just one of thousands to cross his desk. Still, it might mean a modest plum someday. At the moment I confess I am not much interested in God damned plums.

P.P.S. Pray, tell Doolan to wrap up a blanket and a shirt or two, and to throw them on the return mail, as my packing was hurried, and I forgot a few items. I am glad not to be there, so as to avoid his crowing over how I need him.

P.P.P.S. I do, though, wish I was there. I find myself realizing how much I do need you.

*****

Three days later, the same mail coach, having survived an eventful journey across West Cork, rattled through Bandon on its return trip to Cork Town, but not before dropping off a bundle and a letter addressed to Ensign Lockwood. The letter's author had, as usual, written in a mad hurry, with little care for punctuation, penmanship, or legibility, but with an obvious, overriding affection.

My dear, dear, husband,

It is with such relief that I received your letter and I knew at last that you were indeed unhurt. The yeoman corporal who rode back from the Big Cross told me he saw you well, and Colonel Sutherland, who has been a kind, if a rather odd man, much given to Highland pipes, has spoken of you in the most flattering terms.

Though Colonel Sutherland has been kind, he has not, despite my repeated entreaties, some of them, I confess, delivered in a strident manner, reined in Captain Lewis, that small-souled príompallán, mallacht Dé air, (I shall not translate, but you might surmise, sir, my intent) who has made things here in Clonakilty so very much worse. No matter how I or the people beseech him, Sutherland cedes responsibility to Lewis, pleading Lewis has more experience in dealing with the Irish. I fear Sutherland is a very weak fellow.

After the battle, Sutherland pulled his men (Scots, and by nature decent men, I think) into the barracks and left the Big Cross field to the yeomen. Doctor Trevelyan, a good-hearted man from here in town, volunteered to go into the field and treat the Irish wounded, but he was turned away, Lewis telling him there were no wounded rebels, only dead men, which is the most vile lie, as I spoke to Lt. Telfer of the Caithness who said they left many rebels still alive on the field — oh, I am so very angry with Lewis and his like!

He had been eagerly anticipating a letter from Brigid, but as he read it he surprised himself by growing increasingly annoyed with her. He had always had trouble deciphering her handwriting when she was upset, and it was obvious that she was very upset. He had hoped for a letter of kindness and support, but was instead faced with yet another problem to manage. He read on, feeling put upon, giving his annoyance free rein.

There were more than a hundred Irish men who were killed in the battle, or likely murdered afterward, but the families were not allowed to claim the bodies, and to further torment the People, Lewis ordered his men to drag the bodies behind their horses down to the town and leave them in front of the town's market house for several days, with guards posted to keep the families away!

such a cry was raised, but it was only after
Father Cassidy came to beg, on his knees, for
Sutherland to release the bodies, that he finally
relented. But, dear James, when Lewis was ordered
to release the dead, he had them dragged down to
the crab hole at the far end of town, to Deasy's
Quay, where the fish mongers dump their slob, the
foulest of places, and there he had them thrown in!

Lockwood pushed the letter away, and hissed, "Christ, how can she possibly think I have anything to do with how the dead are treated? I have enough to deal with without... oh, God damn it anyway." He stalked off to see Colonel O'Reilly, finding him behind a desk in the headquarters building, busily crafting letters to Dublin Castle. Lockwood strode into the room, slapped the letter down, and said, "Sir, Mrs. Lockwood informs me that the bodies of the rebel dead in Clonakilty are being defiled. Our victory is tainted, sir. There can be no honour, sir, in such wanton cruelty—"

"My dear James!" said O'Reilly. "My goodness... I was... quite unaware! Pray, let me see what your bride tells us...." Pulling the letter to his side of the desk, he quickly read the portion James pointed out. "I am shocked, sir, shocked! I am, of course, unacquainted with Colonel Sutherland, and while I knew of Captain Lewis's... well, let us call it 'disdain' for the peasantry, I would be shocked if these accusations prove true."

"Accusations, sir?" said Lockwood, his brows rising in surprise. "My wife's account cannot be challenged, sir! She holds my implicit trust, Colonel, and I am disappointed that it is you who should doubt her."

For the first time of their acquaintance, Lockwood found O'Reilly eyeing him with annoyance, perhaps even dislike. "I shall look into it, Ensign," said the Colonel stiffly. "But I cannot but mention that it was the rebels who first introduced atrocity to this conflict, and if they are repaid in the same coin, they can only blame themselves."

*****

Brigid Lockwood draped her best shawl around her shoulders, and said, "Diarmuid Doolan, I am going to Mass, and I am going alone."

"Now, Missus, himself would never forgive me if I were to let you walk alone on those streets, the world as it is."

"Nonsense. Things have been quiet all week. Have I not lived in Clonakilty all my life? There is not a soul here who would say an unkind word to me, let alone touch a hair on my head." He heard the catch in her voice; she was no longer certain that was true.

"All right, then," he said, ignoring her flicker of hesitation; he was, for all his faults, not entirely without grace. "It is Sunday morning, and you're going to Mass. I shall go as well, being a man of the Catholic faith, I am."

She sniffed in amusement as she moved toward the door of her rooms in Clonakilty Barracks. "Diarmuid, I believe that if you stepped into a church of any kind you would instantly burst into flames."

"Not instantly, I think?" he muttered to himself as she passed by, herself young, strong, and with at least a mask of certainty. "Sure," he wondered aloud, "God would grant me a moment or two of... well... smoldering, first?"

"In any case, you will remain here, *le te thoil*. If I see you following me, I shall see you shot for desertion."

"We're usually just flogged for desertion, please, Missus."

"Very well, then, flogged, but mercilessly. By the way, I saved you some cake from Colonel Sutherland's party last night, and there is some very good cheese in the larder as well. I shall be careful, Diarmuid, *a grah*, and I'll return before you ever miss me, so."

She was bound for St. Brigid's, the modest chapel allowed the Clonakilty Catholics by their Anglican masters. It stood on the west side of town, but she was determined to go first to Clonakilty pier, and so turned herself east on that densely foggy Sunday morning. Very few people were out, and those few were flitting shadows in the mist. At the far end of the pier stood the Facheen's Bridge gallows. As she feared, two bodies hung there, unattended in the silent gloom. She then forced herself to the edge of the crab hole. Empty, now, the corrupt bodies dragged away, but the stench of the rotted dead was so overpowering that she retched over and over. When she could stand again, she turned away and ran.

She had regained her composure by the time she reached St. Brigid's, but she was disappointed not to find her father or sisters there. Many of her neighbors and old family friends were present, but few acknowledged her, and none spoke to her. She found that she was not surprised when she saw suspicion in their faces. When she reached her pew, Father Sheeran stepped out of the sacristy, ashen, and with a strain in his voice he said, "My dear friends, I am... honored... to allow the Reverend Horatio Townsend, Vicar of Kilgarriffe and chief magistrate of Clonakilty, to address us this day."

It was unheard of, a blasphemy, sure, but the priest nodded back toward the sacristy, and a gaunt man dressed in black stepped out and took Sheeran's place behind the pulpit. There were gasps and cries of surprise and anger; Townsend, ; the man who had recently sentenced a child to death for the theft of a pocket watch, was widely hated.

Brigid saw other men in the sacristy, and the hint of weapons and uniforms. The vicar was not placing all his faith in God's protection.

With a mix of admonition and venom, Townsend addressed them, "Deluded, though still dear, countrymen, your eyes have hitherto been blinded by passion, your understanding perverted by artifice, your ears shut against the voice of reason. You have despised the admonitions of authority and rejected the counsel of true friends. Reflect with remorse and repentance on the wicked and sanguinary designs for which you forged so many of these abominable pikes. Yield up to justice your leaders and instigators, surrender your illegal weapons, return to your habitations and resume your industrious employments."

Townsend prided himself on his elegant oratory, but his lengthy address was wasted on the congregants. Some had only Irish, and of those who could understand him, most held him in such disdain that they would as soon murder as hear him. Brigid could not bear him, and walked out. She was a red coat's wife, and of the people there she alone could afford to risk offending such a man.

She stepped out into the foggy street and found her father waiting for her. She nearly ran to him, but stopped herself when she saw his face.

He stood with his arms crossed, a standing stone of a man. He did not greet her, only saying, "I hope you're pleased with that boy of yours, quite the warrior, him."

"He did his duty, Father, and I am very proud of him. He was mentioned in dispatches, and shall—."

"The King's men are none too discerning, are they, about who they call hero, when all he did was kill a boy?"

"Father! How can you say such a thing! James would never kill a boy."

"So sure, are you? A boy it was, and indeed one you know."

She felt a chill grip her heart.

"A boy you know," he said, thrusting an accusing finger at her. "One of our own family, yes, your own cousin! The boy Fergal, slain by that bloodthirsty demon!"

"No! That cannot be!" she gasped, recoiling from him. "You lie!"

"Ask him yourself, and see if he'll confess his sin!"

For the second time that day she ran from horror.

Chapter Thirty

Prior to the fighting at the Big Cross, Ensign Lockwood had drilled his men with something resembling severity; following the desperate fight against the rebels he pushed them with draconian harshness. He had lost men, and was determined to lose no more. They had been in Bandon for nearly a week as he exercised the company in close order drills in the barracks yard, determined to make them, and himself, better soldiers. The rebel defeat near Clonakilty had largely quelled the uprising in West Cork, though there were reports of fierce fighting up near Wexford. If Lockwood's company was called upon again, he would have them ready.

Beyond his determination to be prepared, he was also privately sensitive to the critiques, spoken or not, of the garrison officers who casually watched from steps, doors and windows surrounding the cobbled yard. Thus, when Private Malarkey dropped his firelock, a heinous sin punishable by execution without benefit of clergy, all present anticipated the private's immediate crucifixion.

Yet when Ensign Lockwood strode down to Malarkey's place in his second platoon, the soldier, who had hurriedly retrieved his firelock and returned it to his shoulder, deliberately kept his eyes not to his front, but in a wholly mutinous shift to the right, and there they remained.

With equal parts rage and surprise, Lockwood barked, "Why are your eyes not to the front, Private Malarkey?" Noticing then that nearly every eye in the company was turned to the right, toward the barracks gate, he roared, "Christ, have you all lost your minds? Your enemy is to your front! What a pack of God damned moon calves—"

Private Malarkey returned his eyes to his front, but he made a subtle throw of his head toward the gate, and between his clenched martial jaws, he muttered, "Sir, it's the missus."

It was she.

James would not have been more surprised if the King himself had come to Bandon Barracks, but it was indeed Brigid Lockwood who stepped down from the high seat of a jaunting cart with a natural grace that made him catch his breath.

On the far side of the cart, Doolan climbed stiffly down, but James had eyes only for Brigid. He managed not to run to her. "Good God, Brigid! However did you manage to come here! A delightful surprise, I assure you, but—"

She offered him her cheek, but skillfully rejected all but the most cursory embrace.

He went to pay the cartman, but Brigid deliberately tapped her husband's arm and said, "Pray, let us not pay Mr. Keating yet. I have asked him to wait a few moments before he departs, as I may... decide to return to Clonakilty."

Lockwood stood blinking for a moment, trying to discern just what she meant by that remark. Doolan meanwhile had pulled his pack and Mrs. Lockwood's trunk off the rear of the cart, and standing behind her, the gnarled fellow knuckled a salute to his officer. For the second time that afternoon, a man in the barracks yard threw his head toward Brigid, in this case Diarmuid Doolan, with raised eyebrows and stretched eyes, though Lockwood could not decipher the nature of the message. James was astonished and overjoyed by the arrival of his wife, but he now stood puzzled and not a little wounded by the icy reception she offered.

"I had believed, my love," James said, though he felt the endearment sharply deflect off Brigid's stony countenance, as she now stood with her arms folded across her chest, "that we had agreed that you would remain at Clonakilty barracks until after the rebellion was quite over...."

"The drive was quite a pleasant one" she said in a tone of obvious falsehood. "We had very little trouble, even though your *soldier,*" she said with an acid look back at Doolan, which made the poor fellow visibly blanch, "quite uncivilly *insisted* on accompanying me. His red coat brought us some unwanted attention, sure, as we passed Slieveadrohid." She pronounced the name of the place with a silky Irish accent, and while James had no idea where such a place might be, he had sense enough not to ask.

"A couple lads made as to throw stones," said Doolan, by way of explanation, "but I showed them my wee Bess, and their mothers came running out and dragged them away."

"Praise God," she muttered, "another Slaughter of the Innocents averted." Then, more clearly, she turned to her husband and went on, "Pray, sir, where are our quarters? We have several matters to discuss."

Some of the other garrison officers had caught sight of Mrs. Lockwood, the exceptionally lovely Mrs. Lockwood, and though they buttoned up their coats and preened themselves as best they could, they were to be disappointed, as she took her husband's arm coolly and they went directly to his rooms.

He had long ached to be alone with her, but once they reached his quarters he realized the single bed in the far corner was an impossible dream. She spun on her heel, and for the first time since he had known her, she looked at him with something like doubt. "It seems, sir, that your recent actions have ensured that my family wishes never to see me again."

"Brigid! Whatever do you mean? I would never do such a thing! How can you—"

Her challenging tone did not waver as she pointed a finger at him, the slender young woman and her towering, baffled husband. "I took a great leap of faith when I married you. I risked the opinion of my family, my friends, all that was dear to me, because, all for my *love* for you!"

Her voice broke, the first tears came to her eyes, and he stepped forward to embrace her, but she stuck that same finger in his chest, forcing him back, and her voice regained its edge. "Know this: I do not for one moment question your honour, or your conduct. But I must know what happened at the Big Cross. You must swear, *swear*, sir, that you will answer my questions honestly!"

"I have never lied to you, Brigid, why—" he said, aghast, growing angry despite himself. "And yes, thank you, I know that in marrying me you risked the opinion of your friends and family, as did I! Have we not discussed that a hundred times, and agreed that we did love one another enough to override all such nonsense? But now, you ask me to be honest with you? You doubt me?" He coughed an ironic laugh, then added, "Very well, then, my dear wife, ask me your questions, if you must!"

She was nearly crying, but resolute as she said, "You killed someone at the Big Cross, did you not?"

He stood with his mouth open, caught back-footed for two breaths, before he said, on the edge of being exceptionally angry, "Yes. You know very well I did so. I explained that in my last letter. Why is that suddenly of such import?"

He saw her resolution weaken, but through the tears that escaped her, she sternly said, "Did you know this man? What did he look like, this rebel, this—"

"Christ!" he hissed. "You wish to know the particulars? You wish to know the manner in which your husband first became a killer of men?" He barked a mad, furious laugh, stepped over to the battered old sideboard, and poured whiskey into a chipped crystal glass. "If you must know, he was a skinny redheaded boy. And a damned fool." Lockwood took a long swallow, unflinching. "He was in the crowd of rebels fleeing the field, and he might well have gotten clear, but he left the others and deliberately, *deliberately*, I tell you, ran at me, as if he had no other purpose in life than to slay me." Another swallow and looking into the bottom of the glass, he added wonderingly, "A little idiot with a homemade pike. Why in the world would he be so determined to kill *me*?"

She fought back her tears, and choked out, "He was my cousin."

"Jesus," he eventually whispered, with a mix of astonishment and sadness. He sat heavily on the bed. Wide-eyed, he took another long pull at his whiskey.

She stepped over to the sideboard, poured a healthy splash of whiskey into a dented old tin cup, and turned to sit on a dusty old chair in the opposite corner of the room. She sipped the whiskey without a flinch, the daughter of Michael O'Brian.

He tried to gather himself, and said quietly, "Very well, then. I apologize for growing angry, but you must surely realize that I had no way of knowing that fellow was your cousin. And more than that," he said, with pain in his voice, "why would someone in your family wish to do *me* harm?"

After a long pause, she said in a hesitant voice, even softer than his, "Before I came here I knew, but I am now certain—I realize that sounds foolish, but it is how my emotions work, so you had best learn, sir, to allow me my ways—that you did not know who he was. He was a stranger to you." She wiped a tear away and said, more strongly. "You did not know him, but he somehow knew you." Holding her cup with both hands, she said, in an exhausted voice, "As to why he sought you out? He has always been such a foolish boy; a boy in every sense. I suppose he wanted to impress my father, to impress all the O'Brian men, to defend the honour of the clan. Blind damned foolishness."

They both tended to their cups for long minutes, until he said, "In any case, Brigid, I am very sorry to have caused you pain."

"And I, my love, am sorry to have... no, I never doubted... that I had questions about what happened between you and Fergal."

"Fergal, then? Fergal O'Brian. I shall remember his name."

She fiercely nodded, then they sat long minutes, drinking, thinking, growing certain and strong, until she sighed, and said, "I find I must apologize, too, for being... foolish, emotional, say what you will... as I have lost much of who I am, what means most to me." She paused, wiped tears from her cheeks, and more calmly she went on, "They were, I suppose, what *once* meant most to me. Now, I find that my old world has quite fallen away. I cannot go back there. I realize, now, that my life is with you. I trust you do not find that too great a burden?"

He grinned, and said, "So, you are resigned to long years with the tall, handsome bloke who stole you away, eh?"

The whiskey had flown through her, and she barked a quick laugh, caught herself, then barked another, a hand to her mouth. "Oh, that's you, love, sure." She sighed in frustration. "Fergal threw his life away, his rebellion a dream, and so succeeded only in sowing doubt in the minds of my family, and pushing me to the life of an army wife." She then raised her cup and added, "Fergal was always a fool. Still, *ar dheis Dé go raibh a anam.*"

James raised his glass, and softly said, "May it be so."

"And so he is gone, and so, too, will my family forever see you as his murderer, and me as the girl who chose to stay with her redcoat husband rather than return to her ancient Irish ways."

There came a cursory thump at the door, followed by the stumbling entrance of Private Doolan, carrying Mrs. Lockwood's trunk. He set it down with an obviously deliberate crash, and said, "I paid that felon Keating and sent him back to Clonakilty."

With no response from the two people who sat in opposite corners of the small room, he sniffed disapprovingly, then went on, "Two shillings, four pence, he called for, to carry one wee woman and one honest Irishman a few gentle miles," then adding, *sotto voce,* "hazard pay, my dying arse." Looking for some type of response, and receiving none, he added in the same muted tone, "Every penny I had in the world." A master of expressing his opinion in any situation, he stowed her trunk by the bed, sarcastically whispering, "'*Oh, thank you, Diarmuid, you noble man.*' '*Oh, dear, Ensign and Mrs. Lockwood, you're quite welcome, I'm sure. It's my feckin' pleasure.*'"

In an exhausted, exasperated voice, Lockwood said, "Christ, man, I shall reimburse you in the morning. For this evening, you are dismissed."

Doolan stood up straight, crossed his arms, looking at one, then the other, in obvious displeasure, and did not move.

A long moment passed before Mrs. Lockwood wiped her eyes, and said in a surprisingly strong, brokenly cheerful, voice, "Diarmuid, *a grah*, I wonder if you might seek out the Mess Officer and ask if I might be added to his list as Ensign Lockwood's wife. I shall take up residence here with the regiment."

She got to her feet with determination and not a little spirit. Shooing Doolan out with both hands, she said, "Out with you, now, Diarmuid, *mo stor*. I must dress for dinner. I am an O'Brian, an Irish gentlewoman, and an officer's wife, and I shall not disappoint."

*****

She was by no measure a flirt, but at dinner she quickly became the favorite of the officers of the garrison and the envy of the officers' wives. Still, those ladies had no fear of the flawless, clever, young woman stealing away their husbands. The other wives envied her, less because she captivated their husbands than because she so thoroughly captivated her own. Mrs. Lockwood and that quite darling young man surreptitiously held hands under the table throughout the evening, as the two young people—they were impossibly young—clung to one another with something like desperation. That obvious devotion sparked reactions ranging from amusement to animosity among the six other married couples in the mess, sniffing nostalgia among the seven married men whose wives were still at home, and frustration among even the most ardent of the fourteen bachelor officers.

*****

By any math, James and Brigid ought not to have both fit in that narrow bed, but with great satisfaction they found they did so, with room to spare.

The room was cold, but they had little use for the blankets. A sconce by the door held a flickering candle, light dancing over the perfection of her skin. Resting at last, she sighed contentedly, then in more animated tone, said, "Oh, I forgot to mention that before I left Clonakilty I received the most charming letter from Ensign Mainwaring of your regiment."

"Tom!" cried James, raising up on one elbow, brightening further, if that was possible. He then busied himself with kissing the back of her shoulder.

"He received your letter, telling of our wedding." Then laughing and squirming, she went on, "You must stop that, sir, if you are to hear my news. Very well, then. He sends us both his heartiest congratulation and best wishes. He also warns me of your violent temper, excessive drinking, and your... how did he phrase it... your *rampant womanizing—*"

"Did he, the dog!" James said with a bark of laughter, then resuming his attention to her shoulder.

"It seems our Ensign Mainwaring—"

"Tom, my love, he will insist on you calling him Tom."

"Tom, then, is a bit of a wag. I shall call him Tom between us, but I cannot refer to him by his Christian name until we become acquainted." She paused for a long moment, and her tone turned serious. "I am a proper Irishwoman, *a grah*," she said with a catch in her voice. "My father raised me to be a gentlewoman. My father, who might never speak to me again." She was quiet for another moment, her head in the crook of his arm, then added, "Will my sisters come to hate me as well? Surely not, James, oh surely not them as well?"

He held her as she wept, the strong young husband, ashamed to find himself at a loss of what to say, what to do.

Chapter Thirty-One

The renewal of mail service included newspapers reaching the barracks, and Colonel Montgomery was delighted to call the barracks officers to the mess to hear the latest news. Reveling in the attention, Montgomery read many of the dispatches aloud, relating stories of how the forces of the King, aided by prompt reinforcement from England, had achieved victory after victory. Rebel atrocities were trumpeted: in Wexford, where innocent Protestants had been burned alive in a barn, and several loyalists had been hoisted on pikes on Wexford Bridge. But those deaths had in turn been avenged by a great victory over a rebel army at Vinegar Hill.

Ensign Lockwood was certain there were an equal number of atrocities perpetrated by the King's forces, but the dispatches were silent on that subject.

The rebellion in West Cork had largely been quieted by the Crown victory at battle of the Big Cross. The Yeoman cavalry of Bandon Barracks thus had little to do but to make wide sweeps across the area to intimidate and terrorize, and the garrison infantry was only rarely called upon to perform any duty beyond standing watches. Lockwood was quite content to keep his battered company of Westmeaths contained within the barracks walls.

The meeting dragged on, as the senior officers had a tendency to prate, referring to the rebels as peasants with sharp sticks; Lockwood and the other officers who had battled the rebels at the Big Cross held their tongues.

When Colonel Montgomery finally dismissed his officers, the ensign took the opportunity to stop by the quartermaster's office to see if the coach had carried mail as well. He was pleased to find two letters in his box, but noting the clock on the wall, he grimaced and headed back toward his quarters, pausing for only a moment in the yard. His company's afternoon drill session would begin soon, and he needed to change out of his best coat. More than that, he found that even a few minutes with Brigid had a remarkable effect upon his mood, and he took every opportunity to see her.

He found her sitting on the bed, wearing only her shift, languidly brushing her hair with one hand as she held a book in the other, her cheeks rather flushed as she read. Her shift was not completely buttoned up, and he had to force himself to be no more than usually interested in her bosom.

She looked up, and brightly said, "Hello, *mo mheile stor.*" With a discernable teasing tone, she went on, "Your meeting lasted an age; I trust you found it deeply moving?"

He smiled as he pulled his coat off, and said, "Yes, thank you; I can think of no finer way to spend a morning. If you have any trouble sleeping tonight, I shall tell you all about it." Gesturing toward her book, he asked, "I see you finally found something worth reading?"

"Oh, yes! Mrs. Hill has kindly loaned me her copy of *The Italian.* The author is a Miss Radcliffe, a woman, mind you, *mo stor*, and she writes with such artistry! The antagonist is so well drawn, this Father Schedon… oh, if I should come across him I would give him a piece of my mind, I quite assure you, priest or no."

He folded his coat across the back of a chair—Doolan would give him hell if he did not care for it like Christ's own shroud—as he added casually, "Another mail coach has come in." He pulled a crumpled letter from his pocket, held it up with two fingers, and said, "A letter from my father; always the supportive patriarch."

He flipped it into the fireplace.

She watched his face closely, but said nothing.

He watched the letter curl and slowly blacken in the coals until it burst into flame. Turning to her with a wry smile, he said, "Just a few lines; I read it out in the yard. I was surprised to find his tone to be almost conciliatory. In fact, he says it is not too late for me to save my place in the family. He was kind enough to in offer to have a churchman of his acquaintance, a Reverend Autry, annul our marriage—"

"An annulment!" she cried with clenched fists. "Oh, what a terrible man he is, to suggest such a thing! You must write to him this very minute and tell him, *Go ndéana an diabhal dréimire de cnámh do dhroma ag piocadh úll i ngairdín Ifrinn!*"

With a playful look, he said, "I am sure that is a suitable reply, my dear, but perhaps we might first… well, discuss this notion of annulment." She scowled at him, a combination of amusement and annoyance, as he went on, "By happy coincidence, one of my proctors at school was an expert in matrimonial matters, as he had an unfortunate tendency to marry any bar maid of an affectionate nature. He taught us, among other things, that consummation is not a legal requirement for marriage. Even if some poor fellow's new wife has not granted the final favor, that is still not grounds for annulment."

"If you continue with such glib dismissal of our marriage, sir," she said as she set aside her book and deliberately buttoned up her shift, "you need not concern yourself with matters of consummation ever again."

He grinned, and with an exaggerated shrug, said, "Well, one other option is for me to be declared impotent, but church law requires that I first be tested by three court-appointed courtesans."

She rolled her eyes, returned to her book, and muttered, "And they say Catholicism is burdened with ludicrous tradition. Jesus, Mary, Joseph and their wee donkey!"

He barked a laugh, then, more seriously, said, "I hope you'll forgive me for first dealing with my father's ludicrous letter." Pulling a bulky letter from his pocket, he handed it to her, and added, "This came as well. Perhaps it might lift your spirits."

As he handed it to her, he leaned over and kissed the top of her head. "I had best hurry; drill waits for no man."

She gave him a sweet smile as he left, and turned to her letter. In an instant she recognized the hand on the cover. She sat silent for a moment, staring at *Mrs. James Lockwood,* written by her sister Anne. Slowly opening the letter, she found a note and a beautifully embroidered handkerchief. Irish families traditionally gave their daughters a decorative kerchief on their wedding day, one with a special dual purpose. The bride could wrap her bouquet in the fabric, or simply have it on hand to collect the inevitable tears. Sometimes called a magic handkerchief, this same fabric would then be repurposed into a Christening bonnet for the couple's first child.

With welling eyes, Brigid held the kerchief to her cheek as she read,

Our Dearest Sister,

Please, please accept our apologies in not having this modest gift prepared before your wedding, but Caitlin and I so wished to finish it as best as our skills allow. We miss you so, but we are certain that you are happy with Ensign Lockwood, our brother James! And we so look forward to you coming back home to visit when opportunity allows.

Your loving and most devoted sister,
Ann O'Brian

Brigid, Ann didn't want to let me rite anything, but I told her I must, so that I might tell you that I speak to Father about you <u>Every Day</u> and I am certain he is softning about your handsome soldier even though some of Father's friends even deer Uncle Tadg were killed in that awful fighting and Father was so sad and Ann is scolding me for riteing to much so I must close Your <u>Favrite</u> Sister <u>Caitlin</u>

****

The next day, Brigid Lockwood held her husband's arm more tightly than usual as she picked her way down the steps of their quarters in her best shoes. It was a misty afternoon, and the soles were slick. She and James had been invited to dine with Captain and Mrs. Geiger, and she had some hope of Lisa Geiger being her first friend at the barracks.

They paused at the bottom step when the front gate was thrown open and a dragoon on a lathered horse came galloping into the yard. The horse was clearly exhausted, but the dragoon repeatedly spurred her up to the headquarter steps.

James was enraged, calling out, "You, sir! Stop that God damned spurring or I shall—"

The dragoon, however, ignored him, instead leaping from the staggering beast and bolting up the steps and into the headquarters.

James moved to follow him, but Brigid held his arm, quietly saying, "No, stay, my love. Something is afoot." With something like fear in her eyes, she added, "Do stay with me, won't you?"

"Why, my love," he said with surprise and kindness, "I am sure this is nothing—"

The duty drummer, still in his shirtsleeves, burst out the door of the headquarters and frantically beat out a thundering Officers' Call.

Suddenly as alert and distracted as a retriever, James spoke without looking at his wife, though she studied his face, searching for the calm garrison officer she had known just moments before. "You'll excuse me for a moment, I trust, my dear. I shall be back..." he was two steps away before he finished, "...in just a moment."

She watched as all the garrison officers ran to answer the call, and in the beautiful August evening—the weather had had been glorious all that summer—she saw many of the enlisted men, as well as many of the garrison wives and children, step out into the yard, all eyes on the headquarters.

From down the block of the Officers' Quarters, Lisa Geiger, a pretty, dark-haired woman, stepped out her door. She caught Brigid's eye, and they exchanged a brief, meaningful wave.

Only a few moments passed before several officers—Brigid, a soldier's wife, noted they were all Westmeath and Royal Artillery men—dashed out into the yard, calling for their sergeants.

In another moment the barracks was a tumult of activity, drums beating, men shouting orders, men in red coats and blue running about. Doolan emerged from the crowd and ran past Brigid, saying only, "Beg pardon, Missus," as he bolted up the stairs and into their quarters.

After a few minutes James finally trotted over to speak with her, hurriedly saying, "The French have landed in Sligo. We are away. Cork, for now, then God knows where. Every man who can bear a musket is to march... I hope you'll not mind being without Doolan? I shall send for you as soon as ever I can."

"May I not come?" she said, knowing the answer.

"Oh, goodness, my dear, this will not be a march fit for you, or for any of the wives and children. But I am certain—" noticing a discussion out in the yard, he turned away and called out, "Sergeant Fitzgerald! Have McKenna and Duffy show their muskets to the Armoury Sergeant, and right quickly! I won't have them marching with those worn springs!"

She took his arm and pulled him back to her, fiercely saying, "James Lockwood! Sure and there may be Frenchmen in Sligo, but that is more than two hundred miles from here. Why on earth are you being called to march like the world is ending?"

With genuine pain in his voice, he told her, "Pray do not spread the news, but Sligo is lost... a God damned catastrophe. Only a thousand Frenchmen landed, but the local people—they had been quiet as mice until the damned French arrived—rallied to them by the thousands. Still, our forces there should have handled them without issue. But the French and the rebels have *routed* our men at Castlebar. Our regiments ran like sheep, General Lake galloping away, behaving worse than any of them. Our troops all across the island are shifting, trying to recover and respond. A God damned catastrophe...."

*****

An hour later he was gone. Brigid paced around their room, now her room, wondering if the French could possibly tip the balance of the rebellion, praying they would not.

She then thought of Lisa Geiger, as her husband had marched out with the artillery. Brigid pulled her shawl around her shoulders and strode to her door. She paused, however, with her hand on the doorknob, thinking for a moment, then turning back to the little cabinet by their table, she pulled out a bottle of their cherished stock of claret. Trusting Lisa would have two glasses, she set out to make a friend, and perhaps a comfort.

Chapter Thirty-Two

In the days that followed, Brigid made a deliberate effort to ignore any news from outside the barracks walls. She clung to the knowledge that the French were in Sligo, and very far away. Determined not to worry about James, she instead distracted herself with fulfilling her role as an army wife, an officer's wife. The garrison culture in Bandon was much the same as in Clonakilty, though she soon learned an additional lesson: a woman whose husband was away from the barracks, no matter the reason, might find herself subject to unprovoked slights from the other women. It began with the senior hens, but soon some of the very junior women found themselves free to subtly insult Mrs. Lockwood and the wives of the other officers who had marched off to Cork. Brigid had known that her husband's rank played some role in how she was treated; she now learned his presence shielded her from vindictive little *soithí* who now felt free to kick her, knowing their husbands were nearby and would protect them from repercussion.

Bristling to think that her worth as a person, in that society, at least, hinged upon her husband's protection, she worked to unravel that knot of status, appearance, and liking. Brigid had some support from other wives whose husbands were away, but they had little influence on the older women. Those pecking seniors were privately dismayed that darling Ensign Lockwood, a perfectly respectable young man, the son of a prominent family, a Protestant family, would marry such a person. In short, they expected this Mrs. Lockwood, a woman so young, so pretty, so Irish and so Catholic, to be a thorough-going ninny, likely even something of a slut, and they were more than a little put out when she proved otherwise.

At a tea for the officers' wives, hosted by Mrs. Plant, Mrs. Lockwood very nearly corrected that lady, only at the last moment keeping herself from pointing out that Elsinore lay in Denmark, not Italy. Mollified by the young woman's retreat, the older ladies allowed the rest of the tea to wind down without further swordplay, though Brigid left Mrs. Plant's quarters with her head down, a determined stride, and flushed cheeks.

On her way back to her quarters Brigid's resolution crumbled. She was heartily tired of being mistreated and tears came to her eyes. Thoughts of James came to her, and she wondered what this life and its endless separations might hold for them. She was in an uncharacteristic state of self-pity when she found Lilian Garrigan, the seasoned wife of the barracks armourer, waiting at her door, clutching a letter.

Mrs. Garrigan started to curtsy, a reflex of long habit, but Brigid hurriedly waved it away, sniffing, saying in Irish, "Oh, Lilian, *a grah*, you mustn't think of me so. I am Michael O'Brian's daughter, and no more. Still, that is for me, is it?"

Many of the wives of the enlisted men thought highly of Mrs. Lockwood, marked in this instance by Mrs. Garrigan's hurrying the letter from the barracks postmaster up to the Lockwood's quarters as a token of her respect. Brigid appreciated the gesture; as with the officers' wives, among enlisted families there were some who eyed this Mrs. Lockwood with keen suspicion, this young woman who could travel in each world with such evident ease. As anxious as Brigid was to read her letter, she needed to first thank Lilian in the formal fashion required by their language and culture. Brigid asked after her children, and complimented her dress, though she longed to be alone and tear open the seal.

Lilian Garrigan, however, was not easily dismissed. She frowned at the younger woman, and said, "Tears, Mrs. Lockwood?"

Brigid used an index finger to wipe her cheeks, saying, "I am so very worried about my husband. You understand."

To Brigid's surprise, Lilian sniffed in derision. "I understand the worry, sure. But no true soldier's woman will cry and play the child. Your role here is to support your husband, come hell or no, and support the families of his men, and show them how it's done. Being a soldier's wife, and, more than that, an officer's wife, can be far harder than any soldier's lot."

As she turned to go, Lilian added, "So, you wipe those tears and hide them away, young gentlewoman. Be who you must be, and find joy in that."

Once inside, Brigid stood with her back to the door for some minutes. With trembling resolve, she opened the letter, and read.

My dearest Brigid,

After our march to Cork we were promptly hustled aboard a frigate, the Amethyst, *if memory serves, and like so many kittens stuffed into a trunk, carried up to Dublin, then sat there in an odorous old warehouse for a few days. I do apologize for not having written earlier, but I had little to report other than my attempts to keep the men from thumping the locals, until, in complete darkness and a driving rain, some ill-mannered staff officer pointed us up the road toward Mullingar, with little ceremony and even less to eat, but we are arrived here at last. And what do you know, as soon as we staggered into the regimental barracks we were informed that the French and their rebel friends have been crushed by Lord Cornwallis at Ballinamuck, wherever that is.*

As you might imagine, the French landing came as a great shock to Government, though it is rather an anti-climax to learn that France sent only a thousand men. While those Frenchmen incited large numbers of the people of Sligo to join them, their army was overcome with comparative ease once Lord Cornwallis gathered his forces, forces which did not require the presence of the Westmeath Militia Regiment in general, and your beloved husband in particular.

All that being said, please know how desperately I miss you, and how very sorry I am that I left Bandon in such a callous hurry, and to no purpose.

The good news is that Colonel Montgomery is in soaring spirits, (I would say this to no one but you, my dear love, but I believe his most earnest wish is to avoid anyone, of any nationality or persuasion, from shooting at him, perhaps even speaking harshly to him, ever again) and so he is offering to have the regiment pay for the officers' families to be carried up to Mullingar by post carriage, and for the enlisted families to be borne by wagon, which is most generous, and I wonder how he shall ever be able to explain such an expenditure to Dublin Castle, but we need not concern ourselves with such a thing, and I hope to see you very soon indeed!

Your loving and most <u>affectionate</u> husband,
James Lockwood

*****

"Do pass that bottle, won't you?" growled James to Tom Mainwaring. "Your childhood, your evidently Godless, soulless childhood, seems to have lacked instruction in any human behavior as basic as *sharing*."

After handing over the bottle, Tom turned to where Doolan was unpacking the meager Lockwood possessions, and said, "Doolan, be a good fellow, won't you, and open that bottle of claret. Yes, the one with the yellow label... I wager Mrs. Lockwood's glass is empty."

"*Go raibh maith agat, Thomas, a grah,*" Brigid called from the next room, where she sat writing once again to her father, secretly in agony over his lack of response. She addressed Tom in Irish upon every occasion, subtly teasing him, as they had become fast friends since she had rejoined the regiment in Mullingar.

Smiling at Doolan when he stepped into their tiny dining room, she placed her open hand across the mouth of her glass, and whispered to him, "I've had quite enough for tonight, I think, Diarmuid, *a grah*. Please take the rest of that bottle back to your quarters with our compliments. Good night, now, and God bless."

Doolan nodded his thanks, though after closing the door behind him and thumping down the steps, he muttered, "Wine... thin as water... no drink for a man, is it... no hope of a Christian whiskey... Christ, what a life."

In the parlour, on a comfortable chair opposite Ensign Mainwaring, Ensign Lockwood had reason to be delighted with the recent turns in his life. He had, to begin with, consumed enough wine to render him content with any condition short of the rack; Brigid had arrived in Mullingar, beaming, a few days earlier, to his infinite pleasure; the rebellion was over, and there was hope of something resembling peace; the regiment's consolidation at Mullingar Barracks entailed a reunion with dear old Tom; and, lastly, he took great pleasure, and a degree of relief, in Tom and Brigid becoming the friends he'd hoped they might be.

The full regiment's return to Mullingar had resulted in the barracks officers' quarters being assigned to the higher-ranking men and their families. The ensigns of the regiments, married and unmarried, were sent to seek quarters in town, and freed of the sonorous presence of their seniors, those young people had been turned loose on Mullingar like so many beagles off the leash.

Mullingar was not a large town, and the selection of available rooms was limited. An observer devoid of romance might then have regarded the rooms secured by the Lockwoods, the second story above a draper's shop, as poky and inconvenient, perhaps even shabby, but the Lockwoods were perfectly happy, indeed enchanted, with their new home. A supplement to the apartment's charm was Tom taking the windowless garret above them, a windowless, dusty, but secluded and wholly affordable retreat.

On that evening, the Lockwood's apartment was alive with the chatter of the three inebriated, intelligent, happy young friends. There was a small, and thus inexpensive, fire in the hearth, and Brigid had gone to the wild extravagance of lighting four candles. Her hair was down, and in her plain dress she was unconsciously, softly, beautiful. James and Tom, young, strong, and without pretense, were in their shirtsleeves, in an essentially continuous state of hilarity.

Secure in the knowledge that his bed was, if need be, within crawling distance, Tom was as deep in wine as his friends, his very dear friends. He took a deep swallow of wine and, barking a laugh, said, "Oh, I must tell you this: do you know, last month, while my company was still in Athlone, there was a woman, a woman I scarcely know, upon my honour—"

"Bah! sir, bah!" cried Brigid from the other room in good-natured feminine disbelief.

In pure delight, James waved a finger to claim the floor, and said, "Oh, come now, brother, methinks thou protests *too* much—"

"Well," said Tom, raising his hands, and with a confessional tilt of his head, "I confess, we spent... some time... together, but I assured her on several instances that I had no intention of an attachment—"

Brigid howled a triumphant laugh from the parlor.

James grinned, tossed his head toward the other room, and quietly told Tom, "I married her for her laugh."

Tom grinned, and raising his glass to his friend, quietly answered, "You are a very clever fellow."

Louder, then, so that Brigid could hear, Tom went on, "To continue: this lady, a widow a bit older than I, but a lovely woman, I assure you, made a wholly outrageous offer: that I, an officer in His Majesty's service, during time of war, should resign my commission, and move into her manse! I should perhaps mention that she is a person of some property... half of Roscommon would tip their hat to her... and despite my remonstrations, she persists in her affections! Just this morning I received yet another letter from her, posted from The Black Horse here in Mullingar, begging me to come to her. I am at my wit's end, I do confess."

Brigid's laughter from the next room reached a level very much like hysteria, and James was not far behind her.

"Hence," said Tom, attempting sobriety, "I am determined to find a path by which to honourably... well, absent myself. Now, I beg you both to listen to me on this point: I am informed by Major Morton that the Twenty-Seventh Foot... the Inniskillings, a *line* regiment, mind you ... has been authorized to add another battalion, and they are recruiting officers from among the best of the militia regiments. As they are headquartered in Ireland, they desire first to recruit from among the best of the militia regiments on the *Irish* establishment!"

"Yes, yes, that is very good in them, of course," said Brigid in a knowledgeable, good-natured voice, as she came to lean on the frame of the parlour door. She glanced at James, and thought him the most handsome man she had ever seen. She went on, "I am informed, however, that an ensigncy in a line regiment costs precisely four hundred pounds."

"On top of which," added James, "one must consider the four pounds, six and ten in agent's fees, not to mention the customary guinea to the agent's clerk, who does little more than shuffle paper and hold out his greasy palm upon every occasion." Turning to Brigid, in very good humour, he went on, "And I believe, my dear, our domestic funds currently hover somewhere close to zero."

"There are still twelve pence in my purse, but tomorrow is the first of the month, so our fortunes will improve by... let us see.... a thirty-one day month... eight pounds, two and nine, which will be most welcome, but is not quite four hundred pounds."

"But you have, at least, discussed it, then?" asked Tom, intrigued, serious, his eyes flicking between Brigid and James. "You would take a posting with a line regiment?"

James said nothing, though Brigid thought she saw a look of realization cross his face. After giving her husband a quizzical look, she swallowed hard, and said to Tom, "Well, yes, we have discussed it at some length. A commission in a line regiment is what all you militia fellows aspire to, isn't it? James is always on about how amateurish the militia is, but the financial aspects of a line commission seem a bit... I don't wish to offend... a bit mercenary, I suppose."

"Buying rank might appear unseemly, "said Tom, "but it is has long been the tradition, and for officers' commissions to be so costly certainly ensures their undying loyalty to the *status quo*."

From down in the street below there came the sharp sound of raised voices, several men calling out, and the three friends fell silent, heads cocked to listen. Brigid walked over to make sure Doolan had locked their door, and both James and Tom glanced over to see that their swords and pistols were at hand. They listened a few seconds longer, until James relaxed back into his chair and said, "English." The men in the street must have been drunken yeoman from the garrison; no rebels would have spoken English.

As if nothing had happened, Brigid went over to stand behind her husband's chair and kissed the top of his head, saying, "Beyond the financial concerns, I would be unhappy if Ensign Lockwood was sent overseas. We have agreed, though, that if that should ever happen, it would be best for me to remain in Ireland. The lives of women following the colours are... infamous. There are so many tragic tales."

James looked up to smile at her, and said, "Still, it has been nearly twenty years since His Majesty's forces have been sent on foreign service, so, unless the French start kicking up a fuss, we have a good chance of a long spell of home service."

She leaned down to kiss him, then looking up, said, "But tell us, Thomas, *a grah*, would you take such a commission yourself?"

Tom leaned back into his chair, sipped his wine, and with an amused smugness, he said, "Oh, I have every intention of taking a commission with the Inniskillings. But, of course, I am my own man, free to make my own decisions. I know little of tortuous decision-making, not being a married man, and so not yet acquainted with the various surrenders involved."

Brigid Lockwood scowled at him, and pointing a finger, she said, "Thomas Mainwaring, you are on very thin ice, sir."

The three of them laughed until Tom waved the Lockwoods down and went on, "In all seriousness, now! I have been invited to vie for one of the postings, and I have it from Morton that you, James, are on their list as well. You were mentioned in dispatches, after all, and Lord Cornwallis has noted your name and conduct!"

"Oh, fine, sure," said Brigid, her accent enhanced by wine and glee, "we're on their cherished list, but the four hundred pounds!"

"It seems, my dear bride, *mo mheile stor*," said James, "that our friend is alluding to recruitment as an entrée to an ensignship in the line. There are rare occasions when a man might be given a commission, free of the normal purchase price if he can persuade... ten?"

"Fifteen," said Tom with raised eyebrows.

"*Fifteen* of his men to volunteer into the line with him."

"Well, then," said Brigid, brightly, "the issue is resolved! Your men adore you, sure, and you'll have a hundred or more volunteering!"

James gave Brigid an appreciative smile, but said, "Keep in mind, love, that thirty-six of my men are married, whereas a typical line company allows only six women in the whole company to travel abroad. Not many families are willing to risk the wife and children being stranded in Ireland while their man is sent off to war. Unmarried enlisted men might be enticed by the small recruitment bonus, and the hope of a pension after twenty years of hardship. The life of officers on foreign service is little better—"

"Nonsense, brother!" cried Tom, holding his glass aloft, "There is unflagging honour! Adventure in foreign lands! A long career, glory, and once you're a general, a half-pay retirement in a neat little cottage in the country!"

"Oh," cried Brigid, suddenly enthused, "we might find a wee place near Clonakilty! My father and my sisters nearby!"

James smiled weakly, and after a brief pause, said, "That would be lovely, my dear."

*****

The next day was a Sunday. The day dawned cool and wet on Mullingar Barracks, very nearly cold compared to the warmth of their long summer. Eight Company of the Westmeaths had been given the guard, so the remaining nine companies had relaxed schedules. Few of their officers were about; many, including both Ensign Lockwood and Ensign Mainwaring, had been left off the duty roster. The rebellion was over, and the King's forces in Ireland were taking their ease.

It was with surprise and anger, then, when the men of Eight Company were roused by their sergeants, told to stand to, hurry up, you loathsome bastards, stand to, now, a flogging for you, Brady, if I hear one more fucking word, as Himself has returned from leave and wants to see how you've grown, you stunted brutes, stand to, stand to.

Eight Company, then, clattered out of their barracks, the weather not improving their mood, for the wind was cool, sharp, with bouts of slashing rain. They were unhappy, but they were soldiers now, and they formed up with real competence.

An officer, heavily cloaked, strode out of the headquarters building. As he drew near, there was discernable grumbling in the ranks, one of the louder voices calling out, "Fuck me, it's Barr!"

The company's sergeants were hard-pressed to restore order, Barr standing silent in front of the company. When they were at last quiet, Barr called out, "Men of Eight Company! I am sorry to have been away on sick leave for such an extended period, but I am at last returned to command you." He smiled his razor, soulless smile, and went on, "More than that, I have come to offer you an opportunity. After long consideration, I have decided to transfer to the line, as the 27th Foot, the Inniskillings, have offered me a commission in their new battalion. I desire fifteen of you men to join me. Who wishes to volunteer?"

With the cool wind snapping around them, not one man stepped forward.

Nonplussed, with a tilt of his head, Barr said sharply, "Be damned to you, then, you sheep. You shall all stand there until I get my fifteen." Turning to the senior sergeant, he went on, "Sergeant... oh, what's your name, damn you?"

The sergeant had served under Barr for months before the rebellion, though he did not sound surprised to be forgotten, as he rumbled, "Gibney, sir."

"Very well, then Gibbey. Keep them here until fifteen come forward."

"I might point out, sir, that the men have not had anything to eat—"

Barr sniffed in amusement. "Poor lambs. Perhaps a few of them will fall over, *pour encourager les autres.*"

"Beg pardon, sir?"

"You should brush up on your Voltaire, Sergeant." Seeing no flicker of response in Gibney's stony face, Barr went on, "When you have fifteen, you can find me in the mess. Short of that, you had best bloody leave me in peace."

It was nearly thirteen hours before a shivering Sergeant Gibney stepped into the officers' mess, where Lieutenant Barr sat, surrounded by empty plates and bottles, numerous letters opened and scattered across the table, warm, dry, happy and drunk as a lord. "Beg pardon, sir," said Gibney in a shaking voice, "but fifteen men have volunteered to the line."

With a mirthless grin, Barr asked, "About fucking time. I wonder... are you one of the fifteen, Sergeant?"

"I have a wife and two boys, sir—"

Barr hissed in derision, and said, "You are a cowardly prick. The fifteen men who discovered their stones may return to the barracks. The rest of you curs will remain in your ranks for another hour to remind you to heed your betters." Taking another long drink of wine, he waggled his fingers at the sergeant, and said, "Now, fuck off."

Alone again, Barr picked up one of the letters and read, with great amusement, every word. Each of the letters was from Colonel Edwin Montgomery to a man named Wesley

Chapman. The letters revealed Edwin's deep love for Wesley, a love which Wesley returned, with great devotion. Wesley had left Dublin to attend to business in England, but planned to return to Edwin come winter.

Some months before, when Ensign Barr had been subjected to his final unpleasant session with Colonel Montgomery, Barr had noticed a letter addressed to Mr. Chapman on the Colonel's desk. Late that night Barr had broken into the Quartermaster's office and rifled through the outgoing mail bag, where his wildest hopes were rewarded. The letter was deeply scandalous. Barr carried the letter to England, to Wesley's stylish home, and confronted him. It had required a brutal beating before Wesley revealed the bundle of letters from his dear love, hidden in the wainscoting.

It was possession of that correspondence that guaranteed Barr a glowing letter of recommendation from Colonel Montgomery, a letter praising Ensign Barr's martial prowess, discretion, steadiness and devotion to the King.

Barr sat grinning, flipping through the letters with something like mania. The notion of honest, true, guileless, love amused and confused him in equal measure. His thoughts wandered to Brigid O'Brian... Christ, how he would have ruined that girl... and James Lockwood, the insolent puppy... he refused to think of them as a married couple.

With each passing day he hated them more.

Chapter Thirty-Three

When he awoke, James lay very still and recalled something his father had once told him: "Only the weak and infirm feel the after effects of excessive drinking, though a gentleman, on occasion, might find himself '*tired*'." He slid out of bed, thoroughly tired, and got dressed as quietly as he could. As hard as he tried, he made more than a little noise, stubbing his toe and dropping his boots. As he opened the door of their bedroom he heard Brigid mumble from under the blankets, "Have a good day, *mo cuisle*."

He awkwardly tip-toed back to her, leaned over gently to kiss the top of her head, and whispered, "Go back to sleep, my love." She mumbled something in sleepy agreement, and he tucked her in, softly kissing her hair and neck, and then slipped out of the room, deeply in love.

He met Tom in the street, where they traded pained grins, and walked down Linen Street toward a baker's shop for a quick breakfast of scones. They both had a sweet tooth, and the porridge provided by the mess held little appeal.

"You know," said Tom as they walked, "you could forego all this business of raising volunteers and simply ask your family for the money to buy in."

"Stuff and nonsense. You know very well that my father would not give me tuppence."

"Yes, yes, your father has no hope of heaven, but what of your mother…?"

"I could ask, but it's the principle of the thing, don't you see?"

Tom sniffed and said, "You and your principles; I personally gave up on my principles some weeks ago."

"Really? I hadn't heard."

"It was quite touching. I gave each of my precious little principles a pat on the head, and then sent them tumbling out into the street, each with a shilling in their virtuous little hands."

James swallowed a smile and asked, "Pray, what happened to your principles once loosed in the wild? I study such things, recreationally."

"I hesitate to admit it, but our landlady's puppy found them in the garden and tore them to bits. It was quite awful; I can hear their plaintive cries even now. I suppose I should have intervened, but I was… indisposed.

"That is doubtless the puppy that she wants to give to Brigid. A likeable little brute—"

They were interrupted by the sight of Diarmuid Doolan running across the Royal Canal Bridge, calling to them.

Panting up to James, Doolan said, "It's Barr, sir! He's returned, like the Sluagh of old. Last night he tortured fifteen men from Eight Company into volunteering for the 'Skins."

"Barr!" cried James, his eyes wide. "Here! And raising volunteers! How in God's name could that bastard garner a recommendation for the line?"

James broke to run toward the barracks, but Tom grabbed his arm and said, "We'll go together, but we won't run. We'll not give Barr the satisfaction, will we? So, so at the route step... forward, Ensign."

It was thus some time later before Ensigns Lockwood and Mainwaring, consciously casual, chatting and munching scones, reached the barracks gate. Private Doolan walked in their wake, doing his Donegal best to look dangerous, a scone tucked into his pocket.

Charles Barr stood in the cobbled yard, immaculately turned out, a cigarillo fashionably dangling from his lips. As a groom brought up his glistening black mare from the stables, Barr exhaled smoke through his nostrils, flipped the cigarillo off in an elegant sweep of his arm, and said, "Oh, my goodness, the wise and the good are afoot. Do pardon me if I flee in villainous terror." As Lockwood and Mainwaring stepped up to him, he sniffed in derision, and said, "Fucking puppies."

James clenched a fist, but halted just short, and said, "I thought we were done with you, Barr. Your cowardice is the talk of the regiment."

"Such an unfortunate misconception. It is fortunate that Colonel Montgomery, at least, is aware of my manly conduct, and so has been good enough to expedite my commission with the 27th. Now that I have seen to the fifteen men to volunteer with me—the merest formality, I assure you—I now depart for Enniskillen. Perhaps, though, I shall call on O'Brian on my way out of town..."

"Oh, yes, do," said Lockwood, doing his best to match Barr's *sang froid*. "Every morning I leave my pistol with

Brigid. How surprised you should look if she put a ball in your head."

With an absent grin, Barr said. "She would too, would she not? God, what a girl." Swinging himself up into the saddle, he went on, "No matter. I have, by chance, come into a tidy sum of money, so the ladies of Enniskillen, and every house between here and there, had best stand warned."

"Before you go, Barr," said Tom—James had never seen such tethered anger in his face—"tell us how you managed a recommendation to raise for a commission."

"You boys had best learn that I have friends, important friends. I help them, in my own modest way, and they in return do me the occasional kindness. One in particular comes to mind. Mainwaring, your posting to the Inniskillings is of no concern to me—you are, frankly, a nonentity, pretty face or no." He then looked down at James, a look of utter hatred growing in his face, saying, "But I have arranged that you, Lockwood, be denied any place, any promotion. I shall see you broken."

Barr put the spur to his horse, but Lockwood called out to him, "You know, Barr, every time I see you there is more madness in your eyes!"

Harshly reining in his horse and spinning in the saddle, Barr looked back at Lockwood with a flash of terror on his face. Only Barr and Lockwood understood the true import of that comment, but still Barr's eyes darted around the barracks yard, as if every man there knew of his pox, his secret, his shame.

He galloped off as if pursued by demons.

*****

Ensigns Lockwood and Mainwaring spoke to the men of their companies, and in both cases more than fifteen rankers opted to follow their officers into the line. In fact, twenty-one of Lockwood's men chose to follow him; deeply touched, he carefully wrote their names in his pocketbook, privately vowing to watch over them as best he could.

A week later, Tom's commission arrived, and while the elegant document was duly celebrated, the collective joy was muted by the lack of a similar document for James. His commission did not arrive in that day's mail, nor in the days that followed, however much each day's mail coach was watched.

Ensign Mainwaring received orders to march his fifteen volunteers up to Enniskillen, and the garrison major tasked him with the unpleasant duty of escorting Barr's thoroughly unhappy fifteen as well. Tom delayed as long as possible, thinking that James and his men could march with them, but each day's mail, eagerly anticipated, proved disappointing. After several days had passed, peppered with comments from senior officers about young pups not appreciating their good fortune, Tom could find no further excuses for not setting out. He rode off on a borrowed horse, thirty redcoats in his wake, and his cherished commission in his breast pocket.

*****

The weather was changing. The first chill of fall came, and all that day cold hard rains pounded Mullingar. Brigid did not feel well, and the cold seemed to seep into her, no matter how she bundled up, but she knew the state of their finances, and despite James's urgings she allowed the hearth to burn low all day. It was only late in the day, when James was due to return home, that she would stir the fire and add two peat logs. At ten pence the load, her budget required each load to last four days. She dreaded the full onset of winter.

James eventually came thumping up the stairs, in a foul mood and soaked to the skin. As she helped him pull off his wet coat, she said, "You are so late, my love. Come, let's get you into some dry clothes. Was your day as miserable as it seems?"

As he changed, he said, "Miller ordered three companies, mine of course being one of them, to march out to Skeagh Deg, ten miles out and ten miles back, just to intimidate some poor people who had complained about tithes. Tithes, for God's sake." He pulled a new shirt over his head, and went on, "When we got back to the barracks there was again no commission. The men who volunteered to go with me are asking when we are to march, and I have no answer for them. Two months have passed, and I am afraid that I have made a fool of myself."

"This is all so very wrong! Can you not write to General Moore, even Lord Cornwallis himself? After all, you were mentioned in dispatches for the Big Cross action."

He relaxed as he pulled on the fat wool socks Brigid had knit for him. "It is one of nature's great pleasures, to have warm feet. Thank you, dear." Wiggling his toes, he added, "I hesitate to write any more entreaties, if for no other reason than I do not care to play the beggar. I simply cannot understand why there is still no reply from my Uncle Montgomery; is his silence a polite way of saying I am denied a posting to the line? If I go over his head I may be exposing myself to insult or a drubbing. Can it be possible that Barr was not lying, that he could indeed thwart, even end, my career? If I push, do I risk even my current post with the Westmeaths? I just do not know."

She draped his wet things across the backs of chairs and the headboard, kissed him, and said, "Come, warm yourself by the fire. We shall have our tea and our supper, and you can tell me more about the poor people of Skeagh Deg."

*****

Another cool, misty afternoon, as Brigid readied herself to do her shopping. She still did not feel well, and she found that her feet had swollen to the point where her shoes were uncomfortable. It was not a long walk, and she had been in town long enough to know the shops, and, for better or worse, the shopkeepers. The baker was a kind man, who typically sold her a small, older loaf for a penny. The wine merchant disliked her for being a Catholic; the vegetable seller disliked her for being married to a Protestant. The woman who sold eggs disliked everyone.

She sighed and opened the door, only to find her husband bounding up the steps, his eyes aglow, waving a letter, crying out, "The post is come, and such glory!"

He swept her up and twirled her around the room, kicking the door closed with a sweep of his heel. He spun her around twice more before finally setting her down, and she held her hands to her face, laughing and crying. Holding the letter aloft, in roaring spirits, James went on, "At last! The letter from my Uncle Montgomery... here, I shall read you some bits... his heartfelt apologies for the delay... what a grand fellow he is, the best of men... clerical errors and such... sadly, he is resigning his colonelcy, and retiring to London...my mother shall be so disappointed. But this bit! He pledges his devotion to us... he sends his love, by the way, I shall let you read the whole thing... so beautifully phrased."

Laughing and crying even harder, she punched him in the chest (she was a small woman, but one who knew how to deliver a blow) and cried out, "Enough of his compliments, James Lockwood! Do not tease me one minute longer! What of the *commission?*"

Laughing and wiping away tears of his own, James finished the letter by roaring, "*and* one of his last official acts as Colonel of the Westmeaths is to see me posted to the Inniskillings!"

They clung to one another for long minutes, until he turned and laid his uncle's letter on the kitchen table. Then, reaching into his coat, he pulled forth a large envelope, and opening it with something like reverence he placed an elegantly written document on the table, and together they read,

GEORGE R.

GEORGE THE THIRD BY THE GRACE OF GOD, KING OF GREAT BRITAIN, FRANCE, AND IRELAND, DEFENDER OF THE FAITH; &C.

TO OUR TRUSTY AND WELL-BELOVED <u>JAMES LOCKWOOD</u> GREETING. WE DO BY THESE PRESENTS, CONSTITUTE AND APPOINT YOU AS ENSIGN TO THAT COMPANY WHEREOF _TO BE NAMED_ IS CAPTAIN IN THE CORPS OF FOOT, COMMANDED BY OUR TRUSTY AND WELL-BELOVED <u>LORD ENNISKILLEN</u>

YOU ARE THEREFORE CAREFULLY AND DILIGENTLY CHARGED TO DISCHARGE THE DUTY OF ENSIGN BY EXERCISING AND DISCIPLINING WELL BOTH THE INFERIOR OFFICERS AND SOLDIERS OF THAT COMPANY, AND WE DO HERBY COMMAND THEM TO OBEY YOU AS THEIR ENSIGN. — AND YOU ARE TO OBSERVE AND FOLLOW SUCH ORDERS AND DIRECTIONS, FROM TIME TO TIME, AS YOU SHALL RECEIVE FROM YOUR CAPTAIN_ TO BE NAMED_OR ANY OTHER YOUR SUPERIOR OFFICERS, ACCORDING

TO THE RULES AND DISCIPLINES OF WAR, IN PURSUANCE OF THE TRUST HEREBY REPOSED IN YOU.
GIVEN AT OUR COURT AT ST. JAMES, THE 1ST DAY OF NOVEMBER 1798 IN THE YEAR OF OUR REIGN, THIRTY-EIGHT,

BY HIS MAJESTY'S COMMAND,
PORTLAND.

ENTERED WITH THE SECRETARY AT WAR.
COMMISSARY GENERAL OF M. LEWIS MUSTERS.
WM. WOODMAN.

They celebrated the good news in the joyous fashion typical to young couples, until some time later, when James pulled himself away, saying, "I really must return to the barracks, dear. I ran home to you as soon as I read the letters, so it's likely they have assumed by now that I've deserted. My God you are beautiful... but, no, really, I have to go back and speak to Major Miller and do the proper."

As he dressed quickly, he brightened even more, if that was possible, and said, "Oh, I forgot to mention that Uncle sent a most handsome gift! It is still in my coat... a draft for a hundred pounds!"

"Oh my God! A hundred!"

"Yes, indeed! He wishes us all the best of luck, and hopes it will help us get us off to a proper start."

She sat up in bed, his heart skipping two beats as she did so, and said, "Oh, we must get you a new coat! And the line officers wear shakos, do they not? With those lovely brass plates. It shall be such fun to go shopping for you!"

"And a new dress for you," he said as he pulled on his boots. "But tonight, we must have a splendid dinner to celebrate, and damn the cost!"

"I will get dressed, and we shall go down to the Clovergreen and book a table."

"We?" asked James. "Will you need Doolan?"

"Oh, not Doolan," she said, giving him an innocent look. "It's the baby and I who'll be going."

There came to James the moment common to men when they realize the enormity and joy of imminent fatherhood. He tried to speak, found nothing, and simply sat and held her, very much blending into one person.

"Now," she said, finally, wiping her tears, "you had best return to the barracks. My baby must not have a deserter for a father."

"Yes, I suppose I must. But you should rest, I think? Yes. You stay under these blankets, now. I will send Doolan to book dinner. I shall be back as soon as ever I can!"

Ensign James Lockwood ran down the narrow steps to the ground floor, sounding very much like a squadron of dragoons at the gallop. He bolted down the narrow hall to the rear of the old building, calling, "Doolan! Doolan, there!"

Doolan, playing at deaf, sat by a window in his shirtsleeves, bent over his officer's second-best coat, with a needle in his hand and thread in his teeth.

Lockwood quickly said, "Never mind my coat—"

"What! Never mind these buttons, each one of them loose as a queen's ass?"

"Damn the buttons, man! Run down and book a dinner at the Clovergreen... a good roast, puddings... she likes trout... the best of everything, you hear me, now? My commission is come through, and Brigid is going to have a baby!"

"Well, now," said Doolan, rising to shake his officer's hand, "I give you joy, sir." With something like tenderness in his voice, he said, "The Missus shall be the great mother of the world, sure. May St. Brigid watch over her." But then with a cough, his usual whine returned, and he went on, "Still and all, they'll be more work for me, won't there? The fucking line. New lodgings, new facing colours on these old coats—buff for the Inniskillings, never keep that clean, Christ —and new feckin' buttons and all…"

Lockwood's roaring spirits would not be dampened, and his huge smile never faded. "The Inniskillings! What opportunity! We'll have Barr to deal with, of course, but with Tom Mainwaring and my men with us, there shall be great days ahead!" With that he bolted down the hall and out into the street, gleeful as a boy.

Doolan set aside his sewing, and as he put on his coat and bicorn, he muttered to himself, "We'll be seeing what tomorrow brings: endless sorrow, likely, but we'll see. We'll just see." Still, as he headed up Bridge Street, the hard, gnarled fellow walked with something like a spring in his step and something like joy in his eyes.

The End

About The Author
Mark Bois

In 2006 Mark Bois fulfilled a long-time ambition and returned to school to earn a Master's degree in history. His Irish ancestry and a fascination with military history prompted him to write his thesis on the Inniskilling Regiment and their bloody stand atop the ridge at Waterloo.

Amongst the dusty rosters and letters in the British National Archives, and then in the artifacts and records of the Inniskilling Regimental Museum, he found what he needed to write his thesis. He also discovered the fascinating personal stories that inspired *The Lockwoods Series*.

As a happily married man and the father of five, Bois finds it interesting to tell the stories of families. He thinks it especially important to share the stories not just of soldiers, but also of those who wait for them to come home; the burdens they bear alone, and together.

If you enjoyed this book,
please write a review.
This is important to the author and
helps to get the word out to others.

Visit:

PENMORE PRESS
www.penmorepress.com

The Lockwoods

of Clonakilty

by

Mark Bois

Lieutenant James Lockwood of the Inniskilling Regiment has returned to family, home and hearth after being wounded, almost fatally, at the Battle of Waterloo, where his regiment was decisive in securing Wellington's victory and bringing the Napoleonic Wars to an end. But home is not the refuge and haven he hoped to find. Irish uprisings polarize the citizens, and violence against English landholders – including James' father and brother – is bringing down wrath and retribution from England. More than one member of the household sympathizes with the desire for Irish independence, and Cassie, the Lockwood's spirited daughter, plays an active part in the rebellion.

Estranged from his English family for the "crime" of marrying a Irish Catholic woman, James Lockwood must take difficult and desperate steps to preserve his family. If his injuries don't kill him, or his addiction to laudanum, he just might live long enough to confront his nemesis. For Captain Charles Barr, maddened by syphilis and no longer restrained by the bounds of honor, sets out to utterly destroy the Lockwood family, from James' patriarchal father to the youngest child, and nothing but death with stop him – his own, or James Lockwood's.

PENMORE PRESS
www.penmorepress.com

Lieutenant James Lockwood

By

Mark Bois

"Captain Barr desperately wanted to kill Lieutenant Lockwood. He thought constantly of doing so, though he had long since given up any consideration of a formal duel. Lockwood, after all, was a good shot and a fine swordsman; a knife in the back would do. And then Barr dreamt of going back to Ireland, and of taking Brigid Lockwood for his own."

So begins the story of Lieutenant James Lockwood, his wife Brigid, and his deadly rivalry – professional and romantic – with Charles Barr. Lockwood and Barr hold each other's honor hostage, at a time when a man's honor meant more than his life. But can a man as treacherous as Charles Barr be trusted to keep secret the disgrace that could irrevocably ruin Lockwood and his family?

Against a backdrop of famine and uprising in Ireland, and the war between Napoleon and Wellington, showing the famous Inniskilling Regiment in historically accurate detail, here is a romance for the ages, and for all time.

"... Bois' meticulous research and command of historical detail makes this novel a must read. He sets the standard for research and understanding... and the audience will demand more novels from this new author. Historical fiction welcomes Mark Bois with open arms." – Lt. Col. Brad Luebbert, US Army

PENMORE PRESS
www.penmorepress.com

Midshipman Graham and the Battle of Abukir

BY

James Boschert

It is midsummer of 1799 and the British Navy in the Mediterranean Theater of operations. Napoleon has brought the best soldiers and scientists from France to claim Egypt and replace the Turkish empire with one of his own making, but the debacle at Acre has caused the brilliant general to retreat to Cairo.

Commodore Sir Sidney Smith and the Turkish army land at the strategically critical fortress of Abukir, on the northern coast of Egypt. Here Smith plans to further the reversal of Napoleon's fortunes. Unfortunately, the Turks badly underestimate the speed, strength, and resolve of the French Army, and the ensuing battle becomes one of the worst defeats in Arab history.

Young Midshipman Duncan Graham is anxious to get ahead in the British Navy, but has many hurdles to overcome. Without any familial privileges to smooth his way, he can only advance through merit. The fires of war prove his mettle, but during an expedition to obtain desperately needed fresh water – and an illegal duel – a French patrol drives off the boats, and Graham is left stranded on shore. It now becomes a question of evasion and survival with the help of a British spy. Graham has to become very adaptable in order to avoid detection by the French police, and he must help the spy facilitate a daring escape by sea in order to get back to the British squadron.

"Midshipman Graham and The Battle of Abukir is both a rousing Napoleonic naval yarn and a convincing coming of age story. The battle scenes are riveting and powerful, the exotic Egyptian locales colorfully rendered."* – John Danielski, author of *Capital's Punishment*

PENMORE PRESS
www.penmorepress.com

RAIDER OF THE SCOTTISH COAST
BY

MARC LIEBMAN

Which serves a Navy better? Tradition and hierarchy, or innovation and merit?

Two teenagers – Jaco Jacinto from Charleston, SC and Darren Smythe from Gosport, England – become midshipmen in their respective navies. Jacinto wants to help his countrymen win their freedom. Smythe has wanted to be a naval officer since he was a boy. From blockaded harbours and the cold northern waters off Nova Scotia and Scotland, to the islands of the Bahamas and Nassau, they serve with great leaders and bad ones through battles, politics and the school of naval hard knocks. Jacinto and Smythe are mortal enemies, but when they meet they become friends, even though they know they will be called again to battle one another.

"This is Marc Liebman's first foray into the age of sail, and what a densely packed, rattling yarn he has produced... The twists and turns of the breathless plot see the two main protagonists cross again and again in a story that never lets up its pace." ~ Philip Allan, author of the award-winning Alexander Clay series about the Royal Navy during the Age of Sail.

PENMORE PRESS
www.penmorepress.com